Never Sleep with a Suspect
ON GABRIOLA ISLAND

Sandy Frances Duncan & George Szanto

TouchWood
Editions

VICTORIA • VANCOUVER • CALGARY

TouchWood Editions
#108 – 17665 66A Avenue
Surrey, BC V3S 2A7
www.touchwoodeditions.com

TouchWood Editions
PO Box 468
Custer, WA
98240-0468

Library and Archives Canada Cataloguing in Publication
Duncan, Sandy Frances, 1942- Never sleep with a suspect on Gabriola Island : an islands investigations international mystery / Sandy Frances Duncan and George Szanto.

ISBN 978-1-894898-89-8

    I. Szanto, George, 1940- II. Title.
PS8557.U5375 N48 2009   C813.54   C2009-900842-4

Library of Congress Control Number: 2009920164

Cover design by Chyla Cardinal
Front-cover photo from iStockphoto
Interior design by Duncan Turner
Maps by Darlene Nickull

TouchWood Editions acknowledges the financial support for its publishing program from the Government of Canada through the Book Publishing Industry Development Program (BPIDP), Canada Council for the Arts, and the province of British Columbia through the British Columbia Arts Council and the Book Publishing Tax Credit.

BRITISH COLUMBIA
ARTS COUNCIL
Supported by the Province of British Columbia

Canada Council   Conseil des Arts
for the Arts   du Canada

PRINTED IN CANADA

1 2 3 4 5 12 11 10 09

For Marilyn and Ian, Phyllis and Vic,
and all the NDWs
for your ongoing support.

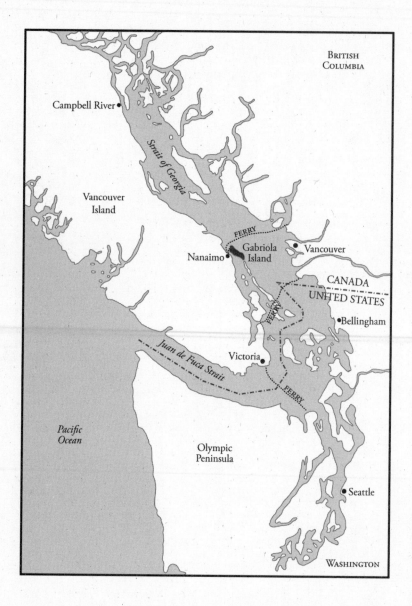

BRITISH
COLUMBIA

Campbell River •

Strait of Georgia

Vancouver
Island

FERRY

Nanaimo • Gabriola
Island • Vancouver

CANADA
UNITED STATES

FERRY • Bellingham

Juan de Fuca Strait

Victoria •

FERRY

Pacific
Ocean

Olympic
Peninsula

• Seattle

WASHINGTON

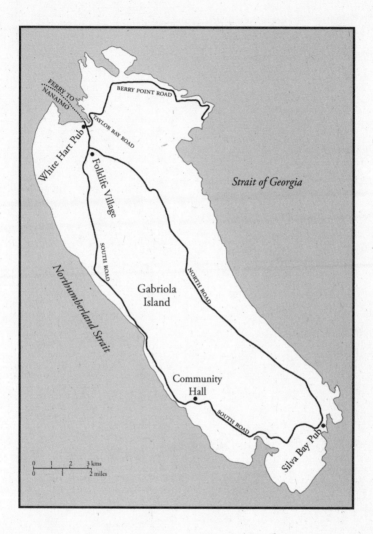

FERRY TO NANAIMO

BERRY POINT ROAD

TAYLOR BAY ROAD

White Hart Pub

Folklife Village

SOUTH ROAD

NORTH ROAD

Strait of Georgia

Gabriola Island

Northumberland Strait

Community Hall

SOUTH ROAD

Silva Bay Pub

| 0 | 1 | 2 | 3 kms |
| 0 | 1 | 2 miles |

ROSE MARCHAND PRESSED the remote button on the arm of her chair, and the door to the deck swung slowly open. She stared up at the bluing cloud-free sky. After a night of light rain it was a perfect morning. The world washed clean.

She pushed on the chair's guide wheels and propelled herself forward, onto the low, narrow deck. Behind her the door closed with a small squeak. Why did it squeak on closing but not on opening? She'd get Roy to oil it. She rolled over to the ramp and let herself glide down. Though the day should warm nicely, now at 6:00 AM it was cool.

She gripped the wheels and started her roll along the circular asphalt drive. Another thrust, another, another, and she was rolling faster than most people jog. Great to be alive.

The air past her face felt soft, and now she could see the sun rising beyond the tall, straight firs and the angled arbutus trees. Their home and the Gallery backed to the ocean. In front, a long avenue led from the circle drive to the road. The circle served as her track, about thirty metres in diameter. Artemus had designed it well.

She pushed hard, past the path to Tam's cabin, eyes on asphalt ahead. But her peripheral vision noted a dark bundle to her left. She sped up, she needed to get her heart rate higher. Back to the house, second circle. Arm and shoulder muscles now fully awake. Around again. She slowed a little, glancing ahead to spot the bundle.

There, on the grass. A dump of clothes. Or a person? Flat on his face, dirty jeans, faded shirt, no cap. Damn! She had to break her rhythm, deal with whoever lay there, some drunk? Here? Drunks didn't casually pass out on the Gallery grounds. She guided her chair toward the person's workboots. "Hey! You!"

No movement. She rolled by him and leaned toward his head. Oh dear god! "Roy! Roy!"

She rolled her left wheel against his side. No response. Oh god, was he dead? She reached down to check for breathing. None obvious. Damn it to hell, she thought. And then she thought, Call the police. At last she thought, Poor Roy.

It would not be a first-rate day.

ONE

KYRA RACHEL STEERED her Chevy Tracker behind the row of cars moving down the Horseshoe Bay parking lot and onto the 10:30 ferry to Vancouver Island. Ten minutes late loading, but she'd still be in Nanaimo in good time. On board, she turned off the engine, locked the doors, walked up three flights of stairs to the front lounge and found a chair by the windows. A ferry was a place out of regular life, good for reading, people-watching and, despite the quality of ferry food, eating. No. In two hours she'd be lunching with Noel, and besides, her father had just made her finish a stack of his superb blueberry pancakes.

Kyra stared up Howe Sound. White-topped mountains shone in the sunlight. Dulcet tones on the loudspeaker: "Welcome aboard BC Ferries. Our sailing time to Nanaimo will be one hour and thirty-five minutes." The ferry departed. Kyra stared out. An immense green mound hove into view—Bowen, the island of her childhood. Early autumn maples dotted its flanks with a golden tinge. She remembered it as, mostly, a satisfying place. But way more houses there now than then.

Slowly Bowen Island's western tip slid behind the ferry. Go outside? Maybe later. When she'd smoked she'd headed outside even before finding a seat. Even after six months the desire for a hit of smoke in throat and lungs often consumed her. Now she breathed deeply, smokelessly. The lounge had filled with people, the general noise level increased. Get coffee? She continued to sit, deeply inhaling no-smoke.

Before boarding, she'd called Noel in Nanaimo. The answering machine had come on. She figured he'd be monitoring his calls. "Noel, I know you're home." No response. "I'm on the next ferry from Horseshoe Bay. How'd you like to go out for lunch."

Noel had picked up. "I don't want to go out for lunch. I'm fine as I am."

"The convention is first you say 'Hello.' Hello, Noel."

"Hello, Kyra."

"Anyway, I'm not fine. It's the three-month anniversary."

"So?"

"So we'll go for lunch at the Acme."

"I don't want to go to the Acme."

"Yes you do. We'll toast Brendan."

"Don't be so bossy."

"Not bossy. Efficient."

Silence. Then, resignedly, "We'll see when you get here."

"You'll be fine." She closed her phone. Three months since Brendan's death. Noel still needed time for his mourning to wind down. Had she herself fully dealt with Brendan's death?

Her own mourning, she realized, was for the on-top-of-everything Noel, the funny Noel she'd known for years. Then three-plus years ago, when Brendan's company moved him to Nanaimo, Noel's deflation began, tiny bit by little bit. Could Noel, a first-rate investigative reporter for the *Vancouver Sun*, still do the job from Nanaimo? Sure, both he and Brendan agreed. But the real answer was, No.

In the women's room, Kyra washed her hands and stared in the mirror. Lipstick needed repair. She unclipped her hair. Curly dark brown wisps tickled her neck. She dragged a comb through the mass and clipped it back in place. She felt torn about how to be with Noel— assertive as just now, or something gentler? She'd not seen him since the funeral but they'd e-mailed three-four times a week, and spoken on the phone. When Brendan was still alive Noel was at least there—angry, caring, ironic, devoted, whatever. But these last three months . . . Shake him out of this withered sense of himself he'd allowed to take him over. She had to.

Her brows looked thick. She wet a finger and stroked them. The weight she'd added since separating from Sam made her chin bulge. How could she not have noticed that? She sucked in her gut, thrust out her chest and pulled herself up to her full five foot six and three-quarter inches. Yep, Noel needed a little tough affection.

Ten minutes before Kyra's call, Noel had folded the last letter, addressed and stamped the final envelope, and set it on the small pile. He leaned back and gazed at the framed photo of Brendan. He'd stood it on the dining table a month ago, when he began writing wearying thanks-for-your-condolences notes. The picture was a head and shoulders portrait taken a year before Brendan had been diagnosed: a man in his prime, sculpted features, straight black hair greying at the temples, lips curved up as if smiling at a joke only he—and maybe Noel—knew. Lips that now, achingly, Noel could feel on his own. He pulled his gaze away. A month of replies, the four piles to mail each over ten inches high. Now what was he supposed to do? Today, tomorrow, the next day?

Brendan had had a wide range of friends; so much sympathy. Damn you, Brendan, who gave you permission to die?

Getting up, Noel took the envelopes to the hall table. He thought: wallet, keys, shoes— The phone rang. He shuddered, a mechanical reaction by now. At least it wasn't three in the morning. Still, he didn't want to answer. He easily might be not here—gone out the door two minutes ago to mail the thank-you notes. Anyway, he couldn't locate the receiver, damn cordless phones. The ringing stopped, the answering machine cut in. Kyra's voice. Talk to her? He glanced around the living room. Hard to locate a receiver that's stopped ringing. She was inviting him to lunch. He looked at his watch: nearly ten. He lifted yesterday's newspaper from the coffee table. Aha. He picked up the phone. Listened, answered. Smiled, relieved she couldn't see him.

They talked. He suddenly looked forward to seeing her. Briefly. "See you—" But she'd already hung up. How did she know he'd be fine? And why has she gotten so bossy these last few months? He wanted to call her Kira again as he had years ago when she was in a mood. She hated Kira. She used to shout at him, "Keera! Keeeera!" He set the receiver onto the newspapers, on second thought carried it to its base. Way too soon for a fun lunch at the Acme.

He poured more coffee and took it onto the balcony. He stared and sipped. A tug trailed two barges of sawdust. A seaplane ratcheted out from its dock by the hexagonal pub and restaurant. Four yachts churned by, only one under sail. He took another sip. An immense gleaming white motor launch was tied up in the marina. You're ostentatious, Noel told it.

Noel had gotten used to living on Cameron Island. Despite the name, Cameron Island is not an island. It had once been an island but early on Nanaimo city fathers had filled in part of the harbor with coal-mine slag. Now Cameron Island was an upscale condo development that jutted into the harbor next door to the Gabriola Island ferry slip. He liked his condo well enough, and the view. But in the last weeks he'd begun thinking, Should I stay here? Every detail reminded him of a Brendan project, a Brendan comment, a Brendan splurge. Should he even stay in Nanaimo? Since leaving Vancouver he'd shifted his pace of living, had come to like the more casual life, gentler, way less tense. Move to one of the Gulf Islands, even more relaxed than here? Island time, little pressure, tasks that didn't get done today could be worked on tomorrow, or next week. By next month it would become obvious the job didn't have to be done at all.

He finished his coffee. Damn Kyra, why is she being so pushy? And so pious, giving up her esses. Good thing booze doesn't begin with an ess or she would've quit that too—no sex, smoking, or swearing was bad enough. Her "dang" and "schmidt" sounded so precious. Except he did, after all, adore her. But no lunch out.

The phone rang. Good. Kyra, calling to moderate her efficiency. "Hello?"

"Is this Noel Franklin?" A deep, pleasant voice.

"That's right."

"This is Artemus Marchand. I'd like to engage your services." Worry in the words.

A familiar name. "What services?"

"A dead man was found on my property." Agitation, and insistence.

"What does that have to do with me?"

"I need your help. It's my groundskeeper, Roy Dempster. The Gallery's groundskeeper. The Eaglenest Gallery. He's dead."

That's how Noel knew the name, from the Gallery. On Gabriola. He'd been there with Brendan.

"My wife found Roy's body. I'm concerned about the Gallery's repu-tation. And about Roy. Though it's too late for him."

"You need my help?"

"You come highly recommended. I'd like you to make it clear to everyone that Roy didn't die on Gallery grounds."

"I don't know what you're talking about. Bye."

"Wait. Please. Is this the Noel Franklin who used to write investigative columns for the *Sun?*"

"Used to is right."

"I'm told you're discreet and thorough." Marchand's voice quavered. "That's what I need. Roy may have been murdered. Or maybe not."

The conversation was beyond Noel. "What on earth do you think I can do?"

"Would you come over to the island? I'll explain everything."

"If it's maybe murder, aren't the Mounties handling it?"

"There's a column in our newspaper— I'm deeply concerned. I've got to stop the gossip. You can read it for yourself. Give me your fax number. I'll send it over."

"Listen, I don't investigate anything any more. Okay?"

Silence. Then, "Very well. Sorry I bothered you." The line went dead.

⎯⎯

Tam Gill tucked the brown-paper-wrapped painting under his arm. A. would be in his office, and big sister Rosie in her greenhouse. Such creatures of habit.

He walked down the steps from his cabin, passed through the little copse of fir and high salal, and strode across summer-burnt grass to the big house. He inhaled slowly, deeply. Fresh September air, tang of sun-warmed cedars and fir, bit of salt from the chuck. Great. Bucharest had been all bus and ancient-taxi exhaust.

He let himself into the house and climbed up to A.'s second-floor office. A., always with the period after, was how Tam thought of his brother-in-law, Artemus too big a mouthful, Art wrong, and certainly not Artie. Tam knocked lightly on the closed door.

"Come in."

He opened the door. Sunshine flooded the office and glittered off the whitecaps in Northumberland Strait. In the distance lay Nanaimo's sprawl with Mount Benson beyond, a green guardian. An empty easel stood beside the black-and-silver-striped sofa.

Artemus glanced up from a pile of files on his open roll-top desk. He studied Tam's tawny long-planed face, so similar to Rose's. Except for his short curly hair and of course the mustache. "You seem okay. Rosie said you looked like hell last night."

"Hello to you too," Tam laughed. "Sleep and a shower helped. Jet lag's as bad as a hangover."

"Twelve hours?"

"Fourteen. Feels like twice that." Tam set the package on the coffee table.

"No trouble at customs?"

"No. But it still pisses me off, the security guys making me take my shoes off. Passed them through the X-ray separately." He shrugged. "Me and everybody else."

Artemus remained silent, possibly imagining a grim-faced airport guard. "Okay. Ready?"

"Yep." Tam undid the string and pulled the paper off the painting. "Got the tape in?"

"Yep. Rab really enjoys these little backgrounders." Artemus combed his thick silver hair with his fingers, then reached into a desk pigeonhole, found a remote and flicked it toward the sound system on the far wall. A tiny whirring hum as a tape began to record. "Go ahead."

The painting, an oil nearly a metre high and two-thirds as wide, featured three pink and orange angels, fingers angling toward a point just off the canvas, set against ruddy sun-smeared clouds in a lowering sky. The thick, battered frame had lost most of the original gilding. He carried the painting to the easel. "It is, as Dorstel reported, a School of Correggio."

"God bless Dorstel." Artemus studied the oil painting. "Very very nice."

"Almost certainly from the Parma period, possibly done by Lanfranco himself. Right where Enfrescu said it was, a small town southeast of Bucharest. About a hundred fifty k over a road from hell. My rental never heard of shocks."

"What was the name of the town?"

"Polorescou. You won't find it on the map. The painting was hanging way back around a dark corner. If the shop sells anything else this month it'd be a miracle."

"You sure it's from Correggio's school?"

"See the way that right one's finger's pointing? Some say he copied it from Leonardo. Also, Correggio worked on that kind of illusion, like it was actually all happening up in the sky. Well, after Mantegna

TWO

NOEL AND KYRA h...

"Yeah. Peaceful."

"And the drive up...

"No trouble. But...
Peace Arch."

"Give yourself tir...

"Dang right I wi...
drive to the Acme?"

"No lunch out, ...
cheeses. Some pretty...

She could push h...
had to want, from d...

"Okay. I'll set the tal...

"Please."

Sitting at Noel's...
on salmon sandwic...
salmon, did you?"

"At the fish coun...

"When were you...

"Not since Bren...

A shame, Noel u...

"You want to go aga...

He glanced over...
the mood for much,...
a few months befo...
container gardenin...
nasturtiums, anem...
less than tender ca...
make them die. Ma...

Kyra raised her...

"To Brendan."

They sat, silent...
Noel's narrow face.

developed the technique. Likely one of the sketches for the Dome of Parma Cathedral."

"That'd make it, what? 1520s?"

"Yeah. He had a commission in 1526 for an Assumption of the Virgin. See that figure, foreshortened? I'd say he sketched a few like this, then his students filled them in. The pigmentation isn't the Master's but the positioning of the figures sure is." Tam shook his head in admiration. "Correggio really is undervalued."

"Barnabé did the authentication?"

"Yes."

"Good." Artemus gazed at the angels. "Well done, Tam. Thank you." He stopped the recording.

Tam sat on the sofa and propped his runners on the coffee table. "It cost us 4,200 new leis."

Artemus reached for a small calculator. "Still about three leis to a dollar?"

Tam nodded.

Artemus tapped some numbers. "You paid $1,400 US—"

"Plus change. But as usual, over half the cost was for the beautiful thick frame."

They laughed.

"What do you figure it'll go for, half a million?"

"American," Artemus said.

Tam crossed his arms behind his head. "Will you put it in the Thanksgiving show before Rab takes it?"

Artemus' smile turned smug. "The community does enjoy the shows, don't you think?" A faux-naive question. "The Eaglenest Gallery Schools-of Open House." He savored the words. "Our sixth annual. Then on to Vancouver. You'll hang them."

"Of course. But I was thinking, getting them down to Rab—you're not worried about the border?"

"Relax. Paintings don't wear shoes." He laughed.

"Tell me something, A." Tam spoke quietly. "Do you—trust Rab?"

"Trust? Of course I do. What do you mean?"

"Not sure. Just that, sometimes he, well, scares me."

"Don't be silly. He's a friend. Completely trustworthy. Ask Rose."

"Yeah, okay." Ta
"What's in the fridg
"I made *coq au v*
"Great." Tam he;
new on Roy's death
"No." Artemus l
article about the bo
taking matters into
hiring an investigat
Tam's eyes narr
"To protect the
"Did you discus
"No need. The (
"For shitsake, A
"Roy's death ha
"Who thinks it
Artemus went t
ping. "Here."
Tam took it, a c
Artemus thoug
that. He wondered

Could his fine hair have thinned further over the last months? "So. What's new here?"

He thought for a moment. "I finished all my thank-yous. For the condolence notes."

"Well hallelujah. A weight off your brain."

"Brendan knew way more people than I did. Do."

"And what'll you do now with that exhausting job out of the way?"

"It really was, you know. All those nuances."

"Sorry, Noel." She patted his forearm. "And nothing else new?"

"Well, not really—" He stared at the last half of his sandwich.

"What?"

"No, no."

"What's up."

He let out a dramatic sigh. "Phone calls."

"Someone calling you? Or you calling somebody?"

"Calls at 3:00 AM. Half a dozen in the last five or six weeks."

"From?"

"No idea. The phone rings, I pick it up, there's some exaggerated breathing, the line goes dead." He shrugged. "After the fourth call I just let it ring. But I could hear somebody on the answering machine. Breathing, then the click."

"Did you call the phone company, get them to trace the calls?"

"Yep. The breather used a throwaway cell phone."

"What about the police? Did you report the calls?"

"Just to Albert."

She'd heard Noel talk about Albert Matthew, Nanaimo RCMP, but had never met him. "What'd he say?"

"It's no real threat. Harassment, yes. He said the best way of dealing with the calls is to ignore them. Told me to turn the phone ringer to off, leave my watch on top of the machine to remind me to turn it on in the morning." He smiled. "It works. But I still get the recordings."

"You could change your phone number, not list it—"

He shook his head. "For half a dozen calls? Not worth it. He'll get bored and stop."

"Or she. When was the last call?"

"Couple of nights ago. The sun was high in the sky when I got to hear the breathing."

"Waking up at three in the morning to breathe on the phone, now that's work."

"Maybe he—or she—gets off on it."

Kyra set down her sandwich. "And what else is new?"

"That's it."

He asked about her life in Bellingham, the work, any new cases? Three quick ones since they'd last talked at length, all assignments from the insurance company. And what about the Sam front? No, she was done with him, over and out. Anyone new on the scene? She was living alone and enjoying it.

Noel rinsed plates and cutlery and slid them into the dishwasher. He laughed suddenly. "Oh, something sort of funny this morning. Funny now. Irritating when I got the call."

"The breather?"

"No, a guy from Gabriola. He wanted me to investigate a death. Can you imagine?"

"Maybe if you told me more." Noel described the conversation with Marchand.

There it was. A natural outlet. She said, "I think you have to call him back."

"What for?"

"Tell him you'll look into it for him."

"Why?"

"Because the idea feels right." Because Brendan was dead but Noel remained. "Because you're good at it."

"That was a previous life."

"And what's your life now?"

"Just like a year ago, my book. I'll get back to it."

A venture three years old and nothing to show. He had to get out, not sit in this condo staring at a blank page. "You need a project for now. And you can do this."

"Kyra, I don't want to get involved in any investigation. Been there, caused too much harm."

"That was completely out of your hands."

"I wrote the series. I didn't understand the situation well enough. The woman was only peripherally involved and I made her central."

"You corrected that."

13

"Sure. After the damage was done. After she nearly killed herself. After her kids were hounded out of school. Nice correction."

"But this time you're right in place."

"They came down hard on me—the public, my colleagues. I don't want to be any kind of public figure again, not even a reporter with a byline."

"You could use a pseudonym—"

He shook his head.

"Listen. If you take on this Gabriola case, three things. First of all, you don't have to write anything people will read."

"That'd be good."

Which was why he'd likely never write his book. That thought absorbed, she said, "You could solve a problem for someone. Without making yourself public."

"I could. But why would I want to?"

"Because, third of all," she realized he was taking the hook, decided, and grinned, "you'd be working with me."

His brows went up. "You want to work together?"

"Why not?"

"We never have."

"Lots of stuff we've never done together." She grinned bigger.

He snorted a laugh. "And never will."

"But," and again she took his forearm, "getting involved with this dead man thing could be interesting. We've got different ways of looking around, so we'd learn twice as much as you would working alone." There, that was good—build in some assumptions. And she had his attention. "Go on, call this guy. Say you'll be over soon. When's the next ferry?"

"What about you?"

"I'll be with you. But don't mention me till we get there. I'll be your, uh, associate. Now go call him."

"I don't know, Kyra. I don't even have his phone number."

She headed for the telephone rack, grabbed the book, found the number, read it out, handed Noel the phone.

Pushy. He dialed, mainly because he had no reason not to. Marchand answered. Noel said he'd reconsidered.

"Oh, very good. Could you come soon?"

"Well, if you want, this afternoon."

"Excellent. There's a ferry in forty minutes."

Noel glanced at his watch. "Okay." Then he had another notion. "You have some sort of column about the case?"

"Yes, that's right."

"Can you fax it to me right now? Same number as the phone."

"I appreciate this, Mr. Franklin." Marchand gave him directions to the Gallery from the ferry.

Noel set the phone down. "Wonder why he called me? I'm not listed anywhere as an investigator."

"Don't look at the gift horse's teeth."

He picked up Brendan's photo, gave it a moment's loving stare, and carried it back to its proper place on the bedroom chest of drawers. "Well," he muttered to the photo, "I guess that's what I do with the rest of the day."

The phone rang. The faxed newspaper column. They read it together.

WHAT IS THE CONNECTION?

By Lucille Maple

What is the connection between the body of Roy Dempster, long-time island resident and noted birder, and Artemus Marchand, world-renowned gallery operator?

This question is being asked in the market, in the Credit Union, in the restaurants and on the ferry, wherever more than one Islander is gathered.

What happened on Marchand's property that got Roy killed?

Who would want to kill such a nice man? Granted, Islanders know that Dempster was wild in his youth, coming to Gabriola as part of the 70s "hippy" movement, working as little as possible and spending his days (and nights) in a haze of various drugs, but he'd "turned over a new leaf" a number of years ago and had recently joined the "Bearers of Eternal Faith." As a member of that upright organization, he was crusading against the vile vices of drugs (he knew them all) and was attending The Church of the Strait at the Narrows.

Someone (who shall remain nameless) was overheard to say that it can be no "coincidence" that his body was found on Marchand's property. Others speculate that the connection must go back to before Mr. and Mrs. Marchand [née Rose Gill. Ed.] arrived on our beautiful island, some sixteen years ago, after Mrs. Marchand's tragic diving "accident."

Now how can this be? Everyone knows that until his "conversion" to the church Roy Dempster was a "layabout" who probably dealt drugs. He was not likely THEN to have had an opportunity to "hang" (as the youth say) with someone as important and influential and generous as Artemus Marchand. Dempster had been working for the Marchands as general factotum and "dogsbody" for only a year, long after he cleaned up his act. It is important for Gabriolans to remember how lovingly Roy tended the grounds of the Eaglenest Gallery.

On the other hand, "life is stranger than fiction" and so might there be a previous connection?

Or did the two have a serious falling out, as some Islanders, recalling Roy's old temper, have asked? Was Marchand about to "fire" Dempster?

Unless the Mounties are able to solve this heinous crime, Gabriola's tongues

will continue to wag. But I caution our
citizenry against "besmirching characters"
and spreading possibly baseless rumours.

Noel finished after Kyra. He flicked the fax onto the table.
"Total drivel."

"Yeah, it is." She ran her hand through her hair but failed to
untangle a bunch of curl. "Still, Marchand wants to talk about it."

"It's tripe and innuendo." He glanced at the byline. Lucille Maple?
Gawd. "Maybe this is a bad idea, Kyra."

"It's a new idea. And you have to head in a new direction." She
set her hands on his shoulders and stared at him. "You'll always love
Brendan. But you have to do something new and you don't know what.
We'll take your car. Since I've paid for all-day parking."

"Okay. You win. But slow down, Kyra."

"And this evening I'm taking you to dinner."

"You don't have to go back to Vancouver?"

"I'll stay over. Unless somebody's trying to scam my poor billion-
aire insurance company again and they need me tomorrow."

He glanced at his watch, then down at the ferry parking lot. Not
too full and they still had twenty-five minutes. "Let me find a map
of the island." He activated his computer screen, poked around the
Internet and printed out three sheets.

Knows-where-to-look Noel. She smiled. He hasn't lost it. "So
what did you find?"

"A map, ferry schedule, some tourist info. And the Gallery's
home page."

"Good."

He looked out his window. The cliffs of Gabriola three kilometres
away backgrounded the approaching ferry. Nice day, he thought. Sun
on water, all that stuff.

"Tell me about the Gallery." Kyra collected her purse and followed
Noel to the front hall.

"Let's get on the ferry first." From a little chest under the mirror he
took a key. "Here." He handed it to her.

"What's this for?"

"The front door. Just so you have one."

17

She squinted at him, but took it. "Okay."

He grabbed the printout information sheets, folded them, stuck them and a small notebook and pen in his shirt pocket, stuck the map in his leather jacket, corrected the angle of the inside floor rug to 30 degrees and locked the door behind them. "You know, I was on Gabriola once and met Marchand. A friend of Brendan's had a show at the Gallery. That painting above the couch? Lyle Sempken did it. Brendan bought it. You met Lyle at the funeral."

Kyra remembered Lyle. Lyle had given Noel a hug of the sort, Kyra figured, Noel might one day have to think about. Handsome fellow, tall, elegant. When he slumped he still stood a couple of inches taller than Noel's five-ten.

"He's invited me for lunch a few times— No, not like that!" as she raised one eyebrow. "He's just someone to talk to, for god's sake. Brendan and I saw him now and then. Anyway, I said no."

They headed for the stairs. "What's he like?"

"Who, Lyle?"

"Marchand."

"Oh, cashmere sweater, silk shirt. Arcadie tie. He stood out."

"Yeah?"

"It was an island opening, right? A few people in fluorescent sport pants and jackets, the Vancouver-on-holiday look. Mostly the usual small-island Gore-Tex and jeans. Clothes say it all." He shook his head. "Put Marchand in overalls, I wouldn't recognize him."

Across the lobby Noel unlocked a door and they stepped into the parking garage. Kyra wished she weren't wearing khakis and a casual shirt. For cashmere she ought to be in a suit, but at least she had her teal sweater to go over her shirt.

"I explored the house part of the Gallery. Marchand had lots of paintings on the wall. I'm pretty sure one was—you ready?—a Titian."

She turned to Noel. "You don't find Titians just hanging in island living rooms."

"It sure looked like one. It was oil, not a printed copy."

"Then we know he can pay for your services."

Noel took out the key to his new Honda. Something felt wrong. The chassis was down too low. He stepped back and scanned the car. "Shit."

"What?"

"There." He pointed to the front tire. Flat. He glanced to the rear. Flat too. "Shit shit."

Kyra ran her fingers along the sidewall. She passed around the back of the car and stared at the tires on the driver's side. "All of them," she said. "Slashed." She glanced about at the other cars in the garage. Their tires appeared fine. "Don't you have any security here?"

"I thought we did. You saw me unlock the door."

"You've got enemies, my friend."

Noel stood still, his arms folded. "What's going on?"

He looks green is what's going on, Kyra thought. "One thing it means is we have to take my car."

"Hey! I have to have my tires fixed. I have to report this to the police."

She took his right elbow and gently pulled. He refused to unfold his arms but did let himself be drawn back. "We have an appointment to keep." She spoke calmly. "The slashing probably happened last night. Your tires will still be slashed when we get back. We'll call the cops, then you'll deal with the tires. And maybe even figure out who you've pissed off."

"We can't just leave—"

"Yes we can." She fast-walked him to the long-term lot, opened the passenger door of her Tracker, and nudged him in. They drove the two hundred metres to the ferry booth without speaking.

Noel passed her two twenties. She gave the bills to the attendant, asked for a receipt and got very little cash in change. They pulled into the ferry lot, nearly three-quarters full. She turned off the engine and faced him.

He spoke evenly. "The 2:00 PM is a good ferry. The 3:45 is full of high school kids. A boatload of giggling and flirting and touching. Makes my skin crawl."

"I thought you'd been to Gabriola only that once."

"Even from there," he pointed vaguely up to his third-floor balcony, "I hear them down here. Louder than gulls squabbling over a rockfish corpse."

She knew what he was doing. She pulled her cellphone from her purse. "I'll just call my father." No answer at the shop. She phoned his house. His answering machine advertised the concert he was playing in tomorrow evening. He must be rehearsing. She left a message: "Sorry, I have to stay over in Nanaimo. See you tomorrow. Love you." Same message to her boss, minus love.

In the rest of the world Nanaimo has a certain fame, such as it is, for two things. First, for the annual Bathtub Race featuring motorized fibreglass contraptions that zip in a looping course around the Strait of Georgia. And, second, for Nanaimo Bars. Noel claimed he hated Nanaimo Bars—a sweet, sticky, gloppy mess, he said. They were really, she knew, a firm layer of sugar, butter, nuts and coconut; a yellow layer of sweet custard; and a top layer of thick semi-sweet chocolate. Deadly. Yum. She too could keep herself from thinking about Noel's slashed tires.

The ferry slipped in between the dock supports. An attractive ship in BC Ferry colors, white, a red and a blue line running its length. It clanged into place and tied up. Foot passengers strode off. Backpacks, strollers, a roll-along suitcase. Someone disembarking waved to someone waiting to get on. Pieces of a self-contained society. A white-haired woman strode along the ramp, followed by a giggle of teenagers and a couple around Kyra's age, their arms about each other. Then a rumble of cars, maybe fifty in all, island beaters, pickups, SUVs, a Mercedes and a cement truck, driving off. She looked at her watch. The precision of ferries, here and for most of the islands, Canadian and US, had impressed Kyra for years, and especially in the last months—half of her cases for Puget Sound Life Insurance had been on islands.

Before, as a kid, as a teenager, she had regarded islands and ferries as magical. In fact, a family story had it that Kyra, on her first ferry trip, cried because the fairy didn't have wings. Now she saw ferries and islands as twin parts of a privileged life—living close to the bustle of the mainland or, like Gabriola, to Vancouver Island, but separated from all that noise and impatience.

Noel had been addicted to islands long before she was. For years his parents had owned a cottage on Bowen Island, only a short ferry ride from Vancouver. Then her family rented the summer place next door, and she and he became friends. Noel had taken her fishing. She was ten and had never caught a salmon. He was eighteen and knew where they ran. She remembered her first one, flopping in the bottom of the boat. He showed her how to club the fish—the skull, right between the eyes—so it wouldn't suffer. Back at the cottage, with her father watching, Noel made her gut the fish. She could still hear Noel saying, You shouldn't ever keep more fish than you'll eat. Now she said, "You've never wanted to explore Gabriola?"

"Brendan and I went there." He pointed at Newcastle Island, a provincial marine park, no cars, no homes, only half a kilometre from shore. "That was our island."

She'd been there with them twice, first a pleasant picnic for three, second time with Sam soon after their wedding. Sam had gotten along well with Noel. But the foursome made Sam uncomfortable, which Kyra hadn't expected.

She'd loved Sam, or thought she had. Then. She'd left Sam. So she had left sex behind.

Question: How bad is life without sex?

Answer: Not bad at all. Because sex involves you in some of the world's biggest messes.

Tam set the *coq au vin* going in the microwave. Then he strode to the end of the hall, through his sister's suite and out the door to the pergola leading to the greenhouse. Where he met Rose, wheeling toward him.

"Tam, dear, what were you doing in my room?"

"Rushing through. Sorry. But Rosie—"

"Please stay out of my room."

"I said sorry. But listen, A. may be messing up."

"What're you talking about?"

Tam stared at Big Sister Rose, eleven years older. BSR, the way he'd thought of her since learning to spell. "He wants to hire a detective." His whisper was hoarse with a suppressed shout.

"What for?" Her eyes slitted.

"He's worrying about the Gallery's reputation. We don't want any detectives here."

"Of course we don't."

"Okay, tell him. I'm off to town." He'd discharged his responsibility and turned back toward his *coq au vin*.

"Do not go through my room, please."

He hunched his shoulders in mock-fear. "Yes, BSR." But he did understand. She had her private spaces, her room, her greenhouse. Just as he had the cabin to himself. And of course Artemus his aerie. He headed for the kitchen by way of the front door.

Just here to eat, that boy. Now he'll bike to the ferry and Nanaimo's charms. Rose wheeled to the water side of the pergola and took in Northumberland Strait, a freighter, two sailboats, Nanaimo buildings, mountains. She loved this view. Then she wheeled back to the greenhouse. She'd talk to Artemus when Tam was gone.

The walk-ons walked on. The ferry worker signaled the front car. When the row beside her had boarded, Kyra started up and followed the vehicle parade across the ramp, bump up, bump down. She cut the engine and slouched into a renewed pleasure of ferry travel, a stretch of peace until it docked again, and all the more so on a small ferry where she could remain in the car.

This slashed tire business had gotten to Noel. Yes, and to her. Slashing tires of a single car in a garage shouted out serious personal venom. She wondered if it had anything to do with the 3:00 AM phone calls. Wondered too if Noel had made a connection. What could he have done to bring on slashed tires and deep-night phone calls? She glanced at him. He was staring straight ahead.

This was a bigger small ferry than to Bowen in the old days, five lanes for cars, and it looked like passenger lounges on both sides. On the Bowen ferry you climbed up the stairs for a great view. "Tell me about Marchand's gallery."

Noel blinked, and jerked toward her. "I just want to say, I'm glad we're coming over together." He folded her in a solemn hug. "You know— Oh, you just know."

She hugged him back. Her one-time mentor, become her friend. She kissed his cheek.

Noel pulled away, leaned against the passenger door and again fell silent.

"Okay," she said, "the gallery on Gabriola Island."

He nodded, and took the printout sheets from his pocket. "Eaglenest has a show coming up, Thanksgiving weekend. Some old paintings Marchand's located. What they are is a big secret."

"Heck of a way to attract an audience."

Noel glanced at the second sheet. "Gabriola's full of artists and weavers, potters, alternative wellness workers."

"Wellness?"

"Massage, reflexology, acupuncture. And colon hydrotherapy."

She shuddered. "Yuck."

A sudden chilly breeze blew through the window, the salt-breath of ocean, early fall. "Come on, let's go up front. I want to see the island as we approach it." He grabbed his jacket and the printouts and stepped down.

They passed the rows of cars, maybe fifty on board, two-thirds full, mostly British Columbia plates. Before them lay a broad landmass, high cliffs to the right, thickly treed with Douglas fir or so it seemed from this distance. On the left, a shoreline of hollowed sandstone beach at low tide. On the cliff above, red arbutus, some with their bark peeling, sun-splattered bright green leaves. On deck, people in groups chatted or perused the oncoming island, the gulls, the blue-grey water. A couple of cyclists, helmets at their sides, sat on the deck playing cards.

"It's strange," said Noel, "I look out at this island every day and I don't know much about it at all."

"Mmm." Suddenly Kyra was standing up front on the ferry to Bowen Island watching Snug Harbor approach, she was ten, her bony collarbone pressed the rail, she could smell the salt tang of back then, see salmon jump— "Read some more about the place."

He scanned the printout. "About fifteen kilometres long, a third as wide. Three provincial parks, some regional pocket parks, golf course, tennis court, couple of marinas. Local history museum."

"Sounds pleasant enough."

"About 4,000 population year round, 6,000 in summer. Three pubs. RCMP detachment with three Mounties, two medical clinics."

Kyra's eyes followed a flat-bottomed boat travelling toward them at remarkable speed. "Hey, look at that thing."

Noel glanced at it. "Pretty good engine." He squinted to make out a sign on the cabin. "Arbutus Water Taxi." The ferry approached a dock. "Descanso Bay."

"Look up there." Kyra pointed to the top of a fir to the left. A bald eagle, white head gleaming, watched the ferry approach. "You rarely see them around Bellingham."

Noel said. "Majestic." He turned to her. "Kyra?"

"Hmm?" But she knew his question before he opened his mouth.

"You think there could be a connection between my tires and those phone calls?"

She spoke slowly. "They're two different kinds of things."

"The tires were likely slashed at night. And the calls—"

"So now we know your enemy's an insomniac."

The ferry slid into docking position. "Come on." Kyra walked back and sat in the car. Noel got in. A ferry worker lowered the ramp. "Read me whatever you've got about Marchand's Gallery."

Noel glanced from the printout to the map. "Eaglenest sits on that cliff we saw." He read on. "Marchand opened the Gallery about fifteen years ago. Two areas of expertise." He glanced down the sheet. "First, discovering new painting talent. Some from around here but others from as far away as California and Alaska. He also acts as agent."

"Good for him, I guess."

"Yeah." He read on. "Area two, he tracks down lesser classics, sixteenth- through eighteenth-century works from the schools of master painters. He shows them first at the Eaglenest Gallery. Wonder if Gabriolans can afford to buy." He slipped off his jacket.

Foot passengers, bikes and motorcycles streamed off the ferry. Kyra turned the key. She looked up toward the eagle tree, but the bird was gone. And their row was rolling. "Here we go." She drove up the ramp, along the trestle and onto Gabriola. In the parking lot, cars picked up the walk-ons, and new passengers waited to board. Outside the lot, a row of cars was lined up on the hill, heading to Nanaimo and beyond. Cars approaching from the right were blocked by the cars from the ferry. A small traffic jam on Gabriola.

Rose met Artemus in the kitchen. "Hello, darling."

He beamed down at her, bent over her wheelchair and they kissed. He straightened. "Your brother's eaten all the *coq au vin*." His disapproval was mild.

"Did you like the find he brought? He wouldn't tell me a thing last night."

"Excellent." Artemus gloated. "A school of Correggio." He rummaged through the freezer.

Rose gazed up his back. Thick silver-grey hair rested on his blue shirt collar. Time for a haircut. "Tam tells me you want to hire a detective." She kept her tone flat.

Artemus took out a long package, and turned to face Rose. "It's the Roy rumors."

"The RCMP's on the case."

"Rosie, I can't stand it. I go shopping, and people stare. 'Hello, Artemus,'" he mimicked, "'so sorry about Roy and how come at the Gallery, tsk, tsk—' He put the package on the counter, turned again, a pleading look. "The rumors'll hurt us if we don't nip them in the bud. Like last time."

She tapped her long fingers on her wheelchair arms "A whole salmon is too much for just two of us, dear." She watched as he placed the frozen fish back in the freezer. "No detective, Artemus. He'll ask questions all over the place. There's too much risk. Think of the Foundation. Think what that solar generator means to that Somali village."

"Oh, Rosie, what could he possibly—"

"Roy's death is unfortunate, dear. But rumors pass." Had two segments of Artemus' mind somehow disconnected? "Forget about the detective. The Mounties can manage."

"I've already hired him, Rose."

"Then call him back and unhire him."

Artemus took a can from the cupboard and looked at it. "Bamboo shoots?"

Rose shook her head.

He put the can back in the cupboard. She was a tough woman, his Rose. But he would be cleverer. His call would come too late. "Okay." He pulled a piece of paper from his pocket, picked up the phone, poked in the numbers. "Artemus Marchand here. I won't be needing your services so I'm canceling our appointment. Thank you."

"If he shows up, dear, pay him for a day. How about tuna steak tonight?"

THREE

TAKE A RIGHT in front of the parking lot, Marchand had told Noel.
Kyra did. The Tracker turned up a steep slope. The road narrowed to
a single lane. Kyra noted a mirror, a foot and a half in diameter, angled
to show traffic coming around a blind curve. They reached the crest,
dipped down and left the ferry commotion behind. "Okay," she said,
"what else did you find about the island?"

"That's about it. Except for a bit that came up when I googled
Marchand."

"Yeah?"

"He got into some trouble about four years ago. He bought a
forgery and didn't know it. A miniature School of Hals. Donated it to
some gallery in Salmon Arm. The Feds were most unhappy."

"Why donate a picture to a small-town gallery?"

"For the tax write-off, I assume."

"Oh." She waited. "And that's it?"

"How much do you want for a couple of minutes' research?"

They drove along a little beach littered with sun-bleached tree
trunks, escapees from passing log-booms. Across the bay Kyra
saw their ferry. It suddenly seemed a friendly symbol of union, a
moving bridge holding pieces of land together. Her father, in the
days when they all spent summers on Bowen Island, saw ferries
as unreliable modes of travel, precarious links to the mainland.
But Kyra loved ferries. Their double meaning fascinated her, that
they were at the same time a connection between island and mainland, and proof beyond doubt that an island is separate, different,
special.

Noel gave a self-conscious laugh. "You know, I don't have a clue
what I'm supposed to be doing."

"Neither have I. Yet."

"But you've done investigations of all sorts."

"About a dozen cases. One and a half sorts."

"The dead body sort?"

"No."

"With Marchand, when I'm fumbling around, you've got to take over."

Aha, permission to be bossy, she thought, even as she said, "You've spent years finding the truth in really messy stories. You'll be fine."

Kyra drove uphill. The road flattened. To the right, a clear space between the trees—a glimpse of Nanaimo's sprawl across the water. They passed some houses, then a stretch of undeveloped land. Finally a sign, low relief on a cedar slab, told them they'd arrived at Eaglenest Gallery. Open gates invited them in. The tires hummed over asphalt. Where a wide path led off to the left into a wooded area, another sign, GALLERY, pointed right. They cruised a curve, part of a round drive. Flower beds encircled both sides of a small pond. To the right, a late vegetable garden. A large house stood before them, an elegant stretch of first floor, a smaller block on top at the right. To the far left, a pergola, then a greenhouse. Parked between the pergola and the front entrance were twin white vans and a beige BMW.

Kyra stopped the car and pointed to the second floor. "Is that the eagle's nest?"

"The gallery's on the first floor." Noel gestured at a low extension on the right surrounded by shrubs.

Kyra checked her face in the visor mirror. Enough lipstick, and her corkscrew curls were no messier than usual. "If the gallery is separate, how did you see the so-called Titian in the living room without snooping?"

"Well—people were milling about—there was a door into the house—" He sounded lame and knew it.

She shot him an arch knowing look as they got out. "You're a natural for the detecting business."

Carved on the double doors were eagles, on the left in flight, on the right perching. Noel glanced at a smaller door, labelled GALLERY.

The large left door opened as they reached the flat slate stoop. "Mr. Franklin?" A nod from Noel. "I see you didn't get my message. Well, come in. I'm Artemus Marchand."

"My associate, Kyra Rachel." Greetings, handshakes, and they entered. Noel noted Marchand wore loafers, so left his own shoes on. "What message?" An ample tiled foyer brought them into a living room. Noel recognized it.

Marchand said, throwing the words away, "Oh, my phone call . . ."

Kyra examined Marchand: in his fifties, six feet, thick hair almost white, a mild tan on an inoffensive face, blue silk shirt covering the hint of a paunch, light grey trousers. She glanced around the living room: it ran the depth of the house. On the near end three long windows overlooked the driveway. On the far end a wall of glass featured a grand view, framed by two immense cedars and a small arbutus grove, of Northumberland Channel and the Vancouver Island mountains beyond. Kyra stared out. Far below she heard the muted crashing of surf. "Magnificent."

"Yes, isn't it." Marchand smiled. "Have a seat. A drink?"

Noel turned to Marchand. "Thanks. Some water. But what message do you mean?"

"It's not important now."

Noel pointed to a windowless side wall. "I was here a couple of years ago for Lyle Sempken's show and you had what I thought was maybe a Titian madonna hanging right about there."

Kyra looked to both side walls. They were covered with paintings, representatives of the history of western art from the fifteenth to the twentieth centuries; must be worth a fortune.

Marchand's smile had deepened. "A favorite. From the school of one of Titian's students, Cesare Franco. Filled in by Franco's own students. It's a copy of a Titian original, the Mary Magdalene in the Pitti Palace." He turned to Kyra. "In Florence. And what would you like to drink?"

"Nothing, thanks."

Marchand went out to the kitchen. Oh damn, should he hire them? First get a glass, Rosie would say. Rosie also said he didn't need an investigator. But Rosie didn't know how people talk, she was impervious to people's opinions. But the art world ran on opinions, it wasn't botany. I'm an art professional, he told himself, I can't stop these rumors. I need professional assistance. The Mounties are pros, but Roy's death is only one of their cases. He peeked into the living room. Franklin, alert, slim, quick movements, soft white shirt, he knows his clothes. Rachel, casual wear, dressed for gardening, but a strong capable face, frizzy hair. I do think they'll be helpful. I'll explain it to Rosie later. He filled a tumbler with water.

Kyra and Noel stood at the glass wall, staring out. One panel, a door open to a deck, allowed a breeze to enter. Kyra whispered, "I'm some bumpkin who's never heard of the Pitti Palace? Heck, I've even been there."

Noel gave her an eye-raise of a mental nudge: sympathy, and cool it.

Marchand returned and handed the tumbler to Noel. "Do sit down, please." They did, Noel and Marchand on the sofa, Kyra in a chair. "Mr. Franklin, Ms. Rachel, I have to apologize. My follow-up call was to say I wouldn't need your services. But on further reflection, I do."

"I see," Noel said. "Go on."

"The RCMP has been on the case for ten days. Every day people suggest the Gallery might've been involved in Roy's death. But damn it," he shook his head, "what Lucille writes in her column is all mixed up. Most Islanders don't take her seriously. But still, I worry."

"Let me get this clear," Noel held up one finger. "This morning you were upset about the Gallery's reputation and called me," a second finger, "and later you called to cancel our appointment," finger three, "but right now you're worried again."

"That's right." Marchand nodded.

Kyra nudged him on. "And gossip should be taken seriously?"

"Well it's not really serious." Marchand blinked. "Just—a nuisance."

"Particularly on a small island."

A bite to Kyra's words. Noel liked it.

"Yes. On this island you have a lot of privacy but very little secrecy."

"Islands are great places but people do like to talk. Have you lived here long?"

The question seemed to catch Marchand off guard. "Why?"

"Curious."

"Sixteen years."

"So you must have experienced a certain, well, chattiness in your fellow islanders."

Marchand sat forward. "You're right, yes. It's a community. People care about each other. But what you say is also true."

"Two sides of the same coin." For someone like Marchand, Noel had to use his clichés ironically.

"It's important to keep the Gallery's reputation untarnished. And see justice done. So could you learn what you can? For, say, a couple of days?"

Noel said, "You mean, prove the Gallery's non-involvement."

"Yes, right."

"It could take more than a couple of—"

Kyra stood up. "Could I have that glass of water now, please?"

Artemus turned to her, not understanding. Then he too rose. "Of course." He headed for the kitchen.

Kyra cocked her head toward the deck. Noel followed her outside. "Just let him talk. He's got to convince himself that hiring you is a really good idea."

"But he's already said—"

"He shilly-shallies. But he spoke his real intention when he phoned you. Let him convince himself." She heard Marchand step out onto the deck. He handed Kyra her water. "Thank you."

"Shall we go back inside?"

They took their earlier seats. "Okay now," Noel said, "what can you tell me about Roy Dempster."

Marchand looked relieved. "Roy was with us for just over a year. We hired him first as a general handyman and now he's our grounds-keeper. Sorry. Was. He helped my wife Rose with her flowers." He smiled. "Rose is a marvel with flowers. She's grown everything from Angel's Trumpet to *Zantedeschia*." An increased grin showed his plea-sure at ranging the flower alphabet. "You'd call that a calla lily, the *Zantedeschia*."

Oh, Kyra nearly asked, do they have those in Florence too?

Noel said, "Did Dempster keep regular hours?"

"He was here as the garden needed him."

"But he worked most closely with your wife?"

"And she found his body." Marchand's expression softened into sympathy. "She admired Roy. He planted her greenhouse flowers in the outside beds. Sometimes where Rose suggested. But often where he thought best. Rose said he had an eye."

"That newspaper article you faxed me talked about his earlier life, drugs and so on. Did Roy—"

"No. I've spent years supporting the war against drugs. A drug user couldn't work at Eaglenest. Years ago Roy realized drugs were a huge mistake."

Noel opened his notebook. "Did he drink?"

"I don't know. Not on the job. He'd joined a men's group, they insist on living clean lives, Faith Bearers. Bunch of wackos, but they helped Roy."

"Did he live by himself? Have a partner?"

"I don't think so."

"Close friends?"

"Danny Bourassa. Roy brought him in sometimes for seasonal clearing. Another ex-hippy, I think. And someone else too. Jerry something."

Noel scribbled in his notebook. "Any relatives?"

"A sister. Charlotte Plotnikoff. A so-called painter."

Kyra said, "Any enemies?"

"None that I know." He smiled. "But we didn't socialize."

"When did you see him last?"

"The day before we found him here. About mid-afternoon."

"What else?"

Marchand shook his head.

"We should see where Roy's body was found." Kyra got up.

"Yes. Of course." Marchand stood.

"And," she slung her purse strap over her shoulder, "we should talk to your wife."

"Oh. Do you have to?"

"She found Roy's body, right? So yes."

"You mean now?"

"Now would be best." Kyra said. "Or rather, when I come back from the bathroom. May I?"

"Over there." He pointed down the hall. "The door's open."

Kyra stepped inside and closed the door. She chose not to lock. One time in a strange house she'd locked, then hadn't been able to get the door open again. Anyway she wasn't here to pee. Time to snoop. Bathrooms tell you a lot about people. Medicine cabinet over the sink: first aid kit, small bottle of hand lotion, two combs, unused toothbrush, new razor. No perfume, medication, make-up. The guest bathroom? Floral cotton hand towels. Terracotta tiles. Clean toilet.

One of the sparer bathrooms. What did she learn from this room? The Marchands have guests rarely. Somehow too sterile.

In the living room, Marchand said to Noel, "Then you will look into this problem for me?"

Noel plunged. "You still want me to what? Prove Roy didn't die here."

"Yes please, and thank you. What do you charge?"

From plunge to scramble— "A thousand a day. That's for both of us. Plus expenses. And we need a retainer of a day's fee." Making it up as he went along. A thousand suddenly sounded excessive. Well, not compared to lawyers' fees.

"I'll get a check." Marchand took the stairs to his office two at a time, as if afraid Noel would change his mind. Kyra returned from the bathroom. Marchand came back with a check.

"Thank you, Mr. Marchand." Noel slipped the check into his shirt pocket.

"Let's go meet your wife."

"Of course. And as we're working together, please call me Artemus. This way."

Okay, Kyra realized, they were linked. Time to ask some obvious questions. "Just out of curiosity, Artemus, where were you the evening before your wife found Roy's body?"

"What? You think that I might have— You're being ridiculous."

"Which doesn't answer my question."

"Do I have an alibi? I was right here. In my office, reading files. Ask Rose."

"I will. Was she here as well?"

"Of course. And I find you insulting."

"Think of it as doing our best for you. Not insulting, just thorough."

Marchand glared at Kyra, then nodded. "Okay." He led Kyra and Noel out the front door and around the house to a pergola-covered asphalt path that ran from a side door to the greenhouse. Thick wisteria drooped from the pergola slats. As they passed the two white vans, Kyra noted each passenger door said, Eaglenest Gallery. A white and blue handicapped symbol hung in the front window of the second van. They reached the greenhouse, heavy opaque plastic stretched over curved metal ribs.

"My wife designed it," Marchand said. "Many of her tools too. Because of her disability, you know." He knocked on the wooden door. Silence. He knocked again. He opened the door a few centimetres. His body blocked their view. "Darling?"

The inside smelled humid as well as hot. Marchand pushed the door open a little wider and called, "Are you there?" Kyra and Noel saw splashes of color.

A woman's head at the far end turned to face them. It moved smoothly their way between the rows of flowers. Noel spotted a raised bed of carnations.

"Close the door, dear," she called. "I'll come out."

Marchand pulled the door closed. "Ah, there's a danger of bringing contaminants in. On one's clothes. She doesn't let other people in there."

Noel and Kyra backed away.

"She's protective of her flowers," Marchand continued. "She wins prizes everywhere. She's named lots of new hybrids and two are named after her."

The door opened and the woman, head now attached to a body in a wheelchair, exited. She stopped, reached behind and pulled the door closed. Greying black hair in a chignon, high eyebrows over dark eyes, lips tight beneath narrow nostrils: a handsome face. She wore a faded T-shirt that read, Picture Yourself At The Hermitage, and a denim skirt to her ankles.

Tragic accident, Noel remembered. Disability, Marchand had said. She looked athletic. Mediterranean blood? East Indian? The chair would have done Rick Hanson proud. From each side hung panniers. A metal apparatus protruded from the right-hand bag.

"And who are these?" She addressed Marchand.

"Oh, the investigators I told you—"

"My husband is being too careful." Her eyes flicked from Noel to Kyra, back again. "We don't need your services, excellent as I'm sure they are. The RCMP will manage."

"Rose," Marchand said. "We have to consider the Gallery's reputation."

Noel turned to Marchand. "Yes, I understand you had some trouble a couple of years ago. That forged picture at the Salmon Arm Gallery?"

Marchand looked startled. "How do you know about that?"

"Research."

"That was a blow. I do know my art—just as my wife knows her flowers." Noel noted the plea—warning?—Marchand sent her. "I donated that picture in good faith."

"Do you need me further?" Mrs. Marchand turned her wheelchair to the greenhouse.

"I'm Kyra Rachel. My partner, Noel Franklin. We'd like a few minutes of your time."

Marchand said, "Oh, sorry. My wife. Rose Gill. That's her professional name."

Rose turned, eyed them, nodded, and ran her hands along the wheelchair's turning rails.

The sun reflected off the plastic greenhouse wall. A good-size place, Noel thought.

"It must have been terrible finding Mr. Dempster's body," Kyra said to Rose Gill Marchand.

"Yes."

"Would you show us where he was?"

"Why?"

"It'd be helpful."

Rose took off to her right along the circular drive, wheeling hard. Noel marched after, nearly running to keep up. Kyra and Artemus followed.

With a firm grasp on the wheel Rose halted and pointed. "There. His head was over there, his feet here." She pointed to some grass by a broad path that took off into a little wood.

"Can you show us exactly where?" Kyra took a camera from her purse.

Rose smiled tightly. "I can't quite get up and walk the site, you know." But she drew the metal apparatus from the side sack, elongated it and rolled off the asphalt. Her chair easily accommodated a few bumps. Using the metal stick's end-knob to point, she circumscribed the area. "About here."

"And he wasn't here the evening before?"

"No."

"Were you here, Mrs. Marchand?"

Artemus broke in. "She's asking if you have an alibi, Rose."

Rose glared at Kyra. "I didn't leave the property. And yes, Artemus was with me."

"Was Dempster on his stomach?" Kyra asked. "His back?"

"Stomach."

Marchand said softly, "There was a lot of blood on the back of his head. I saw it."

Kyra glanced at Marchand. "The blow that killed him?"

"That's what the police said."

Kyra pointed her camera, then clicked shots of the ground where the body was found, and of the surroundings. Another click, and the film rewound automatically. Damn. Wouldn't have happened with digital. But real film had higher quality. "Where does this path go?"

In his notebook Noel sketched the lay of Roy's body on the grass.

A pause. "My brother's cabin."

"Oh. We should talk with him," Kyra said.

"He's not here," explained Marchand. "He's gone to Nanaimo. Just back from a trip."

"Was he around when Dempster died?"

"Yes," said Marchand.

"Then we better hear what he has to say."

Noel asked, "How do we find him in Nanaimo?"

"Oh. Likely at his condo or his karate club."

"Artemus," Rose broke in. "Leave the boy his privacy."

Noel said, "Perhaps you can show us his cabin, Mrs. Marchand."

"I don't go in when he's not here."

"And I don't go in at all. Tam is an artist. We don't invade his space."

Some kind of threat in Marchand's voice? Noel wasn't sure.

"We just walk down this path, do we?" Kyra started off.

More trees here, suddenly heavily wooded, already out of sight of the Gallery. It smelled like Bowen Island at years-ago Thanksgivings, a dying-leaf smell Kyra could all but taste. Rose rolled reluctantly behind Kyra down the hard-packed path, Noel and Artemus following.

"What's your brother's name?" asked Kyra.

"Tam. Gill." A neutral tone.

About a hundred and fifty feet along the path Kyra reached a low house, clad in cedar siding over a poured-concrete foundation, set among close-growing firs and a few ruddy arbutus. Shady, almost cool. Kyra liked it. What might she find in its medicine cabinet?

Some stairs and a ramp against the wall allowed access to a wide oceanview deck and side door. The ground sloped downhill toward the cliff. The deck, at its highest, stood about five feet above the ground. Kyra started up the stairs.

"Please," Rose Marchand said, "not unless Tam is here." She turned her chair.

Kyra shrugged, and stepped back down.

FOUR

AN EXCHANGE OF goodbyes. Noel and Kyra headed for the Tracker and got in. They drove out the gates.

"Well," said Kyra, "what do you think."

"Not very much, just yet."

"At any rate, you're working again."

"We are." Was she backing out? "You pushed me into this."

"Let's talk about it. I'd like a beer."

"That'd be good." He scanned his printout. "There's that pub by the ferry dock, and one at the south end." She'd better not be backing out.

"The south end pub." Kyra accelerated. "Get an overview of the island."

Noel checked the map. "Turn right. Looks like about twelve kilometres." He shoved a Nina Simone CD into the player to keep his imagination away from slashed tires, and her elegant rendition of "Wild as the Wind" kept night phones from ringing. Back to the ferry dock, up the hill, past the post office and the museum. They passed a house with a duck pond and a greenhouse that wasn't open today before Kyra said, "What about Roy and that religious group? Ever hear of them?"

"Bearers of Eternal Faith? I did a story on them years ago. A hint left of Jerry Falwell and somewhere to the right of the Promise Keepers. Upright stalwarts for Jesus. Human perfection and celibacy unless married. Not even lip kissing."

"Back to medieval times."

He grinned. "The dark ages were way raunchier than that."

They passed a golf course. They wound down through a forest of mainly fir to the water's edge, a flat beach. Noel pointed to the land across a narrows, "That's Mudge Island, population fifty-one. No ferry or bridge."

"How do you get there?"

"Row or outboard, I'd guess. Islands are like that, you see."

"Thank you, Noel." They were both smiling.

Away from the water again, flat fields, sheep grazing, a pretty bed and breakfast place. Oh the pleasure he and Brendan had found in sneaking away for a couple of days, staying in little places like this. And their vacations, country inns in the Dordogne or in Tuscany, museums by day, fine local food in the evenings—

Kyra swerved the Tracker around a hard left curve. Noel grabbed the door handle. The speedometer said 50 MPH. He said, "Uh, are we late?"

"For what?"

"I don't know."

"Then why'd you ask?"

"You're driving too fast."

"I'm only doing fifty."

"That's miles per hour. The limit here is 60 KPH. Remember what country you're in."

"Oops." She slowed to forty-two.

"You don't want to hit a deer. We need a driveable car."

"You're right."

Close to the ocean again, past a graveyard, past the island Community Hall, at last the south end, large pastures with more sheep, turning right at the drive to Silva Bay Marina and Pub. Nina Simone intoned, "Please don't let me be misunderstood . . ."

On the deck overlooking the water, protected and warm enough to sit outside, each a foaming pint in hand, Kyra offered, "To islands and marinas." They sipped.

In the harbor two dozen substantial yachts lay at anchor, as many more tied up at the marina. Noel said, "Maybe there is enough money on this island to buy a Titian."

"Yeah." Kyra took another sip.

"Okay. Are you going to do this job with me? You said you would."

"If I said no now?"

"I guess I'd do it myself." He leaned toward her. "But it'd be way better if we worked together."

"Well— Yeah. Okay. A deal." She lifted her hand to shake. He took it. A firm double squeeze. Clear Eaglenest's reputation together, then Noel's going to be fine on his own.

"Now," Noel took a drink, "what do we know? And what do we need to find out?"

"Okay. Roy Dempster is dead. Looks like a blow to the back of the head. He was found lying on his stomach." Kyra sipped more beer.

"Do we accept he was killed?"

She shrugged. "Maple's column said so. Marchand thinks so."

"So we start with that assumption."

"Let's brainstorm. Start with extremes. Every idea is equally valid."

"Yeah. Focus afterward."

"Okay. He had an epileptic attack, bashed his head, flipped onto his stomach and died."

"Oh sure."

"Don't eliminate anything before considering it."

"We'd have to find out if he had fits."

"Okay. He was a pothead, now reformed. A member of the Something Bearers."

"Bearers of the Eternal Faith."

Kyra said, "Not suicide. You don't kill yourself with a blow to the back of the head. What if Marchand himself bashed Dempster, created the uproar, then hired us as a cover?"

"Except why? Anyway, he didn't strike me as a murderer."

"How many murderers do you know?"

"Who knows who's a murderer." Noel thought for a moment. "Okay, what do we know about motives?"

"Blackmail? Jealousy? Maybe Dempster was having an affair with Rose. In the greenhouse. He lifts her from the wheelchair and lays her on the flowerbeds." Kyra grinned. "Why is she in a wheelchair anyhow?"

"I think I heard at Lyle's opening she had a swimming accident." Noel sipped, and thought. "The newspaper column hints at some sinister connection between Marchand and Dempster. Would people take that paper seriously?"

"Maybe. It's Marchand's second mess-up in the last few years, remember. Tell me more about that fake picture he sold."

"He didn't sell it." Noel picked up one printout. "This is from Exhibitors' Art On-Line. The article implies it was an honest mistake. Written as a cautionary tale. A charitable donation, and he got a tax break. That's what made it complicated. You sell a forgery, it's a crime against the buyer. But if you take a tax break it's a crime against the government. Marchand paid $152,000 for the painting, so in fact he was the one who lost out." He read to the bottom. "A School of Hals. Supposedly painted by one of Hals' students, somebody Spätzler."

"I am impressed by the speed of your research," Kyra said, half wry, half amazed.

Noel heard both halves. "Good." He read the rest of the printout. "Yeah, I see." He glanced over to Kyra. "It sort of pushes what fake is— the painting's been bought and sold as legit three times since it first got catalogued in 1876. But there's some new test for figuring the age of pigments and the best guess is Marchand's fake was painted in the 1860s. It's been a successful counterfeit for a long time."

"Who'd you say Marchand gave it to?"

"A private gallery."

"Hmm." Kyra sipped. "Oh great, thanks," she smiled at the buxom crewcut server who put down their order of nachos loaded with cheese, jalapeños and olives.

"Okay. What else do we know?"

Kyra shoved two nachos into her mouth, chewed, swallowed. "We know Rose Marchand, or Gill, has a greenhouse. And it's easily contaminated."

"Would Dempster go inside?"

"We don't know. Or where he died, or was killed. And what Rose's brother knows. And the Mounties are still investigating. We need some hard information. Can we talk with your friend Albert?" Another nacho.

"I think so." Noel reached for the plate. "What else?"

"I don't know."

"Okay then, tactics."

"We ask some people a few questions. Who first?"

Noel checked his notebook. "Local Mounties." He looked at her. She nodded. "And Danny Bourassa. Lucille Maple of the egregious column. And Tam Gill, I guess. The painter-sister Charlotte whatsis. And that Jerry something. Then Albert back in Nanaimo."

They finished their beers and food, and checked out the bathrooms. Noel caught his face in the mirror, a face he thought he knew well. Adequately formed, in balance, but nothing exceptional about it. He remembered Brendan telling him that he had a great face, that he loved Noel's face, across the table, as they drove down new roads, beside his own on the pillow. For a moment an image of Brendan's face came, not as in the portrait in their bedroom but as it had drained and yellowed over the last year, so slowly Noel had seen no change from day to day, so quickly as to horrify them both when a photo or a friend provided a point of reference. Noel ran cold water, rubbed it into his face and didn't glance up to the mirror again.

By the time he returned, Kyra had found addresses and phone numbers for Danny Bourassa, Charlotte Plotnikoff and the Mounties, the latter's building close to the ferry. They retraced South Road up-island.

In the Mounties' parking lot a young woman officer told them Corporal Jim Yardley, in charge of the Dempster case, was gone for the day, he'd be on again in the morning. Noel checked his watch. Right, nobody commits a crime on Gabriola after 4:33 PM.

Back in the Tracker, Kyra called Charlotte Plotnikoff on her cell-phone. The machine asked her to leave a message. She didn't. At Danny Bourassa's home a woman answered, "No but I expect him just after five." Kyra said they'd like to talk with Mr. Bourassa about his friend Roy Dempster. The woman hesitated, then gave Kyra directions and identified herself as Patty.

They drove over to North Road and came across a small shopping center, Folklife Village. "I need to buy film," Kyra said. She turned into the parking lot.

Noel turned back to the printout. "This place was part of Expo 86 in Vancouver. They dismantled it there and recycled it here."

Kyra scanned the little horseshoe mall. Wooden sidewalks all around, covered on the left and right sides. The cedar-sided build-ings with large display windows housed a food market, pharmacy, clothing store, art gallery, café advertising jazz on Saturdays, hard-ware store, small library, wine store, DVD rental, and a realtor. "Not bad for an island mall." She bought her film at the pharmacy and rejoined Noel.

"Check out the local denizens."

"What?"

"Like at that Eaglenest show I went to. Take a look."

Kyra glanced about. The men: jeans or tan chinos, and T-shirts or sweatshirts, work boots or Birkenstocks, more chins unshaven than razed. The women: jeans or blue or brown chinos, and T-shirts, one tank top, running shoes or Birkenstocks. On men and women, lots of long hair on many tied back and, more often than not, smiles or grins. The young, though, looked like teenagers anywhere, sloppy boys' pants and bare young midriffs. "Gotcha," Kyra said.

"And the clothes don't say who's on welfare and who owns a yacht."

Along North Road, then down a hill to a subdivision called Whalebone. The streets had names like Moby Dick's Way, Quequeg Place, Captain Ahab's Terrace. "Turn right," said Noel.

They stopped in front of a green clapboard house. A large dog, part shepherd, mostly many other breeds, growled as they approached. "Nice mutt," Noel muttered. The dog's rumblings broke into a series of deep barks.

A woman wearing a yellow turtleneck and jeans appeared at the door. "Stop that, Princess!" Princess slunk around the corner of the house. "She's really very gentle. I'm Patty."

They introduced themselves. Patty's head, Noel noted, was round. Hair cut to helmet her head, no protruding ears or extended chin, and eyes wide, in echo of her overall face. In fact she was round all around, not fat but large-curved, round fingers, short round forearms, rounded breasts, and, when she turned, particularly round buttocks. Trim bare feet in thongs, with round toes. She led them into a small living room. Chairs and the couch were protected by slipcovers, a red and yellow plaid, frills on the arms, each looking ready to head off square dancing. "Danny's showering," Patty said. "He just came home." A large print of a down-home Jesus dividing up a small fish hung on one wall. On another, a wedge of varnished fir, the words "Jesus is Lord" etched in. Noel stared at it. Patty said, "Danny carved that," with hesitant pride.

"He's a woodworker, then?"

"Oh no, just a hobby. He's in site preparation so he gets real dirty, that's why he's showering. He doesn't like to be dirty." Patty giggled, and her lips rounded.

Noel said, "About Roy Dempster. What kind of guy was he?"

Patty thought for a few seconds. "I guess you'd say Roy liked to help people."

"Help?"

"You know. Like if a person needed her wood split or gutters cleaned, Roy'd be there."

"Did he have any special friends?"

"Sure, Danny. And Steve Bailey. But Steve's not a Faith Bearer."

"You have his address?"

She found Bailey's address and wrote it on a scrap of paper.

"Did Roy have a girlfriend?"

The giggle again. "Lots. As many as you can on a small island." She caught herself. "Oh, I don't mean all at the same time. But Roy really wanted to get married. He must have proposed three times in the last couple of years." Another giggle. "That we know of."

"Was he dating somebody special?"

"Sue Smith. Friend of mine." Patty took back the scrap and wrote another address.

"Did he propose to her?"

"Oh yeah." More nods.

"Did she accept?"

"She said she needed time." Patty sighed. "I just wish I'd never introduced them. She's so broke up about him dying and all."

"Good evening, folks." A tall man in his mid-forties, jeans and a white T-shirt. Newly shaven tanned face, brown hair greying, well-muscled arms. Beginnings of a belly-bulge. "My good wife not offered you a cuppa?"

Introductions, and Patty said, "Some Beach Reflection? Or juice?"

Both Kyra and Noel declined. "Get me some tea, would you, hon?" Danny smiled. "Puts your insides in real good harmony." They sat. Patty left them. "You want to know about Roy."

"Your wife was giving us a few details," said Noel.

"About Sue," said Kyra.

Danny frowned. "A good kid, Sue. Should of agreed to marry him. Maybe would of kept him home with her and he'd be alive now." He suddenly shifted his tone. "Why you want to know about Roy?"

They were looking into Roy's death. No, they couldn't say who hired them, confidential.

"Roy used to say, 'My dad worked hard all his life and got nothing, so I'm going to retire early.' He was nineteen then. Spent twenty years floating high." He grinned, suddenly abashed. "Me too. It was the times."

Yeah, Kyra thought, the generation halfway between her parents and herself. Just about Noel's generation, in fact. The islands used to be sprinkled with these guys and their women in Indian print granny dresses stoned at the side of their men. Grass, acid, sex, and off-key Lightfoot imitations. "But he wasn't retired. He was working for the Gallery."

"Part-time retired. Long ago he got into woodcarving. Roy was good with his hands. Except when he was high he couldn't carve. Then one day he came clean. Overnight. Taught me to carve but I'm nowhere good as Roy. I used to drink." He chuckled. "I go to AA now. And I'm a Faith Bearer too, I brought Roy in. You know The Bearers Of Eternal Faith?"

Noel nodded, and Kyra said, "Mmm."

"Best thing ever happened to him. He was strict about doing the important things." Patty returned with a steaming mug for Danny. "Thanks, Hon."

A faint aroma like mudflats at low tide reached Noel's nose. "The important things?"

"Yeah, important. Every man's got to become an agent of revival, practice personal integrity all the time."

Noel pulled away from Danny's track. "Why would anybody want to kill him?"

"Dunno." Danny shrugged. "But we're pretty broken up about it. Aren't we, Hon." He half-turned to look Patty's way.

Patty said nothing. A sloppy silence hung in the room.

Danny sliced into it. "Patty didn't take too much to Roy." This time he turned fully toward her. "But we shouldn't speak ill of the dead, should we, Hon."

"Roy was okay," she said. "He just got a little eager sometimes."

Noel said, "Eager?"

"He'd take the—the important things, maybe a little far."

"What she says is true," said Danny. "He kind of meddled too much with some good friends. People got to learn their personal integrity from inside. Nobody can push it on you."

"He mucked around when my sister's marriage was breaking up."

Patty stared at the floor. "She and her husband Joe, they're good people. Just not so thoughtful." She sighed.

"About themselves," said Danny. "Not like we got to be."

Kyra said, "Would either your sister or her husband have tried to hurt Roy?"

"They're not here. They left last year. It was supposed to be a trial separation." She looked at Kyra. "The last straw was their compost, see. They couldn't decide which of them should get it. So Roy told them that was a divine sign they should stay together. My brother-in-law socked him and they took the next ferry off and haven't been back since."

"The road to hell is lit with good intentions," Danny added.

"Sue should of said yes." He looked hard at Patty. "Why you figure Sue didn't say yes?"

She stared at the ground. "Maybe she wanted to be part of a team with Roy."

Kyra said, "A team?"

"Maybe she didn't want to live in a household headed by her husband." She turned to Kyra. "Obedience. That's a Faith Bearer thing. Maybe she wanted to share, not obey."

Danny tapped his left palm with the side of his right fist. "They could of shared. F.B. doesn't mean not sharing. Just mean's a man's got a duty to head the family. Like a volleyball team. Ya gotta have order. Like ya gotta have a coach and a manager."

Noel said, "Did Roy owe anybody money?"

Both heads shook.

"Did he ever harm anybody?"

Patty looked at Danny. He said nothing. She said, "The painter. Tam Gill."

"That was a long time ago," said Danny. "Before he joined F.B."

"Two years." Patty nodded. "My birthday. We were down at the pub by the ferry. We'd all been drinking. Gill and some other guy was there. And then, you know how a crowd sometimes goes silent, and we hear Roy call Gill a ragtop or something. Which is silly, I never seen him wearing a turban. But they went at each other. And we all got thrown out."

"Did they ever fight again?" Kyra recalled the grim sister, Rose.

"Just that once." Patty turned to her husband. "That I know of. Roy worked over there at the Marchand place where Gill lives and they got along okay."

Noel nodded. "Can either of you think of anyone who'd want to kill Roy?"

"Gee," said Patty. "Like who?"

"You tell us."

Patty and Danny shook their heads. "Roy was a good guy. A good all-round guy."

Noel stood and took out his notebook. "You know a friend of Roy's, Jerry something?"

Danny's eyebrows lifted. "Sure. Jerry Bannister. He and Roy hung out sometimes."

Patty asked her husband, "Didn't they have some big argument a while ago?"

"Yeah, but they got over it quick."

"What was it about?" Noel asked.

"Roy got a bit eager about Bearing Faith, and it ticked Jerry off."

Noel made a note, turned the page, wrote his own name and phone number, tore out the sheet and handed it to Patty. "If you think of anything, please call me."

When Noel opened the front door, the dog lay splayed across the walk. Kyra and he held back as Patty went out and knelt beside her. "Such a good girl, Princess." Princess licked Patty's round face.

Noel and Kyra walked across the grass, got in the car and drove away.

———

Sue Smith's home, on Elizabeth Close, was off Mary Avenue, off Jeanette Drive, off Bertha. Noel raised his eyebrows. "What's with all the girl names here?"

"The developer's mistresses?"

"Or his wives."

"Better than Sperm Whale Lookout." Kyra pulled into a short driveway.

"I don't know about that," Noel retorted. "I loved Moby Dick."

"Okay, let's get serious." She stopped the car, and opened the door. "Though when I think of that compost, I giggle inside."

More like the old Kyra, Noel thought.

They were high up on Gabriola, way above Whalebone. The boxy house provided a peekaboo view of the Strait of Georgia. A ferry chugged through tree branches down the hill.

The front yard was unkempt grass littered with rubber doggy toys, bones, balls. A doghouse sided with cedar shakes sat in slanting sun near the overgrown gravel path to the front door. No dog visible. Good. On either side of the front door, curtains protected windows from the bright sun. Noel knocked.

A mousy blonde woman opened the door. "Evangelists? I wish you the best in Jesus' Name but I found Him another way."

"No—"

"Oh I certainly did. I was worried sick about getting a job, I was down to four dollars when this great peace came over me and I heard 'Stop worrying' and I knew it was Jesus who'd taken me in His Hands, why I could even feel Him soothing my forehead and the next day the job just came to me." She closed her eyes and bobbed her head and smiled brightly at them. "So there's my revelation."

Chri— Criminy, Kyra thought. Noel spoke quickly. "We're not Evangelists. We're investigating Roy Dempster's death and if you're Sue Smith we'd like to ask you some questions."

"Oh." The woman studied their faces. "I always give the missionaries my story and then we talk about Jesus. You have Jesus in your lives?"

"Uh—"

"Sure," Kyra announced firmly. "But we'd like to talk about your earthly boyfriend."

Sue nodded and held the door open. "Poor Roy. Does anyone know yet who killed him?" They crossed the lino area in front of the door past shoes neatly aligned.

Murder does seem to be the accepted version of Dempster's death. Kyra shook her head. "We're still investigating."

Sue was barefoot. Noel wondered, should we take off our shoes too? Sue didn't ask them to so he didn't. She led them over to a worn sofa under the front window. The thin red-flowered curtains didn't shut out much light, but, Noel noted, they did clash admirably with the green and yellow floral fabric of the sofa.

The sun's rays reached two chairs at an arborite table in the dining ell. Kyra looked for another place, then sat beside Noel. "Our sincere condolences on your fiancé's death, Sue."

"Death means being with Jesus so you shouldn't condolence." She wore a short tight T-shirt that told Kyra, Island Time is Jesus Time, above tight jeans. Her bare feet were dirty.

Noel's first impression of her prettiness gave way to an awareness of weather lines around her mouth and eyes. Jesus hadn't soothed her face. Her mind, then?

Kyra asked, "Do you know where Roy was the day before he was found dead?"

"Off birding." Sue pulled a chair out from the table. "Birds gave him peace, he said."

"Alone?"

"Yeah, he liked being out there, standing all quiet looking for birds. He said Carl said there was a strange bird near the bog so he went up to see."

Kyra asked, "Carl?"

"Carl Pocock. Our pastor."

"Here on the island?" Noel took out his notebook.

"Not this week. He's up north. Birding."

"And where's this bog?" Noel made a couple of notes.

"By the clearcut." Sue's words came out disinterested. "He said it was a great place to see different birds since it was logged. It's not a clearcut any more now it's growing back, but everybody still calls it the clearcut. Roy said it used to have eagles and ravens and hawks, but now it gets strange little birds."

Noel jotted some notes.

"Roy came by around six," Sue continued. "He already had his binoculars around his neck like he'd maybe see a weird bird right here in my backyard, so I knew he was getting on his one-track. He asked me if I wanted to go but I had a dog to groom. That's the job Jesus got me, grooming dogs and exercising them." She wound her arms around her knees and her face became animated. "Roy wouldn't let me bring the dog 'cause dogs scare the birds. He thought watching them was a way of worshipping too. I keep wondering, if I'd'a gone, would he still be alive?"

Or you might be dead too, Noel thought.

Sue blinked hard. She leapt up, rubbing her eyes, and padded down the hall. They heard the rattle of a toilet paper holder and a noseblow. She returned, still wiping her face. "Sorry. I should be glad Jesus wanted him. But sometimes I think it'd be nice if he was still down here. Except now I don't have to decide whether to marry him or not."

"You were unsure." Kyra's statement a question.

Sue nodded. "He used to have a bad temper. Patty said I should wait and be sure he had it really under control." Sue wound her arms around her knees again, a bundle of thin limbs. She looked at Kyra as if deciding how much to tell. Kyra let her face take on a sympathetic-keeper-of-female-confidences look. Noel dropped his gaze to his notebook. "See, the real problem is, I'm preparing to be a Born Again Virgin."

Noel kept his head down only by force of mind. Kyra turned her smile of amusement into one of sympathy. "What's that?" she asked.

"We're bringing it back at our Church," Sue announced. "It's for Jesus," she hastened to assure. "See, long ago, if a woman didn't have sex for seven years she could call herself a real Virgin again and go into a nunnery. So some of us are doing it. Or not doing it, I guess." She smiled.

Kyra returned the smile. "How close to the seven years are you?"

"Eight months without sex," Sue announced. "Well, next week. And I've given my past sins to Jesus too. Our Church doesn't like sex without marriage. And all that AIDS stuff."

"Lot to be said for celibacy," stated Kyra.

"Yeah, that's the word." Sue nodded. "Roy joined the Faith Bearers, they're celibate too. Just till marriage. You see the problem, if I married Roy he wouldn't let me be a BAV. Also maybe I want children. It's just been hard to decide." She scrunched up her face.

"That is a dilemma," Kyra nodded in A+ confidante style.

After a moment Sue said, "Well, I guess it isn't now."

"Did Roy have any enemies?" Noel asked, needing to change the subject. Though he thought, three celibates in one room talking about a dead celibate, is that some sort of record?

"Enemies?" Sue, picking at a hangnail, thought about that. "No, Roy liked everybody. Even if he didn't really, I mean. Maybe before

49

he'd get drunk and there'd be some clowning around, you know how guys are. He had a fight in the pub once. With the Gallery guy."

Carefully Noel repeated, "The Gallery guy? Artemus Marchand?"

Sue blurted a laugh. "No, the cute one, Rose's brother."

"What was it about, the fight?"

She shook her head. "I dunno. I wasn't there."

"You must have heard something—"

She turned to Noel with defiant squinting eyes. "I didn't see it, I said." She shook her head. "I don't spread gossip."

"Well, your opinion then. Could anyone at the Gallery have had it in for Roy?"

"What a terrible thing to think!"

Kyra changed tack. "Patty Bourassa told us Roy meddled in her sister's marriage."

"I wouldn't say 'meddle.' It's just, Roy was really keen on the Faith Bearers and one of the faiths is to help others." Sue seemed to have succeeded with the hangnail. She turned to Noel. "I know this because Roy told me. So it's the truth, not a rumor." She glanced at Kyra, almost shyly. "There was a guy Roy wanted to get into the F.B.s and kept inviting him and one day his wife yelled at Roy, right in the parking lot, 'You leave us alone and don't ever talk to either one of us again!' and a lot of swearing." She shook her head. "Some people are just really hard to save."

Noel smiled. "Anybody else he tried to save?"

"Mmm—he wasn't really keen on the homos on the island. He was thinking it was maybe his duty to show them a better way."

Oh dear, thought Noel. "Did he approach any of them?"

"I dunno."

"When did you last see Roy?"

"Oh, late that afternoon. He liked to go birding toward evening when the birds come home."

"Did Roy live near the clearcut?"

"Nope, he's over on Berry Point." Noel unfolded the map and Sue got up to show him.

"What's the address?"

"I don't know. It's just past Seagirt," she pointed. "Brown with pink trim. You can't miss it."

Noel scanned the map. "And where's the clearcut?"

"In here, behind the Community Hall." She pointed to the middle of the island. "The trees are growing, it's being renewed." Suddenly she looked shy. "Just like himself, Roy said."

"How did Roy get to the clearcut?"

"Drove." Sue looked at Noel, a guy who'd flunked Basic Knowledge 101. "Mounties found his truck at the Community Hall the next day. Maybe whoever killed him put it there." Her tone doubted Noel could figure this out for himself.

Kyra stood. "Thank you, Sue, you've been helpful."

Noel scribbled his name and phone number on a blank page in his notebook, tore it off and handed it to Sue. "If you think of anything else, give us a call." He crossed to the door, opened it and nodded goodbye.

Back in the car, Kyra said, "Truck at Community Hall, body at Eaglenest Gallery. We really do need to talk to the Mounties before we go much further." She started the engine. "Compost *and* Born Again Virgins!" She backed onto the road.

"Amazing how much people talk," Noel said. "I'd've figured islanders would be more closed-mouthed to off-islanders."

"Except most people love talking about themselves."

"'I am the most fascinating person I know. Want me to tell you all about me?'"

"And most people like being asked their opinions."

"Let's go see where Roy lived."

"Now?"

"Sure. Check the ferry schedule."

"We've got forty minutes." He wanted to be on that ferry. He wanted to have dealt with his tires.

"Too bad the sister's not home."

"It's okay, I'm peopled out for today. We can see her tomorrow."

"Find Berry Point Road."

They passed a garden store, a road called Tin Can Alley, the fire hall, an elementary school, then drove through Gabriola's downtown: small white mall on the right, Folklife Village on the left, and quickly by a gas station.

"Turn right down the hill," Noel said.

A curvy road cut through Douglas fir, maples, and arbutus. Houses nestled comfortably on their lots. Around a bend, a block of shops.

"We've segued onto Berry Point Road," Noel announced.

Past a beach with majestic mountains across the Strait of Georgia. Then Seagirt: a badly marked road. Beyond it, a white house, a brown house with no pink trim, more driveways, and the start of a hill. Berry Point curved around a bay to the left. "We've gone too far," Kyra said. "Let's try those driveways."

"Let's not intrude."

"We'll make like we're turning around." She pulled into the first driveway, and rounded a curve. "Bingo! You can't miss it. Hah!" The house was small and old, stained brown with fading pink trim. Kyra stopped the car.

"What if he has a housemate?" Noel whispered.

"Nobody said." Kyra got out. Trees had hidden the house from the road. The grounds looked neat, as did the weeded deer-fenced vegetable garden—a few last tomatoes and some bolting vegetables.

Kyra walked up two steps to a front deck and knocked on the pink door, Noel following. No answer. She cupped her hands to her temples and stared into a kitchen.

"Kyra—"

High gloss clutter-free counters, empty dishrack, bare wood table. A folded dish towel hung from the stove handle. She moved to the window left of the door. Noel glanced through the window she'd just vacated. She surveyed the living room. Mustard-colored sofa, armchair with hassock, straight chair. TV. Wood stove. Well kept, Kyra thought. On a stand in the far right corner were four birds—are those Roy's carvings, she wondered? She returned to the front door and tried the handle. Locked. "I thought people on islands never locked their doors."

"There's evidence inside. The Mounties would have locked it."

"Evidence is why I want in."

Noel again followed, exasperated and admiring at the same time. Years ago, as an investigative reporter, he'd have acted like this. He was out of practice.

Across the back, Kyra shifted past the door to the last window. "A bedroom. Double bed, chest of drawers."

Noel stared in. A spartan room. "Let's get out of here." He looked at his watch. "Fifteen minutes till the ferry."

FIVE

ON THANKSGIVING WEEKEND, Rose Gill Marchand would unveil her triumph at the Annual Fair in the Agricultural Hall. But her creations were born for a world far from home. Her floricultural transformations had brought the botanical journals' high priesthood to Gabriola to exclaim, to interview, and to write about each new success. This time her mastery would be broadcast beyond the confines of the discipline to millions who found delight or solace or enlightenment in remarkable hybrids. For she had bred a black *Chrysanthemum morifolium*.

Her excitement had been muted by dear Artemus. Mostly he thought and acted as she did. Now Artemus had struck out on his own. And screwed up.

Tam would have gone first to Jenny or Gretchen or Betsy, whatever her name was this month. Usually, Rose didn't interrupt him in town, the boy needed to entertain himself. She consulted her watch—4:30, by now he'd be at his *dojo*.

She double-locked the inside door, wheeled her chair through the trough of disinfectant and along the track beside the carnations. This generation was so gloriously slowed, the flowers had bloomed ten weeks late. Rose drew her cellphone from her pocket and called Tam in Nanaimo. A female voice explained he was in the midst of warm-ups. She left a message.

She rolled to the outside door, drew it closed behind her, and turned off her phone. She settled squarely into the chair. She'd not done this since the morning she found Roy. Poor Roy. Damn Roy. She grabbed the turning rail, burnished oak, and concentrated on its warmth. Felt one with the chair, her spine its spine, its wheels her legs, she and the chair a single energy. The chair and Rose thrust forward onto the asphalt. Her lungs screamed, "YyiiiYyy!!" She was rushing ahead, hard as her hands could pull at the wheels, fierce as the wheels could draw from her hands, around the circular drive, around again.

She'd given birth to the cry in her first triathlon year, a triple trumpeting: to the water as she rose from her dive, to the wind as she mounted her bike, to the hills as she started her run. Her coach had warned her, the cry was a waste of breath. She knew it doubled her energy.

Around a fourth time. Till, her heart pounding, the chair slowed to a stop at the path to Tam's cabin. She breathed in to the depths of her lungs. She glared at the ground. What was Roy doing here at night, what got him killed? She'd checked the greenhouse right away. All had been in order. Roy, a good worker, finally just another handyman, a human being sure, but as a gardener replaceable. And hiring detectives? Let the police earn their pay. Having the Mounties on the case was bad enough, but at least they were respectful.

She still breathed hard. Slower in her recovery time, but not too bad. She studied her hands. Wrinkles by the knuckles, blue veins too. Old woman's hands. Better than her useless legs. But she wouldn't vegetate! Vegetating was for plants. She laughed aloud. Eighteen years ago even Artemus thought she was half finished, vegetable from the waist down. He'd bought her a cat, a rag-doll. The beast climbed onto her lap and lolled there. Artemus had assumed—and feared— that a cat was all her lap was good for. Hah! She'd hated that cat. Like she hated dwelling on her past. Slowly she rolled her way along the pergola to the house.

Artemus stuck his head out the doorway. "Tam's on the line, dear." He handed her a cordless phone.

She stared at Artemus. She felt a sudden pang of warmth toward him and took the receiver. "Hello."

"Exercising, were you?" Tam asked.

She saw Artemus' small smile as he turned and disappeared into the house. "Spying, were you?" Tam hadn't called her cellphone? Oh yes, she'd turned it off.

"Can you talk?"

"Yes."

"Did A. unhire him?"

"Them. Artemus agreed the detectives—two, the other's a woman—weren't necessary. But as soon as they appeared he changed his mind. Again."

Tam swore under his breath. "They smart?"

She realized she didn't know. "Not particularly." Added, "The woman seems cleverer than the man. And younger by maybe ten years."

"Cute?"

"Pudgy."

"Bosomy?"

"Stacked. Like teenage baby fat. They want to talk to you. About Roy and so on."

"Sure. I'll tell everything. Which is nothing."

Rose nodded.

———

Back in his condo, Noel checked his e-mail. Spam; a note from his brother; his server's monthly statement. An unknown address: great-art@brokernet.com. *Hi Noel, Since you keep saying no for lunch when I call, how about an electronic meal invitation. In the next few days? Like to see you again, buddy. Lyle.*

Noel hated *buddy*. He replied, *Hello Lyle. Next few days pretty full. Maybe later.*

Noel made two vodka tonics and joined Kyra on the balcony. She had her feet on the railing, watching the lights of a late-arriving sailboat slide across the harbor's twilight.

"Thanks." She sipped. "Now what do we know?"

Noel sat and sipped too. "The preliminary work on the Dempster case was done by the Mountie on Gabriola. Yardley. He brought in Victoria."

"You reached Albert?"

"Yep. And guess what. He's become head goose in Victoria—"

"Head what?"

"Head of General Investigative Services. Plainclothes. GIS. Geese In Suits. For Vancouver Island and the Gulf Islands. He's coming up tomorrow."

"Good. What else did he say?"

"Not much. We can talk when he gets here."

Kyra nodded. "What about your car?"

"He was irritatingly blasé. No chance the police could track down the culprit. Easy enough for him to say about my car. I called the Honda dealership, they said simplest thing was I should buy new tires, they'd bring them by and install them tomorrow. By 8:00 AM."

She glanced at him. She suddenly saw what else had seemed different all day. "You took out your earring!" Some sleuth.

Noel said, "Yeah." Two days ago he had linked his earring with Brendan's, its twin, the rings of their compact, and put them in a velvet jewelry box in his dresser drawer. "It was time." Which reminded him to look at his watch. 7:30. "That's the trouble with Tuesday night at Enrico's, not enough delivery guys on."

True, the pizza was taking forever. Kyra's stomach gnawed.

"Maybe I'll grow a mustache." He set his glass on the rail, and sat back. "Used to be a time, ring in the left lobe meant who you were." He stared out over the harbor. Nothing moved.

"When you talked with Albert about your car, did you mention the late night calls?"

"Course not. He'd think I was paranoid."

"Try it out on him."

"You think there's a connection?"

"Don't eliminate anything without giving it some credence."

Noel's lips tucked in.

———

Kyra had had an easy relationship with Brendan. And Brendan had loved many things about her. Like her juggling. Soon after Noel and Brendan had moved to Nanaimo she'd juggled on the lawn late one afternoon. They'd had a couple of bottles of wine but her hands were steady. Two balls in the air, bright red, "Noel and Brendan, Noel and Brendan," a label for each. She'd reached for a third, chanted "Kyra, Noel, Brendan, Kyra—" added a fourth, "Sam, Kyra, Noel, Brendan, Sam, Kyra, Noel, Brendan," around and around, her yellow sundress swirling, the green grass her stage, cheers of delight from Brendan and Noel. A fifth ball, and she swirled toward it, reached, found, flipped it up—too high! She waited that instant too long, missed, and all the balls plopped down. She fell to the lawn, laughing beside Noel and Brendan, who were whooping with pleasure. One of those crystallized moments of pure happiness. For all of them.

Fifteen months ago Brendan had made the Great Mistake. When the last of the tests came back, Noel drove down to Bellingham without calling ahead. He'd burst through her front door into the living room. Sam wasn't home. Kyra was on the phone. Noel had collapsed on the large sofa as if he couldn't travel any farther.

"Call you back." Her instant fear, Noel has AIDS. "Tell me." She sat beside him. He shook. She took his hands. "What?"

He breathed deeply. "Remember last month, Brendan went to San Francisco for that conference?"

Kyra nodded. It poured out. Brendan confessed he'd had unprotected sex with a guy from Atlanta. For a week and more Noel had seethed with anger, hurt, betrayal. How could Brendan jeopardize all they'd built, just like that? First he'd withdrawn into punitive silence, turning away from Brendan, refusal of warmth, no intimacy. Then he came to take the confession as a sign of Brendan's love; sometimes people played around at conferences and didn't say a thing; Noel would never have known. He and Brendan put the incident in a kind of temporal parentheses. Hell, everybody slips up somehow, Noel had allowed. And anyway, Brendan joked bleakly, he'd been too drunk for anything like a good time.

Brendan had been really scared. Every jab of pain became a symptom of guilt. His gums felt swollen, his bones often ached, he was tired a lot of the time.

The tests brought good news and unsettling news: definitely not HIV-positive. But the blood work showed some weird results. More tests needed, more tests done. Then the really bad news: acute nonlymphocytic leukemia. If his blood hadn't been analyzed so carefully he'd be beyond repair. "Good thing I've been so afraid of AIDS," Brendan had said, and shivered.

As it was, he needed massive chemotherapy. If the chemo took, a bone marrow transplant. If a donor could be found. They'd already checked Brendan's sister. Not a match.

"Fuck." Kyra had put her arms around Noel and tried to bring him to her. But he sat rigid. She'd driven back with him to Nanaimo. She spent three days with them, sharing their despair and fear. In the next months Brendan received a wide range of chemical soups, methrotexate injected into his spinal fluid. The National Bone Marrow Registries of Canada and the US couldn't come up with a match. Brendan lost the little hair he had left, and grew weaker. On one of the few better days Noel told Brendan he, Noel, forgave him, Brendan, the one-night stand.

Now Kyra shivered a little in the cooling air. Down below, the ferry pulled in. She glanced again at Noel. His head was shaking.

"Did you see those carnations in that greenhouse today?"

"No. What about them?"

Noel remembered a bad moment before the funeral: no carnations available. Now he said, "Simple carnations, that's all I wanted for Brendan's funeral."

"I remember." Kyra reached out and patted Noel on the arm. "Maybe it's time to give Enrico's a call, see how close that pizza is?"

He phoned. "It's on its way." He pointed a finger at her glass. "Some more?"

"With the pizza." She sipped melted ice. "So. Tomorrow. The cops and the newspaper lady over there, Marchand's artist brother-in-law over here? The sister and that other friend? And you said Albert is coming."

"A lot for one day."

"Should we divide up?"

"At least in the morning." He sat back. "I will now change the subject. Tell me about Sam."

"Nothing to tell. Sam's out of my life. He does seem to be coping."

"That's final?"

"Noel," she took his forearm, "there are two men dear to me these days, you and— Oh dang—!" She leapt up and looked around for her purse. "I told my dad I'd call tonight."

"Call from my phone. And ask him how much a school of Titian goes for these days."

She dialed. Lucas answered. "Hi Dad. Sorry for not being there, I'm still here."

Her dad told her he understood. He always understood.

"How was your day?"

"Fine, thanks. And how is Noel doing?"

"Oh, okay. He really appreciated your note. I'm helping him with a little detecting."

"A case of his, not yours?"

"Yep."

"Is everybody becoming a detective? Can you talk about it?"

Could she? Why not. "Well, a body was dumped at an art gallery on Gabriola Island and we're hired to prove the owner didn't kill the guy." She heard a tinkling of ice from the kitchen.

Lucas chuckled. "Islands seem to need a lot of investigation work."

"Really." He knew that several of her jobs for Puget Sound Life were on islands.

"What sort of gallery?"

"A snazzy place. Noel was there a couple of years ago and he saw a painting by someone from the school of Titian. What would something like that be worth?"

For a moment Lucas didn't speak. Then he asked, "Who's your client?"

Kyra almost gave him the stock "That's confidential" response, but what difference if her father knew? "The gallery's owner. Artemus Marchand."

Lucas sniffed a laugh. "I've met him a couple of times, Marchand. At auctions. Our paths cross in the eighteenth century. But his choice of paintings wouldn't fit well over my settees."

Stop talking about the client, Kyra. Except, as long as she only elicited information . . . "What do you think of him?"

"Affable." Lucas was mulling. "No strong opinions. Attitudes neither here nor there."

"That's him."

"A man who's found luck. Over the years he's earned a respectable reputation and a large amount of money. No, that's unfair. He makes his luck. Like most of us."

Kyra said, "Oh?"

The doorbell rang. Noel went to answer.

"He finds good examples of paintings done by gifted students of great masters. Like the school of Titian you mentioned. I don't know how much it would be worth actually. Depends on size, on quality. Maybe in the mid-six figures. Was the dead man connected with Marchand?"

"The gallery's groundskeeper." Time to back off. "Whoops, got to go."

"What I and my friends consider a mystery is how Marchand finds the paintings. If you and Noel were to solve that you'd be doing our section of the art world a favor."

"Dad, there's a pizza calling me. See you tomorrow. I'll try to be there for the concert."

"Give Noel my best. He's a good man."

"I will."

"Bye." Lucas said goodbye and she put the phone down. Vancouver in time for the concert would be a trick.

Noel reappeared, large box in hand. They shared an excellent vegetarian pizza and vodka tonics. She told him her father's guess of the price of the Titian school. And that Lucas had met Marchand.

"The world runs on coincidence," Noel said.

As she undressed for bed in Noel's study, Kyra thought: schmidt, what did Lucas mean, the mystery of how Marchand found the paintings?

———

Women who work out are better in bed than women who run. Greater range of movement, more muscle control, more subtlety. Tam felt his blood stirring again, pressed himself into Gloria's back and rubbed her flank. Sound asleep. He raised himself on his elbow and peered over her shoulder at the clock. 2:12 AM. He wasn't near close to sleep, damn jet lag. Karate workout hadn't helped. But okay enough to make it a couple more times with glorious Gloria.

Tam flopped onto his back and put his arms under his head, clipping Gloria's ear with his elbow. She burrowed deeper into the covers.

An okay-plus day. A personal-best bike ride to the ferry had used up his anger at A.'s stupidity. Descanso Bay had sparkled in the sunlight, Nanaimo and Mount Benson stood out razor sharp. He'd breathed in deeply and coughed out. The last, he hoped, of Bucharest phlegm. The ferry was on time. He didn't know any of the walk-ons so found a little peace going across.

A fast pump up the hill to Machleary Street and his karate club. His master said he'd be ready to try for his fifth in black before the end of the year. A shower, then downhill to Heritage Mews, the studio apartment he'd bought two years ago, a sweeping view of the harbor and the islands. With binoculars he could make out Eaglenest. Even the hideous Cameron Island tower had begun to blend in.

Gloria lived conveniently in the same mews, a one bedroom. At four o'clock she'd gone to work at the Health Club, finished massaging people by eight. At 8:40 she called, ready to go. He knocked on her door. Tall, blonde, full lips, open smile. White mini-dress with a deeply scooped neckline; Tam was partial to clavicles. He'd thought about painting her, all warm bare breasts and pink round hips.

"Missed you for four whole hours," he whispered after their third athletic kiss. She kissed him again, nodding. He envisioned hoisting her over his shoulder, carrying her to the bed, and spreading her out. But she'd got so dressed and made up, better to wait.

She poured him a Scotch. She'd bought his favorite single malt, Loch Sneead. Better watch that. They'd agreed, not too serious. She draped a red shawl over her shoulders and they set out in her car.

Late dinner at Amrikko's Indian Grill, a shared ginger beef and a vegetarian red curry, back for a small drink. He'd been judicious with the Scotch. Gloria was his nightcap.

Mm-hmm, he mused, why can't you remember the whole thick rich experience of sex until you're having it again? You recall movements and touches but the sensations blur, like a watercolor background wash. He rolled onto his side and pulled up the duvet. Gloria understood comfort: a king-size duvet for a queen-size bed.

Thank god he was here tonight. He could imagine what was going on at the Gallery, he'd seen versions before—free-form battle tangos, cha-cha-cha, or venom polkas, A. and BSR shifting the steps to trip the other up. The one he remembered best came just after Rab—Peter Rabinovich, as A. had still called him then—had made the initial phone contact with Eaglenest. Tam had seen the dance starting and got up with his plate to leave. He couldn't understand why they insisted on drawing him back to the table. Not just to finish Artemus' excellent duck with cherry sauce, artichoke hearts and *pommes de terre Lyonnaise*. Tam ate little fowl or fish, and almost never red meat, but the *canard aux cerises* had been superb. Till Big Sister Rosie started in.

A. was jocular. He'd agreed to sell a school of Celesio to Rabinovich for $376,000. And Rabinovich might want other paintings. Tam had said, "Great! Congratulations!" Then BSR glared disapprobation.

In Tam's memory A.'s right hand was 80 degrees up, his left at 60 behind. Rose took the tango lead. "The guy's built a hotel in Las Vegas?" Cha! "You want to sell to him?" Cha! "That's gambling money, we don't do gambling money." Cha! Cha!

A. spun and straightened, soft-shoe shuffled, trying to lead into a verbal waltz. "Three seventy-six, darling. A three-thousand-room hotel. Multiply, multiply." Their dinners cooled.

Rosie clicked flamenco: "No hotel is built in Vegas without Mafia money. I draw the line," a hand slice, snap snap snap of fingers, "at selling to organized crime."

Tam remembered cheering to his forkful of duck: That's my BSR.

"Oh darling," A. into Strauss now, "You understand, this fellow," swoop "has turned over a new leaf," longer swoop. "Russian, a Jewish type." Skaters' Waltz on the Neva?

Tam put down his fork. He chewed slowly.

"Peter Rabinovich," march march, tramping Cossacks, "couldn't stand the Soviet system, he went to Israel," a faint ram's horn?

Tam took a bite of excellent potato. "Why don't you eat," he'd said. They both glared at him. Intermission?

No, back at each other.

Why, Tam wondered now, was he remembering the fight in dance?

"This poor guy," A. had pleaded, "he went to the States from Israel because Israel was even more socialist than the USSR," whining Rimsky-Korsakov violins.

"He's taken you in." Rosie Kurt-Weilled, And his name is Rab the Knife. "You're so soft!" She was actually wheeling around the table double speed. "You fall for any sleazy story!" She was going so fast, Tam couldn't choreograph— Ahh, fast as she used to swim! Memories from around their parents' kitchen table, his swim star, the family so proud, he'd worshipped her.

"Will you please stop moving? Let me explain!" A.'s firm soft-shuffle. "The money for the paintings, it's for the Foundation!"

"Gambling money, gambling money, gambling money!" His sister speeded up yet more. Tam leapt out of the way so suddenly his chair fell back. Rose wheeled around again. Tam took a protective karate crouch. "No!" he yelled. "Talk about this deal!" Her wheelchair stopped in mid-roll. He reversed her gently 180 degrees, left her facing her husband. Who was stuttering, hands out minstrel style, about his Foundation project.

Lying in Gloria's bed, he thought: Well how about that, karate is dance. So I danced the final steps of the dance with Rosie that night. I turned her in just the direction she wanted to go. To A. And therefore to Rab.

Lots of money did come in. The Foundation benefited as A. had hoped. BSR got to muck around with her flowers in world-class style. Turning Rose around wasn't the worst thing in the universe, was it?

Tam buried his nose between Gloria's scapulae. He breathed her scent. No more thinking. Skin, and wet, and the brain turned off.

SIX

AS PROMISED, FOUR new tires had been mounted on the rims of Noel's Honda Civic. Clipped to the windshield wiper, a bill for $544.23. Alone on the ferry he wondered, should he file an insurance claim?

Corporal Jim Yardley greeted Noel in the vestibule of Gabriola's RCMP headquarters. "Heard you'd been by." Yardley in full uniform, including a tie. Solid jaw, bushy eyebrows, brown hair cut short. Some would say handsome. "Come into the office."

"Thanks." Noel followed him to a double-windowed room, a desk against the wall and a small conference table at the center.

The Mountie gestured to a chair, and took one himself. "The Dempster case, right?"

"Word gets around."

"You know how it is on islands." Yardley glanced out the window. "I was told I could answer your questions."

Probably phoned Albert, Noel thought. Albert Matthew had helped Noel a number of times over the last few years, most recently when he needed information from the Nanaimo Mounties in the early research for his Chung murder book. Albert proved himself an excellent source. He was a bloodhound for old unsolved cases, especially if his damned rivals at Canadian Security Intelligence Service might have messed up an investigation. He made files available Noel could never have located. In the early days of their acquaintance Albert had been the kind of homophobe who acted the liberal so thoroughly he'd actually befriended Noel to show he had no problem with queers. Noel had played into this relationship in part because he believed that education takes place in mysterious ways: if he could break down Albert's fear of gays, BC might be a bit better place to live. They'd argued often—which Noel realized was a major step—and with decreasing rancor. Whatever works, Noel had decided.

"So how can I help you?" Yardley was asking the window.

"We need some fill-in on what happened." Noel took his notebook out.

"Who's we?" Yardley moved his gaze back to Noel.

"My associate, Kyra Rachel, and I."

"Who're you working for?"

"Can't tell you."

"Ten to one Artemus Marchand hired you. You want help from this office, you cooperate. Right?"

"Okay. Marchand."

Yardley sat back, hands behind his head. "Here we're second-level. General Investigative Section took over the case right away." Read: Never give the field guys a chance. "They're handling it out of Victoria. They keep us up to date, forensics, whatever." Read: As much as they have to. "And we feed them reports." Read: Since we have to.

The local field unit handles the initial stages, Albert had explained, then turns it over to Nanaimo's GIS. But Nanaimo doesn't have the technology for complex cases so Victoria does the fancy work. If there's no arrest in the first couple of days, the case passes back to the on-site unit.

From a desk drawer, Yardley brought out a thin file, laid it flat, opened it, took out a sheet of paper. "Dempster's body was found on the grounds of Eaglenest Gallery September 19. A contusion on the side of the head behind his right ear, heavy hemorrhage. Bruises on his left cheek and ear. No trace of a weapon."

Noel nodded, and scribbled.

"Found about 6:15 AM by Mrs. Marchand. She called 911, I went over. It had rained, back of the body was soaking wet. His chest and face were muddy, the ground underneath was dry. Clearly not killed where he was found. Coroner's report says he'd been dead since early the previous evening. Mrs. Marchand had wheeled around the place just at twilight, nothing there then."

"So Roy was definitely killed and the body dumped."

"Yep. The most recent dirt on his shoes didn't match the dirt there. He'd gone off to the old clearcut the previous afternoon. Same kind of dirt up there as on his shoes but there's dirt like that all over the island, thin ferrite clay."

"How'd his body get to the Gallery?"

Yardley sighed. "Car, truck, something."

"What did Dempster drive?"

"A 1999 Toyota pickup. And yes, same ferrite clay on the tires and undercarriage as on his shoes. The truck turned up in the community hall parking lot. Smeared prints everywhere, mostly Dempster's. Except on the steering wheel, that was wiped clean. Bird guide on the seat."

"Binoculars?"

"Nope."

"Have you pretty much ruled Marchand out?"

"Nobody's in or out."

"What else? Enemies?"

Yardley closed the file. "No, far as we know. He was in some men's group, called—" he searched—"Bearers of the Eternal Faith. No apparent enemies there."

"And the GIS in Victoria?"

"You can ask the guy. He's in Nanaimo today. Inspector Albert Matthew."

"Thanks." The many roads to Albert.

———

The map of Nanaimo showed Tam's karate club eight blocks from Cameron Island, walkable Noel had insisted. The most important thing Kyra knew about sea level was, from there it's all uphill. She took her car.

She turned right, past a marina with commercial fishing boats, sailboats and the Protection Island ferry—called, quaintly, The Protection Connection. Then across the street the concrete concert hall, its glass facade reflecting sky, marina, and the rear of Cameron Island.

At the Coast Bastion Hotel she turned left. The bastion itself, a last remnant of Hudson's Bay Company days, now painted white and blue, disappeared in her rear-view mirror. Past a First Nations art outlet and onto an overpass. She found Machleary Street on the left, and a parking space.

Mid-Island Karate Association was in an old wooden building that had once been an elementary school. Kyra all but heard hordes of students thundering down worn stairs from the front door. Inside, a young bleach-blonde receptionist sat at a desk that held a telephone, a computer, and an empty in-out basket. "Excuse me, I'm looking for Tam Gill."

"He should be done soon. Take a seat." Bleach-blonde looked at her as if she were sizing up the competition. Kyra gazed back professionally, glad she'd dashed to a store first thing this morning. New tan wool slacks and loose green woven top reassured her. She'd also found a comfortable pair of black suede shoes which, as she sat, she admired.

A man appeared. Tam. No doubt about it; the family resemblance was marked. As handsome a man as Kyra had seen in months. Six feet of taut brown skin, curly black hair still wet from the shower, a dominant nose. Black cycling shorts, brown T-shirt. Bleach-blonde lilted, "Someone for you, Tam."

Tam rewarded her with a smile and a wink. "Thanks, Deb honey." The smile dropped away as he turned to Kyra and raised his eyebrows.

Kyra stood up. "Mr. Gill? I'm Kyra Rachel. Could we go somewhere and talk?"

"About?"

"The Dempster death."

He looked her over appraisingly. "I really don't know much. I left for Europe that evening, just got back." He nodded as if she'd passed muster. "But sure, if you insist. I'll buy you a coffee." He smiled at Deb-honey, who'd been glaring at Kyra, but Tam's smile quickly set her Deb bones a-melting.

At the bottom of the stairs Kyra asked, "Where to?"

"A place down there," he pointed, "the green sign. I'll get my bike and meet you."

"You can ride with me. I'll drive you back."

"I'm going that way." He walked to the bike rack and waved.

Kyra drove around the block and back down Fitzwilliam. By the time she'd found a parking space Tam Gill was sitting at a table in a little courtyard. She thought, he's damn beautiful. Then she thought, damn, I swore and damn, he's turning me on. Get professional, Rachel.

"What will you have?" Gill asked as she sat.

"A latte, I guess. You?" She started to rise.

He jumped up. "No no, I'll get them."

"Business expense."

"My treat. Hold the table for us." He went inside. She sat again.

This is a controlling dude. Through the window she watched him laugh with the server. He runs on high-test allure. Ten-twelve years younger than his sister? Late thirties somewhere.

He returned with a steaming latte for her, what smelled like a lemon something for him. "Thank you." He sat. She sipped, and licked her upper lip. "Now, about Roy Dempster."

"Not much to tell. You've talked to my sister and brother-in-law, right?" Kyra nodded. "I doubt I can add anything."

"What about the fight at that pub, the White Hart?"

"That was years ago."

"Two."

"Yeah, could be. Roy apologized. Actually, he apologized half a dozen times. He'd joined some men's group. He was into apologies."

"What was the fight about?"

"Aghgh. Roy was with a bunch of guys at the next table. I was with a friend from Victoria, another artist. We're talking about—" he raised one eyebrow, "—important things. Roy's group's getting piss-loud so I lean over and tell them to shut the eff up, we're talking business and can't hear each other. Roy leans over and squeals, 'Why don't you ragheads go back where you come from!' And, can you believe this, the guy giggles. My grandfather came from the Punjab eighty years ago and my friend is third generation Iranian-Canadian." He smiled. "I found out later Roy's father arrived from Cornwall after the Second World War." He sipped his tea. "Easy to talk about now, but I felt kind of furious."

She was intrigued. "What'd you do?"

"My friend figured what set Roy off was me saying Roy's neck was so red his father must've been a peckerless rooster. He came at me swinging— You really want to know?"

"Of course." She enjoyed hearing his voice. And saw that Tam Gill knew this. "Tell me."

"Well, Roy gets his right arm back for a roundhouse and lets swing but I duck and bring up my own arm so that the tops of our arms make contact—here, bring up your right arm."

"What? How?" She extended her arm.

He slid the two cups aside, reached over the table, took Kyra by the elbow, made an ell, brought her arm up and toward her so as to bring her to half-standing. The tops of their arms touched halfway between wrist and elbow. "Now push."

She pushed. Her heart was pumping hard. His forearm angled below Kyra's, pushing back and up. She was swung to his right, instantly off balance. Tam laughed. "Exactly!"

She ran the fingers of her flipped arm across her hair. Her forearm tingled. "Okay."

"You see what happens. I go with his swing and take it in the direction it's going. He doesn't make contact so he goes half-around. My hand slips to his wrist, I grab it and hold on. When you swing like that and suddenly your arm stops, your body keeps going, your shoulder gets caught up, you fall to your knees or flat on the ground, depending how hard you swing. I catch Roy with a kick in the ribs and knock the air out of him, and it's all over."

"Wish I'd seen it." Their eyes locked. Exceptional large dark brown eyes. Quick pulse, as if she'd been in the fight. Say something else. "Did you hurt him?"

A chuckle from Tam, and his gaze dropped. "I figure he ached for a few days. But a medium-low rib kick won't break any bones. I could've taken out his knee easily enough, or the dramatic kick to the head. But this wasn't a big-deal fight. I shouldn't have lost my temper but I'd had enough to drink, and he was a loutish bully."

Loutish. No one says loutish any more. Kyra breathed deeply. More relaxed now, and she was charmed. Roy had been provocative and racist. And loutish. "And then he changed his ways after that, as Lucille Maple wrote?"

"Oh, Maple. My brother-in-law pays too much attention to her. You must have more important cases to investigate." He sipped his tea, looking at her. "Anyway, it's not Artemus' business to find out who killed Roy." He leaned back in his chair.

Kyra, pleased he'd accepted her professionalism, tried not to look his way. But her gaze was drawn to his cycle shorts, T-shirt, gloves, cycle shorts— Concentrate!

Gill said, "Do you get many murders in your business?"

"Do you think Dempster was murdered?"

He shrugged. "Seems that way."

"Actually my experience of murder is rare. I investigate divorce cases, insurance claims, that sort of thing. And you, you paint?" She would ask the questions. "Are you successful?"

"Moderately."

"Ah." Modest or truthful? "I gather you spend time in Europe." It was all becoming too much let's-get-to-know-each-other, not enough wily-snoop-collects-information. "Doing what?"

"I sniff out schools-of paintings for the Gallery. Know what a school-of painting is?"

Kyra nodded. "Done in the school of some major painter."

"Sort of. It's how we attribute anonymous paintings to the area or artist their styles most closely resemble. Since Eastern Europe opened up there's a lot of stuff out there that hasn't seen the light of day in sixty-seventy years. Also paintings that were hidden from or stolen by the Nazis are being rediscovered. Well," he reconsidered, "a lot in the early nineties, less now. We buy paintings like these, show, and sell them."

"I'd like to see some."

"The Gallery's having a show Thanksgiving weekend. You live in Nanaimo?"

"Bellingham."

"The University Gallery there's got a fine example of the Sienese School. Fourteenth century."

"Oh," Kyra said. His tone was kindly. Her voice sounded dumb.

"Are you going home soon?"

"Pardon?" She gave herself a mental shake.

Patiently he repeated his question. She nodded. "Well if you're here around Thanksgiving, come by. Our Thanksgiving, not the American one." Tam drained his tea and stood. "I'll show you what we have." He shook her hand. "Nice meeting you." He put on his bike helmet.

"Nice meeting you," she said. Dumb and fatuous, both.

"Maybe we'll meet again." Still smiling, he lowered his eyelids in apparent invitation as he straddled his bicycle and wheeled away with a wave.

Kyra started to leave, then got out her notebook. *Tam Gill*, she wrote— She glanced at her watch. Nearly 11:30! She bolted to her car. Next ferry to Gabriola left in minutes. The time on the meter had expired. No ticket, but a uniformed parking-checker half a block down was fining away.

Kyra should be taking on Lucille Maple. Nice insightful chat between two women of the world, he'd said to her. And she said, You want to deal with Tam Gill instead? Maple lived in a rambling rancher off South Road back from the water just east of Brickyard Beach. No large trees but many tended garden beds. Each segment held one kind of flower only—blue buttony ones here, fading reddish somethings there, feathery climbing things at the side of the house. Each bed, Noel noted as he turned off the engine, set off by a border of shells, old butter clams in various sizes.

Beside the carport, a kayak. In the carport, that had to be a TR6. On thick grass to the left a green table, a closed sun umbrella listing in its hole, and matching plastic chairs.

Noel had telephoned. Now a woman opened the front door as he walked up her flagstone path. "Step on the stones!" A brisk contralto. "That's grass seed between them!"

Noel, usually a reserved man, found his legs bopping along the flagstones as if his feet were playing hopscotch. And—where'd that come from?!—a pirouette, Noel a giraffe in ballet shoes. In order, he realized as he reached the stoop, to make Lucille Maple laugh. Why? Because her article was so ridiculous?

She laughed. "That was silly." She pulled her face into a line of composure. "Just what kind of detective are you?"

Missing no beats, Noel said, "An effective detective."

She tried to keep her face straight but another laugh escaped. "Oh stop."

"Actually, I'm just a researcher. For example, why grass seed in September? Isn't it too late for seeds to germinate? And once the rain comes, won't it rot?"

"I'm ever hopeful," Ms. Maple said. "Gardens grow years after they were planted and stuff that was composted sprouts."

They grinned, each recognizing the other: failures in elementary gardening.

Noel followed her into a cool, bright, long hall. Shoes off? She had shoes on. She led him to a neat Edwardian sitting room on the left.

Through glass doors Noel noted a desk, a computer, a chaos of paper.

"Sit down. We will not talk about gardens."

"Good." Noel sat on a suede ottoman.

"You would like some tea."

"Of course," Noel agreed.

She headed down the hall.

He looked about the room. One wall held a floor-to-ceiling shelf filled with books. A quick scan showed Lucille Maple's range, at least as represented here: from sixteenth-century poetry to sci-fi power-women, from European and Latin American travel to biography, mostly about or by women. And a separate section, books about islands; shelved, Noel noted, alphabetically by name of island. A high cupboard with china cups below, china dolls above. Against the side wall, Maple's music center—a CD player, tape deck, turntable and pre-amp.

Maple returned with a tray holding a pot of steaming water, milk in a plastic container, sugar in a silver bowl, and two tea bags on a plate. She took cups and saucers from the cabinet, set them down, dropped in the tea bags. "A godsend, microwaves, know what I'm saying? Sugar?"

"No thanks." Tea bags were bad enough but a microwave to heat the water?

She handed him a cup, tea bag soaking. "Now then, Noel Franklin, ask me your questions. But since I usually ask the questions, I know all the tricks."

He pressed a spoon against the bag, put it on the saucer and sipped. Bitter, already cooling. Then he sat back and put on a facade that suggested deep thought. He evaluated Lucille Maple. Early sixties, he guessed. Tall and fine boned, alert eyes, short curly grey hair, good muscle tone on her arms She wore a red-print blouse, denim skirt, ankle socks and running shoes. Tanned calves, he noted, also firm and trim. "I'm investigating Roy Dempster's death."

"Silly twit. Do you know that since white settlement in the 1880s we've only had three murders on the island? Till this one."

"So you're sure he was murdered?"

"Killed, anyway."

"I read your article. You seemed sympathetic to him—"

"When you were at the *Vancouver Sun,* you wrote what you thought, yes?"

"How'd you know I was at the *Sun?*"

"Answer my question, I'll answer yours."

"Okay. I wrote what I thought."

Maple nodded. "Helps explain why you never became an editor."

"I was an editor. Well, acting. How'd you know, anyway?"

"Young man, I've been raking muck for fifty years. I have my sources."

Fifty? "Tracked me down between my phone call and now?"

"Of course."

"Fast work." He sipped the tea. "And your sources for the story about Dempster?"

"Dempster was an ass. But when I write for the *Gabriola Gab* it's not my role to take down Roy. Especially now he's dead."

"Why lay his death at Marchand's door?"

"I didn't. The killer tossed the body there, not me. I ask: Why?"

"To throw the cops off-track? To lay the guilt on someone at Eaglenest?"

"Maybe. That'd be a little progress." She squinted at him. "But again I ask, why?"

He laughed. She was questioning him. "You're very good." Progress?

"Lots of experience." She lowered her eyelids demurely.

Noel sipped more execrable tea. "Okay, could anyone there be guilty?"

"Oh, all of them, know what I'm saying? Guilty of something. Murder? I don't know."

"Marchand himself?"

"Artemus Marchand is a gentleman."

"Then why'd you light into him in your column?"

"Can't let prejudices show in a newspaper, know what I mean?"

No, he didn't.

"Listen, he discovers new young artists. Many aren't very good, but lots of artists from previous centuries weren't much good either. And the Marchand Foundation funds small projects in developing countries and stays out of the clutches of the IMF and the World Bank. That's enough in itself, but he also contributes to our charities.

Without him, the Walk-In Breakfast Program would have died last year. He's put thousands into the Wildlife Conservancy. And anti-drug programs in Nanaimo. I can't imagine him hurting another person. My money'd be on his wife. A cool one, needs to hear regular glorious things about herself. Works with flowers. Some big surprise at the Thanksgiving show, I have to cover it. What can you say about a flower show."

"What's the story with her? The wheelchair, I mean."

Maple sipped. "I interviewed her when her gardening aids for the disabled were patented. Pretty and talented is Rosie Gill. You know Gill Timberlands Inc.?"

"Vaguely."

"Her grandfather was Sihan Gill. Gills have been in the Cowichan Valley since the early nineteen hundreds, one of the first Indo-Canadian families on the island. Business goes to the eldest son, Nirmal, then to Nirmal Jr., Rose's older brother. But the others have to make their way with talent. 1978 Commonwealth Games, Edmonton, gold in the butterfly, silver in the relay. Montreal Olympics in '76, two golds. Glory. Her two greatest competitions and she never got to leave the country. She retired when she graduated from UBC, straight A grades in her majors, botany and chemistry. Didn't go on, though. Married Artemus, oh he was a dish, they met at a party a year after he finished at Princeton. Oldish whitish BC money marries oldish brownish BC money. By old I mean fifty to a hundred years in BC And what a wedding, Noel, what a wedding. Enough multiculturalism there to satisfy a decade of liberals."

"You covered the wedding?"

"Yep. A ten-minute interview turned into a ten-second clip. Editors! Just as bad in TV as in newspapers, right?"

Noel didn't bite. "What did she say?"

"I interviewed her earlier. Told me how she became a sports-woman around town. Triathlon was her thing, she fought to make it an Olympic sport. Tennis of course, and charity golf. Then she takes up diving. Looked gorgeous on the high board, flips and double twists. She got a lot of TV time, being who she was. And her body was stunning. She'd organize performances for the cancer society. As if they need more money. For kids with cystic fibrosis.

And one day, practicing, she springs, and comes down so her back catches the tip of the board. When they pull her out of the water they don't think she'll live. She was thirty-six. Paraplegic ever since. She your client?"

"Maybe my client's the brother. Tam Gill."

"Tamar Gill. Artist. Nirmal's other pride. Art and sports, the lifeblood of the nation. But Tam never made it beyond Nanaimo. Not even into his brother-in-law's gallery. Good craftsman. But an artist has to grow, know what I'm saying? Not Tam Gill. A gallery in Nanaimo hangs him every other year and every show he's on a new tack. Three years back it was all abstract flowers in greys and browns. Before that, soft pinks and oranges for triptychs of nudes— men, women, kids. Last year he did super-realistic mechanical objects—inside of a stove, gearshifts, teeth of a water wheel. I have to review these things because he's a Gabriolan. How much can you say about a naked orange baby?" She finished her tea, not bothered by execrable.

Noel nodded his sympathy.

"'Naked orange woman cute, naked pink man with large parts hairy.' Can't say too hairy, even if you know it. Not in a family newspaper."

"Ms. Maple, how long have you lived here?"

"Forever. First time I came over was 1963, to visit a friend, and in half an hour I knew the island was made for me. One of those rare perfect matches. Before I retired I came here every time I could. And make that Lucille."

Noel nodded. "And you came here. To write for the *Gabriola Gab*?"

"Not intentionally. I'm an old lady, Noel. Haven't you noticed?" She sounded, after angry, almost wistful. "Nobody wants a seventy-four-year-old muckraking old-lady TV journalist. Hell, no one wants a fifty-four-year-old female on TV, even if she looks thirty-four. Dumb pricks."

Noel laughed and placed his cup and saucer on the tray.

"Sorry. That snuck out. No, life's fine here. But it's hard to get the hang of this writing stuff again when you're used to just talking. And my editor keeps sticking comments in my articles! Damn editors." She snorted. "I love islands and this is a great one. I like it out on the water too—I kayak around the islands, camp sometimes. Old Maple fits right in, know what I'm saying?"

Noel figured he did. "Yep." He stood. "Thanks for seeing me." He shook her hand, a sincere shake. From both. "It's been a pleasure."

She saw him to the door. "I'm a good interviewer," she said, "and I know when I've met another. Watch those stones."

"Won't take my eyes off 'em." He wrote out his name and phone number, and handed the paper to her. "You learn or figure anything interesting, let me know."

"About Roy Dempster?"

"Or whatever." He stepped down to the walkway. At each flagstone he bent low.

"Hey! What're you doing?"

He turned back. "Watching the flagstones. Don't worry, they'll be okay."

SEVEN

KYRA PARKED THE Tracker in one of the guest spaces at Cameron Island and ran. The ferry was already unloading. She paid her fare and hurried down to the crowd of foot passengers. After the last car drove off, she walked onto the ferry and strolled to the front. Really the front, not the bow; bow and stern were interchangeable, depending on the ferry's direction. A shuttle ferry, she thought, back and forth, back and forth. What would it be like to work on? What—Nonsense questions. Why? Nonsense questions were like juggling. Admit it, Tam Gill turned you on.

No way for a woman of thirty-six, married three times, given up on sex, to feel. Such a woman controls her hormones, right? But how do I know how I'll react to strangers? Like why did Marchand get to me, with his Pitti Palace throwaway? And Tam? And Tam.

She headed to the back of the ferry. Halfway there she noted a familiar white van. A white-on-blue handicapped logo hung from the rear-view mirror. Eaglenest Gallery. The greenhouse. Rose Gill Marchand. Another stranger I didn't take to. Kyra glanced toward Gabriola. Lots of water before we get there. She walked around to the driver's window. "Hello."

Rose Marchand looked up from her book. "Oh. Hello."

Kyra introduced herself again and looked into the van. The driver's seat had been removed to accommodate a wheelchair, clamped down left and right. "What a fascinating adaptation," she enthused. "How do you manage the gas pedal? And braking?"

With a small why-does-everyone-ask smile, Rose said, "This is the gas. This is the brake." She indicated levers on either side of the steering wheel.

"How do you get the wheelchair in?"

"With my pneumatic lift. Here." She indicated her door with her head.

"So you can be completely independent?"

"Independence is important."

"Indeed it is," Kyra agreed. "I must say I admired your garden yesterday. I tried gardening once but I have a real black thumb." A glimmer of interest from Rose? Or vexation? "The only plants I didn't kill were dandelions. Shouldn't gardening in Bellingham be just like here? I mean, no real difference in climate or anything?"

Rose closed her book and set it on the passenger seat. "Depends. Rainfall, sun, exposure. Something in your soil. Have you had it tested?"

"No."

"It could be too alkaline." Rose's expression turned less pedagogic. "Or acidic."

"Maybe the previous owners did something." Gardening, one of Kyra's weaker topics. "Do you grow all your flowers in the greenhouse?"

"I start the seeds there."

"And Roy helped you with your flowers."

She hesitated before saying, "Yes."

"I suppose he'll be hard to replace."

"He had a good eye. But Gabriola has lots of good gardeners."

"Though not nearly as good as you. I drove around the island."

Rose bowed her head slightly but did not demur. "One must strive for mastery."

"Like your diving?"

Rose squinted at her. "Of course," she said, dismissing both question and Kyra.

Kyra considered leaning her elbow on the window frame, but decided against it. Blundering should not be overdone. "The accident must have been terrible."

Rose shrugged.

Kyra flinched in sympathy. "Your husband said some flower species are named for you?"

Rose tightened her mouth. "*Chrysanthemum articum roseum* and *Gladiolus callianthus gillis*."

Kyra shifted to wide-eyed enthusiasm. "Will other new flowers be named after you too?"

"Probably."

"Are your flowers available?"

"I suppose so. But that's not the point."

"Oh? What is?"

"To create one perfect plant." Rose half-lidded her eyes. "When you've done that, there's nothing left to prove."

"Oh. Well. Your husband must be so proud of you."

Silent, Rose stared out the windshield.

"And you're so careful, you worry about germs getting on your plants." Kyra looked forward. The wall of trees behind the Descanso Bay ferry dock loomed.

"One must be careful. More and more diseases are air- and water-borne."

Kyra stood instructed. "I hadn't noticed." She stared at the gas lever, the brake lever. "You studied botany?"

"Yes." The silence grew thick.

"Where'd you go to university?"

"Excuse me. I have to prepare to unload."

"Oh." Too direct. Slow down—no, let it go. For now. "Well, good luck." Kyra stepped back. Rose inclined her head in dismissal. Kyra joined the foot passengers at the front. Tam clearly owned the Gill family's allotment of charm.

———

Kyra found Noel at the pub by the ferry, sitting in a large chair at a table. She plopped into another chair. "Golly gee."

"What do you know?" Noel asked, his tone bright.

"I've just had an unsatisfactory conversation. 'One must strive for mastery.'"

"I agree with that."

"You wouldn't if you'd just heard it from Rose Marchand."

"Yeah?"

Kyra reprised her conversation with Rose. "And I had my meeting with her brother."

The server arrived, a tall woman. They ordered beers and hamburger platters.

"Tam Gill," said Noel.

"They have people in Europe locating these schools-of paintings. Gill checks out each one."

"So now you can tell your dad how he finds them."

"Okay," said Kyra, "your turn. Tell me what you know."

Noel filled her in: Dempster's body dumped, his truck at the

79

community hall. Bird book yes, but not the binoculars Sue had mentioned. "Maple's sure he was murdered."

Kyra said, "Then it wasn't Marchand. He wouldn't dump Roy's body on his own front lawn."

"Unless he's extremely devious."

"Don't see him as devious. Now as to Rose—"

"Why would she want to kill him?"

"They're having an affair, Roy calls it quits, she kills him. If she can't have him no one can."

"Oh sure, she wheeled up on him in her sporty wheelchair, he knelt down, put his face in her lap and she bashed the back of his head in with her trusty trowel."

The server set down their mugs of beer, and they drank.

"How about blackmail," said Kyra. "Roy discovered Rose's deep dark secret—"

"Which is?"

"Everybody has one."

"Oh yeah? What's yours?"

"If you don't know," she smiled sweetly, "I won't tell."

"What's Rose's?"

"Murder, maybe? Roy and Artemus are having the affair, Rose gets jealous, she kills Roy to save her marriage."

Noel shook his head. "Not the homophobe Roy whom born-again Sue knew."

"Still, we can't rule out blackmail. Even if we don't know who was being blackmailed." She saw Noel's grimace. "Okay, we weren't hired for that. Just to clear the Gallery."

Noel considered this. "The body was dumped there. That clears the Gallery."

"Except Marchand didn't need us to get that information. The Mounties already knew that."

"But they never told Marchand. We have to."

"And we also have to talk to Roy's sister, and the friends."

Noel took a mighty glug. "And Albert at six. Maybe he'll dot each *i* and cross each *t* for us."

"Great." Kyra glugged too. "Tell me about Maple."

"She's quite the gal. Seventy-four, has a kayak and a vintage TR6.

We talked journalism. Nose like a ferret. Anything she may know she kept to herself. So I decided just to chat her up. Maybe tomorrow she'll open up some more. My sense is, she figures if she keeps digging she'll beat the Geese to the perp."

"Jeez, Noel, who writes your lines?"

"I'm learning to talk the talk, don't you think?" He consulted his notes. "She insists there's no way Artemus had anything to do with Dempster's death."

"But that column practically tried and sentenced him."

"She said she was being objective. Oh—she's written an article about Rose Gill's inventions. Remind me to look it up."

The food arrived, hamburgers with lettuce, tomato, mushrooms, onions, jalapeños, mayonnaise, relish, and mustard. The fries were crisp and hot. He told Kyra about the two Thanksgiving shows weekend after next, art and flowers. She told Noel about Tam's enactment of the fight here in this pub. "Tam's more of a charmer than his sister. But, like her, he insisted Marchand didn't need to hire us."

"We all agree, then." Noel chewed and swallowed. "Still, why get so het up about it?"

They finished their hamburgers. They munched their fries. Noel reached for the bill and stood. "Roy's sister, the friend, and Albert. Then we turn in our report." He paid, they left. Working with Kyra made him feel like her contemporary. When he'd been her age he'd felt he could do anything, all options available. A long time ago, so few years back. They reached his Honda Civic. He glanced at the tires. Fine. He'd be sorry when she went home to Bellingham.

Roy Dempster's sister Charlotte Plotnikoff lived on Malaspina Drive. Noel turned at a sign pointing to Malaspina Galleries.

"More galleries? Schmidt, another artist? Doesn't anybody here work for a living?"

"You don't think art is work?"

"Not what I meant."

"Anyway, it's not an art gallery," Noel said, recalling his research. "Naturally scooped rock formations. Apparently pretty dramatic." Two minutes later he stopped. "Here's the house."

Charlotte Plotnikoff's home had to be on the waterfront, but from the driveway the house blocked any sense of beach. Half the door was glass. Noel knocked on the wood frame. Through the glass they saw a staircase.

A minute passed. Kyra noted a rope dangling from a cowbell and pulled. It clanged. Below it an oyster shell overflowed with butts. She wanted a cigarette—No, she told herself, no you don't.

A glaring woman in an ankle-length batik dress and no shoes pelted down the stairs. She opened the door. "Yes?"

"Ms. Plotnikoff?" The woman nodded. Noel introduced himself and Kyra. "We've been hired to investigate your brother's death."

"Oh god, Roy," the woman's face crumpled, she blinked fast and opened the door. "Let me put the lids on my tubes." She dashed back up the stairs, calling, "Come in!"

Noel glanced down the hall, a high-sheen oak floor, to a living room wall-to-walled with thick white carpeting. "Shoe removal," he said, kicking his off.

Now that she'd lived in the US all these years, Kyra found shoe removal a drag. In snow or mud it made sense. But September on Gabriola? With an eye-roll at Noel, she slipped off her shoes.

The woman came rushing back down the stairs. She led them into the living room. Noel's socked feet sank into the carpet. Beyond a wall of sliding glass doors, the view was a panorama of the Strait of Georgia from the hills behind Nanaimo to the Sechelt Peninsula. Texada and Lasqueti Islands were framed by two smaller islands. A short flight of stairs led to a sandstone beach and some tidal pools. A large bleached log nursed salal and a couple of cedar seedlings.

"Beautiful spot," Noel exclaimed.

"We're very lucky." Her tone indicated this to be her automatic response.

"Our condolences about your brother, Ms. Plotnikoff," Kyra started.

"Charlotte, please. Oh god it's dreadful, dreadful." The rims of her eyes reddened and she blinked rapidly.

Noel took control. "May I?" He dropped into a rose velour-covered armchair. Kyra chose a matching sofa.

Charlotte folded her arms and paced. She was a plump woman in her early fifties with short grey-blonde hair. The red-purple dress, hanging from her shoulders, suited her in an aging hippy manner. "I've been over it and over it. I just don't know who could have done this."

Had she been in young Roy's druggie crowd? Noel wondered. "Roy have any enemies?"

"He was Mr. Kindness. My husband is phobic about heights so Roy cleaned our chimney. And the gutters." She sighed. "I just wish he hadn't gone to work at the Gallery!"

"Why?" Noel asked.

"Marchand's such an arrogant, patronizing bastard. Like he's God's Gift to Gabriola."

"God's gift."

"Yeah, he wants to be a citizen of the world. And if the world comes to Gabriola because of him, then Gabriola becomes the world. You know he's got this foundation that gives away millions? Not to any of us, heaven forfend. Give it to us and nobody'd hear about it. Give it to somebody in India or Timbuktu and you're a great man. That's Artemus."

Jealousy? "You say he ignores Gabriola artists?" Kyra wriggled the bait, a slow retrieve.

Charlotte bit and ran. "Damn right!" She dropped into a wood-armed chair. "He only shows from off-island. For me it's okay now, I've got four galleries that take my work. But it sure would've been easier if I'd had Marchand's support."

"He outright refused to hang your work or just paid no attention?"

Charlotte turned to Noel. Her eyes narrowed. "I took him some pictures. He said he was booked up for the next two years."

"You know he wasn't?"

"Look, I live here so I can't be any good. Heck, even his brother-in-law's in my boat. But I'm okay, I've got lots of support, other artists, my husband." She considered this, and nodded. "Walt's very supportive."

"Is he an artist too?"

"He has a denture clinic in Nanaimo. Making false teeth is a lot like sculpting, he says."

"But," Kyra observed, "Roy did decide to work at the Gallery—"

"Too damn right!" Charlotte spat the words. "Roy didn't understand. 'Just get over your feelings,' he'd say. 'Get over your feelings and let your heart lead the way.' Bull."

"Can you think of anyone who might have wanted to hurt him, anyone at all?"

"Nobody'd want to hurt Roy, ever."

Noel stood, then Kyra. "We won't take any more of your time," Noel said, "but if anything comes to you, please give us a call."

"Of course."

He gave her his number. His notebook was thinning. Should he get cards made up? She followed them down the hall. Crouching to tie his shoelaces, he asked. "Did Roy work anywhere else?"

"He was caretaking someone's garden while they're away. The United Arab Emirates, he said. But I don't recall their name."

In the car, Kyra announced, "Dentures as art."

"*False Teeth In Water Glass.*" Noel laughed.

Kyra pulled out the map. "This Steve Bailey lives on Harrison." She showed him.

Noel backed out the driveway. "She sure has the venoms for Marchand."

"She's the first person who's been down on him. Except for the Lucille article."

"Lucille would know who from the island has gone to the UAE. I could ask her."

"Good."

"No investigation untried, right?"

They drove in silence for a couple of kilometres. Kyra said, "Listen, try this. Charlotte gets angry at Roy, they fight, she kills him—accidentally, on purpose, I don't know. She dumps his body at the Gallery to blame it on Marchand."

Noel scowled.

"At least it's a hypothesis."

A deer darted out of the bush and froze halfway across the road. Noel slammed on the brakes. "See? Like I said yesterday. Deer."

The deer stared at the car, trotted to the shoulder, turned and stared some more. "Point taken," Kyra said.

Noel drove on. Okay, start thinking hypothetically. He slowed and stopped behind three unmoving cars.

Kyra said, "Remind me who this Steve is."

He looked in his notes. "Another buddy, Patty said. Non-F.B. friend."

"Oh yeah." They were stuck at a stop sign while cars, trucks and a school bus roared up the hill from the disgorging ferry. "What a drag," she said.

Noel made a note about Roy's other job. "With luck we'll have time to check out Jerry Bannister too, the guy Bourassa mentioned."

"If not today, tomorrow." Kyra popped the glove compartment button. "What've you got for music?"

"Not much."

She rummaged, and pulled out a computer floppy. "What's this?"

A wry grin from Noel. "Backup of the Chung book." She didn't respond. "In case the condo burns down. Just leave it there."

She rummaged some more, came up with a caseless tape. "Holy schmidt, this Grateful Dead's thirty years old!"

The ferry unload ended and they turned left. Past the museum, right at the cop shop, left and a final right. Noel cruised slowly. Kyra peered at addresses.

Bailey's turned out to be a mobile home, double-wide, with attached workshop and woodshed. Four tall cedars shaded the trailer. Summer-brown grass on all sides; no mower had visited it this year. On the far side stood a limp apple tree.

Noel's knock was answered by a man in shorts and a faded T-shirt. "Steve Bailey?" The man nodded. "We'd like to ask you some questions. About Roy Dempster."

"We're making some inquiries." Kyra held out her hand and introduced herself and Noel.

They waited for Bailey to ask the usual, Who hired you? but he didn't. "A real tragedy about Roy. Come on through to the deck. It's pleasant out there."

They passed a shabby couch in a comfortable living room. Kyra noted maybe a dozen clocks. Bailey slid open the screen and shut it behind them. On the shaded deck stood a picnic table scattered with wood, metal gears and pieces, and a clock face. He sat. "Ask away, I'll just keep working."

"You making a clock?" Noel asked, with real interest.

Bailey smiled. He was in his late forties, thinning reddish hair, blue eyes and florid cheeks growing today's stubble. "Yep. From a kit. This one's an authentic fourteenth-century replica, it only has one hand. Two hands didn't come in until the sixteenth century."

"I like clocks," Kyra stated. "My father's an antique dealer."

"Kits are way cheaper than antiques," Bailey stated, picking up a half-inch gear. "I have one antique, a nineteenth-century spring-wound Westminster chimer. I wouldn't part with it," he added hastily, as if Kyra's father were making an offer.

"Was Roy into clocks too?" Noel, conscious of the ferry, reclaimed the conversation.

"Nope. Damn, I miss him. He was a good head. He tried so hard."

"We hear he put people off sometimes, trying too hard."

"Yeah. He couldn't get it through his skull that everybody didn't share his enthusiasm for turning themselves into perfect people." Bailey fitted the small gear against a larger one.

"What about Roy's fight with Tam Gill?"

"Oh yeah. Roy got mouthy. We all got the boot for it. But you know, after he went to work at the Gallery he changed his attitude to Gill. Apologized for that ragtop stuff. Gill isn't, of course, but anyway turbans are no weirder than crucifixes. In my book."

"Steve," Kyra said, "do you have any ideas who might have killed Roy?"

Bailey picked up an oblong gear, sat still and stared into space. "None."

"However far-fetched."

Bailey shrugged. "I wish I did. For whatever good it might do Roy. Who'd want to kill a birdwatcher, for god's sake? Birds and the clearcut, that's what mattered to Roy—well, this religion stuff now too. He was broken-hearted when they logged it, he made the loggers leave an eagle-nesting tree standing. For a few years he wouldn't drive down South Road so he didn't have to get close to that bare hill. Then, about the time he got religion, he started going back. The alders were already maybe fifteen feet high, the arbutus and fir were getting tall too. Also some new birds were using it, rails, he said, and something else." Steve laughed mirthlessly. "The tree with the eagle nest is still there, but no eagles. Poor old Roy."

"Do you know whose house he was looking after?" Noel interjected.

"No. Didn't know he was."

Kyra asked, "What about Roy in his drug days? Did you know him then?"

"Sure. Ten or twelve of us arrived the same time, most from the East or the States. We grew good dope, had a couple of nude beaches, fished, beachcombed, built houses where we wanted to. The living was easy."

"We hear Roy gave up drugs," Noel said.

"Oh yeah. Most of us have, except the occasional joint. Can't cope the way we used to. But there's still some damn good weed growing on this island."

Noel looked at his watch. Kyra smiled; he could have glanced through the door at any of the clocks. "Oh, Bourassa said Roy sometimes hung out with a Jerry Bannister. Do you know him?"

"Yeah, part of the old crowd."

"Where's he live?"

"First road past Bertha off North Road, Bridie, I think. A brown trailer."

"If you remember anything else, phone, okay?" Another sheet from his notebook.

"Sure." Bailey stood. "But I been thinking and thinking and I've got no place."

———

Rose had arrived home seething. In the kitchen she found Artemus chopping onions. A moment of memory: Artemus cooking, meal upon meal, for nearly two years after her accident. And most meals since. She stared at him in silence.

He turned. "What's wrong?"

"Your detectives, Artemus, that's what's wrong." She wheeled into her bedroom.

Artemus blinked, suddenly remembered an important phone call, and rinsed his hands. Onion flakes glistened on the block, but two of his wife's understated furies in two days were two too many.

Rose left a message on Tam's answering machine in town. She phoned his number at the cabin, left the same message. Dialed his karate club, gone, another message with the dulcet-toned receptionist. Drummed her fingers on the chair arms and sighed. She felt studied and sullied by the woman detective. She needed a shower.

When they had designed the house to accommodate her wheelchair, Rose decided they'd have separate bedrooms and baths. At the shock on Artemus' face, she added, "With visiting privileges of course, darling." Artemus had not been happy but agreed it was best. His suite upstairs included his office. Rose's bathroom, tiles sloping to a central drain, allowed her chair to roll easily from toilet to vanity to shower, the latter separated from the rest of the room by a tiled wall. She could wheel up to the shower bench, hoist herself onto it, and push the chair to dryness just beyond the wall. Afterward, she retrieved it with the Extendiarm, her own patent. The bathroom design gave her an independence that had encouraged her slow journey out of depression.

No, no shower now. She changed from town clothes into an old T-shirt and greenhouse skirt. Back in her chair she pressed the remote, and the door opened. She wheeled over the threshold and heard the door squeak closed. She remembered she'd been going to ask Roy to fix it. She whipped across the deck up the short side path that led to the pergola and greenhouse. She unlocked the two deadbolts, ran the wheels of her chair through the trough of disinfectant and busied herself with stamens and pistils. Forget the detectives. She listened for any sound to suggest Tam had returned.

She'd buy him a cellphone. Stripped people of their privacy, he said. So what. He'd get used to it. Everybody did.

Concentration on microscope and miniaturized tweezer probes drew her in. Hours went by. The phone startled her. "Yes?"

"Hi, I'm home. What's up?"

"I'll be right over." She closed the phone, put it in her pocket and, with a fond smile at her chrysanthemums, bolted the inner door. Outside she turned and locked the greenhouse door. A fast wheel along the path gave her the momentum to carry the chair up the ramp onto Tam's deck. He was waiting with two bottles of uncapped beer. He held one out. "Thanks." She took a sip. "That detective snoop accosted me on the ferry today. She wanted to know about my van's alterations and my flowers and," Rose give full vent to her ire, "did I study botany and at what university?"

"Which ferry?"

"Eleven-forty."

"I'd just left her." He stretched out in his deck chair, raised his arms over his head, yawned, lowered his beer and drank. "Don't worry, BSR, she's going home to Bellingham soon. We won't see them again and A.'ll feel he's done something when he pays their bill."

Rose drank and considered. "The woman was tenacious today. I hate being questioned. What did she ask you?"

"Oh, about Roy." He grinned. "And if I was a successful painter."

"What did you say?" Rose was suddenly curious.

"'Moderately,' I believe is what I said. 'Moderately' covers a lot of ground." Tam sat up.

Rose gazed into middle distance, her focus blurring the brown of a log boom, wanting to be convinced.

"Rosie, stop worrying. They're inept."

"I worry."

"Okay." He threw one hand up in mock concern. "Phone your friend, discuss it with him." He nearly added, Rab won't say anything different from me.

She finished her beer. Rab would not want detectives around. Sticking their noses into everything. "I dislike that woman."

"I think," Tam stroked his mustache, "she's sorta cute. If you like Renoir."

"And you do," his sister declared.

"Oh you know me," he smiled, mocking, flirting. "I like 'em in lots of different styles."

She thought about Rab, hoped he'd always remain her friend. She did need to speak with him. But not about this.

EIGHT

NO TROUBLE FINDING Jerry Bannister's brown trailer. It hadn't traveled over any macadam in a couple of decades. Once-yellow latticework in front of cement blocks anchored it to the ground. Someone had built a fifteen by ten deck along the front by the entry-way. A blue canopy covered the right half, picnic table and benches underneath it. These, together with a gas barbecue, gave the exterior of the Bannister residence an air of aging comfort. The garden was limp with spent daisies, and the grass and weeds, uncut, showed the usual September burn.

Noel stopped the Honda behind a recent model long-box Sierra. He checked his watch; the ferry left in forty-two minutes. They walked toward the deck.

"Yo!" The voice came from the side of the trailer. A tall man with sloping shoulders, sweatshirt hanging from them, dirty jeans, brown ponytail poking through the back of the ball cap, waved their way.

"Hello," Noel called.

"You folks doin' okay?"

"Fine," Kyra answered. And whispered to Noel, "Stoned."

The man walked toward them. He could have been fit for fifty-five or wasted for forty. He scraped the smoking tip of a lit home-roll against his jeans, and stuck the butt over his ear. "What can I help you with?"

Noel asked, "Are you Jerry Bannister?"

"Yep." He gave a little laugh.

"You were a friend of Roy Dempster?"

"Hey, I am a friend of Roy's." He scowled. "Roy's a good guy."

"You do know Roy Dempster was killed?"

"Yeah yeah yeah, I heard all that. But death don't take away friend-ship, right?"

Kyra said, "I suppose not."

"Glad we see eye to eye, Miss." The lines at the edges of his eyes deepened. "Care to sit?"

"Uh, sure."

"On the grass," he swept his hand across the weeds, "or up there," he pointed to the deck, "or inside."

Kyra's medicine-cabinet curiosity took over. "Inside, I think."

"Place is a mess but if that's what you want." Bannister led the way. They entered a kitchen that affirmed his promise: just enough light to show no surface without litter—half-empty bottles, piles of cans, packaging on the floor, chairs overturned, sink full of dirty dishes. A stench of low-level decay permeated the dead air. Bannister righted two chairs, took a pizza box from another, found a bare spot on the floor, and they sat at the table, inspecting each other over dirty glasses and desiccated pizza now of interest only to a whorl of sow beetles.

Kyra introduced herself and Noel. "We're investigating Roy's death, Mr. Bannister."

"Jerry, my name's Jerry, you say Mr. Bannister and I look over my shoulder for my old man." He stared at her. "You guys want a beer?"

"No thanks," they chorused.

"I do." He headed for the fridge. Kyra tightened, fearing what might be dead, or worse, living inside it. She looked away. Her eyes, now more accustomed to the grey of the kitchen, swept the walls. From counter height to the ceiling, in fact tacked to part of the ceiling, were dozens of girlie magazine centerfolds, dim glossy pink skin in startling curves, featuring wide apart red lips, raisin nipples, haired or shaven pudenda, clothing limited to an occasional pair of stiletto heels. She took Noel's elbow and gestured with her head. He nodded, he'd noticed. They heard the fridge close, and Jerry say, "It's my collection."

Noel said, "The posters?"

"Yep. I got three from the first year of *Playboy*. They're in the bedroom. Wanna see 'em?"

"That's okay," said Kyra.

"Got a real treasure in there, hold on, you don't wanna go in there, I'll get it." He took his beer down a hallway.

Kyra said, "Let's finish double quick and get out of here."

"Meantime, just don't breathe too deep."

Jerry marched toward them. "Here she is." He handed Noel a scantily clad figure with 1940s permed hair, holding a bottle of pop. "Recognize her?"

"Rita Hayworth?"

"Hey, you're good. Gorgeous, eh? She's older than my mother." He giggled. "But Ma never looked like that."

"Now, about Roy Dempster."

"Yeah, I miss him every day." Jerry took a swig of beer. "A real good head."

"Were you a member of his church?"

"Fruitcakes." Jerry snorted. "Tuttifrutticakes. Nope. I know which half of my head to shave. Nope. Roy and me did jobs together, you know, painting, bucking, splitting."

"Did you ever work together at the Eaglenest Gallery?"

"Yep, cleanups and so on. But I don't like gardening, making things neat and clean." He swept his arm around the room, showing it off. "See what I mean?" He giggled.

"Can you think of any reason why anybody'd want to kill him?" Maybe, Noel surmised, Roy came in here to clean the place up, slipped on some pasta and cracked his head open.

"Nope nope nope. Nobody'd want to kill Roy."

Kyra took over. "Did he have any enemies?"

"Ha!" Jerry gave the tabletop a grim stare.

"Did he get into fights?"

"Come on, Roy didn't fight."

"What about the fight in the pub with Tam Gill?"

Jerry gave Kyra a long stare. "The son of a bitch provoked Roy."

"How?"

"Picked on him. Called him names, like. Listen, what're you asking?"

Noel stepped in. "Roy sometimes put people off by trying too hard to help them, right?"

"Shit. Why'd you have to come here? I was feeling good. Now I feel like shit."

"Why's that?"

"'Cause he's dead, don't you get it? Christ." He took a long swallow and drained the bottle. "Great guy." He fumbled at his ear, and located his weed. He found a match in his pocket, lit it, and breathed in deep. Seconds of silence and he released the smoke. He nodded, more serene, and offered the butt to Kyra. She shook her head. As did Noel. Jerry said, "But he's still dead."

Noel pushed his chair back. "You and Roy never argued?"

"Don't get me wrong, he's got a right to be dead. If he wanted to he'd still be alive."

"How so?"

"I wish I knew," Jerry said.

"Well, yes." Kyra stood. "Thank you for your time."

Jerry took another long toke. "Thank you for yours, too."

"We'll see ourselves out." Noel followed her to the door.

"I'll come with you," said Jerry. But he didn't move.

The Honda backed to the road and headed for the ferry dock. Noel drove for a couple of minutes before either spoke. Then he said, "Why didn't he tell us about that falling out he had with Roy?"

"Didn't Patty say they made it up after?"

"Mmm," Noel agreed. "Waste of time, talking to him."

"I don't think so." She smiled. "We now know some of Roy's friends aren't neat and tidy and religious. What made Roy and Jerry friends? A side of Roy we don't know."

"Why didn't we ask him if he had an alibi?"

"We don't care who has an alibi. We're not trying to find who killed Roy. We were hired to clear Artemus, and we've done that. In spades."

Ten minutes later they arrived at the ferry lineup to find no cars, the *Quinsam* still at the dock. They drove on. "Just made it," said Noel. "Lucky." They waited. And waited. "Weird. Why doesn't it go?" Suddenly they heard the screaming of a siren.

"Aha," Noel realized, "an ambulance run."

"With us as a bonus," Kyra added.

The ambulance loaded, and the ferry pulled away. Noel said, "Pass me your phone. I'll call Lucille."

Kyra dug it out of her bag and snapped it open. "You know her number?"

He pulled out his notebook and took the phone. "In here." He looked at the phone, handed it back. "It's so damn small. You dial." He gave her the number.

She heard the ringing and handed it back. Noel made a face at it, then put it to his ear. "Hello Lucille, this is Noel Franklin . . . Dempster was caretaking a house . . . Somebody now in the United Arab Emirates . . . Know who that would be?" Lucille's voice came through as tinny squawks. "Taggart, eh?" Noel repeated and made scribbling motions to Kyra. She wrote the name and the address he repeated. "Where's that?" He nodded. "Thanks, Lucille."

In the Coast Bastion lounge they found Albert Matthew sitting at a window table. A short man but, he liked to say, Mountie-height when the recruiter signed him up. His broad face, greying slicked-back hair, and gentle brown eyes suggested an open, generous man; his flat nose and the thin white jag of a three-inch scar on his right cheek called for a more complicated reaction.

To Noel the generous side had long ago won out. They'd met ten years back when Gabby Bingden disappeared from her parents' summer home on Thetis Island and Noel was covering the story for the *Vancouver Sun*. When the girl wasn't found the story died as news but Noel was familiar with similar cases so saw a pattern at work, and he kept up his investigation. Gabby's mother Clara thought the RCMP were doing nothing to find the girl. By nothing, it turned out, Clara meant she didn't think those First Nation natives the Mounties were forced to hire knew the first thing about where a respectable suburban-Vancouver upper-middle-class kid like Gabby might disappear to. If Clara had been his mother, Noel figured, he'd have disappeared too. As it turned out, Albert Matthew knew a lot about suburban kids running from island to island. With Noel's alternative-press research they tracked her down to Hornby Island, where she was hanging out with a bunch of other middle-class kids who thought slumming meant breaking into houses during the week while the owners were away and living on the beach from Friday to Sunday. They brought the girl home, filthy but alive. Noel wrote the story, "Suburbia, Runaways, Islands," giving Albert great credit, adding some stinging comments about Clara. Gabby ran away again the next year. As far as Noel knew the girl hadn't been heard from since.

Albert stood as Noel approached. Each opened his arms to a flirting width, a half second later they shrugged the other away—a lost cause—each laughed. Each took a light affectionate punch at the other, and the ceremony ended. "*Inspector* Matthew. Congratulations."

"We are such a liberal bureaucracy."

Noel shook his head in dismay. "Once you let those Sikhs wear their rags, anything's possible."

Albert nodded. "Least we're still free of fairies."

"You sure?"

"Hey!" Kyra grabbed them both. "Bend your heads so I can see whose neck is redder."

"Don't be upset." The dark brown of Albert's eyes sparkled. "We let the babes in. Babes is just like guys."

Noel said, "Kyra, my friend Albert. Albert, my friend Kyra."

They shook hands and made pleased-to-meet-you noises. They all sat.

"So," said Noel, "this is where Inspectors water, eh? A step up from the pubs of old."

"I've got serious responsibilities now." He turned to Kyra. "Got to live up to the image."

"In that case," said Kyra, "I'll have a margarita."

"You know, my dear, I'd love to buy it for you, but the taxpayers wouldn't approve."

Noel sighed. "Civilians to the rescue once again."

"Great. Margarita sounds pretty good," Albert said to the waiter as he arrived with a bowl of peanuts.

"Make that three," added Noel. "So. How is it being a Goose?"

"Has its moments. More positive policy-making, less positive time on the beat." They dug into the peanuts and talked about Victoria and Bellingham. Their drinks arrived. They sipped. "You're on the Dempster death, are you? You going to make a business of this?"

"Just research," Noel said. "Kyra investigates for an insurance company. I talked with Jim Yardley this morning. All the details, all the correct talk. No new information."

Albert smiled. "So. Where are you?"

They told him what they knew, Kyra appending Noel's narrative, Noel developing Kyra's.

"So you're stuck." Al nodded. "No hard evidence your client had nothing to do with Dempster's death but a pretty good surmise, no way to know who killed him. But Marchand got his money's worth so you'll be signing off."

Kyra leaned forward. "And you're not stuck?"

Albert said, "You didn't speak with Carl Pocock, the Pastor."

Noel shook his head. "He's gone off birding. Upcountry. You had a talk?"

"Before he left," Albert said. "He knows the woods. He spotted a pair of Virginia rails in the clearcut. He told Roy about them."

"So?" Noel sipped his margarita. "You figure Roy was killed for following birds?"

"Possibly. But a better question is, where was he killed?"

"Maybe in the clearcut," Noel suggested. "Roy was caretaking for a family named Taggart. They've been in the UAE since April. They have five acres in the middle of the island, near the clearcut."

Albert scooped up some peanuts. "Yeah. Jim Yardley took a look around but didn't find anything. Of course it had rained that night."

"Would it be the right sort of dirt?"

Albert nodded. "A lot of the island's the right sort of dirt." He caught Kyra's glance at Noel. "And you two," Albert said, "watch your snooping. Don't get hauled in for trespassing."

"No sir," Noel mock-saluted.

At six-thirty Kyra left them to line up for the seven o'clock Vancouver ferry. Chat had turned to old times, Albert telling investigation stories. Noel and Albert figuring where they'd go for dinner—aha, Noel, willing to eat out! Both had tried to persuade her to join them. But she'd promised her father she'd be back in Vancouver tonight, and she'd already canceled yesterday.

At the end of Stewart Avenue she bumped into the lineup poking out of the parking lot. "A one-ferry wait," the worker directing traffic told her. "You'll be near the head of the line for the nine o'clock." The woman grinned, too cheery behind dark-tinted glasses. She handed Kyra a color-coded bit of cardboard. "Pay when you get to the booth, ma'am."

Kyra called her father to apologize, left a message not to stay awake, they'd have a long catch-up in the morning. She sat in her car in the line. Damn!

Stop. You like ferry lineups, right? Waiting for a ferry forces you to slow down. Nowhere to go till your ferry gets in. So chill out.

For five years, age ten to fourteen, ferries had meant Bowen Island and Noel in the cottage next door, eighteen when they met, Noel who took her questions seriously. Handsome, intelligent, exciting Noel. He taught her about salmon and tides, currents and seaweed. They built a birdhouse, he made her listen to birdsongs and how to distinguish them. And every summer three or four times the two of them had walked onto the ferry and ridden across to Horseshoe Bay for fish and chips at Troll's.

Then came the worst summer of her life—yes, it still qualified, she thought now. The summer she was fifteen William had moved in with Noel. They'd sat on his deck with their arms around each other and there was no room for her. Oh he was still friendly but he wasn't her Noel. She felt All Of Life pulling away on a train and she was left in the station. She hated William, she hated Noel, she hated her parents and most of all she hated herself for feeling this way. She couldn't remember talking to anyone the whole summer. Corroded by jealousy. Noel and William took her fishing, took her over to Troll's; she hated it. Years later she realized that she really liked William all the time she was hating him, which had made it worse.

She reached over to the passenger seat and flicked open a small leather case. In padded pockets lined with blue velvet, six red balls each an inch and seven-eighths in diameter. She squeezed one. She'd started to juggle as an escape from girl's gym. To graduate from high school she had to pass a swimming test—no problem—plus one more gym course. She waited till her last year. She wanted sailing but signed up too late. Which left only basketball and soccer. Yuck! But wait: juggling was still open. She discovered she had good eye-hand coordination. She also discovered that four young men she knew each insisted she was his girl. She liked them all. Choosing one would eliminate the others. As a joke she named the balls Terry, Dave, Tommy and Gordon. All in the air, which would fall first? But none of them did! She could keep them all in the air at the same time.

Last year before she and Sam split, they'd argued about everything: the toothpaste lid, the time for dinner, where to go on vacation, risky investments, soggy washcloths in the sink, her job. Afterwards, she'd juggle. Even now she heard Sam's voice: Why do you always juggle when things get tense? She had claimed she juggled any time. But his words continued to niggle at her.

She dropped the ball into its pocket. The truth was, juggling kept her hands busy; in her smoking days, she couldn't juggle and light up at the same time.

What could she juggle in this investigation? Dempster dead. Marchand and his gallery. Rose and her flowers. Kyra and Noel, private investigators. Yes, working with Noel had given her a neat quick high. Too bad it ended.

———

Noel got home from dinner with too much wine in his brain. The conversation with Albert kept returning to Dempster's death, and Eaglenest Gallery. So he visited the *Gabriola Gab* website and tracked down references to Artemus Marchand. Passing an article about a possible bridge to Gabriola from Nanaimo via Mudge—a bridge!—he found:

A BRILLIANT GABRIOLA INVENTOR IN HER OWN RIGHT

By Lucille Maple

Yesterday I had the extreme pleasure of interviewing Ms. Rose Gill about her brilliant inventions to aid and succour handicapped gardeners like herself. Ever since she fell into that category (a diving accident left her "paralyzed from the waist down"), she has swelled the ranks of passionate Gabriola gardeners, but with a twist, to make gardening easier and therefore more enjoyable to the Disabled.

Arriving at the gates of the Eaglenest Gallery [See Gab article on Artemus Marchand and his Gallery, November 20, 1993. Rose Gill is Marchand's wife. Ed.] and driving through to their beautiful grounds, I was met by Ms. Gill, who wheeled out to meet me in her wheelchair that she has specially modified and now patented. (Readers: I knew of Ms. Gill's inventions two years ago and asked to interview her then, but she made me wait until the patents were secured, that joyful event happening this past spring.)

Ms. Gill's inventions were spread on a table outside her large greenhouse for my perusual and delectation. It was a good thing it was not raining. Ms. Gill does not let anyone into her greenhouse because of the "dangers and diseases" strangers might unwittingly transport on their apparel. (Gabriola Gardeners, take heed!) She had, however, kindly taken photos of the interior. These were available to me.

One is struck by the raised beds lining each wall and down the middle, easily accessed by the wheelchair gardener. I did not dally over the bright splashes of color however, which attest to Ms. Gill's "green thumb" since my task was the implements. Ms. Gill assured me that for the non-wheelchaired gardener (including us able-bodied folks), she could easily design a little motorized railway car which would run up and down the aisles on a rail. I was assured that a wheelchair is just as mobile as a rail car.

I examined the first invention, a long-handled trowel, hoe and rake combination, useful, I was told, for weeding, although Ms. Gill was quick to point out that greenhouses not troubled by visitors were weed-free.

Next came the lightweight tools in bizarre and intriguing shapes, for garden implements. Arthritic gardeners (like we all may one day be) should "flock" to these. Or should that be "phlox?"

Rose Gill's final invention (and her most

interesting, in my own personal humble opinion, but I'm sure it will be the general consensus of all before long) is her Extendiarm. "It's like having your own personalized Canadarm. It opens, shuts, twists, grabs, rotates, holds, tilts and picks up, it will do anything you need to do but can't reach to do it," Ms. Gill assured me. She demonstrated by picking up ONLY ONE blade of grass. The Extendiarm would be indispensable when you're recovering from your hip or knee replacement or when you've broken your leg. Short people (or should I say "height challenged") would love it for reaching overhead cupboards.

I asked when her inventions would be on the market for ordinary folk and was told Soon, but she didn't know how much they'd cost.

Gabriola is a fortunate community indeed to have such a brilliant and dedicated inventor. After a companionable cup of tea in their elegant living room overlooking Northumberland Channel, we parted. Good luck, Rose Gill, with your Future Inventions!

The distance from Lucille Maple in person to the tone of her prose was impossible to fathom. Noel turned off the ringer of his phone, lay his watch on it and went to bed. Only when his head hit the pillow did he realize he'd eaten at a restaurant. Was he moving away from total bereavement?

NINE

LUCAS HERSCHEL FELT a disappointment he knew Kyra didn't share: she'd arrived too late for the concert. She loved him, but not his music. And he loved her too, but not her ever-present psychologizing, as if the pleasures and injustices of life could be explained by the workings of the human mind. As if one could ever discover more than a detail or two of these. As if history didn't exist. As if one could avoid politics, the evils of the right, the dangers of the left.

It was 9:30 AM and Kyra still slept. He'd returned the living room to its usual state, couch under the window, Bösendorfer realigned with the wall—how well Brina had played last night, her fingers leaping through the *Trout Quintet*, he'd not heard a single false note. He stored the folding chairs away.

He squeezed some oranges. As he hoped, the old juicer's whirring woke Kyra. She came out of his study rubbing her eyes, wearing only a black T-shirt and her underpants. "Good morning, Little One." A long time since she'd been small enough to deserve the name but for him she'd always be that.

She hugged him. "Morning, Dad."

"Breakfast?"

She nodded. "A quick shower." Her father, ever a skinny man, had put on some weight. His tennis tan showed how much his hair had receded. Lucas. She'd begun addressing her parents by their first names the summer she was fifteen. Sometime later Lucas had reminded her he was the only person in the world she could call Father.

The hot water woke her. Noel's study couch, her father's study couch—she looked forward to a real bed tonight, alone at home. She felt a little guilty about the concert, but missing it was a relief. Lucas' group was adequate at best and her father as violist the weakest of the five. The strongest player was Vera the cellist, an antique dealer like the others. Her keeping Lucas as part of her quintet had long made Kyra assume more than music was involved here. She didn't have much of an ear but she could hear timing and when Lucas came in a sixty-fourth of a beat late, it jarred. She dried, pulled on clean underwear and the new clothes she'd bought yesterday—her father liked to see her well-dressed. She sat down with him at the table. Through the window she noted that the vine maple was tinged with fall.

"Fresh coffee?"

"Yum." And an omelet *aux fines herbes*, and toast. Pretty good compensation for the lumpy couch. And she knew how pleased he was that she didn't step outside for a cigarette any more. She took a bite of omelet. "Yum."

"Thank you."

"Love you, love your omelet."

Lucas patted her hand. "And how's Noel? Still suffering?"

"Actually, he's pulling himself together."

"I'm glad you spent the extra day there. Noel cares for you greatly." And vice versa, he thought. Oh, what might have been . . .

"I know that!" She laughed a little as she heard her adolescent tone.

"And what happened with Mr. Marchand?" Lucas raised his eyebrows.

They were done with the case so she could tell Lucas, and did. "There's no motive for Marchand to be involved in any of this."

Lucas smiled. "The man I met didn't seem capable of killing. But he's most able to find lost schools-of paintings." Lucas poured them more coffee. "I've seen them, they're often fine work. Dealers who locate schools-of usually come up with pieces that should remain lost."

"Why?"

"Nowhere close to the standards of the master."

"And you want to know why Marchand's so successful."

"I do."

"It's his brother-in-law, Tam Gill, who goes to Europe. He talks about sniffing out the paintings."

"How does Marchand hear about them? What are his methods? Why is he so successful?"

Kyra sipped her coffee. "Can't he be successful?"

"But why only he?" Lucas, long-time member of a small antique consortium, had left his tenured position in Political Science at Simon Fraser University fifteen years after he'd begun teaching there, furious at academic bureaucracy. He started his antique shop and became a happier man. Years ago he had explained to Kyra that his antiquarian friends and he helped one another. They were too old to compete. Now he said, "Marchand seems to have no help from anyone. Could he have a secret cache somewhere?"

"If he did, would he pull out one or two paintings at a time to keep the price high?"

"That'd make sense. If it's a cache, for example, he must have gained access to some old Nazi or Communist hoard."

"Isn't that possible?"

"There'd have been rumors. We haven't heard the least rumble."

How well connected was her father? "Could someone be forging them, selling them to him?"

"Extremely doubtful. The paintings Marchand's found have been well authenticated. Most of them by two of the best people in the field. I've seen them. They all come with their provenances."

"Maybe stolen?"

"It's a mighty small world. Theft, even from obscure sources, gets whispered about."

"Is there big money in these schools-of paintings?"

"There can be. In good condition, a School of Cranach or Ghirlandaio, with a few discernible brush strokes of the master, a metre by a metre-three," Lucas shrugged, "half a million to a million? Way more than a few years ago. Size, condition, scarcity, recognition factor all play their part."

Kyra sipped coffee. "Yep, big money. Who's buying them?"

"People with big money."

"Do you go looking for schools-of?"

Lucas raised his eyebrows. "In the old days we didn't have to, the news would come to us. My friends and I share costs. We still have scouts across Europe. Since the late nineties, they've found very few. Two summers ago I wrote Marchand, asking him to talk to our small group. He wrote back saying he was far too busy. Last year I wrote again, but he never replied."

"Why didn't you just phone?"

"In our world we're not quite so abrupt."

"Did you write him with a fountain pen?"

"With a quill." They smiled.

"What makes Marchand such a good hunter?"

"We'd like to know. Should we hire you?"

"We?"

"I believe the others would also be interested."

She thought about it. "Chances are pretty good I won't be able to find out anything. If you and your friends who know the art world can't figure it out—"

"We don't know Marchand and Gill. You and Noel do."

She raised her eyebrows. "Got a lot of money?"

"No. But a little."

"Okay." Ethical to investigate an ex-client?

———

Not till he'd finished breakfast did Noel notice the red light on his answering machine blinking. Maybe Kyra, trying to reach him? Damn those breather calls, blocking them cut out everything. He pressed the playback button. A moment of silence— Shit! The breathing again, then a raspy voice, ". . . nice new tires . . ." He squeezed his eyes shut. A click, and the message ended.

"You fucker." For minutes he didn't move. All coincidence had vanished. Someone has it in for you, Noel. Who, damn it? And why? Call Albert— No, try to figure this out by yourself.

When had the phone calls started? Five weeks ago. When he was already beaten down by Brendan's death. Someone who knew that, wanting to beat him down some more? Whoever was calling, and had slashed his tires, had succeeded in rekindling Noel's discomfort in being a visible person. Except there weren't any newspaper articles with his byline, let alone media interviews. His only public activity was this investigating, only since two days ago. And Kyra had it right, asking people questions is hardly a public act. So timing made any relationship between clearing Eaglenest Gallery and the breathing caller impossible.

Could it go back to that poor woman he'd maligned? But that had been years ago; why now? Anyway, since then he'd practically dropped from sight. Kyra was one of the few old friends he still saw. And he'd not accepted invitations from any of Brendan's friends.

Who the hell had it in for him?

Maybe the time had come. Up on a high shelf he found three packets containing the notes for his book on the Chung murder case and the file holding forty-six pages of printed-out manuscript. He piled it beside his computer, clicked from standby to active, pulled up the Chung directory, and opened the paper file beside him. He reached page seven without taking in a word.

He leaned back and stared at the ceiling. Couple of cobwebs up there. At least some spider was catching flies. The book needed a few active cobwebs. He could phone his editor. He had nothing to say to her. Too bad Kyra had gone. Call her? Tell her about the phone call too.

Or go back to Gabriola and check out the property Dempster was looking after? But Yardley had found nothing. Anyway, the investigation was over, they'd done what Marchand wanted. Just write the report. Could Roy's side job have had anything to do with the Gallery's reputation?

⸻

Question: What is worse than sitting in your car for an hour and a half, minutes from the border, on a sunny fall afternoon as the engine idles, breathing in poison from the exhaust of the ancient truck to the left, all for the privilege of crossing back to the US?

Answer: Knowing you chose the wrong lane. The car to the left and the van to the right had shot so far ahead they're likely already in Bellingham. That, and the dull hard pounding of too-heavy metal shaking the SUV coming up on the left, vibrating through your tires, deep into your buttock-bones.

Kyra turned on her CD player to drown out the sound, but the Bare Naked Ladies disk Noel had loaned her couldn't stave off the pulsations. And the other CDs were no better, Moxy Früvous, Nina Simone, Liz Phair. She took her foot off the brake. Her Tracker rolled one car length. The throbbing kept pace, her seat a-buzz with it. Good thing she'd prepared herself for this with extra weight, some flesh to keep the bone from grinding away inside her derrière skin.

Two lengths up, the thump-thump from the van softened; three. A car full of dogs now, German shepherds, three huge heads out the two side windows. She loathed dogs. A few weeks after she'd started investigating, Sam had begun pushing. Their conversations were versions of him saying: "Get a dog, when you're alone it's not safe."

"A dog?"

"For your line of work."

Sam could rarely bring himself to say the word *investigation*. Or *detection*. "Not safe in Bellingham, Washington, for shitsake? Nice-salt-of-the-earth town like Bellingham?"

"Sure." Sam would shake his head, his show of weariness. "You're out alone all the time."

"All the time? A couple of cases."

"Gone all night—"

"It's called a stakeout. What're you saying?"

"I'm saying you're not here. With me. Next to me. In bed with me."

She'd say, "Sam, you were the one who said it'd do me good, getting a job." And he'd say, "But not this kind of job." And she'd say, "I like this kind of job." And the anger would build. "Sorry."

"Think about getting a dog," he'd say.

Dogs are so fucking dependent. Hours of that going for a walk thing. And they drooled. Saliva all over your sweater. Your crotch. Maybe not from a small dog, a poodle, but who in her right mind wanted a poodle. Anyway, when she was alone on a case, a dog would get in the way. Sam just didn't get her detective work.

The dogs had moved five cars up.

Sam never did buy her a dog. For safety's sake, he'd bought her the Chevy Tracker. Perfect for your work, he'd boasted. And gas, insurance, maintenance get to be business expenses. She'd hugged him. She'd stared out the window at the white box on wheels. This was absolutely not the car she wanted to be seen in. Why hadn't she sold it? Because Sam had given it to her?

She needed food. Why couldn't some enterprising lad with a hot dog cart decide to take on the border crunch? A big fat hamburger, heavy with relish, half-sour pickles, lightly fried onions, tomatoes, crisp lettuce—

Two lengths forward. She looked at her face in the rear-view mirror. Hair sticking out more than usual. Eyes bright and brown as ever. She squinted at her reflection. The new weight padded the curve of her cheekbones. When she was fourteen Noel had told her her cheekbones were her finest feature. She believed him instantly. Did she really want admiration for her cheekbones? Her three ex-husbands had all raved about her lovely cheeks. With that much agreement, should she argue?

Eight car lengths farther. Ahead, the Peace Arch: *Children of a Common Mother.* The usual question waiting: Citizenship? Born in Brooklyn, a year old when she moved to Vancouver. Became a Canadian citizen at eighteen, just before going back to the States, Oregon, Reed College. A legal citizen of each country. Some border officials don't like you to have dual citizenship. So when she entered Canada she said Canadian, and the other way around. Six car lengths.

Five cars from the booth. Finally her turn. "Hello."

Two officials, a crewcut male and a hang-jowl woman, who said, "Nationality?"

"American."

"How long have you been in Canada?"

"Three days."

"Purpose of your trip?"

The familiar guilt, border guards and police aroused it, clearly she'd done something wrong. "Family business."

"Anything to declare?"

"No."

"Please get out of your car and open up in back." She did. Crewcut left the booth—taller than he'd seemed. "Would you open the suitcase, please?"

"Sure." She did.

Crewcut wore gloves. He shuffled around in the case, looked under a couple of layers of clothes, closed the suitcase, slid it to the right, on the left he lifted the carpeting. Ran his hand along the metal, took a small baton from his belt and tapped first the side then the floor. A hollow sound. He dropped the carpeting and smoothed it flat. "Please open that case on the back seat."

Kyra reached in, and passed him the open case.

He took out a ball. He squeezed it. "What's this?" He took out another.

"Standard juggling balls." He looked at her suspiciously as he felt the rest. Then he tilted his head at the unsmiling woman. They stepped aside and conferred.

Kyra's guilt increased even as she told herself it was irrational. Did people really smuggle stuff in juggling balls?

The man and woman returned. He put the balls away, closed the lid and handed the case to Kyra. "You may go. Have a good day."

"Thanks." For letting me into one of my own countries? After an hour and a half in line? Gee whiz.

———

On the ferry Noel consulted the map of Gabriola and, once off, drove along South Road to Brickyard Beach and up Ferne Road—he hadn't been this way before—to the Taggart property. A long winding driveway passed through fir, cedar and broadleaf maples, then a lawn and garden in front of a low house, technically a rancher, one storey, sprawling, imposing.

Before leaving, he'd checked his tires. They were fine. Now he stopped the car and climbed out. And felt foolish for having come. But he hadn't been prepared to write the Marchand report. Or think about the new phone call. And the Chung manuscript had closed his brain down.

He stepped up to the front door and knocked; the family could have returned. Without Roy, who would be looking after the property? He knocked again. He sensed the silence of a long-empty dwelling. The drapes were drawn over the three windows he could see.

Off the deck, along a brick path to the side, more closed drapes. It's true, houses don't like being empty. The yard contained a tree with a tire swing and a garden area, unplanted. What had Roy been caretaking? Around to the back of the house. A nip of autumn held the air, but the sun still shone bright. Here at the edge of a brick patio sat a covered hot tub surrounded by built-in benches and planters. Beside the tub, a brick barbeque. He could live like this, cook a steak, lie in the tub, stare at the stars.

More mown lawn and weeded perennial garden back here. Roy's work? Woodshed, garage on the other side. Beyond the lawn, the property dropped gently to trees maybe thirty metres away. Noel walked down the lot.

A thin path wound through the trees, the duff between them free of windfalls. Then the vegetation changed to scrawny alder, small arbutus, and fir seedlings. Of course, Noel realized—these lots abut the clearcut. Roy would have done his caretaking, then gone bird-watching back here.

The trail, still visible but with more low growth, continued on. A deer trail? Birds rustled and a little stream seeped. In the spring would the ground be covered with those sweet small strawberries? About fifty metres along he was suddenly confronted by an impassable thicket of Himalayan blackberry vines, still a few drying berries, highest growth around. The path, even fainter, headed around the berry patch to the left. An extensive patch. When blackberries find conditions they like, they spread.

Then suddenly the trail ended in a trample of mud facing the tangled vines. The Taggarts' private blackberry patch: wine, jam, pies. Recently trampled, he noted, and the Taggarts had been gone since April. Gingerly grasping a vine between its thorns, he pulled it aside. It caught other vines, separating them from the rest like a door in the thicket wall.

Behind the vines, planted in soldierly rows, thick green cannabis. The center of the blackberry patch was hollowed out. Not a few plants for personal use, but dozens, maybe more than a hundred. It looked high quality and close to harvest-ready. Like the pot Lyle had brought for Brendan. But Roy the Faith Bearer, growing pot? Albert would be most interested.

⌒

I like Bellingham, Kyra thought, as the I-5 bisected the city's northern reaches. Slightly smaller than Nanaimo, about the same age, its history too was coal, logs, pulp and fish. Only 150 miles between the cities, both seaports, both with islands in view, both hilly, both with sprawling malls off a highway. What, she wondered, made Bellingham so not-Nanaimo? She'd thought for years, if she could figure this out she'd have figured out the confusing difference between Americans and Canadians.

It's in the architecture, she used to think. Houses in Bellingham are more, well, American. Verandahs, gingerbread. So she'd studied certain Vancouver neighborhoods, Strathcona, Mount Pleasant, parts of Kitsilano: verandahs, gingerbread. Like Nanaimo. Then she'd got picky; Canadian verandahs are higher, require more steps; perhaps American houses don't have basements.

The flags. Yes, a major difference. Especially now. But even before September 11th there'd been way more Stars and Stripes in American neighborhoods than Maple Leafs in their Canadian equivalent. A lot of Canadians thought it the height of ostentation to fly a flag when you know perfectly well what country you're in. Flags belong at borders and embassies. What do these flags mean? This is the house of a patriot? Death to all terrorists? I grieve for those who died in Iraq? And what does it mean not to fly a flag? Surely not the opposite.

She'd come to Vancouver in 1973 when her parents were hired to teach at the new state-of-the-art Simon Fraser University, a few years after the Maple Leaf was proclaimed the new Canadian flag. Some people missed the old Red Ensign and had refused to fly the new banner. Thirty-something years wasn't long for a flag. Over two hundred for the Stars and Stripes.

The Fairhaven exit, thank heaven. This bit of I-5 was concrete slab, not asphalt, and she always wondered how her castanets of teeth fared as the car bumped along. At least her speedometer matched the m.p.h. signs. Stop at Albertson's for food or check the fridge first? Fridge, she decided, it's only been three days.

The utilitarian side-by-side duplex she'd rented after she and Sam had split was a green box with two doors, four windows, two straight cement walks flanked by two driveways. She parked the Tracker in hers.

In the living room, a nondescript nubbly beige sofa, an armchair clothed in fading spotted blue, and a wood chair awaited her. She was fond of that one, a Hepplewhite from her father. But it wasn't the sort of chair that commanded, Sit in me. The dining room held her computer on a door blank propped on two filing cabinets. The kitchen sported the fridge, a stove, sink, table and two folding chairs.

At least Noel's got a real home. Despite Brendan's death Noel's place is warm and welcoming. I've got a place that sulks, that whispers, I know you don't want to be here.

You're right. But it's not your fault, house. Kyra vowed right then to move.

She opened the fridge and sniffed the milk. Off. She flashed to Jerry Bannister's kitchen yesterday. She poured the milk in the sink and ran the water. Okay, go to Dos Padres for a margarita and chimichanga. Phone Sarah, her friend from the juggling group, also recently separated? Walk the three blocks, she needed the exercise.

She checked her phone messages. Mike, her ex-burglar friend and teacher; a drink some evening? Sam, just calling to say hello. Amy, an old friend from Reed. Not many calls for three days away. Quickly she read her e-mails: no, she didn't need her penis enlarged; a petition about the plight of women in Afghanistan that she'd seen word for word years ago. Noel: pot plants in a berry patch in the clearcut beyond the Taggart property—huh?—and he'd been trying to reach Albert. She wrote him back immediately: What the schmidt are you doing?

"Albert, it's Noel again. Hi . . . I went to see where Dempster was caretaking. Did Yardley say anything about pot production inside a berry patch? . . . Yeah, lots of it. Footprints in the mud, since the rain . . . Right. He should follow the little path . . . Sure. My lips are sealed."

Kyra felt her father's comments tugging at her. Her curiosity itched. And scratching brought back Tam Gill telling her about the Sienese school-of across the cappuccino table— Hmm. She set out for Western Washington University's Art Gallery.

The air felt cooler, wafts of autumn rising from brown alder leaves crunchy underfoot. She liked this campus with its view of Bellingham Bay and the San Juan Islands. A permanent sculpture display studded the rectangle between the Science buildings. She threaded her way through to the Gallery.

Noel backed up his report to Marchand on three floppies and a memory stick. He hadn't mentioned the pot plants behind the Taggart property. Wait for Kyra's reaction, consult with her? No, pot in the clearcut has nothing to do with the Gallery's reputation. He clicked the Send icon. He felt a pang of regret.

Kyra opened a door, crossed a foyer, descended five steps to a room with white walls and pictures. A man at a desk looked up from his book. "May I help you?"

"I understand you have an example of the fifteenth-century Sienese School."

"Right. The far room of our permanent collection." He was young, ponytailed, nose ring. Clearly a Fine Arts student. Or MBA in training.

"Like the pamphlet for our new exhibit? Hiromi Takabuki, we were lucky to get him."

"That's nice," said Kyra. "Local artist?"

"Well, Portland." The kid smiled. "Close enough to be local."

She took the pamphlet. "Thanks." In the designated room, she spotted what she assumed to be The Example between a still life of flowers, a dead rabbit and two pheasants, and a pastoral scene of river with boat and surrounding cows. The Example was a Seated Madonna with Child. What else. The Madonna looked tired, the Child a tiny old man in the Madonna's arms. Something wrong with the Madonna's chair—it tilted forward. Kyra studied it. The Madonna looked as if she were about to slip off. Five centuries of slipping. Poor dear, thought Kyra. Tilted back would give the correct perspective. The Madonna had olive skin and almond-shaped eyes. A lot of gold in the background, and small angels. The image hung behind a Plexiglas screen. Kyra read the information plaque:

> A fine example of the Sienese School, unattributable to any one artist. The Sienese School is the name given to the many artists who produced frescoes, triptychs and icons in Siena from the late 13th or early 14th century until the mid 15th century. Duccio (1260–1318), Simone Martini (1284–1344), Pietro Lorenzetti (1305–1348), and his brother, Ambrosio (1319–1348) were among the notables. Madonna and Child, the left side of a triptych, the part seen here, exemplifies the Byzantine influence that hung on longer in Siena than Florence, where Giotto (1267–1337) was changing the representation of the human form to a more natural look. Donated by Dr. and Mrs. Irving Williams, 1971.

Kyra studied the painting again. A more natural look would help. Okay, I can go. She glanced quickly at the other images in the permanent collection. Twentieth century, names she didn't know. An unrecognizable bronze lump on a stand. Definitely she liked a more natural look.

Kyra passed through the Takabuki exhibit and glanced at the paintings. Naturalistic images swam through abstract swatches of color on heavy canvas. After a few pictures, she got it. A gas pump and a missile amongst trees. A blurb of red that could be a polluted lake, or just rage. Another of birds pecking at piano keys, splotches around the piano legs maybe dead birds. At first each picture seemed painted in a different style, but quickly their unifying intention began to impose itself. Clever, Kyra thought. A special talent. I should give artists more time. Like that Madonna. Was it painted on wood? At the desk, Kyra asked, "What do you know about the Sienese school-of?"

The kid looked up with a sweet smile. "Just what's on the wall. If you come back in December I'll know a lot more, that's a course I'm taking." He stood up. "The Curator's in from lunch. I'll get her and she can tell you about it."

"Oh, that's okay—"

"No trouble." He stepped back to a half-open door behind the desk and knocked.

Kyra stared at a rainy streetscape. A line of giant ants marched down the sidewalk.

"Hello. May I help you?"

Kyra turned. A woman, blonde hair, about Kyra's age, tall and slim, smiled expectantly.

"These are very funny paintings," Kyra said.

"Yes they are," the Curator's smile stretched to a grin. "Takabuki's a great humorist."

"I was wondering about your Sienese school picture. Is it painted on wood?" They walked toward the permanent collection.

"Yes. Until the early Renaissance, it was usually wood. Or painted directly on the wall. It's varnished egg tempera with gold leaf."

Again in front of the icon, Kyra asked, "Do you know where the other two panels are?"

"The right side is still in Siena. No one knows where the middle is." The Curator turned from the painting to Kyra and stuck out her hand. "I'm Ann Blair, by the way."

Kyra introduced herself. "That poor Madonna looks like she's going to slide off her seat."

"It's another century before artists get a sense of perspective." Ann Blair studied the icon. "We're lucky to have it. Only a few public

113

institutions can afford paintings like that, some large museums and wealthy universities. Like Emory, with all its Coca Cola money."

"I'm told newly discovered paintings came out of Eastern Europe, after it opened up."

Ann nodded. "They get bought up quietly. Recently too by resort hotels. And casinos. Atlantic City, Las Vegas. And they get loans, too. There's a casino hotel in Vegas that has a gallery with combined shows from the Guggenheim and the Hermitage in St. Petersburg. A colleague who went to a trade fair there told me about it."

"Really?"

"If that's not enough, there's even a place in Vegas that actually calls itself The Hermitage. It capitalizes on old art. Absolute debasement." Tiny spots of red appeared on the curator's cheeks.

Kyra shook her head in sympathy. "How did the donors acquire your Siena school painting?" They were strolling toward the front gallery.

"I understand Dr. Williams picked it up in the last days of the Second World War." Ann tsked. "A lot of art 'changed hands' in that war."

"I should learn more art history."

"I'm giving a survey course next semester."

"I just might take it. Thank you." Waving in the direction of the kid, Kyra left. Where have I heard of a place called The Hermitage in the last few days? Something I read? Halfway home, she had it. Rose Gill's T-shirt. Picture Yourself At The Hermitage.

TEN

THE PHONE RANG. Noel waited a moment, then picked up. "Hello?"

"Hiya, buddy, how's it going?"

Buddy. Noel paused, then identified the voice. "Lyle?"

"Just calling to see how you're doing."

"Oh okay. How about you?" Lyle had called three or four times since the funeral, just to check, he'd said, that Noel was okay. Right now Noel didn't want to talk to Lyle.

"Pretty good." Lyle's tone was shiny-bright. "Want to get together?"

Why wasn't Lyle off being absorbed by his painting? Or by his teaching? Noel advanced with caution, "I'm finishing some research, don't know when I'll be free."

"I know about your research." Lyle laughed.

"Oh?"

"Artemus Marchand phoned me, worried out of his gourd. I recommended you."

"Oh." One mystery solved. "Why me?"

"Figured you'd be good."

"Well, thanks." I guess, Noel thought.

"So how about dinner. I'm buying."

"Look, Lyle, I'm not really ready to eat out yet."

"What's the big deal?"

"Eating out should be enjoyable, you know? I'm not up to that kind of joy yet."

"Oh. Okay. Well how about a drink. You could come over here but the place is a mess—I'm in the middle of a real creative period."

Then Noel heard Kyra chiding him: Go part way. "You could come over here. A drink."

"Great. I'll bring munchies."

Go on, Noel, Kyra was demanding. "I guess I could cook us a light meal."

"First rate. When?"

Noel checked his calendar. Damn. Nothing on this week, of course.

Get it over with. "How's tomorrow?" Anyway, he'd already dined out. With Albert. Without thinking.

"Terrific."

"I warn you," Noel warned hard, "Brendan was our cook."

"I'll stand it," said Lyle. "What time?"

"Uh, six-thirty okay?"

"Perfect. See ya."

Noel broke the connection. Now why had he done that? If a drink felt like too much, why had he promised supper? For the moment he preferred it alone. Lyle was someone Brendan used to see. Had the two ever been lovers? Impossible to know. One of Noel's and Brendan's agreements, they'd never discuss past loves. Discuss, you begin to compare, which never brings you closer. Noel hadn't ever been drawn to Lyle, but he did admire the man for changing his life. Up to about three years ago Lyle had been, like Brendan, a stockbroker. And a promising painter. He'd always be promising, he told Brendan and Noel soon after he arrived in Nanaimo, unless he gave up his day job. So he took a half-time job teaching a couple of business courses and gave himself over to his painting. He'd chosen Nanaimo to be closer to his agent, Artemus Marchand. Who had hired Noel, and Kyra.

Puget Sound Life Insurance hadn't believed Treatman Taylor's spine gave him only two hours a day on his feet after he'd slipped on seaweed and cracked five ribs. The insurance company was right. Kyra contextualized the fourteen photos she'd taken of Treat happily swinging golf clubs at three separate courses, printed up the report, put it together with photos and invoice in an envelope and drove the finished project downtown to the Puget Sound Life head office. Margery said they'd get back when they needed her for more work, likely soon.

Back home she e-mailed Lucas, telling him what she'd learned from Ann Blair, adding, Found something kind of weird. Did you know casinos and hotels are buying these paintings too? She wrote Noel about the chat with her father, added Rose Marchand's The Hermitage T-shirt and The Hermitage casino coincidence, and described her meeting with Blair.

Too late for lunch, too early for supper. Maybe that new pizza place around the corner from the post office? Their mushroom and anchovy should be researched.

⌐ ⌐

Artemus checked his e-mail. Ahh, the report from Franklin, long and detailed, many interviews. Known that Roy Dempster was killed elsewhere, dumped at the Gallery. Eaglenest was in the clear. A hard copy of the report would follow.

Good. And Lucille would be on about something new this week. A bill for two days, $2,000, which included expenses minus the $1,000 on account. Steep. Worth it.

Marchand sent back an immediate reply: *Thank you. There'll be a check in the mail.*

⌐ ⌐

Good topping, though the crust was too thick. But you can't learn about an *arriviste* pizza joint without trying it. Kyra filed it in her mind under *E* for Emergency, subdirectory Pizza—they stayed open till 3:00 AM. She left her calls unanswered, decided her new-home search could wait, and watched a detective drama on TV. Too exciting. Unrealistic. Before going to sleep she checked her e-mail. One, from Sam, give a call when she got back. She glanced at her watch. After eleven. Too late to call? Sam stayed up late. No, just send him an e-mail. But he asked you to call, Kyra. She picked up the phone, pressed in his number. Four rings. Answering machine. "Hi. It's Kyra. You asked me to call. I'm calling. Call when you can."

She located her leather case in the coat closet, brought it to the living room, took out three of the red balls. They lay comfortably in her right palm. She lobbed the first one up a couple of feet, as it approached its arc the second rose, the third as the first came down to her left palm. Higher. Three feet. Her fingers articulated, the ball spun and rose into the air as the second landed. Three balls going, easy. Six inches higher, a break in rhythm between third and first, her right hand dipped for the fourth ball, up it went. Up and around, down and over, up and around. She caught the balls a pair in a hand, picked out a fifth, began again: one-two-three; four; five. Her mind drained. A flow of motion to arms, hands, balls. She stopped, flushed. Best de-stressing she knew of. She went to bed.

In the morning she bought a newspaper and read the classifieds for new abodes. Rent or buy? She checked her e-mail. A quick note of thanks from Noel for the schools-of and The Hermitage information, nothing further re pot in the clearcut, a copy of the Marchand report and Marchand's response. While she was on-line an e-mail came in from Lucas@fineantiques.com: *Thanks, Little One, for your note. The consortium agrees, we'd like you and Noel to learn more of how Marchand finds paintings. A few days. We are but poor antique dealers. Love, Dad.*

The telephone rang. Noel picked it up. "Hello?"

"Hi. I just had an e-mail from Lucas," said Kyra. "He and his antiques friends want us to find out how Marchand finds so many schools-of."

A moment of silence. "Is that legit?"

"What?"

"Investigating an ex-client."

A pause from Kyra. "We serve only one master at a time."

"True."

Kyra cleared her throat. "Let me ask you something."

"What?"

"Interested in combining our research skills into an ongoing partnership?"

"Some sort of investigating agency?"

"Let me put it this way. I'd rather freelance with you than work for Puget Sound."

This was moving too quickly. One thing at a time. "We better think about that."

"And about Lucas' request?"

Now Noel felt a trickle of excitement. Okay, one thing. "Why not."

"Uh—we couldn't charge them as much as Marchand."

"You're the boss."

Kyra gave that comment an instant of thought. "Tomorrow afternoon. I'll e-mail you my ETA."

"Good. See you then." Noel walked onto his balcony, shoved his hands in his pockets and rocked back on his heels. Strange how Kyra was able to make him feel like a kid. Younger than forty-four, anyway.

Rose rolled in at five. Artemus kissed her and showed her Franklin's report.

"Not much use, were they?"

He'd known she'd say that. "Things calmed down," he soothed.

"You shouldn't get so worked up about appearances."

"Art is all about appearances, dear."

An abnormal acerbity. Rose drew back. Artemus reached an edge rarely; most often she was allowed to blow for both of them. In a jocular tone she suggested, "A celebratory drink?"

"Good idea. Tequila?" He marched briskly to the wet bar and busied himself.

Rose watched him. Artemus brisked when getting control. Did he have that much face invested in his detectives? "Now everyone knows the gallery is irrelevant to Roy's death."

"Right." He turned and handed her a double tequila. "And now you and Tam can please get off my case. Cheers." He smiled, his eyes holding hers. It felt great to be back on good terms with Rosie.

"Right." She sipped, smiled back, and stroked the top of his hand. And you get off your case too.

A fine morning. Kyra felt back in the saddle. Though she hated the idea of another drive, that border, those ferries— Could she fly? She googled airline companies, found a site she'd never seen before, Raven Air, seaplanes daily, Tacoma-Everett-Bellingham-Nanaimo-Comox. She called. No problem, Bellingham to Nanaimo in forty minutes, flight leaves at 2:40 PM. First rate.

She'd have to see Tam Gill again. The final arbiter in buying specific paintings. She stared out the window, then picked up the phone and called information, a number for T. Gill on Gabriola Island. She pushed lightly on the 1, and the ten digits. "This is Tam Gill. I know I'll love the sound of your voice. Please talk to me." How can such mellow tones come through a phone line. The click. "Hello, Mr. Gill. This is Kyra Rachel. You may remember me. I talked to you about the death of Roy Dempster." There. That was easy. "I'll be in Nanaimo tomorrow and I'd like to meet with you. Please call me back." She left her number. The back of her neck prickled. Ridiculous. She was done with all that. She was serving their client, the consortium. She was an intelligent self-controlled person.

Tam Gill studied the painting. That blue needed a deeper tone, maybe more purple. Nice thing about oils, they didn't dry too fast. He stepped out of his orange coveralls made more colorful with yellow, blue and green paint dabs, automatically felt for the key in the pocket, and scrubbed his hands at the sink. In his main room—living, dining, kitchen space—a light flashed on the answering machine: Hello. This is Kyra Rachel— He scribbled down the number.

What now? BSR said A. said the detectives had turned in their report. What the hell did she want? To get laid? He laughed aloud.

He took out the bread and searched the fridge for a sandwich middle. Or had A. ordered the snoops to keep on going? He might have; all summer he'd had these fits of indecisiveness. Shit. Tam closed the fridge and stormed out. He banged on the greenhouse door.

A long wait, then Rose pulled it open. "I've told you and told you to phone first."

"The detective's coming back. She just left me a message."

"What?" Rose wheeled out, closing the door. Her eyes and mouth tightened. Her brother. Her husband. They yanked at her loyalties. "Are you saying Artemus called them back?"

"Or she's after my bod."

Could Artemus have changed his mind again? Why? Today at lunch he'd been fretting about three important critics who hadn't yet confirmed their presence for the Thanksgiving show. "When did she phone?"

"I don't know. What time is it now?"

"Ten to three."

No wonder he was hungry. "Between nine-thirty and now."

From nowhere Rose felt a pang of fear. "Artemus couldn't have." Or, yes he could.

"Where is he?" Tam's stance had returned to focus, legs apart, body centered.

"Probably in his office." She touched Tam's forearm. "We should all talk."

Tam nodded. "I'll find him." He left.

She wheeled in through her suite and along the hall. She watched Tam follow Artemus downstairs. As they approached she launched in. "Artemus dear. Did you rehire the detectives?"

"What?" Artemus squinted at Tam. "What's she talking about?"

"The woman left a message on Tam's machine. She wants to ask him more questions."

"I never revisit yesterday's problems, you know that."

"Artemus." Rose's wife-in-control-of-family tone. "Are you saying, truly, that you've had no more dealings with them?"

"Of course not. Haven't thought about them." Then he did. "So they're still at it?"

"Yes," said Rose.

"But the RCMP will cope now. Won't they?"

Tam turned to Rose. "I'll find out what's up."

———

Kyra took a long walk around Lake Samish. She wouldn't like to live in any of these houses. Too settled and demanding. Clean my eaves, sweep my chimney, paint my doors. Back at her duplex she took a shower. Tonight she'd stay home and read a book. She dried herself off, pulled on her robe, noted a message on her phone. Tam Gill. "Hi Kyra. Sure I remember. Love to see you again. I'll also be in Nanaimo tomorrow, be free by late afternoon. How about a drink? I've got a small condo in Heritage Mews, number 231. About five-thirty? Give me a call to confirm. I'll take a drink with you as reward for a hard day's work."

She breathed way down deep. What would she read tonight? First she'd have a drink. No, first call him back. Again his recorded voice. Did he just pick up messages, never go home? "Great. The Heritage Mews at five-thirty. Number 231."

Coordinate with Noel. She called, told him she was coming up. And felt good about it.

ELEVEN

NOEL'S ATTENTION BELONGED 20 percent to his notes on Eaglenest Gallery: did they make different sense looked at from the consortium's point of view? They didn't. Figuring out how he felt about investigating an ex-client took five percent. A need for lunch held 74 percent. And one percent listened to his *boeuf bourguignon* burbling on the stove. The phone rang. He looked up in irritation. "Hello?"

"Is that Noel?" A shivery whisper.

"Yes."

"It's Patty Bourassa on Gabriola. Danny's wife. Can you come over to the island? Please?"

"What's up?"

"I'm scared they'll arrest Danny. You said if anything else happened—"

"Right, but—"

"They found Roy's binoculars in our shed. Lucille—you know, the reporter?"

"Yes."

"She got a tip and she and Jim Yardley came over and found them. I'm scared Jim's coming back to arrest Danny." A quiver in Patty's voice. "Jim told us not to leave the island."

"Look, I don't know how I can help but I'll catch the next ferry. Make some hot tea, lots of sugar and milk. How's Danny?"

"He's sitting on the stoop."

Noel glanced out the window. "I'll be there soon. The ferry's halfway here."

"Thanks," Patty whispered and hung up.

In fairness, Patty couldn't have known he'd finished working on Dempster. He sent Kyra a short e-mail about the call, maybe she'd pick it up along the way. Then he printed it and left it on the table in case she came in before he returned. He switched off the stove. Why he'd made so complicated a meal for Lyle he didn't know, but he'd enjoyed the process. He set the entry rug at its oblique angle and locked the door. At the mailboxes he grabbed several envelopes and headed for his Honda. He drove to the ferry, paid, and got in line.

A horde of kids walked off, laughing, bumping each other. Then a stream of vehicles. Noel bounced the Honda on. He checked his mail. Phone and cable bills, pre-paid anyway. The ferry began to move. Another envelope, no return address. He tore it open. He pulled out a piece of newsprint. It looked like an obituary from the *Sun*. He read it.

> Franklin, Noel. 1964-2008. One-time star investigative reporter for the Vancouver Sun, Noel Franklin, a three-year resident of Nanaimo, had been working on a book. His naked and mutilated body was discovered in a gully beside Nanaimo Lakes Road. He is survived by his parents, Samuel and Diane Franklin of Parksville, and by a brother, Sidney, of Stanford, California, but not by his partner Brendan Yi. His book would have been a failure. Don't send flowers.

Goosebumps. Okay Noel, easy. Chill out. First, reread it. He did. The words didn't change. He turned it over. Blank. Fake newsprint. He set it on the passenger seat. Fingerprints? But why, why? Why!

The tire-slasher phone-breather. Someone who knew him. Or someone who'd researched him. As he had Marchand.

Naked. Mutilated. Ha! The unkindest cut related to his book. It was maybe correct.

Phone Albert? And Kyra. The ferry arrived at Gabriola. He shoved the obituary to the back of his mind.

He found Danny and Patty on the back deck, empty mugs and Princess beside them. The dog barked without enthusiasm. Patty looked better than she'd sounded but her round face sagged. "Tell me what happened."

"Jim showed up with Lucille right on his tailpipe," Danny said. "They marched over to my shed," he pointed toward the back of the property, "a minute later Jim came out with the binoculars in a plastic bag. He asked me where I got them from. I said I didn't know they were there."

"You sure they're Roy's?"

"Yeah." Danny got up and leaned straight-armed on the railing, still looking toward the shed. "His name's engraved on them, his sister gave them to him."

"Did Lucille say who tipped her off?"

"Not to me." Danny squeezed his eyes closed. "Beats me." His head shook. "Just beats me."

"Had to be planted there," stated Patty. "But why? Danny was Roy's best friend."

"Maybe to turn the attention from somebody else. Show me where the binoculars were."

They crossed the brown grass, Princess too, and Danny opened the door. He pointed at a pile of rags. "Under those."

Noel noted paint tins, pots, shovel, hoe, rakes, lawnmower. Tidy. "This your workshop?"

"No. I've got half the garage. This is just storage."

Noel stepped through the entry and examined the door—a latch and hasp on the door frame, but no lock.

Danny noted his gaze. "Nothing here to steal."

"And the rags, how long have they been here?"

"About a week?" Patty paused. "Last Sunday? When I repotted the African violets?"

Danny nodded. "Before your parents came for dinner."

"They arrived early. I forgot about the rags." She bent to pick them up now—

Noel put a hand on her arm. "Better leave them till you know the Mounties are done." A sudden panic in her gaze. "When was the last time you were in here, either of you?"

"I guess then, Sunday." Patty looked over to her husband. "Unless you've been?"

"No, it's been weeks. Since I last cut the grass." He turned to stare at his brown lawn.

"Who's visited recently?"

"Sue's come for coffee twice," Patty said. "She's dog-sitting, so we take doggie walks."

"Steve came by yesterday to borrow my Skilsaw," Danny offered. "Anyway it's in the garage."

"No one else?"

They shook their heads in unison. "Not while we were here," Danny said, adding, "Jim's a friend. Much as a Mountie can be a friend. They get moved every three years."

Noel said, "I think it's all going to be okay."

He could still make the 3:10 ferry. He was curious now: who had tipped Lucille about the binoculars? Lyle wasn't coming till 6:30.

His knock pulled Lucille from her computer—Noel could see it from her blinking eyes. "Hi. I'm disturbing you, but can I come in? I've got a few questions."

"Tea?"

"No thanks." Then lunchlessness hit him. "On second thought, sure. But would you do a finicky man a favor and boil the water in a kettle?"

"You worried? My well water's just fine, I had it tested three months ago."

"No, no. Kettles heat hotter." He smiled and hoped it looked ingratiating.

"Oh, all right. I think I have a kettle."

He followed her down the short hall into the kitchen. A kind of fussiness here: chintz curtains, matching tablecloth and wallpaper, a round dwarf bowl marked *Cookies*, toadstool salt and pepper shakers. A wall plaque proclaimed the kitchen to be the Heart of the Home. Different from the living room side of Maple. Maybe the side that segregates flowers.

Lucille pointed up over the fridge. "Reach that down for me." Noel handed her a sixties-vintage electric kettle. She filled it and plugged it in. "I didn't think I'd see you so soon." Her tone wasn't displeased. She sat at the table and indicated a chair. "Ask away."

"The tip on Roy's binoculars you got this morning. From whom?"

"Phone call. Probably a man's voice but disguised—high, breathy, muffled—could have been a woman's. He or she said, 'You'll find Dempster's binoculars under rags in Danny Bourassa's shed' and hung up. I phoned the cop shop then drove like a bat out of Hades, know what I'm saying, so I got there just as Jim did." She looked smug.

The kettle's decibels increased from purr to chortle. Noel spoke louder. "Any idea who?" She shook her head. "Somebody who knew how you'd respond."

"That's half the island," said Lucille.

"Knew you'd call the police. Not the Bourassas." She nodded, not competing with the kettle. Now Noel knew why she preferred the microwave. "What happened there?"

Noel watched her set out teacups, sugar, milk. She plucked teabags out of a canister. No teapot, Noel noted, resigned.

"We walked into the shed." Lucille's muckraking voice. "Jim sorted through the pile of rags with an evidence bag and picked up the binocs." The kettle broke into a rolling burble, surf in a storm.

She let the water boil a good ten seconds, then unplugged the kettle and poured the water over the tea bags in the cups. "Thank you," Noel said. "Think Danny or Patty hid the binoculars?"

"Not judging by their shock, know what I'm saying? But they might be good actors."

Noel added sugar and milk to tell his stomach his throat wasn't cut. "I think they're pretty transparent people. Who else?"

"I'd guess an angry islander, pointing fingers in various directions."

Noel plucked the bag from his cup. "You going to write about the binoculars being there?"

"Yep."

"Don't you ever worry about pissing people off?"

"Ah, pish and tiffle. I sell newspapers."

"I thought the *Gab* was free."

"I mean sell ad space, of course! Steamy stuff gets readership."

"I guess." Noel sipped. Still awful.

"Okay, who told *you* about the binoculars? Patty or Danny? You must've been on the very next ferry."

"Patty." He had nothing more to tell her.

Nor did Lucille have more for him. So Noel stood, leaving half his tea. At the door she said, "Don't bother watching the flagstones, know what I'm saying? They're okay."

"Thanks for the tea." He drove off. Unsatisfactory conversation. He glanced at the ferry schedule. Damn! Next ferry was dangerous cargo only, no vehicles or passengers. Over an hour till the one after that.

At the Village Market he bought two apples and a pizza bun, then drove toward Eaglenest. He stopped by a little beach and unwrapped his pizza.

Did Kyra seriously want to be partners in a freelance research agency with someone who got his own obit in the mail? Did he want to be partners with her? The idea didn't appall him. Though it was ridiculous. He had a book to finish writing. Fifty minutes till the ferry. He wished Kyra were here.

———

Bellingham to Nanaimo, middle leg of the flight. The aircraft arrived from down the coast. After Nanaimo it would head north to Comox. At the check-in desk, Kyra learned that the routing, advertised for months, had been approved only five weeks ago. Lucky. A security guard examined her flight bag, handling every item as if it held nitroglycerin.

She was dressed right this time, low-heeled city boots, loose chinos, white top with long sleeves, taupe cotton jacket, Gore-Tex in hand. A blouse, jeans, sneakers and underwear in her carry-on. And her purse was a standard detecting kit—cellphone, flashlight, camera, lock picks, tissues, tampons, two snack bars, lipstick, moisturizing cream and wallet.

The seaplane glided along the dock and stopped. A crew-woman tied it in place. Three passengers and a tall uniformed young man got out. Eight minutes later the man in uniform marched her and four fellow passengers to the end of the dock. She showed her passport, the US one. They boarded a Raven Air nine-seater, joining three others. The left engine sputtered to life. The uniformed man, likely a pilot, closed the hatch and bolted it, the right propeller whirred. He handed them each a customs declaration form. Kyra filled hers out and stuck it into her Canadian passport. He joined the captain at the controls. Yes, co-pilot. The crew-woman cast the plane free. It growled across flat water. How did they know where the runway started? Sudden increase in engine roar, Kyra's back rounded into the seat cushion, and they were in the air.

She stared down, sailboats receding, the town and the bay growing small. On the ground, tiny inlets and tide pools burbling with life fascinated her, anemones and starfish and inch-long darters, sea-worms, mussels, scuttling crabs and dead crabs. Even from up here she could almost feel hard warm wet stone against her palms. From here too she saw the patterns, pools and inlets, land intruding into water, water gliding into land. The inlets down there had to be huge, each with its own mini-inlets and pools. Up here her eye held the overview. Yes, she liked seaplanes. No border lineups in the air.

The plane crossed from Washington into British Columbia somewhere between Patos Island, a state park accessible only by water, and Saturna Island. They skirted Salt Spring Island on the strait side, two humps of land pinched in the middle, then long skinny Galiano, and across the channel to Valdes, Gabriola next, along the northeast. They descended into Nanaimo harbor and slid gracefully to dock at the seaport landing.

On the dock, waiting to meet the plane, half a dozen people. Including Tam Gill! Come to meet her? He couldn't know she'd be on this flight! He waited back from the others, not watching the passengers.

She handed her customs card and Canadian passport to a woman wearing a peaked hat that said Immigration-Customs/Douane, separate functions except at small ports of entry. No, nothing to declare. Nothing but a sudden pounding heart. The woman kept the card, handed back the passport. Bureaucracy done with.

Tam was staring at her. Their eyes met. From him a moment of recognition, then uncertainty. Then a huge smile, a wave, and he elbowed his way toward her. "Hi!"

"Hello. What are you doing here?"

"Come to meet you, of course."

"How'd you figure me on this flight?"

"Just lucky." He grinned. "No, I'm lying. I'm picking up a shipment for the Gallery. Need a ride? I've got the van."

"I only have to go a couple of blocks. It's just as fast to walk." Drat.

"Two blocks are two blocks."

That smile again. She smiled back.

"Let me grab my shipment. Aside from everything else, I'm the Gallery customs broker. Give me a minute."

Her eyes followed him to the cargo pod. A dock crewman unloaded suitcases, small wooden boxes, half a dozen cardboard packages, and three high, wide, thin crates.

Well, darn it. His appearance had thrown her into a fuss.

Tam collected the crates. The dock man handed Tam a sheet of paper. He located a dolly, loaded it, wheeled the packages to the van and piled them in back.

Most irritating was, now she'd have to change. She couldn't meet Tam later in clothes he'd already seen her in today. Professionalism demanded an image that controlled, and that included tactical clothing. Likely, and she let an ironic smile grow in her mind, likely he'd already undressed her. Peeled off her jacket, let her pants fall to the floor. The sex dance.

"You coming?" He opened the passenger door.

She walked over, not managing the brisk step she wanted. He reached his hand over for her elbow but she used the door's armrest to pull herself in. He closed the door.

Only a pair of jeans and another blouse. Dang!

"Where you headed?" He smiled at her through the open passenger window.

"Cameron Island. The whole two blocks south."

"No problem. I just have to stop up there." He pointed. Above the back of the dock, a government placard said, *Customs/Douane.* "Won't be a minute." He headed off.

Two minutes. Three. She could have been at Noel's apartment already. Customs. Voluntary honesty here, pick stuff up, go by, report. What was he importing? She leaned around, supported herself on the driver's seat. Still warm— Well of course it was warm, the whole van was warm, it was a warm day. Five minutes. The three crates lay stacked flat. She eased herself between the seats. Snooping headed the description list of any job she'd ever be interested in. On the top crate, a bill of lading enclosed in plastic. From Sultan Suppliers, North Bend, Oregon—

"Frames." Tam's head stuck in through the door window.

She nodded. "Ah." Getting caught snooping was not in the job description. She sidled forward between the seats. "All done?"

"Yep." He climbed in and did up his seatbelt. "It's quick. They know me." He started the engine. "Three modern antiqued picture frames, value twelve hundred dollars each. Sultan does good work. You need a frame, I can get you a good price. Anything else you'd like to know?"

Kyra produced a mock-feeble smile as she fumbled with the seat-belt. "Sorry. Just curious."

"Must be your profession." He laughed a little, and drove onto Front Street.

She mentioned the new airline route, so much easier. For him too? Before had he used the regular Nanaimo airport? He dropped her on the circular drive in front of Noel's condo building. She realized she was looking forward to their drink. But hmm, Tam hadn't asked which Cameron Island building to drive to.

She thanked him, headed for the outer lobby, and pushed the electronic buttons. No response. But her key from Noel opened the door. She walked up two flights and let herself into his apartment. Was that deadbolt always so loose? A note from Noel: I'm on Gabriola. Dempster's binocs turned up in the Bourassa shed. New stuff on that Vegas casino. Lyle's coming for dinner. You are VERY welcome!

Lyle. Interesting. And the binoculars. Intriguing.

She looked in Noel's study closet on the off-chance she'd left some garment. No, but some other clothes hung there. She flicked through the hangers and paused at a steel-blue shirt. She stroked the sleeve, fine lawn, almost like silk. Yep, it would fit her. Noel wouldn't mind.

From Noel's balcony she watched tourists on the embankment. Couples, all ages. For a moment she yearned to walk along that promenade hand in hand with a man who loved her—

She wrote on the bottom of Noel's note: I should be back before seven. Yes, I'd love dinner, thanks. And I promise to leave you right after. She took a long bath and got dressed. She watched the Gabriola ferry arrive, and depart. She grabbed her jacket. Time to go.

TWELVE

ROSE HAD BEEN thinking about Rab. Rab was Peter, originally Pyotr, Rabinovich, a Russian Jew who'd taken a circuitous path from the old USSR to the USA, stopping in Czechoslovakia as it was then, some years in Panama, then Switzerland and Israel. His most striking feature was an elegant skull, baldness having hit him in his twenties. His face was lean, like the rest of him, with a dominant nose, prominent cheekbones and lips full enough to belie the leanness. His eyes were a pale grey-blue. A scar courtesy of the KGB decorated his left cheek. Why had the KGB arrested him, when had he gotten free? Rab was ever vague on details. His young wife and their little girl had been killed when a suicide bomber had blown up the bus they were on. He had taken merciless private revenge against the faction that had claimed responsibility.

Rose, some years back, was surprised to discover she found bald heads attractive. Artemus had a head of lush silver-grey hair which he'd undoubtedly keep to the grave. His head was attractive too.

They'd all met six years ago, soon after Rab opened The Hermitage, his Las Vegas luxury hotel and casino. He'd insisted on decorating his palace with good European art, his way of reclaiming Jewish-owned art stolen by the Nazis during the Second World War. A consultant had mentioned, among other dealers, Artemus Marchand. Gabriola? A small island? Does it have roads? He was intrigued. Their business association had worked well. Rab and Rose became friends, each someone the other could confide in.

She locked the greenhouse, wheeled in through her bedroom door to the kitchen, wine rack, opener, glass. She took a sip. Oh what the hell. She dialed Rab's private number.

"Hello?"

"Hello, Rab."

"Ah! My favorite *collaborateur!* What wonderful thing have you done now, Rosie-Rosita?" He spoke with perfect English grammar set in what Rose recognized as residual Leningrad nasality layered with light west-Asian gutturals and curlicued Levantine cadences.

"Rab, you're a caress to a woman's ego."

"Tell me more."

"Well, in fact, I have done something wonderful. A new flower. A black *Chrysanthemum morifolium*, the first of its kind."

"Amazing!"

"I'm going to show it next weekend."

"Rosie-Rosita, congratulations. Dumas only created a black flower on paper."

"I accept all laudatory comments." He was good for her. And, she believed, they were good for each other. An affair of the mind, he described their relationship, far more important than affairs of the flesh. Of which he had many, some sweet young plumlet ever on his arm. "But Rab, I'm worried. About our—arrangement."

"Should we speak on the phone?"

"I don't have much to say. Only that— I don't know if we should continue."

"You speak of recent global politics?"

"I worry about borders."

"Yes, we should talk. Oh my dear, I've neglected you. My life has been even more horribly full than normal. And yours as well, I imagine."

"Not really, not on our island." Should she explain? Why not. "Our biggest event's been the death—the murder—of our gardener."

A moment of silence before Rab said, "But that's awful!"

"Yes. I found his body."

"How dreadful, Rosie. How horrible for you. Have the police discovered who did it?"

"No, but they've been around. Artemus was upset. He hired investigators."

"Hmm."

"I agree."

Their Hmm, and, I agree, caught a full summary of Artemus' not-thought-through decision and the problems it might bring. "Anyway, they didn't find anything."

"Still, that was a damn stupid thing for him to do."

"Just foolish, I'd say."

"Did he hire a large agency?"

Strange question. "I don't think so. A man and a woman."

"Their names?"

Why does he want to know that? She told him. "They sent a report absolving the Gallery." She wished she hadn't mentioned the detectives. "So I didn't think to bother you."

"Nothing you do could be a bother to me, my darling."

She laughed. She'd bet Tam learned flirtation from someone like Rab. Or did the ability just arrive on a male chromosome? "You're sweet." They would talk soon about the arrangement. They said goodbye. She finished her wine. The time had come to discuss this with Artemus.

Kyra, jacket in hand, walked up Bastion Street across the bridge over the old Island Highway. Down to the right used to be the whorehouse district. Up the hill along Fitzwilliam to the old city quarter, slowly becoming a boutique and restaurant area, especially along Wesley Street. The houses up here dated from the late 1800s, homes for Hudson's Bay Company overseers and foremen, for managers of Nanaimo's coal industry. The name Nanaimo, she also knew from Noel, comes from *Snuneymuxw*—she said it aloud. Except for the starting *S* and the strange *X* just before the end, it did sound like a mispronunciation of Nanaimo. Rather, the other way around, Nanaimo a corruption of—

Oh, quit maundering! Just do your job. Another interview, another judgment of partial truths told, concealed stories, stances, innuendos. Schools-of paintings and Eaglenest. You're good at interviews, remember? Selby Street. One block. Three-storey modern Tudor condos. The door to the Mews, the name. The number. She pressed.

A voice from a tinny speaker said, "I'll buzz. Come up."

A low whine. She entered and climbed stairs, found the apartment, raised her knuckles, brought them down as the door opened. She caught her balance and her brain said, déjà vu: Tam's karate move on Dempster, going with the other's action.

Tam grinned. "Hi."

"Hello." She smiled and held out her hand. He took it and they shook, his pressure firm but not dominating. As hard as hers.

"Come in." Golf shirt, khaki shorts. Bare feet.

"Thank you." She strode to the middle of the room, jacket in hand.

"My home away from home. Well, my studio apartment away from home."

"Nice." Small kitchen against the side wall—sink beside stove, fridge beneath, microwave above. A wooden table and two chairs by the sliding glass wall, overlooking downtown and the harbor. A couch. Couple of doors, one closed, the half-open one to a bathroom.

"Every now and then I need to get away from Gabriola."

"Oh? Is that important for you?"

He looked at her sharply. "If you want to live more lives than you get over there, yes."

More lives, that's what she too wanted. "It's very attractive."

"I like it. But I like my place on Gabriola too."

Was he yanking her back and forth? "That's also pretty."

"You know why I like it?"

Was she supposed to guess? She was the interviewer here. "Why?"

"See, I start off in some huge place, Bucharest, London, even Toronto, and I take a fast plane to a smaller place, Vancouver. From there it's a small plane to a smaller place on a big island, Nanaimo. Then a little ferry to a small island, and a slow van on curving roads to a house, Eaglenest. Then a path through woods to a tiny cabin. That's my kind of island peace."

It appealed. "Active downsizing."

He laughed lightly. "But I need Nanaimo, too. And Vancouver. And London."

She nodded.

"Now. We can go out for a drink." An inferior option, his tone declared. "Or I have almost everything you might want," he gestured, "right here. We can sit on the balcony. I think it's still warm enough."

"Yes." He was smooth.

He walked past her to the sliding glass door, half-open, and gestured for her to go out, assuming his preferred option had been accepted. "What may I give you?"

"A glass of white wine?" As she passed him her sleeve brushed his arm. The fine lawn of her shirt pressed on her skin. Part of her said, Be careful, Rachel, and another part insisted, If it takes flirtation to get him chatty, two have to play the game. She sat on one of the rattan deck chairs, a table between them, and set the jacket on the arm. Had he edged his shoulder forward as she passed? She faced out toward the harbor but paid more attention to the beat of her pulse. Did it show at her temples? She touched her hair, slid her fingers down the side of her brow. No.

He brought glasses, cut crystal, and a bottle of cold wine, a Caterina Sauvignon Blanc 2006 from Washington State. He displayed it like a good sommelier. She nodded, he uncorked.

An expensive wine. The very wine she'd bought Sam, a case, for their second anniversary—an earlier vintage, of course. A wine Sam loved.

Tam set both glasses on the table, filled them to half, handed her one, raised his, found her glance, no words. The glasses clinked lightly. Excellent crystal. Nineteenth-century Bohemian? She sipped. Lovely. Tam was saying, ". . . can't keep much wine around. Your choice was limited."

"Delicious."

He sat and smiled. "Yes."

She couldn't keep from smiling back. The silence, not more than four or five seconds, for Kyra was a twist down to a pleasant place, a weakness in her thighs, an instant sweet ping at her temples— To be disregarded. "I need some information." She sat up straight. "For another case."

"I'll do my best." He sat back, his eyes still on hers. "And then I'll ask you something." His lip corners turned up, just a touch. "Okay?"

Kyra said, "You can always ask," but felt as if she'd signed her name to a pact she'd not read. Quick, her close-to-the-truth story. "We're acting as agents for a consortium of antique dealers. They know you've found a good many schools-of in the last few years."

"Mmm," said Tam.

She speeded her delivery. "They'd like to buy up to three between them." She took another sip. Superior wine. She sat back. "Will Artemus have paintings soon?" She raised her eyebrows, she hoped innocently. Another sip. What, nearly empty?

He too sipped. "Can you tell me who your consortium is?"

She shook her head. "Afraid not." And only then saw where he was headed.

He nodded. "I understand." His tone, all business. "And as you must understand, I can't tell you anything about the paintings." He shook his head. "If I did, Artemus would have my ass."

It took her half a second but she blurted a laugh.

He laughed too. "It's true, he would." He picked up the bottle and poured her more wine.

She reached over, let the lovely fluid flow, with one finger stayed his hand, "Thank you. So I can't learn anything from you." This time she found his eye.

He smiled.

"I went to see that Sienese school-of painting in Bellingham, the one you told me about."

"Oh good." A pleased smile. "It's a pretty good one."

"Yes. But that poor Madonna, forever sliding off her chair."

A laugh. "A gift to the museum. Probably lost for hundreds of years."

"How do they get lost like that?" She gave him a naive little smile, awaiting his wisdom.

"Sometimes people don't know what they have in their attics. Sometimes they're hanging on the wall, been there so long nobody looks at them anymore."

"And how come they get found?"

"People track them down."

"Oh? Is that difficult?"

"Not if you know the scene. Not if you're smart."

She nodded as he spoke, appreciating his insight. "But how do you know which attic or wall? There must be millions of eighteenth-century attics in Europe."

"No, it's easier than that." He sat back, stretched out his long bare legs thick with dark hair. "We have a team."

"Ah."

"Scouts. I told you about this when we had coffee, remember? Throughout Europe. And we may expand into western Asia."

Her smile must say his words were full of meaning. It wasn't hard. She enjoyed his voice.

"They find paintings shut away in storerooms or warehouses or sheds, forgotten for lifetimes. Literally. Or buried away during World War Two to hide them from the Nazis, only coming out now. Sometimes bedding for rats and spiders, sometimes in strangely good shape. Our scouts are clever. You can't imagine how many unemployed art historians there are in Eastern Europe. One-time university professors. They know their territory."

She continued to nod. "And?"

"We get a report. Sometimes they contact Artemus, sometimes me directly. If the report sounds good I go to examine the painting. I'm a fair historian myself. I evaluate the quality of the work and the state it's in. And I decide whether to buy. I set up authentication tests, that's a necessary part. Each scout gets a finder's fee."

"Is authentication hard?"

"We work with several experts. So, no."

"You buy most of what you hear about?"

"Oh, about half." He sat forward again. "I used to love it, seeing remarkable parts of the world, finding a hidden treasure. A real adventure." He leaned toward her. "But you know, something's new in me recently. More and more, all that feels like part of my past." Even as he nodded he held her gaze. "I've got to change myself."

He sees inside me. Danger. "Yes." She placed her again empty glass on the table.

Tam picked up the bottle and reached over to pour.

She covered her glass. "I think I've had enough." Time to go.

"A little more won't hurt."

She smiled. "Actually, it might." She stood. "I know so little about history. But this has been fascinating. And the wine was delicious. Thank you."

"Do you really have to leave?"

"I think so. Yes."

He stood, never looking away, not for a flicker. She slid through the door, looked back, saw her jacket on her chair. To retrieve it she had to brush by Tam twice. He did not move out of her way.

At the hall door he stopped her. "I had a question, too."

"Yes?"

He reached out his hand and took hers. He stroked her knuckles with his thumb. Brassy danger bells clanged. "May I kiss you?"

May I kiss you? he'd really said that? *Kiss* reverberated among the bells. She felt the blush rising up from the silky collar of her shirt. He was standing close, smelled so tantalizingly male, something piney, soap or after-shave, his dark eyes— Leaning toward her, starting to pull her to him— Kyra shook her head, though her head wanted to nod— "No," she managed to squeak. She smiled so he wouldn't feel too rejected, so he'd realize her *no* was a reluctant one. But now having said *no* did she wish she'd said *yes?* She took a deep breath. Her neck burned with blush.

With a last caress of her knuckles, he released her hand and shifted his weight away. "No means no," he cited, smiling—how had she missed that dimple in his cheek? "It doesn't mean don't ask the question again."

She smiled back, then turned the doorknob, "Bye," and escaped. If she'd stayed, she'd have melted in his arms. Kyra the cliché.

THIRTEEN

IN LATE SEPTEMBER 1996, a Massad agent acting under the alias
Lev Sten—one of four working covers for his rarely used birth
name, Llewellyn Katz—broke into the Jerusalem condo of Pyotr
Rabinovich. From his agency control Katz had received a sweeping
enter-and-investigate order. The Russian Desk, Immigrant Section,
of Massad needed to divine just where Rabinovich fitted into the
panoply of newly arrived exiles under its vigil; or, if he didn't fit, why
not. Katz's agency control did know, from three months of surveillance, that six days a week, from sunset Saturday to late Thursday,
Rabinovich spent much of his time at the Wet Negev, a bar he'd
bought the year before with cash brought into Israel via unknown
routes and from undetermined sources, possibly the St. Petersburg
black market. When Rabinovich first acquired the Negev he kept it
open for business seven nights a week—to accommodate, he liked to
say, his Arab, Christian and heathen customers—but after three weeks
of warnings from a yeshiva around the corner, eighteen baseball-
bat wielding thin-bearded rabbinical students, their prayer-shawls
fluttering, invaded the Negev on a Friday two hours before sunset
and laid its furniture, mirrors and spirits to waste. Thereafter Pyotr
Rabinovich closed the Negev on the Sabbath.

The obscurity of both Rabinovich's principles and the capital that
supplied them had aroused the fascination of the Massad. A chaos of
information had been gleaned from hundreds of debriefings of the
many who joined Rabinovich at his table. Most claimed Pyotr as close
friend and loyal acquaintance. He trusted none of them.

Rabinovich represented too many unknown, therefore dangerous,
possibilities. Hence the door to Rabinovich's condo at 6:15 on a
Thursday evening, hence Lev Sten as telephone repairman with a tool
belt strapped to his waist, hence the electronic lock decoder.

The door opened. Too easy, thought Sten, a short blond man in
khaki shirt, shorts and sandals. He called out in Hebrew, "*Bell Yisroel!*"
No answer. He grimaced thinly, closed the door behind him and felt
the barrel of a pistol at the back of his skull.

A voice said, "I did not order a phone repair."

With thumb and index finger Sten took from his pocket a sheet of folded paper and showed the man the repair order. "Are you Mr. Rabinovich?"

"Yes," said the man in English, "and your Hebrew is lousy. British?"

"Nottingham," and Sten continued in English with a midlands accent, "and you were cursed to be born Russian."

"A metre from the wall. Legs apart. Undo your work-belt. Drop your trousers." Sten did. "Arms apart, high, lean against the wall. Thank you." With his pistol Rabinovich patted Sten along his shirt and pants. "Pull your undershorts down, please. Good. Now spread the cheeks. Kick your trousers over here, please." Rabinovich examined the tools on the man's belt. Among these, a palm-held camera. "All in order, *chaver*. Except your lock pick. Standard Massad issue."

Sten said nothing.

"I assume the camera is normal. Everyone in this country is a tourist."

Sten squinted at Rabinovich as in mild disbelief.

"Please, turn around and raise your scrotum. A little higher. Good, thank you. Now put your pants on. You are here to explore my condo. I am a loyal Israeli. If Massad believes I am a cause for concern, you must do your job." He waved his pistol wide, an invitation. "Please."

"I'm here to fix your phone."

"Go right ahead. But place no listening devices. No, you could not, you have not brought anything with you unless you are wired ve-e-ery deep up your asshole. So. Be my guest."

For the next two hours Sten searched in and beneath drawers and under beds, tapped walls and floorboards, examined letters and notebooks and packages of photos, showing Rabinovich in the company of publicly familiar faces. Also letters in languages Sten didn't know. He found nothing that might prove of interest to his agency control. Which itself was interesting.

Rabinovich asked Sten many questions and Sten, while going about his professionally thorough search, responded with casual truthfulness. Halfway through they discovered they shared Yiddish in common, which shifted them to first name basis. By the end they found they knew British-Jewish and Russian-Jewish versions of the same anti-Israel jokes.

Lev left as he'd entered, through the front door, thinking if he'd stayed any longer Pyotr would've offered him a drink. A convivial man. Lev felt relief that he hadn't been ordered to kill the Russian— not that he'd have been able to till the middle of their joking, then a quick jerk to the side, the wire from the belt, an instant garotting. If Pyotr hadn't shot him first.

He reported his search with precision, suggesting further surveillance. His agency control agreed with Sten's analysis and ordered the agent to spend several late afternoons a week at the Wet Negev. Over a year and a half Pyotr and Lev—Lev even after Llewellyn Katz revealed his English name, Rabinovich exclaiming, "Llewellyn?! Every parent is an anti-Semite!"—talked and joked. In the end Rabinovich sold the Negev to a South African playboy and left Israel for the US, grumbling, "No room to grow in this socialist country."

Six years ago he asked Katz to join him at The Hermitage, head of security, vice-president electronics division. Massad never did figure out what Rabinovich was doing in Israel.

Llewellyn Katz, arriving in Las Vegas, finding the desert landscape eerily familiar and his salary quadrupled, adapted with loyalty to his designated alias, Herm 3.

Rabinovich would this evening send Herm 3 to Nanaimo. His assignment: two detectives.

———

Noel wondered if he actually liked Lyle. At least Lyle was a connection to Brendan. So it was okay to see Lyle. His eye caught Lyle's painting over the chesterfield. Not bad. He loaded some CDs and set the machine to random. Melissa Etheridge sang out, "It shouldn't bother you—"

Except it bothered him a hell of a lot, the obituary that lay concealed at the back of the bottom drawer of the chest. Hidden from his eyes. Not from his mind.

Lyle arrived at 6:30 holding a bottle of 2005 Mercurey. He glanced at Noel's bare feet and kicked off his sandals. Was Lyle's mustache new? Noel couldn't remember. He did remember how Lyle slouched. Still, he looked good in blue open-collared dress shirt, maroon V-neck vest and brown corduroys. Noel took the bottle, nodded with pleasure, and offered Scotch, gin or vodka. Good thing he'd assembled the dinner this morning; he'd arrived back from Gabriola thirty minutes ago. On the stove the contents of the Dutch oven looked after themselves.

"End of September," Lyle announced, "early evening is still vodka-tonic time."

"Right." Noel busied himself with bottles, ice and glasses. Inside, he was wincing. Brendan and he, in summers at 5 p.m. would break into their *v 'n' t* song: Early in the evening, Just as the sun is waning, The Friendly Giant calling, It's vodka 'n' tonic time!

Lyle surveyed the living area. "You still have my painting up." He sounded gratified.

"Yep." Noel handed Lyle a glass, picked up his own, clunked. "Cheers." Noel sipped, Lyle chugged half his drink. Noel sat at one end of the chesterfield. "How's your work going?"

Lyle sat at the other end. "*Comme ci, comme ça.*" He flipped a so-so with his hand. "After the exhibit at Eaglenest I got galleries in Toronto and Montreal. Sold a few small ones. But nobody really cares about painting." He cocked his head.

"That bad, eh?"

"My lectures about the stock market keep me in paint. How's the investigation going?"

"It's okay." But Noel preferred *research*.

Lyle drained his drink, leaned toward the coffee table but couldn't reach it. He shifted to the middle of the chesterfield, set his tumbler down, and turned to Noel. He rested his arm along the back of the sofa. "And how you doing, buddy, really?"

"Okay," Noel said.

"You got to get out more. There's this party coming up, whole community's going, dress as your fave movie star. I've got a great Dietrich schtick." His arm dropped to Noel's shoulder.

Noel turned to face Lyle. "Marlene with a mustache?" He shook his head. "Thanks, but I'm not ready for a party yet." Noel jiggled his glass and sipped. "Kind of you to ask, though." Lyle's arm felt warm, but out of place. Noel inched his leg away, picked up Lyle's glass and stood. "Another? I'll check on dinner." He headed for the kitchen. He realized he was flattered.

"I can make it." Lyle followed Noel. He found the mixings and poured himself four ounces of vodka. "Freshen up yours?"

Noel added a glug of his cooking wine to the sauce. "Fine for now." He poked at the potatoes steaming happily. He felt the pressure of hands on his shoulders and froze.

"It's true," Lyle whispered into his ear, "you are fine." He kneaded Noel's shoulders in gentle massage.

Noel dropped his head. This was ridiculous. But it felt good. But but but. He turned to face Lyle, forcing Lyle's right hand to pull away. He set his own hand over Lyle's left, applied a moment of pressure, then lifted Lyle's fingers. "Thank you, Lyle. We can eat in ten minutes."

Lyle replaced his hands on Noel's shoulders, now facing him. "I want you to know that I've admired and liked you from the day we met. I want you to believe that."

Noel wanted to pull his eyes away from Lyle's. He couldn't. He nodded. "Good of you to say that." He nodded again, harder. "And I like you too. But—" And suddenly Lyle's lips were against his own. Only a little pressure. Enough to spark sensations absent many months. He didn't kiss back. He closed his eyes and waited.

Lyle pulled away. "I know. You aren't ready yet." He grinned. "But you're coming along."

The CD player moved to Cole Porter. Noel said, "I hope so."

Lyle raised his hand to Noel's cheek and stroked it with his fingers. "I can feel it." His amused tone washed into Ella singing, "I Get a Kick Out of You."

Noel reached for his drink. "I do like you. You're witty and intelligent. Even handsome." He took a sip. "But for now, can we just be friends?"

"Rejected before dinner. Mostly that happens after."

Noel smiled sympathetically. He wished he weren't feeling a bit aglow. He hoped Lyle hadn't noticed. The glow felt good. But also scary. As if his face were too close to a flame.

Lyle reached for his drink, raised it to his lips and looked at Noel flirtatiously over his glass. "Doesn't mean I won't keep on trying, you know."

Noel nodded. "Would you mind opening that lovely Mercurey?"

Kyra arrived at Noel's door, still shaken. *May I kiss you?* The words had reverberated all the way down the hill: *kiss you* the electric surge was there, she knew they both felt it. She leaned her forehead against the door frame. She'd said, *No.* This way to Born-Again-Virgin country.

Surely, if one decides to be celibate, one's head rules? She tapped it on the wood. So why the heck had her body responded so intensely? Her skin still tingled. She breathed deeply. She longed for a cigarette. A couple walked swiftly down the hall. Maybe she could bum a cigarette. She got out her keys and fingered them.

Her friend Mike, whose day job was painting houses, had developed a successful career in burglary until a small slip-up landed him three years inside. When Sam said to Kyra, Get a job, and that job turned out to be investigating claims for Puget Sound Life, she mentioned her work to Mike. Just out on parole, he said he'd be delighted to advise her on locks and picks and tumblers. She told him she didn't think she needed that. He'd said one never could tell when an interesting door might turn out to be locked. She'd said, Okay, why not? Mike had found teaching Kyra so satisfying that he'd printed up cards advertising his "School" and soon found a comfortable number of lock-picking students—would-be private eyes mostly, an academic criminologist wanting hands-on training for a research paper. And one or two unskilled burglars? Did he burgle off and on to keep from getting rusty? She wondered how she'd feel breaking into locked places. She had enjoyed the learning. Picking locks was a skill, like juggling. Not needed at Noel's door. Any key would unlock it. She slid hers into the loose lock and pushed the door open.

Noel sprang up from his chair. "Kyra! Welcome back. Glad you can join us."

She noted Lyle move his arm along the sofa's back, the disgruntled expression on his face quickly rearranging itself to blandness. Had that been delight? relief? in Noel's voice?

Noel stared at her, "The shirt—" he forced a laugh, "looks good on you."

"I hope you don't mind," she said, and Noel shook his head. "Listen, you need to change your lock. And the deadbolt only has two screws." She dropped her keys into her bag. "Hi. You're Lyle, right?"

"Yes. And you are?" He stood.

"Kyra Rachel," Noel supplied. "You met at Brendan's funeral."

"Oh yes. Hello."

Noel turned to Kyra. "This is great. Plenty of *boeuf bourguignon* for all."

"Certainly, dine with us." Lyle, now debonair. "I want to hear about Noel's case. Has he told you he's been detecting?"

"Want a vodka tonic? Or something else?"

"Okay." She'd had enough alcohol but needed a drink right now.

Noel zipped to the fridge. He blinked rapidly a couple of times. The shirt—

"We've been working on the case together," Kyra informed Lyle.

He raised an eyebrow. "So you can both fill me in."

A lot going on in the room, Kyra could feel it. She sat in the seat she thought of as hers, an over-stuffed 1920s green and grey armchair her father'd given Brendan and Noel when they made their public mutual commitment.

Noel handed her a glass. She sipped. Noel and Lyle sat. "And how are you doing, Lyle?"

"Not too well." He grinned at Noel.

"We can eat if you want," Noel said.

"Why don't you let Kyra drink her drink? Tell me about the case."

Noel rattled his ice. "Body found on the Eaglenest grounds. The groundskeeper, actually."

"Groundskeeper?" Lyle flipped his wrist in parody. "It's too *Lady Chatterley*. No one on Gabriola has a groundskeeper. Not even Artemus."

"It's a booming business. They just don't call themselves grounds-keepers."

"Groundskeepers." Kyra could feel herself relaxing. "Groundskeeper has a certain—"

"Cachet," Lyle finished.

"Baggage," Noel insisted.

Kyra instantly pictured four variants of sex in the grass. She set her drink aside for later.

Noel stood. "Dinner really is ready." He brought the Dutch oven and a trivet to the table—set, she noted, with Brendan's Royal

Doulton. First time out since he died? Bowl of steamed potatoes, loaf of sourdough French bread, green salad. First time Noel's had a dinner guest since Brendan's death? Who have you invited to dinner recently, Kyra dearie?

They served themselves. First mouthfuls, spoken yums for Noel. A Brendan recipe.

Lyle poured wine. "And the case?" he asked.

"Confidentially, we got paid for not very much." Kyra sipped. "Very nice wine, by the way."

"If I leave teaching, I'll become a sommelier. Contact me then."

"Ah." Two sommeliers today, both flirting. At least this one was gay. Safety there.

"Anyway," Noel could satisfy Lyle's curiosity with common knowledge, "the groundskeeper was killed by a blow to the head."

"I know that. I recommended you to Artemus, remember?"

Kyra looked up from her plate. "You did?"

"Sure."

"Aren't there any established detective agencies in this town?"

"A few. But I've always thought of Noel as a natural investigator."

For how long, Noel wondered, had Lyle thought of him other than as Brendan's partner?

Lyle turned to Kyra. "And you've joined Noel?"

No need to confide totally in Lyle. She fed a small smile a dab of *bourguignon* sauce. "I work for an insurance company."

"Two naturals, are you? Couple of super snoops?"

Was Lyle suddenly, what? peeved? jealous? Noel said, "Investigative research is not the same as snooping."

"But, since you asked," Kyra sopped up some sauce, "we enjoy working together."

"Oh?" Lyle said politely, and glanced to Noel. "You moving to Bellingham?"

"He wouldn't live in the States." Interesting. Lyle knows where I'm from.

"Well, that's a relief."

"He has no need to move," Kyra continued. "We'd work both sides of the border."

"It's only at an early talking stage," Noel said. No. Damn. Sounded like he was apologizing to Lyle. They were nowhere close to working together.

"I like it." Lyle folded his arms. "Always better to go international." He turned to Kyra. "What do you do for your insurance company?"

"Oh, stakeouts, tailing."

"In Bellingham?"

"Mostly on the islands. I've been on San Juan, Waldron—"

"Aha! There's your schtick. An international company detecting on islands. Yeah, guys, this could sell. Get out there. Advertise."

Noel noted the excitement reaching Kyra's face. Slow down, Kyra. "Have some more wine." He picked up the bottle.

"Yeah," Lyle enthused, "it's a great idea. International Islands Investigation."

"Islands aren't international—"

"Okay, International Investigation on Islands."

Kyra tried. "Or Islands Investigations International."

"That's it! I love it. I.I.I."

"Triple-I," said Noel. Why when you name something does it suddenly take on reality?

"Here's your logo," Lyle waxed. "Three wide eyeballs connected at the edges."

"The Cyclops Agency," Kyra threw in, laughing. "Or the Third Eye."

"You have to incorporate," Lyle continued. "I could help you there, I know someone who can— Say, you could make it quadruple I. Islands Investigations International Incorporated."

"No no no, not four." Kyra shook her head. "We wouldn't want a logo that says myopia."

Noel laughed.

Lyle said, with dignity, "Just so everybody can tell who you are."

Noel didn't like this going public business. Let alone being pushed into a partnership in something he might never do. He sat up straight. "You wanted to know about our case."

"I want to know everything, Noel." Lyle chuckled, sharing the joke only with himself.

Lyle's sudden shift from enthusiasm left Noel uncomfortable. "The Mounties found the man's truck at the community hall and his binoculars at another house. The guy had gone into religion. An ex-hippy, ex-druggie. Had to be ex for Marchand to hire him, being so deadset against drugs."

Lyle shook his head. "You know, Artemus isn't anti all drug use. Just uncontrolled use, the street scene. I agree with that—those pushers are evil. And recreational drugs, that sends Artemus into a tailspin. But controlled use for medical reasons is okay, he supports that. Remember how much good that grass did Brendan."

"I do. With eternal gratitude." Noel gave Lyle a weak smile.

"How do you know so much about Marchand?" Kyra asked.

"Hey, he's my agent, right? But also I'm the treasurer of GLANS and I—"

Kyra laughed. "What?"

"Gays and Lesbians Against Narcotic Slaughter. Artemus sends big checks to our annual fundraisers. Some who donate are categorically against drug use, others are just as explicit in demanding legalization. With someone like Artemus—he's considered the nuances—it's a relief."

"Interesting," Kyra mused. "I'd have figured him totally pro war on drugs."

"Seconds?" Noel watched them both refuse. "Salad then?"

"Yeah, he leaves that impression," Lyle grinned disarmingly. "Absolutes are dangerous. I'm with GLANS but I like really good pot." A smile for Noel. "As you know."

Bringing that pot for Brendan: was Lyle already coming on to me then?

Kyra served herself salad. "Tell us about Marchand. He sounded as if he always agreed with the last thing he heard."

"I like the guy. Hey, all artists are a little in love—oh, and in hate—with their agents. He abhors conflict, tries his damnedest to avoid it. Maybe that's what you picked up on."

"Maybe," Noel said.

Lyle sorted through his salad with his fork. "He's knowledgeable on many topics. He went to Princeton, took so many partial majors it took him two extra years to graduate."

Kyra, remembering the lure of arcane courses, nodded sympathetically.

"I'd say, Artemus Marchand is a gentleman in the best sense of the word." Lyle gave Noel a honeyed smile. "A true Renaissance dabbler." Lyle reached out. "I've changed my mind." He served himself another dollop of *bourguignon* and took a chunk of bread. "Actually, we're quite incestuous. Artemus manages my art and I advise him on his portfolio."

"How would you rate him as a dealer?"

"I'd say he has a great eye for art. Particularly mine."

With sudden bravado Kyra asked, "And how good is Tam?"

"Gill?" Lyle reflected. "I'd say very good but," more musing, "there's something missing. The thing that says a work is an original. You know, whatever makes it the artist's own."

"Artist as against technician?" Kyra tried to elaborate. "Imagination? Vision?"

"All that. To see what's out there, and what's in here," Lyle tapped first his forehead and then his belly. "Then meld them, then rise above them. Sort of, a translation." He stared hard at Noel, then nodded to himself. "Like if I were to paint you—" He chuckled, another private joke. "That was delicious, chef. You'll make some lucky man a fine *hausfrau*."

Noel sniffed a laugh. He hoped Lyle would remain this manageable. Meanwhile, it was flattering to be desired.

Kyra got up to clear. "I talked to the curator at Western Washington. She said there are casinos in Las Vegas buying schools-of-paintings." She edged the plates into the dishwasher. "But I also learned they're hard to get now. You have a take on that?"

"Aha, see the detective picking brains. Good investigative technique." Lyle's smile took the sting out of his patronizing tone. "Sorry, the schools-of market isn't my department. I know what anybody who's taken art history knows. Sometimes the technique is fascinating."

Kyra carried the Dutch oven and trivet to the counter.

"Brendan and I looked at some in Europe," Noel said. "They're imperfect, so you can learn a lot about method."

Lyle shook his head. "Some are so imperfect they're junk."

Kyra came back, decided to dive right in, and sat. "What does Marchand pay for them and what does he sell them for?"

Lyle looked uncomfortable. "Come on, even if I knew I couldn't tell you."

"Sorry. Didn't mean to pry." But she wanted corroboration of her father's sense of half a million to a million. "Just, in general. In your artistic opinion, how much would, say, a school of Titian go for? At auction, say." Maybe she'd pop over to Gabriola tomorrow, maybe get a preview of Artemus' Thanksgiving show. Set it up with Tam.

Lyle stared past Kyra, out the window. "Hard to tell about auction houses. Schools-of aren't easy to price in themselves. Good ones are pretty scarce and it depends on who wants them."

"Can you ballpark?"

"Extremely variable. Ballpark? I'd say, depending on this, that, and the other, hundred thou to a mil for an authentic school of Titian, variables being size, how close to the master, if the master touched it. Or a budding student who later became famous in his own right—"

"Or hers."

"If any hers," Lyle said to a yacht in the harbor, "we never her about them, ha."

"Dreadful pun, Lyle," Noel said, but did smile.

Kyra added, having just decided, "I'm going to try for a preview. Of Artemus' new show."

Noel squinted at her. Lyle said, "Good luck."

She smirked. She'd get one. Even if it cost her a kiss.

"Artemus doesn't give previews. But if you can finagle this—" Lyle turned to Noel, "you've got yourself a damn good partner, buddy."

"We aren't partners." Again Noel wished he'd cut that buddy stuff. "You know Marchand got caught up giving away a forgery?"

"He was devastated." A red and white float plane landed smoothly. "An honest mistake. That painting had fooled people for over a hundred years." He laughed, as if complimenting the forger. "I bet the painter's chuckling in his grave. Who was that guy who forged the Vermeers? Sold one to Hitler's sidekick Goebbels?"

Noel realized he knew nothing about forgeries. Tomorrow he'd check out Vegas casinos and forged art. Tomorrow he'd find Albert and show him the obituary. What could Albert say or do about it? Maybe he'd say, a different kind of forgery. He headed to the fridge. "I have procured crème caramel for dessert. It is, I guarantee, superb." Dessert on table, plates, spoons.

Kyra reached for her spoon and ate with great happiness. Then she pled a headache, withdrew to her room, left them to their brandies and cigars or whatever. Noel would take care of himself. But, she hoped, not with Lyle. Lyle made her uneasy.

As for herself, time for a private talk.

———

Noel set the dishwasher going. He wished Kyra hadn't left. He wanted to tell her about his meeting with Lucille who, he realized, had impressed him. Despite her tea.

Lyle hadn't made another advance, not even as a joke. They sat on the balcony and drank port. Warmer than yesterday evening. Lyle wanted to hear still more about Noel and Kyra's investigation. But Noel said, "Sorry, Lyle, that's as much as I can talk about." They watched the dark, silent harbor. The ferry from Gabriola arrived. Pleasant to sit with someone, simply enjoying the evening. Except that the obituary crept across the screen of his mind . . .

Lyle pulled a thin flat silver case from his shirt pocket and opened it. Two large roaches.

He offered the box to Noel. "Care for a toke?"

Noel had smoked pot in his day, and again when it had soothed Brendan's pain. Now its scent would bring back Brendan's sickbed. The pleasant evening had evaporated. "I can't."

"You don't?"

"The last time was with Brendan. I just can't, Lyle."

Lyle nodded, and packed up the case. The ferry departed for Gabriola. Lyle must have sensed the evening was over. "I guess I should be going. Early class tomorrow." He got up.

"Yeah." Noel followed him through the living room.

"Great meal, Noel. Thanks a lot."

"Good. And thanks for the wine."

"And good luck with the agency." He headed for the front door, Noel behind him. Lyle reached for the knob, suddenly turned and gave Noel a large hug.

Though caught by surprise, Noel slowly hugged Lyle back. The momentary closeness felt good. But then Lyle was kissing the side of his neck and Noel dropped his arms. Lyle stepped back, placed both his hands on Noel's cheeks and let his fingers slide down. He reached for the door again. "See you soon, buddy."

Noel closed the door. He was maybe attracted to Lyle, but did he like him? A good-looking man who wanted to be in Noel's company. It had felt just fine to be hugged again, and not by Kyra. But his kiss had felt wrong. The man's insistence made him uncomfortable. Maybe the light of tomorrow's day would clarify the evening.

In Noel's study Kyra had unlocked the leather case and taken out three balls. She'd undressed, climbed into bed and lay still in the dark, the balls by her pillow. She'd been able to hear faint talk from the living room. Her body still tingled. If Tam were here now—*No? Yes?* She got up and took a fourth ball from the case. She lay down again, two balls cupped in each palm. They were good for squeezing as well as juggling.

Celibacy is mind over matter, isn't it? You decided to be self-possessed, to need no one. Now one cute guy comes along and you're ready to sacrifice Born-Again Virginhood?

He was only wanting to kiss.

Sure, tell me another.

Well—

And where has sex ever gotten you?

Kyra tested the heft of the juggling balls. She would juggle her history with men. From the start. Not the year before Reed, that was just heavy necking. The first real one was Jimmy, a quiet sophomore down the hall. It took the two of them a week to admit to each other they were both virgins. They had three months of learning good things about sex till Jimmy the liar went home to Kentucky for Christmas and found his high school girlfriend five months pregnant, so he married her. Kyra was, naturally, heartbroken. Which didn't stop her from having great times. A one-man woman with each of her boyfriends, in four years six of them. Not one of the relationships had ended well: three fights, one dropout, two abandonments. Her fate.

All practice for her real men. Juggle the real men. She got out of bed, turned on the desk lamp, set three balls on the computer table, tossed one in the air. Kyra the juggling nude.

At her graduation dance she had met Vance Perrugia. Instant passion, a love affair for all time. They married in August, white gown and veil. September honeymoon in Italy to meet his aunts and uncles, Venice on his mother's side the first ten days, Naples on his father's the second ten. Then ten days on their own. From intensity as fervor to intensity as triggered temper to intensity as violence. She left him for two days. He found her, all apology and tears. Everything would be okay when they got back to Oregon. She agreed. October proved tense, but that was because they were setting up house. By the middle of November he'd beaten her four times. She filed for divorce in December. Being bashed around by Vance was not her idea of fun. She moved back to Vancouver.

Skiing at Whistler two winters later she met Simon Kerr, a lawyer, early thirties, sense of humor, straight teeth and nice ears, took on immigration cases, some pro bono work, moving up in the world. Ball two in the air. She lived with him a year, making sure he wasn't of the wife-beating persuasion. No, a gentle man, though sometimes given to depression. With Kyra's tender jollying he could snap out of it. They married. Marriage changed Simon. His depressions deepened. She tried to talk with him. "Simon, you really do need help."

"I'm fine. Just a little black sometimes."

"I can't see you when it's so black."

"Just talk to me Kyra. Make me laugh. Like you used to. I'll be fine."

"Simon, I love you. But I don't know what to do."

"I told you. Help me laugh."

But he hadn't laughed in months. He hadn't even smiled. "I can't help you, I want to but I can't. You need professional help."

He was crying by then. "I need you, Kyra."

"If you don't get professional help I won't be able to live with you."

Weeks of arguing. At last an appointment with his doctor, at last a referral to a specialist. The morning before his session, in their third year of marriage, he drove up Mount Seymour and shot himself.

Noel read about the suicide. Simon Kerr, survived by his wife, Kyra Herschel Perrugia Kerr. He phoned in sympathy and invited her for lunch. They talked. She blamed herself. If she hadn't intimated she'd leave Simon he'd still be alive today. Noel suggested to her that she herself could use some professional help. She found herself disagreeing. "Noel, for pity's sake, I don't need to see a shrink. I'm fine."

Noel smiled gently. "Kyra. Did you hear what you just said?"

153

"What?"

"Quote—unquote: I'm fine."

She spent six months seeing the psychiatrist Simon had refused to meet. At the end of that time she told Noel honestly, "I'm fine."

When Kyra had been at Reed, she and Noel sent each other comic postcards with shorthand messages: "Exams! Wish you were here." "Too much rain, not enough brain." After her first marriage they drifted apart; Noel had disliked Perrugia from the beginning. But during the time she spent with the psychiatrist they again became friends, and had remained so since.

It was after Simon that she decided about her name. She'd wanted neither Vance's, nor Simon's. Go back to her maiden name? Her mother's maiden name? She opted for her own, her middle name. Kyra Rachel.

Sam met Kyra while visiting from Bellingham five years ago at a dinner party. He became her third husband fifteen months later. Third ball up, one-two-three, one-two-three, one-two-three, a waltz with Vance-Simon-Sam. Between Simon and Sam, ten months of traveling in Europe and North Africa on an inheritance from Gran; best part of the trip was the week in Siena with Noel and Brendan. Sam, clever and funny and strong, big machines his passion, excavators and derricks, cement trucks. Sam's construction company was based in Bellingham. He'd done well building apartments, an airstrip, parking garages, small-town malls. His work made sense to Kyra. And what should Kyra do with her life? Something, anything, he told her, just make it your passion.

Vance-Simon-Sam-Vance-Simon-Sam-Vance-Simon-Sam. Three balls in the air, around, around— She caught them, retired them, turned out the light, and climbed into bed.

It began just as a job. Kyra met Margery for lunch and after the second martini replayed Sam's plea, passion-job-passion. Margery said, "Well my boss is passionate about not paying out money to some of the people who have policies with us. Maybe you could help him." Kyra followed her natural tendencies and began snooping for Puget Sound Life Insurance. But love for the work and irregular hours upset Sam badly, too full involvement with her work, not fully with him. She kept pointing out it was his idea. Last April they separated.

Three loves in her life, three disasters. She shuddered. Admit it, Kyra, four loves. The summer she was fifteen had been part of her sexual history too. William arrived on Bowen to be with Noel. He was slender and handsome, quick and witty. It took Kyra many agonizing days, that summer from hell, to understand Noel would never be her life partner. They'd become close, and friends. That was a lot. But that was all it could be. Until now. Business partners? Thank you, Lyle, for Triple-I?

Eaglenest Gallery. Triple-I's first case? Gabriola tomorrow. Tam, her secret entry.

He only asked if he could kiss you. And you said *no*. Juggle that one, Kyra.

FOURTEEN

RAIN AGAINST GLASS woke Noel. His window was open. He dragged himself up and pushed it closed. Cold. A major weather shift since last night. He peed, then slid back under his duvet. Quarter to six. Any other windows open? He trudged to the living room. No. Back to bed. Warm. But no more sleep.

He considered yesterday. Take Lyle seriously? With Brendan so recently gone? Think it right: so recently dead.

Suddenly he felt cornered. Lyle had picked up the half-assed idea, a detective agency, named it and thrown in a logo, discussed incorporation, partnered him with Kyra and sent them their first case. Hell, he'd practically sold the Initial Public Offering.

And the obituary, in its envelope. Sunday. He had to locate Albert.

Get up. Get out of this mental loop. Coffee. Breakfast later, with Kyra. Asleep on the sofa bed beside the desktop. Lucky he'd brought the laptop to his bedroom. Lucas' question, How does Marchand find so many paintings? Noel pulled on jeans and a sweatshirt. Steaming coffee mug on the table, laptop open. Wallpaper, a picture of Brendan, warm smile, like on his desktop.

But an hour later, in searching for schools-of paintings around the world, he had learned virtually nothing about where they were found; that an organization called the Monuments Men Foundation had restored many schools-of paintings to their rightful owners, mostly Jews, from whom they had been stolen by the Nazis; that one could buy reproductions of schools-of from several sources; how to get into an art school modelled on the schools of Martini, Lorenzetti, Fungai; thumbnail histories of various schools of great masters; and some information about buyers of schools-of paintings in the last fifty years. Museums, universities, and foundations headed that list. But as Kyra had noted, some large hotels and even a couple of casinos had gotten into the game. In his Lucas file he saved the names of those who had bought in the last five years.

To find sellers, check into buyers? But here a curious discretion pervaded the net: neither source nor price was mentioned. He followed up on the casinos, The Hermitage and The Kingsway, both in Las Vegas. The Kingsway had bought a school of Becafumi two years ago; mostly they were acquiring original twentieth-century art. Saved and filed. More coffee, and check out The Hermitage. Rose Marchand's T-shirt, Picture Yourself At The Hermitage, and a Hermitage casino buying schools-of? Connection or coincidence?

The Hermitage Las Vegas. On the screen, an image of a large hotel fronted with palm trees.

Picture yourself at The Hermitage!
Our three thousand room casino hotel
provides every entertainment!
Fun for the entire family!

Noel skimmed. Three thousand rooms with slot machine and bar in every room. Two hundred-fifty blackjack tables, as many poker tables, more roulette wheels. Amazing.

Eight lounges!
Headline acts!
Koalas!

Koalas? Noel clicked the hypertext highlight.

The Hermitage is undertaking a
world-first environmental project.
We will house ten magnificent koalas in
a fully controlled enclosure.
Here the koalas will live in their
natural habitat, a grove of Australian
eucalyptus trees.
The koala is an endangered species and its
environment is rapidly shrinking.

Then why not plant more trees in Australia and leave the koalas there? Wait, hadn't he read about Siberian tigers in another casino? What, each casino has its own animal?

Back to the main page. He followed a link to Art.

> The Hermitage is renowned for its broad collection
> of European Art.
> Each of twenty-one Master Rooms is decorated
> around the theme of a unique and singular artwork.
> Five more Master Rooms will be available in time
> for Christmas.
> The Hermitage takes pride in presenting to Master
> Room guests paintings in the styles of the Old
> European Masters.

There it was. Then a synoptic treatise on styles, stuff Noel knew.
Then:

> Plan to visit The Hermitage in December!
> A special display of newly acquired examples of Schools
> of Bruschelli, Zurbarán, Correggio, Multscher.
> Also an exquisite example of the later Bruegel School,
> with brushstrokes by Pieter the Younger himself!

Five. All maybe bought from Marchand. A nice bundle of cash.

A floor plan of a suite: bedroom, large bathroom, sitting room and
balcony. A balcony in Las Vegas? Yes, enclosed with heat-blocking
glass, overlooking a blooming desert garden. Hypertext. Noel clicked.
The garden featured thirteen species of endangered Sonora cacti.

Back to the home page. Prices, reservations, e-mail address, restaurants, history. Ahh!

> The state-of-architectural-art Hermitage is both heated
> and cooled by 1,005 solar panels on its acre of roof and
> by underground earth exchange systems.

This plus a desert garden? He made a note: Environmentally
aware? Perverse. Fascinating.

Financing for construction of The Hermitage was overseen by
the Fifth Bank of Nevada and Latuis Interest Corporation through

a series of back-ended debentures. Fifth of Nevada wanted him to open an account and take advantage of a cheap loan to buy a car. With $7.8 billion in assets it had been listed as a bank since the Silver Rush days. Noel saved the names of its President, V-P and Directors.

Latuis Interest Corporation, labelled simply LIC, was a development corporation. Noel read the website twice, trying to figure out what LIC developed.

> LIC works to encourage the evolution of
> developments that excite the LIC assessors after
> a development profile.

Jargon or bullshit? He sipped coffee and scrolled down. LIC had recently assessed developments in the West Indies. Sun and sand for the developers. E-mail address. End of website. Latuis Interest was a private corporation, no need to disclose the names of its head guys.

He mulled. He returned to The Hermitage and checked links he hadn't tried before. Found: CEO Peter Rabinovich. Not highlighted. He clicked anyway. Nothing.

In Google, Noel typed *Peter Rabinovich*. Damn, hundreds of possibilities. A writer hocking his books of flower poetry. A sixteenth-century trader someone had done a thesis on and wanted wider recognition for. A man who spearheaded a move to condemn Ukrainians for their treatment of gypsies. A dozen more. Noel checked them all; likely irrelevant. Then, a maybe: a business journal announcing the winner of an environmental award.

> Peter Rabinovich through his company Latuis
> Interest Corporation has constructed the
> most ecologically friendly Hotel-Casino-Resort
> complex in the Las Vegas desert. His complex has
> only used–

blabbety-blah concrete, blabbety windows, blah.

> An enclosed grove of eucalyptus trees fosters the

breeding of koalas. The handsome marsupials, together with millions of dollars worth of original European art, draw thousands to play the games of chance Nevada's history has so proudly built upon since the original Silver Rush.

Rabinovich arrived in the United States in 1996. Born in a small town near the Caspian Sea in the then-USSR, he suffered greatly at the hands of the KGB, spent time in Europe, then briefly made Israel his home before coming to the US Questioned about his time in Israel, Rabinovich, winner of the 2005 Gladstone Environmental Award, said, Weakling Socialists. I've come to a country I can be free in.

The Award Committee was unanimous in its choice of Peter Rabinovich.

This was followed by two photos of Rabinovich, a handsome slender man, head completely bald as if shaven, strong dark eyebrows, a large nose and thick lips, wearing a pinstripe suit. Noel saved this, backed it up, and saved The Hermitage information as well. What the hell's going on? An award for building a concrete edifice to house thousands of rich tourists in a desert ecology? People who shower twice a day and run the tap while they're brushing their teeth? Old art in fancy rooms. Bought from Marchand? This guy has clout. Wonder how many corpses are buried in his back yard?

A partnership with Kyra?

⸻

Kyra had lain awake for nearly an hour, listening to the rain. Phone Eaglenest Gallery or arrive unannounced? Tam had invited her. Well, for next week after the show opened. A minor detail.

Tam had seen her in both the combinations she could muster. Schmidt. The jeans would have to do. The silk blouse would be okay. What with the rain, good thing she'd brought her Gore-Tex. She heard the knock. "I'm awake."

"Coffee?" Noel spoke through the door.

"Love some."

"Back in a minute." He was, and knocked again. "May I come in?"

"Sure." She sat up, pulled the duvet to her armpits and took the proffered coffee.

He straddled his desk chair. She had draped the shirt she'd worn over its back. Now he stroked it. "This was Brendan's. He bought it for that conference. THE conference."

"Oh Noel, I'm sorry."

"It's okay."

"I didn't know."

"Please keep it." He smiled. "It looks good on you. I'd rather it was being worn. I can't."

She stroked his hand. When he left she stroked the shirt. Then she showered. In the living room she glanced out the window. It was clearing. "Can I take your car to Gabriola?"

"To check out those paintings?"

"Yeah."

"Sure, take the car. I'll work on the Net."

She poured milk on a bowl of cornflakes and blackberries and shoveled them down. He buttered his toast and told her what he'd learned: Rabinovich, the paintings, LIC.

"Well done, head Triple-I researcher."

"We're nowhere close on that."

She grinned, and squeezed his elbow. "So. What about Lyle? He likes you."

"Yeah. He kissed me. Twice."

"What?"

"I didn't kiss him back."

"No good?"

"I'm not ready."

"You've got to start living again."

"Look who's talking."

"Well, you do."

"Some day. I'll let you know. And you let me know too."

"Deal." She got up.

"Kyra?"

161

She raised her eyebrows.

"No, doesn't matter." She cocked her head at him, but he said nothing. He watched her close the bathroom door. He wasn't ready to tell her about the obituary.

By the time she'd brushed her teeth the ferry had turned into the harbor. She put on her jacket, found her purse, dropped her phone and camera in, and slipped her boots on. Went back to the kitchen, grabbed the car keys. "See you soon!"

Noel waved over his head, then half-turned. "Find out what the paintings sold for."

"I'll try." At the door she noted the rug at its angle, shook her head, went out and slammed the door. It bounced open. She closed it slowly and it clicked shut.

She drove the Honda into the ferry lot and followed the line of cars on board. Not many going to Gabriola on a Sunday morning, about thirty cyclists in brightly colored jackets and thigh-tight shorts. She remembered Tam Gill's cycling shorts.

The ferry chugged away from the quay. She got out of the car and strode to the front. Clouds scudded across increasing patches of blue. A warming sun and small breezes conspired to caress her. She stared over to the mainland. The mountains north of Vancouver stood grey and white against new blue sky. The back of her neck tingled with pleasure and she sighed in conscious delight. She leaned against the rail. The pressure against her breasts left her a bit dizzy. Fine day to be alive. She let the sun soak into her skin from forehead to cleavage.

The ferry slowed and drew into its berth, a narrow slot, a perfect fit. A pleasant day on an island, maybe lunch on Tam Gill's deck. She got into the car. Okay, be clear here. Tam Gill is a gorgeous guy. But don't play games. Check out those paintings. Besides, he might still be in Nanaimo.

The ramp came down. She drove off behind the bright gaggle of cyclists and two dozen cars. And Noel's speedometer matched the 30 KPH sign up the hill. Past the mirror at the narrow corner, out along Descanso Bay and the pretty houses by the water, on to Eaglenest Gallery.

She parked on the edge of the driveway by the path to Tam's cabin. Both vans sat in front of the main house. No BMW. She grasped her purse, climbed out, walked down the path, up the steps to the high deck and knocked on the frame of the screen door.

It took a minute before Tam emerged, from the bathroom judging by the towel he was drying his hands with. His face registered surprise and irritation. He opened the door, now smiling quizzically. "What're you doing here?" A dab of purple paint on his temple.

"Surprise! I came for a preview of the art show." She allowed him her winsome smile.

"We don't give previews." He frowned. "Why didn't you phone?"

"It wouldn't have been a surprise. I had a sudden impulse."

"A sudden impulse? When you need to wait for a ferry?" His tone was querulous.

Kyra laughed. "The impulse was sudden, the trip took some time. Do I just stand here?"

Slowly Tam opened the screen door. Kyra stepped in. "Are the pictures hung yet?"

"Of course." He was wearing the same shorts and shirt as yesterday. An automatic closing device hissed as the door scraped into place.

"That's good." Kyra pointed to a painting of flowers in an orange vase on top of an anvil leaning against the wall. Beside the canvas lay an orange vase with different flowers standing on an anvil. "I like that a lot."

"The painting, the vase or the anvil?"

"All three together, actually. Will you show me the paintings in the gallery?"

"Artemus does not allow previews." He pulled himself to a semblance of graciousness. Then he smiled, and half-lidded his eyes. "It'll cost you, you know."

She raised her eyebrows. "Oh? How much?" She tried to breathe against a sudden tightening as her stomach responded to the angle of his head, his hands on his hips.

"One *yes*." He leaned toward her.

She put her hand on his arm, a small stroke, then spun away. "We'll see." She held open the door. They walked along the path and crossed the grass to the Gallery. He put his arm around her shoulder, his fingers pressing her upper arm. Her skin tingled.

Rose closed the inner greenhouse door behind her and recalled Artemus' comment at breakfast: "Are you going to hire another gardener?"

"I imagine so," she'd said.

"The garden needs work before the show."

In truth, she didn't much care. She hadn't replaced Roy. All summer she'd concerned herself less with the garden than she had in previous years. The flowers, grasses and shrubs increasingly bored her. What evolved inside the greenhouse, that alone mattered.

Rain overnight. At least she should go outside and appraise the garden.

Tam unlocked the door to the Gallery and flicked on a row of halogen lights. A dim square space, each side maybe twenty feet long. No windows here, Kyra saw, even on the ocean side. On the wall across from her hung two paintings about two feet high by three wide. Each of the other walls held one apiece. They all gloomed dark. She walked over to the pair. The one on the right was done in shades of black, some browns mixed in, *The Catacombs of Rome* as envisioned by the school of Bruschelli. The other, *The Jaws of Hell*, Zurbarán school, showed a scarlet devil literally defecating the damned into the gaping mouth of a scaly bile-green dragonlike creature. A third in an ornate frame over to the right was a picture of dark-purple angels rising into clouds glowing with a dim sun-heightened orange light. "A School of Correggio," Tam said, smiling at the painting with great pride. The fourth, beside the door, the largest, depicted a rough peasant scene in which nobody looked particularly happy. "From the later Bruegel School, possibly close to the start of Pieter the Younger's career, early seventeenth century. I'm very pleased with it. It came, can you imagine, from a hundred k outside Vilnius. In Lithuania. Don't ask me how it got there."

"Mmm. Where do the others come from?"

He took her hand. "Oh, all over the place. Romania and Poland and Hungry. Found one in Macedonia once. In the old days." He led her to the last and brightest, a Madonna and child.

Kyra's hand squeezed a little pressure back. She made herself concentrate on Mary's tiny face. The Jesus-baby's visage belonged to a miniature and very sinister old man, and featured a leer remarkably close to that of the red devil on the wall across. A joke on God-the-Father? Like the Sienese school-of she'd seen in the WWU Gallery. She thought, I'm not going to remember all this stuff. She took back her hand.

"Attributed to the Swabian school of Hans Multscher." He stared at the painting.

"Do you have pamphlets for the show?"

"Of course."

Kyra smiled warmly. "Could I look at one?"

"I suppose it's okay. I'll go find them." He went out.

Quickly she brought out her camera and opened the shutter wide. She knew better than to use a flash. She clicked fast, circling the room, one-two-three-four-five. And again, closer in. A third round—

"Hey, cut it out!"

"What?"

"Those aren't public till the show!"

"Huh?" She covered the shutter, dropped the camera into her purse and faced him, faux-naive. "Why not?"

"For god's sake, Kyra—"

"What?"

Tam was mad. "You can't use those till after Thanksgiving."

"What's the big deal?"

Tam threw his arms up as in disgust. Then suddenly he smiled. "No, you really don't get it. Just promise me. Keep those private till after the long weekend."

"I will, I'm sorry," she offered, and felt a shock as his palm rested on the skin of her nape. For a second her body stiffened, then relaxed in his direction. She made herself say, "I hope they're valuable. They aren't beautiful."

He nodded, a serious movement, and held her eyes with his. "But they sold well." His thumb and index finger stroked the back of her neck.

Small warm pressure. "Mmm," she said. "For a whole lot of money?" In the voice of one who really didn't get it. "Oh, did you find the pamphlet?"

"Couldn't locate any." He opened the door. "Shall we go back to my studio?"

He seemed eager to get her out of here. "Okay." Push him on prices later.

Tam locked the Gallery door. They walked across the circular drive past the Honda and down the path to Tam's cabin. He told her how *The Jaws of Hell* had been traced for its history, to the extent that it could be determined. She let him talk.

The kitchen garden did need attention. The corn had finished over a month ago and the stalks should have been shredded. The cabbages looked limp, as if the rain reminded them they were parched. Oh well, cabbage was not Rose's favorite vegetable. She wheeled to the flower gardens. She deadheaded the last of the stargazer lilies. Work to be done everywhere. The Michaelmas daisies should be staked. Okay, Artemus did have cause to fuss.

Kyra tried to concentrate. The information kept flowing. That was good. The paintings were ugly. She'd hate to have to live with any of them, even in a hotel room. She held in control the part of her that wanted to ease Tam in among the trees and pull his clothes off. They walked in silence. Sweat dripped warm from her armpits down her side. She felt damp all over. Oh dear.

Motion caught Rose's eye: a man, a woman. Tam. And one of his babes. Here at Eaglenest! Next they'll simper over to the greenhouse or march into the living room—

Something familiar about this babe. Rose wheeled closer. No danger of them seeing her, they were practically a two-headed beast. That female detective? Couldn't be! Yes! She began a violent tack toward them, then stopped. She turned around abruptly. And wheeled away.

Inside the cabin Tam took Kyra's hand. On the walls hung many paintings, a great range. From abstract expressionism to naturalistic portraits and surreal landscapes. Kyra turned to him. "Yours?"

Tam nodded.

"All of them?"

Tam nodded harder.

166

An easel stood by one of the two large picture windows over-looking the sea. On the wall by the kitchen, shelves of paints in tubes. The rack held a work in progress, a kind of diptych. On the right, girls and women in flowing dresses, red and yellow and orange, tiny, against a background of tan hills like desert dunes, but sunless; to the left a kind of sketch in shades of tan of a monster with many feet with a background of reds, yellows and oranges.

Kyra said, "I like it." She did.

He turned to face her. "It's coming along. And now, may I kiss you?"

She heard herself whisper, "Yes."

He touched her shoulder and she flowed toward him, a single movement. He touched her cheek and his hand drifted to her chin. He raised its angle lightly, bent to her lips, touched his to hers, a bare brush of contact.

She reached to his shoulder as if to hold him back. But he was rounded and smooth there and she wanted his shoulder closer to her so she drew him forward. His lips held hers. She felt his hand at the back of her head. She stepped in to him and her breasts spread against his chest. She felt his lips part and she knew she was going, going, Kyra the juggling celibate gone. But suddenly it wasn't okay, not now. She slowly pulled away and could sense he knew the mood had shifted. He let her move-back happen, but slowly, slowly, and she liked that so much, his sense of her wanting it this way, that she nearly came back to him. She looked up at him. "That was nice."

He shut his eyes. Reopened them. Nodded. "Yes." Touched her cheek with two fingers. "There can be more."

Her head could shake, her head could nod. How much would be lost, either way? She knew what a shake would bring, been there for months. A nod was uncharted territory. She gave him a tiny nod.

He let his hand slide down her arm to her hand and took her fin-gers in his. She took his other hand and they drew close. He brought both hands to her shoulders. She felt herself tremble. She dropped her hands to around his waist.

He glanced down at her, deeply serious. "You feel as nervous as I know I am."

She reached up and laid her hands against his cheeks. The smooth skin on her palms sent small quivers from her belly to her pubis. She knew he wasn't nervous, but how sweet of him to say so. She drew his face down and kissed his mouth.

He held the kiss for a long while. Then he picked her up and carried her into the bedroom. "Got any condoms?" she whispered.

"I think I have some left." He winked.

They came for each other twice in lusty succession, and again. He took pleasant minutes exploring her right clavicle, then her left, tracing each with his lips. A bones man, she thought. I have good bones. For a bit they slept. She woke. Well there you are, she told herself, first time. Well, in a long time. Clearly I needed that. Celibate no more. The better or the worse for it? A little of each. She glanced at Tam. A remarkable lover. In each instance able to tell precisely what she wanted, where and how to provide it. She studied his sleeping face, his fine round shoulder, the soft tickly hair on his arm. Was she in love? Don't be silly. She had just had sex with a fine practitioner, that's all. Tam was technically wonderful.

She drifted off again. Woke. He wasn't there. She got up, dressed, couldn't find him in the cabin. In his studio-living room, she examined his work. His range was phenomenal. One of a pretty pink-cheeked child, another of an older couple; both, she thought, impressionist. There were some playful ones with fish and shooting stars, as if done by a ten-year-old. A realistic if sort of smudged landscape with lots of trees and clouds, a seascape of a boat tossed by stormy waves. If the variety of his pictures were any indication, Tam Gill was a complex man.

She went to the bathroom and saw him on the deck when she came out. He kissed her brow. They sat side by side and stared at the water. Then she kissed his fingers. "I should go back to Nanaimo. And home to Bellingham."

He turned to her. "You'll come back." Almost but not fully a question.

She raised her eyebrows. "I might."

———

Noel heard Kyra's key in the lock and looked at his watch: nearly four o'clock. Except for a slow forty-minute walk he'd been at the computer over five hours. He had called Albert at his office, at home and on his cellphone. Answering services all. Lyle had called to thank him for last night. And he'd really enjoyed meeting Kyra. He promised to be in touch soon, they should plan some time together. Most of Noel knew he didn't want to. But the part that enjoyed being liked, appreciated, wanted, gave him real doubt.

He'd copied his laptop Eaglenest files to his office computer. He'd found mentions of the correct Peter Rabinovich scattered around. Rabinovich had owned a hotel in Panama City before The Hermitage. A Panama newspaper, reporting on the Las Vegas venture, stated that Rabinovich had lived in Israel for seven years. Many of the Israeli entries citing Rabinovich were in Hebrew. Two in English mentioned his bar, The Wet Negev.

Noel set the computer on standby. In the living room he found Kyra slumped on the sofa, a beer in hand. "Hi! How'd it go over there?"

"Ask me questions, I'll tell you lies." Code from her childhood: You'll find out someday.

Noel cocked his head in acknowledgment. "Drink that down. Then let's go to the casino. Then I'll buy you a real drink. Then I'll buy you dinner."

"The casino? Why?" Kyra sipped. "When are we going to have our talk?"

Noel held out his hand for Kyra's glass, took it and drank half. "We'll talk over dinner."

She sat up. "Hey, you lose money at casinos."

"It's for research." Noel paced. "I found many Fascinating Facts about Vegas and got curious about the casino in my own backyard."

"Where is it?"

"Back of Port Place. Then we'll go up to Gina's and have Mexican."

"You're on." Wow! An active dinner-out invitation. "And we can clarify what we know."

He said, "I'll bring the laptop."

His security blanket? "Sure." At the door she poked at the weak lock. "Get this fixed, Noel."

Downstairs, and out the door. Tell her about the obit? No, talk to Albert first. "Oh, Lyle called. He enjoyed your company."

"Good." She stopped. "Tell me, d'you think you could get serious about him?"

"Come on, Kyra, how can I know that?"

She looked at him. He really was dear to her. "Watch yourself, friend." She took his arm.

They passed through the cool mall, well-peopled even on Sunday, and out again into the late afternoon sun. The asphalt parking lot intensified the light. In front of the casino, a gaggle of smokers in shirt sleeves. Noel and Kyra walked through a thin tobacco haze. Inside they had to stand a while, adjusting their eyes to bank upon bank of slot machines, most occupied. People pressed buttons rapidly. Decor nightclubby, low artificial light. A clinking rush of metal: to their right a slot delivered a shower of quarters into its trough. The winner remained expressionless. Then she picked up quarters and fed them one by one back into the slot. Where, Kyra wondered, were her friends, flocking to her side, patting her shoulder, Good on you, Mabel, hey! fifty bucks worth! Let's go celebrate with a coffee. But Mabel was in a closed loop, quarters back in, quarters maybe out again. How intimate.

Kyra edged closer to Noel. "Why's she using a machine that's just paid out?"

"There's always more in there. Probability pays no attention to previous amounts."

She squinted. "How do you know?"

"Didn't math class teach you that?"

They wandered on. Poker. Roulette. Eight blackjack games, the dealers, men and women both, wearing tuxedos. The players were mainly old, mainly pale, mainly saggy. The people at the slots inter-acted only with their machines, drop a coin, press a button, drop a coin, press a button. Or just press a button—that guy was playing the slots on a credit card. Ah, a man who reached up to pull a lever on the side of the machine. The exercise option? Tall workers—bouncers maybe?—stood around in orange uniform shirts, men and women. Smaller ones, karate bouncers? Or spotters who called the bouncers?

Vegas casinos would be like this, Noel figured, only a hundred times as large. Three thousand rooms accommodate a lot of people.

Kyra saw a group of twenties-thirties at a poker table laughing, enjoying each other. On Bowen Noel had taught her seven card stud, and blackjack. They'd played for matchsticks or M&Ms. One man smiled at her. She smiled back but the smile didn't get her invited in.

"Enough." Noel pulled her sleeve. "Food."

"We're here, we do research." But she let him draw her to the other exit. "Oh, look, a food court." She glanced at the menu. "Boring. If you lose all your money do they send you to a soup kitchen? Till your next welfare check comes in?"

"Gina's." Noel marched away.

Sometimes you're so old male, Noel. But she followed.

They climbed up the hill. He took her arm. "Thanks for coming with me."

Gina's was bright raspberry with blue trim, a house converted to restaurant sitting on top of a rocky outcrop reached by a crooked road. In front of the door Kyra turned to him. "You know, your teaching me poker took me through my first year at Reed."

Noel quirked his lip. "I corrupted a minor?"

"I only felt corrupted when you won."

"You did develop a good poker face."

Kyra kissed his cheek. No poker face there.

Rose had watched the car drive away. It took her the best part of two hours to feel calm enough to power-wheel herself to Tam's cabin. Letting that woman in there! "Tam!" She waited. "Tam!"

He came out, saw his sister's face and knew why she'd stopped by. So he grinned.

Rose said, "What?"

"She's clay in my fingers." Tam shook his head, grin still in place. "If I were a sculptor, you'd say I created a work of art this afternoon."

"Tam! You let her into the cabin!"

"Don't worry. Like a beer?"

Rose glared at him, turned her chair, and slowly wheeled away.

FIFTEEN

IN GINA'S THE hostess hello'd and how-are-you'd Noel and Kyra and led them to a table.

Kyra glanced at the menu. "I should branch out. But it's always back to a chimichanga."

"You guys ready?" A young man, short hair gelled, three rings in each ear, a nose ring, stud centered in his lower lip, set down a basket of taco chips and salsa.

Noel said, "We'll have a jug of margaritas, please. The small."

Kyra smiled. Sometimes a man being authoritative could be nice.

"And," Noel looked at her, "we're still studying the menu."

"Our specials tonight are—"

A lip stud. How does he kiss? The only special Kyra caught was chicken chili rellenos.

Noel said, "Tuna mole sounds interesting."

"Okay," the ringed man rapped cheerily, "I'll be back."

"—someday," Noel lilted.

A great smile. "Ya got it, dad." Flicked his extra menus and moved to the next table.

"Who is he?"

"Nineteen-year-old tree planter, twenty-six-year-old physics PhD, thirty-one-year-old downsized electrical engineer. He's got a job in a restaurant. The growth industry."

Minutes later the waiter was back with a margarita jug. She settled for chimichanga. Noel ordered the tuna mole. The server said, "You won't regret it, dad, it's some dish."

Kyra poured, sipped, took a chip and salsa-ed it. "Yum. Okay, what do we know?"

Noel opened his laptop and told Kyra about his Hermitage research. "And we know bits of Rabinovich's history. Is it important? I don't know." Noel scanned the Eaglenest directory.

"Okay, why did we just spend time at that casino?" Kyra sipped again.

"Never been before." He grinned. "Check out everything. Like why go to Vegas to stay in an expensive room with a school-of painting." Noel drank too. "Mmm, good."

Kyra mulled for a moment. "We're not focusing. We're interested in the owner, not the guests."

"Eaglenest sells paintings to The Hermitage. Marchand's people bought these paintings—"

"Actually, Tam Gill bought them. Marchand's team just locates."

"He makes the decisions alone?"

"That's what he said." She detailed her visit to the Gallery. "Hey, I got photos of the paintings." She described them. "You figure they're for The Hermitage?"

"'December, special display of five new paintings.' Tam say what they sold for?"

"Nope."

"We'll find out. I've got their names in the file."

"Good. Tam said the names. I don't remember but I'll recognize them."

Noel typed.

"But where are they coming from and why can't others find them?" Kyra took a couple of chips. "Another talk with Marchand."

The waiter appeared with their entrees. He scowled at Noel's computer. Noel saved, slid the laptop into his tote bag and set it gently under his chair. "Enjoy," the waiter said.

They took a first bite, Noel's mole delicious, Kyra's chimichanga fine and spicy. She said, "Okay. Our three Marchand-Gills?"

"Artemus, independently rich, Princeton, won't show island artists, gives a leg up to others like Lyle, finds schools-of Old Masters, sells them for big money. A foundation, grants to small-scale technical projects in the Third World, to moderate drug projects like Lyle's group."

"And his wife."

"Athlete, Olympic medalist, now paraplegic but impressive upper body strength, studied botany and chemistry, perfectionist, mucks around with flowers. Two species named after her. Respected. Botanists come to call. A large greenhouse."

"Right. Invented tools for it."

"Fears contamination. A big shed, plastic covered."

"Big," she repeated, thinking. "Perspective?"

"Huh?"

She shook her head. "And Tam."

"Artist, technically very good, range of styles, buys for Marchand, does karate."

"Control freak," Kyra added, "Handsome and sexy." She grinned naughtily. "Great in bed."

"Kyra!"

"Detecting is a complex art."

"Kyra. For fucksake."

"Precisely."

"But it's the wrong kind of involvement."

"I'm very objective." She set her hand on his. "I'm careful too. Always." Well, mostly.

Noel saw her, ten years old. He put a mental arm around her shoulder. To protect her. To safeguard himself. She had been more intimate with Tam Gill than she could ever be with him. No, he wanted only her friendship. Still it hurt that someone had been closer to her than he would ever be. He tried a laugh but it came out busted. He made himself say, "And how was it?"

"My body felt like it'd been played by a great violinist."

He looked at her, a woman of thirty-six. "Kyra the Stradivarius." A couple of lines on her forehead he hadn't noted before. "One more celibate bites the dust."

"Whatever the investigation calls for." She noted his scowl; disapproving? sad? both, maybe. "I think Sue's BAV stuff got to me. I never meant to be a saint. Even less a born again virgin." But, she wondered, had she just hurt Noel? Not the sex part, that wasn't what she and he had together. Something else. What?

Noel returned to his tuna mole. It suddenly tasted off. He realized it wasn't the mole's fault. "Okay. Could Tam Gill be preventing others from finding paintings?"

"How?"

"Threats? Intimidation?"

"Doesn't sound like Tam. He's a charmer."

"Okay, who does he charm to stay away? Or maybe he paints them himself."

"No way. They test carefully, pigment analysis and all that. You can't forge seventeenth-century paintings in the twenty-first century."

"The forged painting Artemus gave away was viable for more than a hundred years."

"But it was found out." She took the last bite of chimichanga. "Maybe it's just his luck. Like repeat winnings from the same slot machine."

"Maybe others find these paintings, too, but Eaglenest offers the most money."

She shook her head. "My father would've heard about that."

The waiter arrived, took their plates, proffered the dessert menu. They shared a piece of chocolate cake and ice cream.

"Now." Kyra pushed her plate away. "Can we talk about our partnership?"

"Potential partnership. Let's talk on my balcony. Over a nightcap."

"Don't forget your computer."

———

"More chicken, Rosie?"

"A wing. It's delicious."

Artemus knew the paprika sauce was excellent but appreciated the compliment. And dinner alone with Rosie was just fine. The meal was a favorite of Tam's but he had chosen not to join them. So, a good evening and Artemus' private world was in fine shape. Rosie smiled warmly. He was not prepared when she spoke.

"Artemus," she said. "I'm worried."

"Oh?" He put his fork down. "About what?"

"Maybe— I think we have to stop making shipments to Rab."

"I don't understand."

"We've done very well. We've reached a—a kind of peak. But with the increasing fear of terrorism, the country's changed. All this new security. Maybe the time has come to stop." She sighed. "And I worry about Tam traveling so much."

"Rosie— I think that might make Rab very unhappy."

"We shouldn't be greedy. Either of us."

"No telling what an unhappy Rab might do."

She felt a small shiver but wheeled to his side and took his hand. "I think Rab will understand."

"But what about increasing the Foundation's endowment?"

"It's strong enough for what we want to do. We have to leave well enough alone."

"Rosie, do you really think things have changed that much?"

She looked into his eyes. "I do."

"I mean, for all our work."

"Yes."

Perhaps for Rose. But his charitable endeavors couldn't disturb anyone. Just the contrary. Commerce and philanthropy must go hand in hand.

———

They dropped off the film of the Gallery paintings at the drugstore. At his apartment Noel unlocked the door and Kyra entered. He stared down at the rug. "How'd you do that?"

"What?"

"Kyra—" He shook his head and closed the door. "A little tequila?"

She glanced at the rug—parallel to the threshold—then at Noel. "Yeah. Tequila and talk. I'll get the drinks." He suddenly looked worried.

"It's at the back of the cabinet. Use the narrow glasses from the cupboard." The answering machine was blinking. Noel pressed the Play button. Albert's voice: "Got your messages. What's up? Call me at home." Noel did. The machine again. In the bathroom he peed and washed, then returned to the bedroom. Something felt off. He glanced around. In the dim light all looked normal. Except— A chill took him. He flicked the light switch. On the chest of drawers, two photos, himself and Brendan. The third, of Brendan alone? He walked to the chest. The picture lay image side down. He stared at it, reached for it. Stopped himself. "Kyra!" He stepped backward to the door, turned. Bumped against her.

"Hey! Careful." She held out two full tequila glasses. "What?"

He pointed. "Brendan's picture. It's face-down!"

"So? It fell."

"It can't fall forward. It leans backwards." A glimmer of sweat beaded down his forehead.

She put both glasses on the chest and picked up the photo. Brendan smiled out at her. His cleanly etched eyes and lips, in life making him attractive to men and women both, looked weary. "At least the glass didn't break." Noel's carotid artery throbbed. She lay her hand on his wrist.

"How'd it fall?"

She checked the hinge and set the picture upright. "I don't know. A small earth tremor?"

"Oh sure." He pulled his arm away. "Here, but it missed Gina's."

"I have no idea. Come on, let's have our drink and talk."

He took his glass and followed her out of the bedroom. Halfway to the balcony his feet slowed. The rug, the picture— "Wait. I have to show you something." Back to the bedroom, pull open the bottom drawer, reach for the envelope— He thought about it, in the kitchen he opened the utility drawer—

"What's up?"

"Just a minute." He found a package of plastic gardening gloves from Brendan's patio garden days, tore off two, slipped them on, returned to the bedroom, lifted out the envelope. Back in the living room he plopped onto the couch. "Read this." He drew the newsprint obit out of the envelope and unfolded it. She sat beside him. "I'll hold it. You read."

She did. She said, "Wow."

"Yeah."

"When did you get this?"

"Yesterday morning. Leaving to go to Gabriola."

"What! And you waited till now to show me?"

"There hasn't really been a chance. Lyle was here and—"

"You could have told me."

"I wanted to speak with Albert first. I mean, it could just be someone playing a joke."

"Like the tires."

"Okay, the tires. And Brendan's picture. Someone's sending me a message."

"About?"

"No idea. But I do think someone broke in here this evening."

"Wouldn't take much."

"Guess not. Any ideas?"

"Yes. Our drink. Tomorrow you show it to Albert."

"Okay." He sighed. "Uh, let's have our talk in the morning?"

To the bleak look in his face she said, "Sure. We could use some sleep."

He glanced at his watch. Barely 9:30. "Yeah, I'm tired." He drank down his tequila.

"Good night." She kissed him on the cheek, and left him.

He took off the gloves and set the envelope on the dresser beside Brendan's picture. He undressed, lay down, tried to read. The words on the page buzzed into each other. He killed the light, shut his eyes. Did someone break in? He fell asleep. Dreamed of Brendan, a high stone wall in the woods, Noel on this side, Brendan, Kyra, Sam and Lyle on the other. All walking fast, the wall went on, on, he met people—

He sat up, sharp awake. Checked his watch. 1:18. Kyra, Sam and Lyle with Brendan on the other side. He turned the light on. Peed, drank some water. The picture of Brendan, upright as it should be. "Good night, Brendan." He sat on the bed.

Stood. Strode across the living room to the study. Opened the door. Kyra, a fast-asleep lump on the couch-bed. In the corner, his computer. He tiptoed over, turned it on.

Kyra muttered, "I hope that's you."

"Yep." The computer whirred.

"What you doing?"

"Checking. I— Aagh!"

"What? What?" Kyra leapt from the bed.

"There." He pointed to the screen.

"What?" She stared. "I don't see anything."

He pulled away from the keyboard. "Brendan's gone."

"Oh!" The first computer image Noel saw every morning. Erased. "A glitch?"

"Somebody was here." He checked his closet. "Computer glitches don't move pictures. Or a rug." He checked the balcony.

"But why?" Kyra wore her jacket as a bathrobe.

Noel sat. He took a deep breath. Released it. Sat forward. Tapped the keyboard, worked down his subdirectories. Third level, Other. Fourth level, Eaglenest. Fifth, first subdirectory Artemus. Sub-subdirectory, Artists. He opened the first file: some electronic garbage, half sentences about flowers, Hermitage, pieces of words jammed together. "It's fucked." Second file, background, schools-of: snatches on gambling, many smiley faces, e-mail addresses chopped up.

"You sure?"

"Look at it!"

She did. "How can that happen?"

He shook now, furious. "Software virus. Chaotex. Eats files, pukes up their contents in bits and pieces." Upward through subdirectories. The Chung book; files okay. Finances, GICs, stocks— "All okay. Except for Eaglenest." He set the computer on standby.

Kyra pulled him away from the machine and held him tight for a moment. She guided him to the living room, poured him a glass of water, made him sip it slowly.

He stared at her. "I think— Someone is not happy with me."

"An Eaglenest someone?"

"I don't know. The calls started coming long before Eaglenest."

"That virus attacked just one set of files."

"I know, I know."

"Someone at Eaglenest is distressed. Who?"

Noel let out a nervous giggle. "I don't see Rose fucking up my computer."

"Or Artemus breaking in." She stared at Noel. "Tam?"

Noel forced control into his voice. "You'd know better."

Kyra tried to picture Tam sneaking in. No image came. "Maybe someone they hired?"

"Exposing themselves by paying somebody to break in?"

"To get rid of what we know?"

"Everybody backs up their files, Kyra."

"Somebody trying to scare us?"

"They just succeeded."

Kyra considered this. "I think they succeeded earlier. With that fake obituary."

Noel nodded. "God, this pisses me off."

"Good. That means you're not scared any more."

Noel wasn't so sure.

SIXTEEN

IN HIS MOTEL room Llewellyn Katz, Herm 3, considered his report.

The door to Noel Franklin's condo could have been opened by a child. It gave more easily than any Katz had encountered in Tel Aviv or Miami—or Memphis, for that matter. At 6:10 in the evening he'd crossed the threshold, shut the door, stared about and considered each detail. The place sat empty. A few minutes earlier he'd followed Franklin and the woman to the little casino, a provincial joke of disastrous proportions; recycling welfare money with such speed, government check to cash to casino and back to government, was underproductive. Consumer cash needs wide circulation to undermine crime, drugs, disease and ignorance, that was Herm 3's analysis. Then the two had gone to a restaurant. He'd have half an hour easy. Plenty of time.

Nothing about Eaglenest Gallery in the file cabinet except Franklin's final report. Five minutes in closets and chests of drawers produced only shoes and clothing, mostly men's, some female. And a curious fake obituary. Franklin wanting to die, join his partner? On the chest, three photos, two of Franklin with another man, clearly lovers, the third of the lover alone, a Chinese gentleman. Kitchen: dishwasher, sink, cabinets and fridge hid nothing of value. In the clothes washer, a Canadian two dollar coin. He left it.

The computer. The opening wallpaper had been scanned from a photo of the lover. How sweet. From an inside pocket Herm took a CD. He found the Eaglenest directory immediately, no encryption. Naive, these people. He flicked through files. Well, not so naive. Franklin had found traces of probable though not incriminating relationships between the Gallery and The Hermitage. He fed the computer his disk and set its program to invade the Eaglenest directory. Files bled into each other, names changed, files shortened to a few words, lengthened with multiple repetition. There'd assuredly be backups. But Franklin would get the message.

One more gesture, that picture of the lover. Best separate the two dear queers with a minor adjustment. He checked the condo to be sure it was all as his memory recalled it. At the door he noted the rug. It lay at an angle. Had he kicked it? He toed it square, parallel to the wall.

Now in his motel room he poured a large bourbon over ice, encrypted his report, and sent it to Rabinovich.

———

Kyra, awake early, felt wonderful. She dropped her feet to the floor and stood. Her legs were limber. Silence from Noel's room. She peered in. Asleep. She stepped out on the balcony, stretched, bent, twisted, a five minute workout at the railing. Feeling alive and enthusiastic.

Noel dragged himself out of his room and met Kyra at the coffee pot.

"Good morning," she announced. "Coffee's ready."

He watched her bounce to the fridge for milk, bounce to the cupboard for sugar, bounce for crapsake like a pogo stick up for cups. Time to go back to bed.

"Drink this." She gave him coffee with warm milk.

"Someone broke in." His voice was raw.

"I know," she said, all calm, to calm him. "Phone a locksmith."

He held his coffee mug with both hands. "The break-in tells us somebody's trying to scare us."

"And that your lock needs replacing." She sat. She would not let him descend deeper into this mood. Noel was right, this was a campaign of fear. They wouldn't succeed. At the same time, Noel needed a little compassion. Briefly.

He grunted.

"Eaglenest. Why?"

"Either they're trying to find out what we know, or a warning."

"Or both."

"It gives me the creeps. Like somebody's raped my apartment."

"I know." She patted his arm, then squeezed. "But some day even we may have to break in somewhere."

"I'm not ready for this discussion."

"In fact, I've got a lock pick in my purse. I could break in anywhere right now."

Noel nodded. "Great. Your wanting to break and enter makes it okay for me to be broken into." He wandered toward the bathroom but stopped. "Damn, I've got to clean out the desktop." He searched the web and downloaded a generic Chaotex cleanser. "Shouldn't take long."

"Shower time. Go." She ushered him toward the bathroom.

"Okay, all right."

She sipped her coffee. Now take the bull by whatever you can grab. She called Eaglenest. Marchand answered. She gave her name, she'd like to talk to him again. "When's a good time?"

"I don't have a single free moment." Brusque.

"Then tomorrow."

Marchand grudgingly allowed he had a half hour tomorrow at 12:30.

"See you then." She hung up.

A few minutes and Noel came back, his wet blond hair plastered flat. From the fridge he took eggs, milk, bread.

Kyra stated, "An appointment with Marchand, half-past noon tomorrow."

"We're going there? Why? To ask if they broke into my condo?"

"Among other things." She sipped coffee.

"And no doubt they'll give us an informative answer."

"You know, there is someone who could shed light on what they are or aren't capable of."

"Who?"

"Lyle."

"Wait a minute—"

"A consulting meeting. He keeps asking you to lunch. Call him, say that'd be nice." She glanced at her watch. "Today even."

"Why me?"

"He'd figure it pretty weird if I invited him."

"I'll think about it." He dropped a couple of slices of bread into the toaster. "Hey. But I do know who I have to call." And Albert was home. Noel began with the break-in, the obit, worked his way backwards through the slashed tires and the phone calls. "It's getting to me."

"Yeah. But I wish you'd have left everything as it was."

"Left my computer messed up?"

"Left your apartment till someone from here could check it out."

"Hey, I live here."

"Anyway, too late for that. The plastic gloves were a good idea.

Now use them to slide the envelope and obit into a Baggie, put it in a large envelope and drop it off at Nanaimo headquarters. And listen, whoever's doing this doesn't sound personally dangerous to you."

"He's fucking with my psyche."

"Yeah, I know. But we'll get him."

Noel told Kyra what Albert had said.

"Good. Drop off the obit after you've called Lyle. And tomorrow, Marchand. Only way to find out what's going on over there is to get on over there."

"Right."

And maybe, after talking with Artemus, some time with Tam? Maybe smile sweetly and say, Tam, who broke into Noel's condo? Right.

"What'll you do today?" Noel asked.

"Oh, hop over to the casino and feed some slots."

"Great idea, Kyra."

She watched Noel scramble eggs. "Schmidt, lucky you took your laptop to the restaurant."

"I'm old-fashioned. I do floppy backups too. And a memory stick for good measure."

"The Eaglenest files."

"They were and still are in my case."

The toast popped up. She waited as he buttered the slices and scooped on scrambled eggs. A plate in front of her, the other for him. They sat. She said, "Maybe they broke in for a reason other than a warning or to spy on us."

"Like what?"

"No idea." She munched egg and toast.

They finished eating. He put their plates in the dishwasher. "Let's get on with it." At the desktop he clicked on the Eaglenest directory. It came up clean, the Chaotex undone. A breath of relief. Down to The Hermitage, down to painting, and he clicked on the paintings.

Kyra carried a chair over. "Yep, that's them."

"Ah, recognition. So much easier than recall."

"When I get the photos this afternoon I'll write the names on the back."

"You don't have to. The computer labels them."

"Oh." The darned computer would make her redundant. She glanced at him. He was lost in the screen. "Will you stop that?"

"What?"

Now she was irked. "Turn it off, please." Noel opened a new directory. "Noel!"

He looked up. "What?"

"It's all in bits and pieces. I can't get an overview when you've got all those files out. Come over here and sit." His damn computer was an escape from thinking about the break-in.

He got up and sat beside her. "Okay. I'm thinking."

"Good. What—anything, okay?—what itches at you the most about Eaglenest Gallery? Paintings, flowers, artists? Dead Dempster? Artemus? Tam? Crippled Rose?"

"No one says *crippled* since Tiny Tim. It's handicapped now. Or disabled."

"Actually, it's physically challenged."

"Thank you, Kyra."

"All right, maybe not people. Challenged spaces. The handicapped house. The crippled grounds. The disabled Gallery showroom."

"The big house?" No response from Kyra. "The garden? Tam's cabin?" A bit of an itch. Something— What? "The greenhouse?"

"Kyra! What does the house or the cabin have to do with where those paintings come from?"

An itch of memory— She found it. "Your comment, the greenhouse seeming large. The sense I had of the inside—"

"Should be full of flowers, waiting to be transplanted in the garden. There weren't many."

"And why not?" Kyra shook her head. "No, wrong question, it's the size thing. Like we only glimpsed part of the interior."

"Could be. Some lab to develop her flowers? What sort of flowers were there? Flats of carnations. What else?"

"Marchand closed the door too fast." Kyra stared back to the memory.

"One blind alley after another."

She ignored him. "What was it? Perspective?" She got up and paced. She muttered, "How can we get Rose out of her greenhouse?"

"Wait a minute. What's Rose got to do with the paintings?"

"We don't know. But what's she got in there? You noted the discrepancy of space. We have to get her out of there and have a look around."

"Come on, what do flowers have to do with old art? Except as subjects for still lifes."

"Did you check her out on the Internet?"

"I haven't been researching botany."

"You never know what you'll find. Go look."

"Oh for pissake." He headed for the computer. "I thought you hated this machine."

"Call Lyle first."

He glared at her, then found the phone book and called. "Hello, it's Noel, glad you're home. I was just thinking, maybe I'm ready to go out for lunch. Interested? . . . Well how about today? Sure, tomorrow is fine . . . Yeah, something I want to talk to you about . . . Naw, I don't like Charlie's Oven, how about the Crow and Gate . . . Yeah, I really would prefer it. Twelve-thirty? . . . I'll meet you there . . . No, that's okay, I'll be out doing errands. See you." He broke the connection and turned to Kyra. "Tomorrow at twelve-thirty. We have to figure out how to—Damn! We're seeing Marchand tomorrow."

"Hey, it's fine. I'll deal with Marchand."

"I don't think you should go alone."

"If he was responsible for the break-in we have to show we don't scare."

Noel couldn't figure a response so he sat in front of his desktop and got on-line. His mind ran back to the phone conversation. Lyle had been so brisk, no warmth there today.

———

The phone rang. "Hello, my darling Rose, my Peace, my American Pillar, my Queen Elizabeth—"

"Hello, Rab." Rose varieties? Why? "Is everything okay?"

"What are you doing so I may picture you as we speak?"

"I am staring at my black *Chrysanthemum morifolium* and wondering what I could do to augment its perfection in the next generation."

"With perfection, you must admire."

"Do you have something complicated to tell me?"

He sighed. "I took the liberty of investigating your investigators. They're pretty good. They had files on their computer about The

Hermitage, and about me. Including some facts that require serious searching and combining to find. The link to The Hermitage was supplied by the Curator at the gallery at Western Washington University in Bellingham. Your brother told the female, Kyra Rachel, about the place."

"Hell."

"Exactly. The detectives reported to Artemus, but then were hired by a consortium of antique dealers in Vancouver. One of the dealers is the female's father."

Long pause, then, "What else?"

"Of importance? Nothing in the files."

Rose absorbed all this. "I feel—plagued. It's worse than their looking into Roy's death."

"My dear, I don't want you worrying. But be careful. For all our sakes."

"I will," Rose whispered. "Rab, we have to talk."

"Yes. Soon. I'll call you." The line went dead.

For an instant she trembled. Suddenly her world felt precarious. She needed support. Right now she'd settle for Artemus being nearby. She'd lean her head on his hip and bring her arm around his waist.

"Rose Gill doesn't have a website," Noel called to Kyra, "but she's mentioned all over the place." Kyra appeared at his elbow. "Canadian Association of Botanists, American Association of Botanists, International Association of Botanists, Botany Statistics Service, US Botanical Service." He continued to click and save. "It can't be relevant to what Lucas wants."

"What's that you cruised by?"

Noel clicked back. "International Pigment Association."

"Scroll down." She leaned over his shoulder. A sidebar read, in blue print, "About primary pigments."

"Click on that."

He did as he was told, new screen, and she read, "Most primary pigments are derived from flowers, herbs, and grasses—"

"Okay. Let's see." Noel clicked, saving occasionally, until they had several files of information about pigmentation. Interesting too that the International Pigment Association had sponsored a conference in São Paolo, Brazil, at which Rose Gill had given the keynote address: "Pigment Transformation Through Controlled Mutations." Abstracts available. Noel clicked, downloaded and scanned two paragraphs of botanical jargon. He shook his head. "Read this."

Kyra did. "One of us mentioned something about pigment age." Kyra dredged a shadow of memory. "A test."

"The gallery in Salmon Arm. Marchand's forged gift," Noel said.

"Some new method of testing."

"Look—this pigment stuff is irrelevant unless we go back to a forgery hypothesis. But even Lucas said those paintings have been verified by the best in the business."

"Yeah. We're off track."

He blew through his lips. "How do we find out about Rose's research?"

"Translate the abstract into plain English. You know any experts?"

"Nope."

"If we saw what she's doing, we might understand more." Kyra thought for a moment. "Want to break and enter?"

"Looking for what while we contaminate her greenhouse?"

"We get surgical gloves and face masks. Plastic slippers. And leave no fingerprints."

"No. I can't do that."

"Then I'll go by myself. I'll be in and out in ten minutes."

"What if she's there?"

"We lure her out."

Noel stared over to the cliffs of Gabriola. Kyra mustn't go alone. But he did have an idea. "How about, we ask Lucille to get her off the property."

"Maple? You trust her?"

He thought about a younger Lucille. "Yeah, I do. If we set it up right. There's shrewdness there. I think she'd love being a little nefarious." He hoped. Or maybe this was a mistake.

Kyra too looked out to Gabriola. "Let's say she says okay. She draws Rose out, you and I break in." She smiled. "You've come a long way, baby."

He felt his neck flush. "You said it might be necessary."

Beyond the sliding door the ferry chugged into the harbor. She turned back to him. "You know Maple. I don't."

"We're on the same wavelength. Like her repeating she's an old lady. She knows I know she isn't."

"For some people old doesn't exist. What would Maple say to Rose?"

"We give Lucille her assignment," Noel said. "She can choose her own tactics."

Kyra checked the ferry schedule. "Any time after the 11:40 gets in."

Noel bookmarked the entry page of the International Pigment Association.

SEVENTEEN

NOEL LOOKED UP the phone number and poked it in.

"Maple."

"Hello, Lucille."

"Noel. Coming for tea? I've still got the kettle out."

A caller ID, or did she know his voice? He cocked his head, A-okay, at Kyra. "Look, we've got something to propose to you."

"You and your associate I've not met? How does he like his tea?"

"She. Doesn't. Coffee only. Listen, would you do a job for us?"

"What job?"

"Do you need to talk to Rose Gill? For about half an hour?"

"Ah. So you can check out the greenhouse."

Noel, silence. Lucille, silence. Noel looked at Kyra looking out the window. "Let's say, curiosity. Maybe about that new flower. If our research pans out you'll get the scoop."

Long pause. "What do you want?"

Noel nodded vigorously to Kyra. "Invite Rose in. You don't have to give her tea."

"I can invite her. She might come. But she won't stay." She paused. "Or invite her to somewhere else. What's up, really?"

"It's my associate Kyra. She's got hold of a tail and thinks it has a dog attached." Scowl from Kyra. "In half an hour I could prove her wrong."

"Or right," said Lucille. "Okay. I'll think of something."

"Good." Noel, making it up as he went along: "Our consultant's fee for this kind—"

"Oh fiddle, I've got two pensions. All I need is joy and information. I'll have her out from two-thirty to three unless you hear from me within the hour."

"Great."

"The Rottingers next door south are away, their daughter's just had a baby. A boy. Pull into their drive. Get onto Eaglenest land by a deer trail. It heads in next to a fir split by lightning."

"Lucille, you're terrific."

"Then come by for tea. About four."

"We'll be on the 12:40 unless you tell us otherwise." Noel hung up. They'd be early. Didn't matter. "She got us, Kyra. Her price is tea."

"Here." Kyra held out the phone book and tapped a page. "Locksmith."

Noel called a locksmith. Kyra called the ferry. Running twenty minutes late. No problem.

Kyra took advantage of the delay to head across to the mall for the photos, and to buy surgical gloves, carpentry masks, throwaway over-slippers and more film. She passed the condom display and on impulse stopped. Be prepared. Ribbed and peppermint scented? Good grief. She hung it back up, surveyed the rack and chose an old-fashioned plain lubricated pack.

"Uh, hello."

Kyra whirled about. "Hello?"

"Remember me? Roy Dempster's friend?"

Sue Smith. The BAV. At the condom rack? "Hello, Sue."

"I was going to call your friend, uh—?"

"Yes. Noel."

"'Cause he asked did I ever see Roy get anybody other than Tam angry." She fell silent.

"Did you?"

"Not exactly. But yesterday Steve told me about his last conversation with Roy."

Kyra waited. "Go on."

Sue dropped her voice. "Roy told him he'd said harsh things to Jerry. But Roy wouldn't say what. He didn't want those words in his mouth again."

"Did Steve—that's Steve Bailey?" The clockmaker. "And Jerry is Bannister?"

Sue nodded.

"Did Steve say what they argued about?"

"Well, yes." She paused. "Roy wanted Jerry to change his ways. To transform himself."

"Oh? From what to what?"

"Well—to stop being a queer."

Jerry Bannister, the slob with all the centerfolds, queer? Hard to say the word in this liberated time. Gays could call each other queer, like blacks saying *nigger* to each other. Yes, Jerry could have taken offense. "Jerry's gay?"

"I— I don't think so."

"But Roy did."

"I guess. Otherwise why would he have been down on Jerry?"

"Okay. But why did Roy think Jerry was gay? Did Steve say?"

"Because Roy said he knew Jerry hung out with homos, he'd seen him with homos. And Steve said Jerry was really pissed, Jerry told Roy he didn't know what he was talking about, and then Jerry threw Roy off of his land."

"Hmm. Wonder where he'd seen Jerry hanging out."

Sue stared at the ground. "Yeah. I wondered that myself."

Kyra heard worry in Sue's voice. "Sue. Did you wonder about anything else?"

Sue said nothing. Then she looked Kyra full in the face. "Yeah. I wondered about Roy."

"You thought he might be gay himself."

Sue nodded. "I'd been wondering for a while."

"You dated him, didn't you?"

"Yeah but, you know, I was already born again when we met up. So it wasn't a problem."

"But he asked you to marry him, right?"

"He did. But Patty said maybe he wanted to get married in case anybody ever thought he might be a homo."

"Tell me about Jerry. You know him pretty well."

"We go back aways."

"Do you think he's—like that?"

"Jerry came on to me. Couple of days ago." Sue lowered her gaze again. "It was sorta my fault."

"Oh?"

"See, I thought he'd maybe want to talk about Roy."

"Like grieve?"

"Yeah. But he said, Roy's dead, what are you doing for a man now? He grabbed me." Sue crossed her arms over her breasts.

"Did he hurt you?"

"Not really, he was pretty stoned. Just—" She wrinkled her nose. "Ugh."

"Yeah. Did Steve say anything else?"

Sue thought hard. "That's about it."

"And you? Are you okay?"

"You mean about Jerry? Sure. That wasn't the first time. I can handle myself."

Kyra glanced toward the cashiers. "And otherwise?"

"It's hard, without Roy. Hard to continue my beliefs."

Kyra nodded, in sympathy. "Be careful, Sue. And thanks for the info." She headed for the checkout. She turned once. Sue was staring thoughtfully at choices among condoms.

———

Noel phoned Tam Gill's number. The answering machine clicked on. Good, nobody home. Noel broke the connection.

Kyra came back, spitting muttered schmidts. She slammed the door, kicked off her runners, and set a bag onto the table.

"Schmidt what?" He caught the flipped photo pack from Kyra and took out the pictures. The top one was overexposed, the others overexposed or blank white. "What happened?"

"How should I know! The photo clerk said light must've got in the camera. Or the film was bad in the first place. Anyway, we got zip here."

"You leave your camera anywhere?"

"It's always in my purse."

The moon must've been in a bad phase yesterday. For both Kyra's camera and his computer. "In the end, we don't need the pictures." Though his curiosity was up. Then came a notion, hard, hurtful, but he asked anyway, "Look. When you were, uh, sleeping with Gill, were you awake all the time?"

"Huh?"

"Did you actually sleep?"

She thought back. "You're saying, maybe he opened the camera and exposed the film?"

"I'm looking for possibilities."

"Schmidt!"

He let her consider. He followed his own thoughts, a break-in— No. He tried to visualize the back of the greenhouse. Stay out of sight, get in, get away again. But it was crazy! And how could it be helpful in learning how Artemus found the paintings?

"He wouldn't open my camera."

"Did he know you took the pictures?"

"Yes. And he was, uh, displeased."

"And he wouldn't open your camera?"

Kyra shrugged, and told him about Jerry and Roy's argument. Noel rang Steve Bailey's number. "Hi, this is Noel Franklin."

"Oh, hi. Still detecting?"

"Just tying up some ends. Do you know, did Roy have a big argument with Bannister?"

"Yeah, yeah, they argued."

"About trying to make Jerry stop being gay?"

A few seconds of silence. Then, "Yeah. Partly. Except Jerry surely to God isn't."

"Partly. So there was another part? To their argument?" Noel waited.

A long silence. Then Steve said, "About pot. Roy'd gone three months without lighting up. He felt great, he said. And you know how Roy had to help other people."

"So he tried to get Jerry to stop toking?"

"Yeah, that, and . . ."

An even longer silence. Noel gave Steve time.

"I think," Steve spoke slowly, "Jerry had something going, a small patch somewhere. I think Roy wanted to destroy the plants."

"Did Roy say that?"

"Well, not in so many words."

"I wish you'd told us this earlier. Did you inform the police?"

"Jeeze, I didn't think a little argument was that important."

Noel heard: I didn't want to get involved. "They'll want to talk with you."

"I guess. It can't hurt Roy now, can it."

"No." He took a silent breath. "Look, about Roy accusing Jerry of being gay, did he—"

"Dumb mistake. Jerry talks to everybody, even to homos. Especially when he gets stoned. He says he gets stoned to make other people interesting."

"So Roy maybe saw him in with some known gays."

A momentary pause. "Probably did, yeah."

"Why do you think that?"

Another pause. "'Cause Roy told me the same thing. Maybe a week before he died. He cared a lot for Jerry, didn't want him to get all messed up. So he kept his eyes open. And he saw Jerry in one of them fag bars. But that don't make Jerry a homo. I sometimes hang out with bikers, don't make me a Hell's Angel."

"Where did Roy see Jerry? Here on the island?"

"No fag bars here. Over in Nanaimo."

"Any idea where? Or who Jerry was with?"

"Nope. Only that the other guy was buying, and Jerry was drinking whiskey. Roy said he knew who the guy was. Roy said he didn't even want to think about the guy, dressed all nice, what he wanted with a slob like Jerry."

"Did Roy describe the guy?"

"Nope."

"Well thanks. If you think of anything else, let me know."

"Sure. Just . . . I don't want to get anybody in trouble."

"You won't." He put the phone down and gave Kyra Steve's side of the conversation.

She folded her arms tight. "Roy did like to mess with people."

"I better tell Albert." He found Albert at his desk and reported Steve's conversation.

Albert said only, "Thanks for all this. You're a good citizen."

"How are you getting on?"

"Set up video cams around the patch. Slow and steady is the policeman's lot."

"Nothing on my obit?"

"Working on that too."

"Thanks." Was he really? "See you."

Noel and Kyra ate a small lunch, drove into the ferry lot and reached Gabriola at just after one o'clock. They waited for the foot passengers to unload.

"We've got over an hour," said Kyra. "Want to visit Jerry Bannister again? Ask him about his faggot friend?"

"I object to that comment for about four different reasons."

"Three are obvious."

"Stop, Kyra."

"Aren't you just a little curious?"

Noel considered this. "I guess I am."

They arrived at Bannister's trailer. It looked even more decrepit than a few days ago. Noel knocked on the closed screen. A noise behind the inner door. It opened. "Yeah?"

A greyed-out version of the Jerry Bannister they'd seen last time. Noel said, "Hi. We'd like to talk to you."

Bannister squinted at them. "Oh. You guys." He giggled. "Whazzup?"

"May we come in? Or do you want to talk out here?"

"Naw, come in, too bright out there." He pushed the screen toward them.

The mess in the dim kitchen area had grown, but hard to tell what was new. Jerry swept a pot off one chair, a tin can from another. The stuff tumbled along the floor. "Sit. I'm smokin' so you get to join me. Heehee." He pulled an unlit roach from his shirt pocket, lit it, dragged on it, reached it to Kyra. She refused. He giggled again. "More for me." He passed it to Noel.

Noel took it and faked a drag. Jerry was too high to notice.

"Good weed. Right, fella?"

"Good weed," said Noel. "So. You and Roy were big friends, back in the old days."

"Yep. Great friends."

"Got stoned a lot?"

Jerry grinned, and belched.

"Still great friends over the summer."

"Yep."

"But sometimes you disagreed. About things."

"Naw, we were real good friends."

"But you did have an argument with Roy about growing pot. Want to tell us about it?"

A new squint to Jerry's eyes. "Nope. No argument. Nope nope."

"A disagreement?"

"Never talked about pot with Roy. He'd stopped smokin', nothin' to talk about. He was such an asshole. My asshole buddy."

"Did he tell you to stop growing it?"

"Don't grow. That's illeeegal." One more of Jerry's giggles.

"Did you argue about anything else?"

"Nope. Nope. Don't argue with assholes."

"I thought Roy was your friend."

"Yeah. Asshole friend. Heehee."

"Did he maybe say something stupid to you?"

"Lotsa stupid stuff."

"Like, maybe he misunderstood the situation, you with a friend in a bar in Nanaimo."

A quiver passed across Jerry's face. He took a long draw on the roach. "He was an asshole. What're you askin'?"

"When he saw you in a gay bar with—"

Jerry grabbed Noel by the shoulder and leaned his face close. "I go where I go and I talk to who I talk to. Lotsa different places. Got all kindsa friends. You saying I'm a faggot, faggot?"

Noel pulled himself away. "Nope."

"Damn right." He took another draw, then squinted in uncertainty. "How d'ya know?"

Noel grinned. "I can tell."

"Damn right. Damn right."

Kyra started to speak but Noel glanced her down. "We'd like to know, though, why Roy got so angry with you."

"Yeah, he was pissed off, he sure was." One more giggle from Jerry. "He saw me in a fag bar, I had to meet this queer there, he wanted some land cleared." Jerry thought about that. "So I said, 'Sure thing, sure thing.' 'Cuz he couldn't do it himself, he had this bad back. He paid me real good. He's a painter, didn't want to ruin his hands clearing land."

"A painter?"

"Pretty good painter. Roy introduced me to him."

Whoops. Kyra leapt in. "Would that have been Tam Gill?"

Jerry turned to her as if she'd appeared out of nowhere. "Huh? Who?"

Noel asked, "Did the painter have a show at the Eaglenest Gallery?"

"Yeah. Yeah." He took another draw. "Anyway, that's that."

Not for Noel. "Was that Lyle Sempken?"

The squint again from Jerry. For a moment he said nothing, then, "Who?"

"Sempken. Lyle."

"Never heard of him."

"What was the painter's name?"

"Well, I forget. Barry. Barry something."

"Barry." Noel nodded slowly. "Thanks for your time. Come on, Kyra." He pushed open the screen door, held it for Kyra, and they left.

"And thanks for yours," Jerry called after them.

They drove off. Kyra said, "Lyle and Jerry. Good drinking buddies." Noel shook his head, mock disbelief. "How about that."

"You really think Lyle was the man?"

"Does Artemus represent a whole lot of gay Nanaimo painters?"

"You figure Jerry for our pot grower?"

"Could be. What time is it?"

She glanced at her watch. "It's 2:10. Off to Eaglenest."

Back to the ferry landing, past the convex mirror, along the strip of beach, up the road behind the cliff lots, to the house beside Eaglenest. Eight minutes. He turned down the curving driveway as if he owned it and parked at a carport containing two Jaguars, license on the black one Jag 1, the beige Jag 2. They heard a vehicle. "I hope that's Rose leaving."

Their shoes crunched back along the gravel drive. At the road Noel found the lightning-split fir. They proceeded as silently as they could, Noel pushing through salal along a deer trail. Kyra followed. Their legs brushed against salal, huckleberry and kinickinick.

Sluggish flies and those autumn spiders that build webs in empty space—good thing Noel was leading. Kyra waved a wasp away.

The trail led to a grassy patch behind Tam's cabin. Noel pointed to his watch, 2:31. Kyra nodded. For the moment behind a screen of trees, they made their way to Tam's trail. Kyra looked back at the cabin. Under the front deck—Tam's bike? She tugged Noel's shirt and pointed.

"Oh shit," he mouthed. "Other transportation?"

She whispered, "We'll see. Pretend you're invisible." She glanced about, no one, and she muttered, "Come on, let's do it." She strode off quickly, head up, along the trail. In front of the house, a single van and the BMW. She scowled but kept going. They reached the rear of the greenhouse. Noel glided up beside her. No door here. Kyra fumbled in her bag for her lock picks.

They proceeded along the opaque plastic side, pulled on surgical gloves, and draped surgical masks around their necks. Was Tam here? If Artemus came out they were hooped. Kyra comforted herself remembering he had no free moment at all today. In front of the door now. A knob lock and a deadbolt, no great puzzle to Mike's star student. A three, nineteen and six for the deadbolt, an all-purpose Yale for the doorknob. "There," Kyra breathed. They slipped the masks across nose and mouth, slippers over shoes and stepped through the doorway. Cloying air hit them as if all of summer were stored inside. She locked again. Wow, I've really done it in the field! She glanced at Noel for admiration, even congratulations. His face looked a tense nothing.

A hum. Noel stared up. Ceiling ventilators. He willed himself to look around.

Flowers, all sorts of heights and colors in raised beds. They walked single file between metal tracks down the left aisle toward a partition at the back, and another door. A heavier bolt, but after a couple of minutes, open sesame. As Mike had said, no real security anywhere.

A slightly cooler room. Because of the smaller area to vent? Maybe three by four metres, Noel sized to himself; and Kyra thought, about nine feet by thirteen. White tables against the walls, desk high. A sink on the house side. The longest table stood on the far side, its surface hidden by opaque plastic draped over a frame. A round table in the center contained buds or bulbs or pods or hips. Seed things? Tubes, jars, mystery items.

What the hell were they looking for? Earlier the question had been theoretical. Now it was all substance. Noel hated this. Clearly Kyra didn't—she was exploring everything, hopping from object to plant, a happy bee.

Metal cylinders. He picked one up. A hinged top. Kyra snapped a picture. Pictures of the tubes, the pods, the bulby things. On a small table stood a plastic-draped microscope. Shallow drawers were built in underneath. More pods, or hips, dripping a thick black emulsion. Pictures of each table and the contents of drawers. Wide-views of the whole space.

Noel drew back the plastic draping the frame. Flowers in pots, half a dozen, chrysanthemums, blackish. The biggest one stood maybe a third of a metre tall, two flowers fully open, two buds just about to open, more buds. Against their forest-green leaves, the black flowers—well, deep-deep-purple-almost-black—were stunning.

For half an hour Tam's stomach had complained, but his work was going well so he ignored the growls. He loved working in oil, so different from acrylic, acrylic dried fast and pencil outlines showed. Oil is forgiving, it covers everything and gives you time to change your mind. For the hand, for example, he wanted a burnished flesh tone like from years of toil, and gnarled knuckles suggesting arthritis. He'd already redone it five–six times, he'd get it perfect. But right now, food.

He set aside his palette and brush, stood back and looked at the painting. Oh yeah, that fold of robe, the deeper shade suggesting a moving shadow, that had taken time. But when it finally worked, when you got it, yeah it was like sex, both of you humming thrumming strumming together. He had to fix the foot, didn't look as hard-worked as the hand. More splay? Bit of ochre on the side of the heel? His stomach turned on him again. He peeled away his coveralls, checked the key in the pocket, and washed his hands.

In the kitchen he opened the fridge door, examined the contents. Peanut butter, jam, black bean sauce, wilted lettuce, a Dos Equis, two centimetres of milk that stank. Damn, I know I stocked a fridge this week. Yeah, the Nanaimo one. In the freezer a crust of dehydrated bread. A. will have something left over. He always does.

"Get moving, it's 2:53," Noel ordered.

Out the inner door, close, lock. Kyra worked the camera across the larger room. Carnations at the peak of their bloom. More photos. She opened the door, stepped out, peered through draping leaves— Back so quickly she bumped Noel, threw him off balance, stepped on his foot, and he fell. She turned the deadbolt home and dropped to a crouch.

"What?" Noel clambered upright.

She put a finger across her lips. Noel slid into the free area between beds. They waited. Finally Kyra stood. "Tam walked by," she whispered. "I guess he didn't see us."

In A.'s kitchen Tam made himself a cold chicken sandwich. No sign of Rosie's van. Where'd she go? Oh well, back to work.

——

Only when striding down the neighbor's driveway did Noel feel a modicum of safety. Kyra bounced along beside him, all energy. Behind the wheel, starting the car, backing out, the barest bit of his sense of control returned. "I'm wiped," he said.

"Huh?" Only the seatbelt kept Kyra from bouncing against the roof.

"I need to sit still for a while."

"For pity's sake not here. Drive to a beach." She reached into the glove compartment for the Gabriola map. "Back to the ferry, right and then left."

He half-heard Kyra's chatter about the ferry lineup, the curve ahead, highland cattle in a pasture, an oncoming cement truck.

"At those stores, turn left down the slope and park on the right." He did. Kyra said, "Now let's walk on the beach," and was out the door before he turned the engine off.

Noel forced himself from the car. Kyra, on the sand, her shoes off, was high. He had no adrenalin left. He dragged himself through the fringe of trees and plopped onto the white sand. By the water a young woman supervised three preschoolers playing with pails and shovels.

Kyra dug her toes into the sand, arms stretched overhead. "I thought you wanted to walk."

"I just want to sit."

"Don't you like breaking and entering?" Kyra teased.

"I wanted to be invisibly transubstantiated out of there."

Kyra dropped onto the bare log beside him. "We did a great job. We don't know what we found, but we'll figure it out."

"I'll tell you, I'm never doing that again."

She looked at him in mock surprise. "Oh," she said. She stood up and walked to the water's edge. Little waves lapped her feet.

——

By the time they arrived at Lucille Maple's Noel had perked up and Kyra had calmed down. Noel introduced Kyra. Lucille ushered them into her living room.

"First of all," said Noel, "how'd you get Rose away from the Gallery?"

"First of all," said Lucille, "it's five minutes after four. You are allowed the tea you invited yourselves for. Myself, I'm having Scotch. Your choice."

"Scotch," said Kyra. "On the rocks, thanks."

"Damn fool thing to do with single malt. Noel?"

"Scotch, please. Straight. Water chaser."

"Right." She headed to the kitchen.

"If it's single malt, I'll have it the same," Kyra called.

Lucille did not break stride and returned a minute later. Three Dansk crystal glasses, Laphroaig, two tumblers, a jug of water. "There you are." She poured a finger of Scotch in each glass and raised her own. "Cheers." She sat back and told her tale:

She'd called Rose a few minutes after talking to Noel.

"Yes?" The frost of January in Rose's voice.

"I'd like to interview you for an article I'm writing."

"I'm busy, Lucille. The two shows this weekend—"

"The article's on the history of Indo-Canadians on Vancouver Island. The research is done but I want some firsthand tales. It'll take a half an hour. I'll buy you coffee." She listened to Rose's sigh of exasperation. "I won't ask you anything about your shows." Rose's second sigh flowed dramatically along the phone line. "You do prefer that I get the article right, don't you?"

"Oh damn. Sure, but only half an hour. When are you arriving?"

"Interviews are better on neutral ground. The village, two-thirty. Raspberry's."

"Yeah, all right," Rose tsked her tongue again. "But I'll be bringing a stopwatch."

Kyra chuckled. Noel said, "Well done."

"Thanks. I was proud of myself." Lucille sipped her Scotch.

Kyra prompted, "You met her at two-thirty."

"She was late. I'd begun to worry, maybe she'd decided not to come. Worried for you, I mean. Four minutes, forty-eight seconds late when she stopped her van. Three minutes more till she'd lowered the chair and wheeled toward me."

"Did she really have a stopwatch?" Kyra asked.

Lucille smiled. "Not unless her wristwatch doubles as one." She patted her hand across her hair. "I ordered us cappuccinos, set up my tape recorder, and started asking about her growing up in a small minority group in an English-slash-Scots enclave, which is what the Cowichan Valley was, if you ignore the Natives, which everyone did back then. Her grandfather came from the Punjab. He did laboring jobs, the usual racially unapproved-of-immigrant kind of struggle." She sipped her Scotch. "He brought his wife and son over, had more children and supported the family as a logger. Then came the *Komagata Maru* mess in 1914—"

"What was that?" Kyra asked.

"A shipload of Sikhs wanting to immigrate anchored in Vancouver harbor but they weren't allowed to land. They were ordered back to India and some were executed there." Lucille grimaced. "But after the First World War things improved for her grandfather." She sipped. "He started a small subcontracting business, not just labor in the bush. And eventually his son—Rose and Tam's father—turned it into an independent company covering every wood thing from seedling to siding. Their older brother, Nirmal, he's about sixty now, took the company public. It trades on the Toronto Exchange."

Noel drained his glass. "You got all that in half an hour?"

"Of course."

"Impressive."

Lucille looked smug. "Actually, she stayed forty-nine minutes. Two cappuccinos. I had a hard time shooing her home. She told me how tough it was as a child in school. There were other Indo-Canadians in the Valley by then, but she didn't have a white friend until high school."

Kyra nodded. She'd not had a friend of Indian ancestry till university.

"She's a pretty gutsy lady," Lucille said, then, "Okay, now it's trading time. I won't ask what you were looking for. But what's the new flower?"

Kyra glanced at Noel. They hadn't discussed this. Kyra took the reins. "I don't know what it is, but it's black. Kind of a long stem, bit over a foot tall, a bunch of petals."

"Black." Lucille mused. "A tulip?"

"Didn't look like a tulip."

Lucille nodded. "Black." She stood, headed toward the room across the hall, her study. "Help yourselves to more Scotch. I've got some looking up to do."

Noel glanced at Kyra, who said, "Much as I like that smoky taste—"

Lucille was already tapping at her keyboard.

"Thanks for the Scotch. We're going."

From behind her concentration Lucille said, "Come back soon."

EIGHTEEN

THE FERRY PULLED out. They walked up to the front. Kyra stared down at the passing water. "Okay. We know Rose has a double greenhouse. In front, flowers for the garden. In back, a kind of lab with a bunch of near-black chrysanthemums. And seed-pod things with a lot of goo in them."

"And she's damned secretive about the process. She's playing with flower pigments. Well, one flower anyway. Maybe she wants to make all kinds of black flowers?"

Kyra leaned her forearms on the railing. "But why grow black flowers?"

"To prove it can be done? For the genera books?"

The ferry's engines grew from heavy hum to roar. "I guess you have to be esoteric these days to get famous." A hundred feet ahead a cormorant cut across the ferry's path.

"Does she want fame?"

"Maybe more like—importance?" Kyra considered this, suddenly visualized Tam, his face, neck. "Now Tam, I think he'd like a little fame. Except maybe his work's only good. Not great."

"You don't have to do great work to get famous. Just different enough work for some influential art critic to say you're great."

"Hasn't happened to Tam." The *T* on the tip of her tongue felt good. Stop it!

"Think he's still trying?"

She mulled that for a moment. "Yes, I think so."

"How?"

"A painting he's working on." She remembered reds, and yellows. But something felt off.

"Could he be playing around with some pigment his sister's invented?"

"Could be."

"Okay then," Noel said, "we're back to forgery?"

"Everyone says it's impossible. And those paintings are authenticated."

"Yeah, that problem again. Okay, let's leave it for now. Where does Rabinovich fit in?"

"He's the outsider who buys the paintings."

An errant log bobbed by. Noel said, "Maybe Tam's using some color nobody's seen before."

"Maybe I could wheedle that information out of him."

"Stop it!" He was angry again.

"Oh, come on." Literally flirting with danger. She liked the idea.

"Don't get close to him again. He could be dangerous. Remember those photos."

"That's just supposition. And hardly dangerous." She turned to Noel. "Look, somebody's got to work the field. You don't want to. That leaves me. And I can handle myself."

"Not with Tam Gill." Damn her anyway.

"How do you know? You've never even met him." Could she? Yes. On the case, and in the bed. She stared out at flat, heavy water. What was this with Noel? Jealousy? Paternalism? She shouldered her purse, swirled around, and worked her way to the washroom. She sat glumly on the toilet and muttered "Fuck" fifty times. She wished she had a cigarette. Oh fuck to that too. Or— Maybe Noel really is worried about me. The ferry's quieting engines told her to get up.

Noel sat behind the wheel, staring straight ahead.

Kyra glared straight ahead. Tam actually could've messed up the film. Shit.

"So," Noel said. "Supper?"

"I'm not hungry."

"Then you're sick. Or really pissed off at me."

"I'm not— Okay. Shit, Noel, yes I am truly pissed at how much you worry about me."

"Sorry you are. But not sorry to hear it. How about this. Let's not be pissed off." She'd actually said *pissed*, and *shit*, not her stupid *schmidt*. "Let's start over. Supper?"

"I suppose." She smiled. She wasn't pissed off any more. "Where?"

"Want to float while eating?"

"Sounds good." What a relief to say piss and fuck again.

"First we drop off today's film." The ferry docked. They left the car at Noel's, crossed the street to the mall, and left the film. Then they walked to the wharf north of Cameron Island and the twenty-foot passenger ferry, the Protection Connection. A ten-minute ride mostly settled her and brought them to Protection Island and a floating pub, anchored along the seaward ramp of the ferry wharf. They went in. Quiet, half a dozen other guests. They ordered drinks, and fish and chips. They sipped, watched sailboats and cabin cruisers pass by, felt the gentle bob of the wharf from their wake, watched the sun's descent.

All too lovely and romantic, thought Noel. No, think positive, you've got Kyra to talk to. But he sensed an absence in her too, a missing edge. He wished she hadn't forced him to make that appointment with Lyle tomorrow. Especially after hearing about Jerry's meeting with him. All the more after her snippy comment about his unwillingness to work the field. He could if he had to. He just didn't enjoy it. He wondered if the guy who'd broken into his condo had enjoyed it.

Brendan had liked this place, Kyra knew. She listened as Noel talked. What if Tam sat across from her? Goddamn she had it bad. She could feel Noel's mind and conversation coming from somewhere else. Just like her own. Great view of Nanaimo harbor, the city and the mountain. Why was the person who attracted her always the wrong person? At least Noel was someone she could relax with.

They headed back to the little ferry. "You going to tell Lyle about our chat with Bannister?"

"I don't know yet."

"Just figure it out before meeting him."

"Mmmm," said Noel. Bossy again.

At the apartment all seemed normal. The lock didn't look tampered with, but it hadn't last night either. Kyra said she needed a fast walk. She'd be back in an hour.

"Then we'll call Lucas," Noel said.

"Why don't you while I'm walking. You mind?"

"Happy to. I like your father." She left. He opened his laptop to the paintings' descriptions and called. After some pleasantries he said, "The paintings Eaglenest is showing, there're five of them and—"

"Five?" erupted from the phone.

"A lot?"

"A lot!"

"Look, if I describe them, can you ballpark a sales price?"

"I can try. But mostly it depends on how much someone wants them."

"The first one's a school of Correggio." They worked through Noel's list. Minimal information, but Lucas figured them all to be in the mid to high six figures.

When they finished, Lucas asked, "How does Kyra seem to you these days?"

"She seems well. Perky. A bit bossy."

"Oh dear yes. I think she needs to be in control these days. She needs a stable situation, and a sense of direction."

Noel laughed. "So do we all."

They talked for a few more minutes, and said goodbye. Noel tore a clean page from his notebook, copied out the names and Lucas' estimates, placed it on Kyra's bed. Done with her for tonight.

⎯

Kyra walked along the sea wall staring at yachts and yawls, cabin craft and dinghies. Across the water, a few lights from Gabriola. Where Tam lived. Tam who might or might not be a suspect in Roy's death. The case wasn't her problem any more. But about Tam's paintings— New uses of pigments, of color? She decided, took the phone from her purse, and pressed the numbers.

Tam answered on the second ring. "Hello."

No machine! "Hi. It's Kyra."

"Oh, hi."

"I just want to apologize for dropping in at an inconvenient time."

"That's okay. I was surprised."

"I have to be over on Gabriola again tomorrow."

"Ah."

"I should be free after lunch. Will you be around?"

"No. That is, yes but later. Should be back about four-fifteen."

"May I come by?"

"That'd be nice."

"See you after four." She set the phone down. Her hand had gone damp. Damn. Tam Gill. Something about her last time there itched. Something about colors. What colors? She felt tingly warm and let herself smile.

When she got back Noel's bedroom door was closed. She made I-am-here noises but he didn't come out. Yes, a statement. In her room she found Noel's information and whistled. Three to four million dollars for Marchand. She slid the paper into her purse.

In the morning, over breakfast, they talked. Noel had forgotten, he'd need the Honda to get to lunch with Lyle. She called for a rental car. She dressed for the occasion, Brendan's slate-blue shirt, her taupe jacket, and tailored slacks. Right for her interrogation of Marchand. And too bad for Tam that he'd seen her clothes. Anyway, with him she wouldn't be dressed for all that long. She shoved her feet into her boots and bagged her runners.

"Give a call from Gabriola."

She promised to. She picked up her rental, a red Taurus, and caught the 11:40 ferry. Only ten minutes late coming in. She'd arrive in perfect time at the Gallery.

It had been the best of mornings for Artemus Marchand. At 8:15 the last detail for the show slipped cleanly in place. Virtually nothing could go wrong, not at this point. That detail, Gordon Thompson from the *Globe and Mail* saying he'd be at the opening, was a break-through, a fully national contingent of reviewers. Islanders would read about the importance of the Gallery in every major daily and hear about it on the CBC. As well as in the *Gabriola Gab*, couldn't get rid of Lucille. But all that other stuff from her would be gone and forgotten.

The only remaining irritant, that damned detective. Should never have given her half an hour, five minutes was too much. Yes, asking Lyle to recommend an investigator had been foolish. Glad he'd not told Rosie the woman was returning. Rosie was in the green-house. He'd said, Surely everything is ready. The plants keep growing, she'd said.

Artemus sat at his desk. He aligned the pile of Foundation files. He'd been so engaged in preparations for the show he'd not yet sifted through them. Out of curiosity he pulled one from the middle. Stephane Mfane, Mali. Project: Harnessing solar power to drive mill wheels for grinding maize. A possibility, thought Artemus. The kind of project he liked.

The Foundation had been Rosie's idea. A clever woman, and he loved her for this too. But she merely gushed with ideas; he was the one to make it all work. Re-ruralization was essential. When he and Rosie had gone to São Paolo for the International Pigment Association Conference they'd seen for the first time the underside of urban sprawl: a countryside devoid of young people. Plenty of babies, lots of old people. Few in their teens, their twenties. Rosie had been eloquent. Find ways to get the young out of the cities, back onto the land. And don't give people our technology, give them the tools to make the technology they need for solving their own farming problems. Re-ruralize to survive. Artemus, though, was the one who found the wherewithal.

Now the Foundation gave out fifteen yearly grants of around five thousand each, and two for fifty thousand. Since the program's inception the annual big ones had been a follow-up to a successful initial grant. So many good projects. Luckily he could keep it going. Income from the sale of schools-of paintings went directly to the endowment.

A bell rang. Artemus waited forty seconds, then headed downstairs and opened the door. Kyra Rachel. "Please come in." He led her to the living room. "I'm just on the phone. I'll be with you shortly."

"Thank you," said Kyra.

Through the kitchen, back up the stairs. At his desk he opened a second file. Roberto Santangelo, Colombia. Project unclear, something to do with rice mutations growing in very little water. Not much chance for this one, he didn't like sending money to Colombia, too unstable. Never knew if you were dealing with the cocaine trade, FARC, or the government. Still, Rosie should read the file.

———

Noel checked his mail, two flyers and a bill. Nothing untoward there. He checked his tires. Fine. He drove south on the highway. How to handle the conversation with Lyle. Now the idea of lunch left him a bit queasy. Maybe soften Lyle up a little before getting into what Lyle and Jerry were talking about. He turned off toward Cedar and ten minutes later headed down the long drive to the Crow and Gate, an English pub complete with duck pond. He parked, glad he'd arrived here alone. Hey, this was a kind of fieldwork.

Lyle was waiting inside at a table by the window, handsome in open plaid shirt and slacks, grey pullover thrown over his shoulders, its arms knotted in front. He stood as Noel approached and gave him a small hug. Noel returned the hug in smaller fashion.

"So how's it going, buddy?"

"Pretty well."

"Want a beer?"

"Sure."

They headed for the bar to order—steak and kidney pie for Lyle, crab cakes for Noel. Each brought back a pint of pale ale. Lyle asked, "So what's happening?"

Well, his book was coming along, Kyra sent regards, no they hadn't talked about incorporating the agency yet—

"That should be the first thing. Get it all set up legally."

"We aren't there yet."

"Sure, fine by me."

They sipped. Noel said, "Better choice of beer here than at Charlie's Oven."

"Hey, you got a problem with the Oven?"

"Too faggy."

Lyle chuckled.

"You go there a lot, right?" Noel raised his eyebrows and mock-quoted: "Lyle Sempken makes the Oven scene with Jerry Bannister."

Lyle's face greyed. "What're you talking about, buster?"

"Oh nothing much." Buster? "But if Jerry's grubby bawd appeals to you—"

Lyle's smile seemed forced. "Jealous?"

"Lordy-lord. Hardly."

"I was interviewing him. See if he'd be a suitable subject."

"For loveliest fella of the year." Noel sipped.

"If you have to know, it's for a series of paintings with unattractive human beings as their focus."

"And you met at the Oven. Did he know what he was, literally, walking into?"

"Yep. Or he thought he did. I wanted to see how uptight he'd be in a strange situation. Like, some day in my studio undressed. Turns out he's a pretty easy-going guy. Specially when he's stoned." Lyle laughed, lighter now that he'd explained himself. "But if I use him, I'll have to fumigate afterwards."

"Yeah, he's a charmer."

Lyle took a long swallow of beer. "How do you know him?"

"Friend of Roy Dempster."

"Right. You all done now on the Gallery case?" A waitress arrived with their orders.

"Yep." They fell to. Good crab cakes, Noel thought.

"You said you had some sort of problem?"

"I'd like to sound you out on this. Since you know Marchand so well."

"Shoot."

"It could be connected to the Gallery. I'm having trouble figuring out where to begin."

Lyle smiled. "In situations like this I always say, Begin at the beginning—"

"Good." Noel nodded. He forked up more of his crab cake, chewed, swallowed, washed it all down with a little beer. "It started about a month and half ago. About three in the morning, the phone would ring. I hate calls like that, never good news. But with these there'd be no one there. Or rather, someone who just breathed."

"Hey, creepy. Did it scare you?"

"At first. Then I let the machine pick up. But I'd still get the breathing in the morning."

"Shit, terrible. Still going on?"

"Not in the last few days. But then somebody slashed all four of my tires."

"Pretty dramatic." Lyle sipped beer. "You figure there's a connection to the breather?"

"Yeah. I got the tires replaced and the next night I got the call again, only this time the breather said, 'Nice new tires.'"

"Yep, that's a connection. What did you do?"

"Not a lot I could do. I've got a Mountie friend and I told him about it."

"Aha." A renewed grin. "The constabulary on the scene."

"Glad you're enjoying all this, Lyle." Why wasn't Lyle taking the story seriously? He wants to be a friend, you open up to him, he finds you merely amusing. "Forget it."

"Sorry, buddy. But it's a hell of a story."

Noel studied Lyle's expression. Contrite? "Then I pick up my mail and there's a letter. I open it and it's a fake newspaper tear sheet. My obituary."

"'The reports of my death are greatly exaggerated.' Mark Twain."

"Okay, never mind."

"Hey, buddy." Lyle put his hand over Noel's. "I'm not making light. Just that nothing like that ever happens to me, it's hard to know how to react."

Noel removed his hand and used it to raise the mug. "It goes on."

Lyle's brow furrowed. "There's more?"

Noel nodded. "That's why I wanted to talk to you about the Gallery."

"You think Marchand is involved with your phone calls and tires? Look, I know Artemus and, to put it mildly, writing fake obituaries isn't his kind of thing."

"Except a couple of evenings ago I got back to my condo after supper and somebody'd been there."

Lyle squinted. "How could you tell?"

"Little things. Brendan's picture lying on its face. A rug shifted. But mostly, when I checked my computer, somebody'd messed up one of the directories. Only one. All the files I had for our Dempster investigation."

"Now that's scary." Lyle stared at Noel. "Amazing."

"But I don't see Artemus breaking in either, and his wife even less so. Kyra's interviewed Tam Gill and can't see him doing it. But the Dempster file was fucked with. I have to wonder if Eaglenest is connected." He leaned forward. "Any ideas?"

Lyle scowled. "It doesn't make sense. Did you know anyone at Eaglenest six weeks ago?"

"Marchand, from your opening."

"Did you have a disagreement?"

"Nope. We exchanged maybe half a dozen words."

Lyle shook his head again. "It's weird."

"It's like I'm being played with. Stalked."

"Hey, buddy, I know it's scary. But at least nobody's tried anything physical on you."

"The tires were damn physical. And Lyle? Please don't call me buddy."

"Sorry, buddy." He winked. "But nobody's jumped you in the dark, right?"

"I will try to look at the bubbly bright side." Noel tightened one side of his mouth.

The waitress arrived to clear their plates and glasses. "Dessert? Another round?"

"No thanks," said Noel. "No more appetite."

"I hope everything was all right."

Noel gave her a friendly smile. "Loved the crab cakes."

Lyle too was finished. The waitress left. "Anything I can do?"

"You see the Marchands and Tam Gill socially—and Artemus professionally. Any reason why he or whoever over there would want to hassle me?"

Lyle's eyes searched the middle distance for a couple of seconds. "Sorry. But I'll cogitate on it." He grinned. "Hey. Let's talk about better things."

He wanted Lyle to talk about this predicament. But it wouldn't happen. "Sure."

"Like, say," he raised on eyebrow, "you and me."

"You know, Lyle—"

"No, no, don't start with Brendan. Brendan's gone, Noel. Get over him. We're here, we're alive, and we care about being alive. So we should care for each other too."

Noel stared at the backs of his hands on the tablecloth.

"Come on. It's a fine afternoon. Let's spend it together. We can go back to my place—"

"Please, don't."

"Just relax a little. We'll put some music on, I've got a New Zealand Semillon, three years old, I've tried it, it's great."

"I—really can't."

"Sure you can. Everything nice and easy. Maybe a joint to start, that'll relax us both."

"Not a good idea."

He reached over and set his right hand on Noel's left. "You got to start living again, baby."

Noel stared at Lyle's hand on his. He couldn't move it away. Lyle was pressing gently, releasing a little, pressing again.

"You'll see, you and me, we could have a great afternoon. You know you need this. Must feel like forever since you needed to be with someone, right? And me, I need to be with you."

Noel reached for his left wrist with his right hand, and pulled it out from under Lyle's. "It's no good, Lyle. You don't get it. I can't."

Lyle glared at him, sudden icicle spears. "Hey, you cut your balls off 'cuz Brendan died?"

"For god's sake, don't."

"You're an ungrateful bastard, Noel." Lyle sat back and folded his arms.

Noel excused himself, got up and went to the washroom. He didn't need this. He got rid of some of the beer and washed his face. His stomach twisted. Stop it! Just a refused offer, that's all. But why had Lyle come on so hard? Noel had never suggested, not even hinted, he might be available. Nothing to cause so strong a reaction. Goddamn it. Well, was it really that strong? He saw Lyle's stare. Anger? Was he hurt? Pretty powerful stare. He dried his hands. Okay, chill out, finish this off. He saw his face in the mirror. Fine. All in control.

Not much of a lunch. But he had in fact learned why Jerry had met Lyle at Charlie's Oven. Jerry hadn't talked about posing for his painter friend, he'd never admit to it. Why had they met, according to Jerry? Yeah, so Jerry could clear some land for a painter. Noel returned to their table. "Has the bill come?"

"All taken care of, pal."

"Look, this was my invitation."

"Next time."

Lyle did enjoy holding the cards. "Okay." Next time? Not likely. "Thanks."

As they walked out, Lyle said, "It probably won't happen, but if you're speaking with Marchand I'd appreciate it if you didn't mention what my new paintings deal with."

"The beautiful Jerry Bannister?"

"And others."

"My lips are sealed."

Lyle's last words: "Think hard about incorporating." They drove off, Lyle in a black and chrome 1962 Impala convertible, Noel in his Honda. One of the most invasive hours he'd spent in a long time. Could he have brought some of it onto himself?

Kyra waited. And waited. Would confronting Marchand with the break-in be a waste of time? Except, maybe, the surprise element— She stared out the window at the ocean framed by trees. Some early Renaissance seascape? Stick in a Moses figure dividing the ocean in two, and Marchand could display it, sell it. She stepped out to the deck and meandered over to the left. No, Tam's place wasn't visible. She went back in. And waited. 12:49. She waited.

Marchand came down four minutes later. "Please excuse me, the show."

"And no doubt you have another appointment in ten minutes."

"No," he smiled, "but I need to call Toronto at precisely four. Their time." He sat across from her. "How can I help you?"

"I'm curious. Do you ever show local artists, those here on the island?"

"No."

"Why?"

Marchand's head froze in place, a few degrees right of center. He stared at her, eyes narrow. "Because they're bad artists."

She squinted back. "Bad?"

He half rose. "Is this why you came here?"

"Not at all. Do you sell your paintings to clients other than The Hermitage?"

"Why are you asking this?"

"I'm here on behalf of a client, a potential customer for your schools-of paintings. He'd like to know, are you getting more?"

"Of course." Sell to someone else? "When we locate more."

"From where?"

"From Europe, from wherever."

"How much did each of the present ones go for?"

He smiled. "That's between my client and Eaglenest."

She named each picture, each figure a small percentage under the upper-limit prices her father had projected. "Is that about right?"

How did she know? Only he and Tam had the names of each painting. And Rabinovich. And only Rab and he knew the prices. Had Rab already announced his purchases? On his website? He stood, his head shaking. "I have to get back to work."

"It's possible my client could outbid your client."

"I'll consider it."

"He'd also like to know, how do you find so many?"

"The usual way. Now if you don't mind—"

"Where will the pictures hang ultimately?"

"I really have to go."

"Are they in the Gallery now and may I see them?"

"I'm sorry. Please go." He walked toward the door.

"Thank you for your time." She followed him to the foyer and out the door he held open.

He watched her car drive away. Outbid? Rab would be furious. He sat still for a minute. His eyes felt tired. For a moment he thought: a larger budget for the Foundation. He went to the kitchen, poured a glass of water, drank it. Not sell to Rabinovich? Impossible. He'd have to tell Rosie everything the woman had said. But— Rose had insisted they shouldn't sell to Rab anymore. Then, possibly, if the woman's client were really interested—

Home, at the computer, Noel tapped the suspend button and stared at the screen. Basic menu, light blue background. No Brendan. Put Brendan back on?

Why did he come home and turn on the computer first thing? Because he was on a job. But he didn't have to work, Brendan's legacy had left him comfortable. So why had he taken on Eaglenest? But he was enjoying himself, right? Except stay out of greenhouses. Other kinds of fieldwork he could handle. Maybe.

He clicked his bookmark. Pigments, testing age. He clicked to Sources, found an index of books and scholarly papers. Carbon-14 testing, dendrochronology, light-microscopic photon testing— What was dendrochronology? He clicked. Ah, a process that figures the age of objects like antiques, sculptures, wooden musical instruments.

Incredible, by measuring a wood's growth ring curve! He scrolled down. Dendrochronology worked for oak, pine, spruce and others; dating not possible for poplar and linden. So no way to prove the age of a fake linden viola.

Articles on the role of carbon-14 dating in conjunction with either dendrochronology or microscopy: limited to pigments made from recently organic materials, recent meaning the last couple of millennia. So mineral oil bases were exempt. And an intriguing book abstracted a dozen case histories that argued it was relatively easy to prove that any one painting was a forgery but much more difficult to prove that another was in fact authentic. Dating, more an art than a science. Perhaps this uncertainty explained why the painting Marchand donated had passed as authentic for so many years.

But what had a black chrysanthemum to do with paintings? And what else was Rose Gill doing in her inner sanctum?

He sat back. Lyle and Jerry. A strange pairing. Suddenly it made no sense, he couldn't see it, Sempken painting a naked Jerry. Suddenly Jerry's explanation seemed closer to reality: do some clearing. Clearing for what? Did Lyle have land? Did Lyle grow his superior marijuana on his land, did he want to grow more so needed to clear more? Time to check out Lyle's lot.

———

By bad artists does Marchand mean, simply, bad painters, bad sculptors? If an artist is an artist, can she be bad? If an artist produces a work which isn't good, is he an artist?

Kyra had over three hours before meeting Tam. She changed from boots to sneakers. Whoops, this was Canada, runners. Grab a bite at the pub by the ferry? Sure.

What had she learned? Some fear in Marchand? Fear of not selling his paintings to The Hermitage? Maybe Tam would reveal something.

The chowder proved too floury, and the garlic bread was toasted only on one side. Order a hamburger instead? No, she'd have to loosen her waistband.

Waiting to pay she noted a stand with Gabriola propaganda: an island map put out by a local realtor, island artists and craftspeople, a magazine advertising Gabriola merchants, Gabriola Summer Festival of the Arts from July 30 to August 2. Too late for that. And a Gabriola

Food and Farm Guide. Take in a little bad island art? Either that or free-range chickens.

She chose Taylor Bay Road. By 2:30 she'd visited three artists' studios: Simsha, home to objects fashioned from driftwood, seashells and feathers, as well as oil paintings of human faces partially hidden behind growths of barnacles on chins, cheeks, noses (oh dear); Sunday's Harbor, naturalistic watercolors of island birds (well, okay); and The Studio on the Hill, high quality fabric art. As well, she'd heard praise for two island artists, one living and one six years dead. The latter, a sculptor who'd produced her stuff under the tour-de-force name Victoria Vulcana, forged steel and stone into harmonic shapes, gaining adoration and scorn. The former, Os Thiebold, now in residence at the University of New Mexico, married abstract expressionism to island images, mixing sand, sandstone and ground-up shell into his acrylics, the canvases suggesting beaches and cliffs worn down by a relentless sea. Neither Vulcana's nor Thiebold's work was being shown at this time.

She drove past a bed and breakfast place, by the little mall, by the road Dempster's sister lived on. She stopped, U-turned, headed down Malaspina to visit Charlotte Plotnikoff. To see another Marchand-spurned artist.

No studio sign up. If you don't name it, do you get to write it off as an expense? She found Charlotte in the garden kneeling by a plot of frilly blue and purple flowers, a bucketful of pruning and weeds at her side. "Hi! Kyra Rachel." No response. "How does your garden grow?"

Charlotte looked up. "Okay."

"Got a minute?"

Charlotte turned, pushed her legs forward, sat flat on grass. "Find out who killed Roy?"

"No, but—"

"Didn't think so. Nobody ever will."

"The Mounties are still on the case and they—"

"They never look in the obvious places."

"Where's obvious?"

"Where they found Roy. The Gallery."

"And what should they be looking for?"

"At. Artemus Marchand."

"You think he killed Roy?"

"Oh I don't know." Tears again in her eyes. "He's such a terrible man."

"It's a long way from not representing local artists to killing someone, Ms. Plotnikoff."

"He'd like to kill all the artists on this island." A thin nasty laugh. "There was just one on the whole island he wanted to represent. But she didn't want him. And she's dead."

"Dead? Who?"

"A wonderful woman. Victoria Vulcana."

"Why didn't she want him to represent her?"

"She had galleries in Vancouver and Toronto, why give him a cut? And no, he didn't kill her unless he can bring on breast cancer. She got famous without him."

"Why'd he want to represent her?"

"Same reason he does everything, to be bigger than the island. Wants to be a great man." Now the tears came more from anger than sadness. "Roy wasn't a great man, just a good man." She shook her head. "A good man."

Three-twenty. Forty minutes till Tam. Kyra stopped the car at the end of Berry Point Road, surf pounding the logs on the sandstone beach. She got out and read a small plaque, which noted that at this site a scuba diver had drowned—he'd gone down and never come up. A half mile to sea was a long skinny island, home of several quaint red and white buildings, and a lighthouse. A couple of people in a small boat, trolling. Seagulls contesting something edible. What would it be like to live in a lighthouse?

Maybe Tam was back early. She turned the rear-view mirror. Saw a professional face. A professional uses her private life in her work. Her body was private. Her mind investigated. She saw Tam finding her naked in his bed. If she parked where Noel had yesterday, Tam wouldn't see her car. She'd hang her clothes in his closet. Hide her shoes and bag under the bed. When he comes in she says to his surprised face, Your condom or mine? Warmth expanded her middle and she became aware of the demand of her breasts. Afterwards they'd talk about this and that. His paintings. Artemus' paintings. Pillow chatter. Did Rose manufacture pigments for him? Show me how they make your painting unique.

Fantasy, what a turn-on. Sex as a tool of the trade. James Bond would be proud of her. She accelerated, and shivered a little. Scared? It'd been a little scary to sleep with him the first time. Second time? Playing with fire. You've done your share of first times, Kyra. And second times. She felt a sudden low-down twinge. Period coming on? James Bond would not approve.

She drove toward Eaglenest. At the little beach she saw the ferry humming toward Nanaimo. Isn't that wrong? Shouldn't the ferry be coming this way now?

She drove on, turned into the neighbors' drive and parked. She pulled out her notebook and made notes to jog her memory later, short mnemonics: A.M. shaken, C.P. mad, sad. She hunched her shoulders, pulling her breasts in, then filled her lungs, which made her nipples brush along her bra. Her lips parted slightly. Oh, stop it.

She changed back to city boots, not great on unpaved pathways, fine for Tam. To the Gallery land, down the trail. She stared at the high deck. Storage beneath? She checked it out. No doors so not a crawl space. Up at Tam's entry she knocked. No answer. She paced along his deck. Leave? No, wait. She stood up straight. Her lower back ached. Period, hold off. Please.

A door. Between her and inside. The door has a lock. Something interesting behind the door? In her purse, picks to satisfy her curiosity. Locked doors keep out casual burglars, easy-going vandals, ex-spouses. Not investigators with lock picks. To learn valuable lessons, essential to enter. She'd touch nothing she didn't have to. A nineteen and an eleven did it fast.

She pushed the door closed, looked around, sensed his energy in the air. Shoes lined up on a rubber mat by the door. Wooden floors buffed and shiny. Out the front window, trees like all around the house. They blocked the view of the water and Mount Benson but they were cozy, protective. Just about four o'clock. What if Tam walked in right now? She'd hedge: The door was unlocked. He'd say, I locked it. She'd say, you must have forgotten. He'd say—

She took off her boots as some people did on this island. The diptych seemed unchanged. Over there a sofa, chair and hassock in front of a mid-size TV, VCR and DVD under, CD player and a pile of CDs to the side. In the rest of the room many paintings, on the walls and stacked underneath. A table she hadn't noticed before was given over to tubes and other painterly things. The bathroom. Small, a shower stall, sink, toilet. Ah, the medicine cabinet. She opened it. Shaving cream, razor blades. Toothpaste and brush. Nail scissors, file, clippers, Band-Aids, Aspirin, vitamin C. Rethink her theory about medicine cabinets?

She picked up her boots and found herself tiptoeing to the bedroom. She made her stockinged heels touch the floor. She thought: I was invited. Well, sort of. She tried to close the bedroom door fully but it scraped on the floor and stuck, just ajar. The room seemed smaller than it had the other day. The bed big as she remembered, duvet cover in muted blues, purples, greens neatly smoothed. He would come through the doorway and there she'd be, arrayed. A gift, beautifully laid out in his bed, waiting to be laid beautifully. A little giggle escaped.

She took the room in. Chest of drawers covered with papers, flashlight, ring of keys, loose change, scissors. Sliding glass door to the large deck matched the door off the living room. Same shiny wooden floor.

She noted another door and opened it. The closet. Carpeted floor inside. She fingered a tweed sports jacket hanging over beige flannels next to a dark blue suit, pushed to the right. To the left, half a dozen shirts. She realized what she'd seen and looked down again. Odd, a carpet in the closet when all the other floors were bare wood. To keep shoes from scratching it? Not that Tam had any shoes here, in fact nothing lay on the floor. She'd never met a closet without things on its floor, wasn't that the purpose of a closet? Rotted wood under the carpet? She set her purse and shoes down, bent, pried a corner up.

A crack in the floor. The wood splitting? She pulled the carpet back. A trap door.

NINETEEN

ROSE EVALUATED HER seven black chrysanthemums, each sustaining well. So all was fine. Except— Somehow the lab felt off. But she couldn't figure why.

The second-largest chrysanthemum pleased her most, the necessary shade under perfect to reach its quintessence—sheen, size, shape— by sunrise Saturday. She added fifteen millilitres of distilled nutrient complex #6. Her phone rang. She pulled it out of her pocket. "Hello?"

Tam. "Look, the ferry's about a half hour late, there was an ambulance run and I've got Kyra the detective coming."

"I don't want that woman on this property."

"Go over and stick a note on my door. Please. Tell her to wait. I'll be along."

Rose clicked her tongue. "You're playing with fire."

"I hope so."

"Don't actively misunderstand me, brother dear. When's she due?"

"Oh, PDQ. Ten or fifteen minutes. The note?"

"When she's gone, we talk."

"Thanks, BSR."

Rose scribbled the note, spelling Kyra *Keera*, found a push pin, wheeled out of her sanctum, and locked the door. Up the aisle, out, angrier, angrier. Wheel, mutter, steam. Wheel.

———

Kyra stared at the trap door, its handle recessed. She tugged. Locked. A central keyhole. A Weiser. A locked space in a locked house. Maybe she'd ask Tam to show her his basement. Maybe she wouldn't. Terrible to be so curious about what lurked behind locked doors. She found her picks, chose the pattern most likely. Third try, bingo. She pulled at the handle. The door, hinged under the surface, rose toward the wall. Below, steep stairs. A string looped over a nail in the joist. She pulled. Light came on. She knelt and stared down. Holy shit and schmidt as well, a hidden room. She dropped her picks into her purse, got out her camera and the two rolls of film, set her bag on the floor, and climbed down the stairs.

Rose powered up the ramp, turned the corner and pinned the note to the doorframe. There, you'll just have to wait to get yours. Hope you're desperate, dearie—Through the window something caught her glance. The bedroom door pulled near to closed? Tam never moved it, it didn't fit its frame right. She wheeled around to the side deck and looked through to the bedroom. Closet door open. Downstairs light on. Stupid Tam! Rushed out so fast he left the light on and door up? Damn! That woman would be along any minute!

Halfway down, the stairs turned at a right angle. At their foot lay a large space, a table, a bookcase. Two fluorescent tube lights hung an inch below the joists. At the far end stood an easel holding a canvas. Kyra tiptoed over to it. The picture was still in progress. It looked like an old portrait. Like those schools-of-somebody. The obvious clicked into place: Tam paints them.

Rose tugged at the sliding glass door. Locked. She wheeled to the kitchen door, keys from her pocket, her hand fumbling for the correct one. Inserted it— Unlocked! Over the threshold, close the closet and the trap before that woman comes along— Rose pulled open the bedroom doorway and rolled through— A purse. Boots. A noise. Someone—? That woman?!

How about that, Kyra thought. A portrait of a burgher, his breadth of stomach exuding wealth, round ruddy face, purple vest— Aha! The purple she'd seen on Tam's forehead yesterday, the something about colors that had bothered her. She snapped a couple of photos. Next to the wall another canvas, a picture of a vase of flowers. Another school-of-somebody? Other canvases stood stacked, facing the wall. More photos.

If he painted these, why go to Europe? Did he ever go to Europe? The keys, where? There on the chest. Rose reached with the Extendiarm, lifted the keys, rolled into the closet, slipped the key ring around her right index finger and clutched the seat arms with both hands. She slid forward along the seat and silently lowered herself to the floor, leaned forward, forearms holding her in place till she lay flat. She reached, grabbed the trap door, slammed it shut. From below she heard a muffled, "Hey!" Still on her belly she slid the key into the lock and turned the tumblers. She lay there, heart pounding. Pounding in time with the beating on the trap from below. Stupid. Damn! Damn damn damn!

It took more than four exhausting minutes to drag herself back up into her chair.

As the door slammed, Kyra's throat had started a shriek. Only the "Hey!" came out. She ran, slipped, caught her balance, clambered up the stairs. But the trap door had shut tight. She pounded, realized she wasn't breathing, sucked down air. When she'd opened the door it stood angled to the wall, no way it could close by itself. Tam? Had she heard a noise just before the door slammed? Artemus? She sat. She breathed steadily. Okay, explore. Damn, if she'd just held on to her bag. The picks, the cellphone— She put the camera on a step.

Another way out. The walls were unfinished beyond white Styrofoam board insulation. Splotches of color enlivened the grey floor. The ceiling, seven feet up, was bare joists, pink insulation between. She pulled some away. Solid subflooring. She pulled at an edge of wall Styrofoam. She found what she feared, solid concrete foundation. As she remembered: no doors.

A small room kitty-corner to the stairs, two-by-fours and quarter-inch paneling, held a toilet and sink. The seat leaned against the tank. At least she wouldn't have to make a puddle on the floor. Depending how long she was trapped. A non-productive line of thought.

The concrete was impregnable without a jackhammer, the subfloor over her head without a saw. Okay, photos. She grabbed the camera from the step, turned the canvas around—a school of who?—and snapped pictures. Then several angles of the one on the easel.

Against the wall stood a paint-stained bookcase, beside it a wooden coat rack dangling a sweater, a sweatshirt, a carpenter's apron, and orange coveralls. The bookshelves held two flat-bladed knife-scrapers and a cutting knife. She felt the blade; reasonably sharp. Rags, palette, peanut butter jars containing brushes, various jars of colors tightly lidded. She opened one and smelled: oil paint. Jars of clear liquid whose smell she couldn't identify. She took pictures.

On the table lay a used canvas, scraped of most of its paint, stretched on a rack. In some stage of preparation? Books: *Techniques of the Old Masters. Representations of European Art 1400–1700. Five Centuries of Famous Forgeries.* More photos. End of the roll. She removed it, put it in her pocket, inserted new film. Three empty frames hanging on the far wall. From the float plane? Now suspended from the joists by wires. Photos of the ornately carved fronts. Then Kyra thought, better safe than sorry, and rephotographed everything.

Had Roy stumbled on this just as she had? Tam or Artemus killed him to keep him from talking. No, both. Or all three. Just as she and Noel had hypothesized. And dumping Roy's body here on the grounds, a clever ploy. They'd kill her too. Her stomach lurched. She hobbled to the steps, sat, dropped her head, crossed her arms, closed her eyes and tried to think.

———

Noel checked his tires. Nothing slashed. Should he check for a 90 percent slashed fan belt, a punctured radiator, drained power steering or brake fluids? Never in his life had he thought about such things, but now think he must. He looked under the hood, tugged at the belt. It seemed fine. He measured his fluid. Okay too. On with the fieldwork.

He started the engine, turned left, then onto the highway heading south. Three blocks, a right turn, half a dozen streets, another left. The old miners' district here, little houses of two bedrooms, tiny lots. Several near-new condos, the beginnings of gentrification. Many of the houses remained in neglected mode, paint peeling, weeds in front. A time to buy?

He slowed in front of 1131 Angus Drive, a house being transformed, painted facade, bushes clipped. He felt conspicuous and drove on, past 1135, Lyle's place, to the end of the block, turned the corner, parked. He walked back to 1135, a redone single-storey house: bright cream paint, black shutters, molded wooden pillars and latticework around the small porch, a new roof. Well landscaped, bushes along the sidewalk and surrounding the house's foundation, light greens and dark greens, trimmed to just below window level. He took note of the carport: Lyle's elegant old Impala convertible was absent. The guy must do okay with his paintings.

How to handle this? Hi Lyle, I was curious to see where you'll want to paint Jerry's body-portrait? Or, if he were Kyra, Hi Lyle, how about seducing me? Or, basically, Just wanted to see where you live, Lyle. Likely the car not being there meant Lyle wasn't either. Likely this was a bad idea. Just get on with it, see if he's got land to be cleared, and leave..

He stepped onto Lyle's property. Flower beds lined the flagstone walk to the front door; shades of Lucille. He walked up the two steps and rang the bell. Inside, little bells played the first phrase of "Swanee River." He waited, no answer. Again. A reprise. How could Lyle stand it, each time someone came to the door?

Okay, check for uncleared land. He walked around the carport side. Nothing here except a big arbutus tree and shrubs beside a picket fence. A covered walkway connected the back porch to a large shed. "Lyle?" He waited. "Lyle!" No response. At the back of the lot, more fencing.

Okay, he hadn't intruded, a friendly visit, shame Lyle wasn't home. What would Kyra do? The shed. Check it out? He had no lock picks. Anyway, why? Kyra would answer, Because it's there. And maybe not locked. He felt himself drawn to the shed door. He reached for the handle. Okay, locked, that solves the problem. A window? Maybe in back. Noel walked around. No windows anywhere. Sure, if he were going to paint a naked Jerry, better to have no windows.

That was that. Though there was the house— No! Time to get in his car and—

From the driveway, the sound of an engine. Noel fled to the rear of the shed. The engine stopped. A door slammed. Someone strode to the back door. He peeked around. The door opened, Lyle stepped inside and closed it behind him.

Triple shit. What if Lyle comes out, decides to survey his shrubs— goddammit. Okay, take it easy. Dark in a little while, less than an hour. Just wait. It's not cold, not raining. Soon you'll walk silently around the Impala, back to your car, and drive away. Simple.

Four minutes later the back door opened again. He could hear Lyle's voice, one end of a conversation. "Yeah . . . I know that . . . Yeah . . ." Then half a minute of silence. Then: "Jerry, you're an ass-hole, you know that? And from me, that means you're in trouble and you better watch your back." More silence, then: "Well he better not, believe me. You're deep in it . . . Just do nothing. Period. You got that, pal? . . . Good." Then a minute, then two, of the longest silence Noel had ever lived through. Then a whispered, "Shit." The back door closed.

Lyle and Jerry. This Lyle didn't sound like any Lyle Noel had ever met—not even like Lyle the rejected suitor. He needed more information. Ring Lyle's bell again? No way. Wait till twilight settled in, then get the hell out of here.

———

One can never be prepared enough. Or too soon. Four days till the opening and Artemus took pleasure in knowing all was in hand. Not too little here, not too much there.

Strange, that detective acting as agent for someone wanting to buy paintings. To describe them in such detail, to estimate so precisely how much Rab would pay for each. Impressive she'd figured the Zurbarán *Jaws of Hell* at within eight thousand.

Marchand opened the top application. From the Democratic Repubic of Congo, something to do with windmills. He couldn't put his mind to it. Stared out the window at the sea and the mountains. All those people arriving soon. For him, because he'd announced a new show. Satisfying.

He got up, stretched. Through the front window he saw Rose racing up the driveway to the road. She disappeared around the curve. He returned to the applications. No. What was up?

———

Rose rolled back and forth on the twenty feet at the head of the drive, trying to hurry Tam's arrival. She watched a grey car pass. Her brain couldn't shape her thoughts, let alone marshal them; just fear now. No problem, panic, hurting no one, how to hold on to the secrets, why worry, the woman down there, nothing wrong, panic panic. Artemus mustn't find out, no more Vegas, no more schools-of. Panic!

No! Calm. Another car. It sped past the drive. Here is a problem. All problems have solutions. Therefore this problem has a solution. She didn't know the solution but a solution there would be. From an unexpected source. Tam? He knew the woman, could bargain with her. Buy her? Would they ever be really safe?

A sudden hum of tires on the road. Her hands grabbed the wheel-rims and she lunged herself toward the gates. The humming slowed, approached. She saw it then, not the Gallery van but a black sedan, tinted windshield reflecting sun. Rose covered her mouth to keep from calling out. From behind she heard Artemus' voice, "Rosie? Are you okay?"

The sedan stopped beside her chair. The opaque-green driver's window opened.

Rose whispered, "No—!"

Pyotr Rabinovich's tanned pate reflected muted sunlight. "Rosie-Rosita!"

She said, "Hello, Rab. What brings you to Gabriola?"

Rabinovich opened the door and stepped out. A large grin puffed his cheeks. His handsome dark-eyebrowed head looked like a friendly obelisk set on a slender solid torso in windbreaker, white polo shirt and tan linen slacks. "Sweetheart!" He squatted beside Rosie's chair, gave her a hug, and a large kiss on her left cheek.

She held onto him for a moment. "So good to see you."

He pulled away, stood and turned to Artemus, "My dear good friend!" shook his hand and gave him a Mexican-style embrace, the pat on the lower back doubling as a check for hidden weapons. Most unlikely Artemus carried a pistol inside his waistband, Rabinovich found himself thinking, but best to stay in practice. Even in gun-controlled Canada.

Rab here, twice in one summer? Strange, thought Artemus. "Welcome again to Eaglenest." Now thinking, is Rab checking on the quality of the paintings? Could he have somehow learned there might be a bidding competition?

"Thank you." Rab breathed deeply. "Yes, the sea air! You live in paradise, Artemus." He took a step toward the house, then turned quickly. "Ah Rosie, so clever of you to be at the gate. My welcoming committee. How great!" He enjoyed the colloquial phrasing in American speech.

"Come to the house. You look like you could use a drink." She knew she could.

His grey eyes laughed. "How does he who could use a drink look?"

She smiled at Rab. "Thirsty." Get him to the house. She turned.

"Artemus, could you make sure the gate's open for Tam? I need a word with him as soon as he's back."

"All right."

"And then be a dear and bring Rab's car to the house."

Rab raised his eyebrows. "The gate is open. I just drove through."

"Sometimes the wind blows it closed. Tam's supposed to fix it." Rose wheeled away, end of conversation.

"It's not windy." But Rab let it go and followed Rose, thinking she seemed very on edge. He called to Artemus, "There's a case of wine in the trunk for you!"

Twenty metres down the drive, their backs to Artemus, Rab spoke softly to Rose: "And the detectives? What interference from them?"

A whisper from Rose. "They're gone. Also, I didn't bother Artemus with your report."

"Good. And, how nice, you've eliminated my need to be here."

"You can shift from industry to enjoyment."

"Eloquently put."

— —

Artemus watched the wheelchair, accompanied by the white shirt and slacks, leave him behind. He thought of a small parade, a little float and a drum major, passing into the distance. Park the car, dear, park the car. He parked and headed back to the gate just as the Gallery van approached. He waved it to a stop, opened the passenger door, and got in.

Tam looked Artemus over. "Too far to walk to the house?"

"Rose says she needs a word with you." He scowled. "And guess what. Peter Rabinovich just arrived." He rubbed the back of his neck. "He's over at the house with Rosie."

"We must've been on the same ferry."

"Possibly. He drives at Nevada speeds."

"What the hell's he doing here?"

"Maybe he's come for the two shows." He shrugged. "I don't know."

— —

Lights on in Lyle's kitchen, the sound of television news. Get out of here while the getting's as good as it going to get. Noel stepped around the side of the shed away from the porch, past the carport on the neighbor side, across the grass, between two bushes to the sidewalk.

He walked back to 1131, crossed the street, passed Lyle's place on the other side, at the corner crossed back. He leaned against the side of his car and took a deep breath. He unlocked, sat a moment, started it, no lights, did a U-turn and drove away. Well, he thought, I investigated the land-clearing question. With only a bit of that adrenalin fear.

And what had he learned? Improbable that Jerry posing for Lyle was ever in the cards. Had Lyle asked Jerry to clear some other land? Maybe Lyle owned a woodlot, wanted to build a country cottage? Didn't sound like Lyle.

What were they arguing about, damn it.

He stopped at the mall. Maybe the photos were ready. Yes. He took them home. As a reward he poured himself a tall gin and tonic and laid the photos out on the table.

Greenhouse plants. Plants had never much interested Noel, but when Brendan had redone their balcony garden he'd bought some books. They'd joked about putting in a little marijuana. But they weren't into marijuana then, not till Brendan got sick. Thanks to Lyle. Lyle had good marijuana. Would he be involved in growing it? Best way to control quality. Were Jerry and Roy growing the stuff in the clearcut by where Roy had worked? How would Lyle figure in that deal? Maybe not at all, people get their grass in lots of ways. But Jerry had specifically said a nameless painter who'd had a show at Eaglenest wanted him to clear some land, the guy had this bad back. A good lie if Jerry wouldn't admit he'd let Lyle paint him nude. But why meet with Lyle at the gay bar? Noel wished Kyra would get back. He had to think this through out loud.

Her pictures of flowers. Rose Gill's greenhouse, but not full of plants. A tray of crocuses. Crocuses in October? Crazy. And the carnations. Boy, did he miss Brendan. Miss, that was sensible. No agony, Brendan wasn't around, somebody to miss from time to time, time to— Shit.

He searched the bookcases for the flower books. Aha, bottom shelf. Why were flower books so big? He set them on the table and refilled his drink.

Much flipping of pages and he had five groups identified: blue Siberian Iris, red Valerian, Michaelmas daisies, the crocuses and carnations. Normal. Flowers grow in greenhouses.

He poured a third drink and studied the pictures of the inner room. Little round bulby things, plastic bags with a tarry substance. Not pretty but interesting. Track down what they were via the Internet? Where the hell was Kyra?

———

Tam left Artemus in the living room with Rab. What did those two have in common, other than a love for schools-of paintings? He found Rosie in the guest bathroom putting towels out for Rab. Her face seemed pale. "You all right?"

"No." Her eyes met his. "Come here." She closed the toilet lid. "Sit down."

He did. "What?"

She whispered, "Your female detective is locked in your cellar."

Tam closed his eyes. A sigh came from his gut. "Shit."

"Correct," said Rose.

"How?"

"She was down there. I locked her in." She shook her head. "Why'd you leave the house with the door unlocked? And the trap open?"

"I didn't. Honest. She must have broken in."

"How did she know where to look?" Likely spotted something when Tam screwed her.

"I don't know." He pounded his right fist into his left palm. "God."

"What can we do?"

"I don't know." A small sound, almost a hum, came from his throat.

Rose put her hand on his shoulder. "Are you all right?"

He nodded, saying nothing.

She waited, and said finally, "I have to get back to the living room."

He took her forearm. "Just a minute."

"Tell me."

"We have two choices. Or three. First, she agrees to say nothing and we can let her go."

"But how can we be sure she'll keep her word?"

"I don't know. Yet."

"She won't agree to anything."

Tam gave a small shrug. "I don't know very much. Except that we have three choices."

"Okay. The other two?"

"We leave her down there. For a very long time. I would go away."

"Someone would come looking. Her partner. The police. What else?"

"We make sure she never again talks to anyone about anything."

"No. I draw the line right there."

"I don't mean kill her. But an unavoidable accident—"

"No."

He smiled brightly. "And there is a fourth possibility."

"What?"

"We let her out, she goes to the Mounties, we get arrested, sent to jail." His smile grew ironic. "I do hear the women's prisons aren't so bad. But I don't know about wheelchair access."

"My god—"

He stood. "Should I go talk to her?"

She shivered. "You think it'd do any good?"

"You never know." Though he figured he did.

She nodded, still shivery. "If by a miracle we get out of this, no more sales to Rab. Of anything."

"Even those we find?"

"Yes. No. I don't know."

"But what do we tell Rab? And Artemus?"

"You'll invent something."

Tam laughed thinly. "That my sources are drying up?"

"Very good."

⸺

Kyra's only constructive thought was to pick the lock. She wandered the room. Palette knives too wide. Paintbrush ends too wooden—

She went to the toilet. Don't flush after every pee on water-scarce islands but damned if I'm saving these guys' water. She banged the handle. Fuck you, she said to the satisfying gurgle. An oubliette, I'm in an oubliette. On her trip through Europe she'd seen oubliettes in old castles, holes in floors where anybody who disagreed with the duke or bishop could be dropped, the stone cover slid in place, the prisoner left to die among the bones of those who'd died before. She started to tremble. She scrambled up the stairs, banged on the closed overhead door; banged, banged. "Let me out!" She turned around on the step, put her head on her arms. A couple of panicky sobs escaped before she could cut them off.

Her fist throbbed. She moved down, sat to her full height and rubbed her hand.

With every stride up the path Tam had gotten madder and madder. Now he was furious. What to do about her? Why the hell was she in his house? Had she called to find out when he wouldn't be home? How'd she get a key? Oh shit! The key in the coveralls, if she finds that it's all over. And Rab here, what the hell? Most important, don't let Rab know, he'd go ballistic. What would a ballistic Rab do? So deal with Kyra. How? He'd figure something. Wait till Rab is gone. Keep her in place down there.

He opened the door and looked around. The anvil. He set the flowers aside. In the closet he set the anvil over the keyhole. If she found the key and pushed on the trap door, the anvil would wedge against the wall and keep the door from opening.

All he could do right now. He spun around, took a step down the walk— Spun again. Wrong. One more thing. Serve her fuckin' right.

Okay Kyra, you're locked in. This is Not Nice. Sit in their oubliette till you die. Or get creative. How? Can't put a knife in the crack and push up with your back, the deadbolt is a thick steel sheath. So attack the tumblers, get the bolt to slide. She wiped her face. Any sharp objects here? Penny nails? She headed over to the shelves. Just paint supplies. She glanced around. The empty frames, suspended from nails! No, from spikes, hanging by wires. She crossed the room. Each wire was looped over a spike in the joist. She lifted a frame to reduce the tension. Not all that heavy. She unwound one side of the wire and lowered the frame to the ground, then slid her fingers along the facade, its relief of flowers and curlicues. On the back of it, curious, a hollowing out on the right and left frame-sides. Deep, maybe an inch. She leaned the frame against the wall and reached for the wire—

The light went out. "Hey!" she stood still, waiting for her eyes to adjust. Do not panic. You're allowed one panic per case, girl, and you just had it. The fluorescent tubes, burned out? Both? Someone had flipped the breaker, left her in the darkest dark she'd ever felt, she could wait forever for her eyes to adjust. Damn, piss and fuck! The flashlight too was in her bag.

She turned her head to where the trap door should be but no comforting light leaked around it. Okay, don't charge off in nine directions. Figure a plan.

⸺

Rab mixed Rose a strong vodka tonic, as requested, and took an iced vodka with peppercorns for himself. He sat next to her wheelchair. "Your face is full of worries. Tell me."

She patted his hand. An hour ago this would have been fine, this friend at her side, listening to her telling him anything in the world. Just not about the detective in Tam's basement. If Rab knew about the basement, at the very least she'd no longer be his friend. Except his response might be way more painful than that. A violent response.

After dinner would have been better for serious matters, but her nerves were so on edge she had to parade a real problem before him now. "Rab, I'll be completely straightforward—"

"As you always are."

"Yes. I think it's best if Eaglenest makes no further shipments to The Hermitage."

"Of anything?"

"Not of my speciality, at any rate. And Tam tells me his sources are far reduced."

"And what does Artemus say about this?"

"He understands." A small lie.

He stood slowly, his eyes not leaving her. His fingers interwound. "Hmm," he breathed. "You sound fearful."

"Mostly, I'm careful. With these wars going on, our two countries have changed."

He sat again on the arm of the couch. "I would miss our regular contact."

"We'll still talk, and even visit you. And you can come here any time, you know that."

He nodded, though not, she thought, in agreement. "I'll consider what you are saying."

Her eyes suddenly teared. "Have I upset you?"

Artemus came around the corner. "Oh. I thought Tam was here too."

———

With the light dead, Kyra didn't move for what felt like a long time. Now she reached out. Her fingers touched the frame resting where her well-lit mind remembered it. And the wire, fairly heavy, it felt the thickness of a number two pick. What picks had she used on the trap door? She unwound the wire from the other side of the frame. Wire in one hand, waving the other hand in front of her, she advanced by small steps.

Sudden thought: If no light leaks in, how is the air replenished? Would she suffocate in her own carbon dioxide? Stop. Get the trap door open. Her hand touched a wall—damn what's a wall doing here? Styrofoam or wood? She knocked on it, wood, the bathroom, she'd turned too far. Correcting to what she hoped was a straight line, she started off again holding the wire out to warn her. She imagined reaching the stairwell, bashing her shin and falling up the stairs. Stop. She tried to visualize the room. Only a few steps from the bathroom to the stairs, right? Only a few steps anywhere. She moved her hand. The wire touched something. She reached out, knocked it over, a shuffle and a crash. She knelt. The painting and the easel. "Oh shit." She was completely turned around.

She contemplated the layout again. Follow the walls, Kyra. The easel had been at the end on the stair side of the table, the table about two feet from the wall with the bookcase behind. Can't be many more steps to that wall. She brushed by the clothes hanging on the rack, reached beyond it—ah, Styrofoam. She turned right. With one hand on the wall and the wire fishing around in front she came to a corner, turned right again, shuffled a dozen steps and bumped her head. "Ow, damn." She rubbed the bump, and reached out. The stair edge. She stepped back, out from under the upper risers. The wire, then her hand, contacted the right-angled lower stairs.

She crawled up on all fours. No banister here. Her hand brushed against something, it slid away, crashed to the floor. What? Her camera! Oh, god. She backed down the stairs, on the floor on hands and knees, groping. She found it. Oh no! The casing had sprung open. She clicked it closed. It stayed in place. And for a moment she appreciated the dark room.

Up the stairs again, camera in hand. Her head bumped the trap door. She turned and felt for the underside of the lock. Lock-pick Mike had drummed it into her: it's all in the fingertips, reading a lock is like reading Braille. Her fingers stroked the lock. Edge, keyhole, shape. These locks had a small tumbler not reached till two bigger ones were out of the way. Maybe one strand of wire single, one doubled over. She slid down a step and set to work shaping her tools.

TWENTY

WHATEVER ELSE PYOTR Rabinovich could import to Las Vegas, an ocean was impossible. He had suggested a walk over the sandstone of the Malaspina Galleries, where Rose's wheelchair needed only a little help. About ending their commercial arrangement they would speak later. Was she truly afraid of international commerce? Or was there something else? He had never seen her afraid. Now he sipped his drink and smiled at his hosts. "Which shall I see first, my paintings or the wondrous flower?" How tense they all are, he thought. Their collaboration with him? Or stress relating to their upcoming shows? But what anxiety could be born from providing the pleasure of five paintings and a new flower? Despite what Herm 3 had found, surely not some mini-spanner thrown by two rustic detectives? Rab could wait till Rosie or Artemus told him more. And tell him they would. Eventually, people did.

Rab usually managed to beguile Rosie just as he usually managed to get under Artemus' skin. Important to keep the man a little off balance. Or else he could take control, hold on to it with absolute belief in his own infallibility, and bring about some small unpleasantness. In Rab's experience of claiming and maintaining dominance over the powerful or charismatic men he'd known in the last years— high- or low-minded sabras, B'nai Brith moguls, renegade rabbis, Israeli mafia; or oil-and-pride-rich sheikhs from the Arab states; or apparatchniks from the former soviets; or well-groomed grandsons of dons from the old Vegas families that he now dealt with—only Ivy League Protestants eluded him. Men like Artemus Marchand who could stick their bare feet into leather loafers with panache, even apparent comfort. They possessed such a sense of remote natural superiority that the multi-dimensioned webs spun by Pyotr Rabinovich's spiders of machinations melted into air with the lightness of a slivered lemon peel dropped into a Marchand-like martini. Superiority, untouchability, certainty. In the eye of these WASPs Rab became again, and he could hear the whisper, "The little Jew from— where was it?" So he kept Artemus, whom he had in fact learned to like, a bit nettled. "Hmm, Artemus? Since I will soon possess the paintings, why not see them?"

Rose said, "Go ahead. I'll set the table." She gave Rab a smile twice as bright as the moment required and turned to Artemus. "Would you grill your famous lamb chops for us? I'll defrost them while you're in the Gallery."

Artemus gave her a private hard-done-by look, but sighed and said, "Come on," to Rab.

———

"Inconsiderate, Kyra, just plain inconsiderate," Noel said aloud. Had she suggested she wouldn't be back for dinner? You go off in the morning, seven hours later you're not back, at least make a phone call. Screwing Gill again, is that it? Had she promised to call after talking to Marchand? He couldn't remember. He tried her cellphone. "Hello. You have almost reached Kyra Rachel. Please leave me a message."

"Kyra! Where the hell are you? Call me as soon as you get this."

———

Rose relaxed as the Gallery door closed, then tensed again. What was taking Tam so long? He'd refused the beach walk in favor of biking around the island—he needed the speed, he'd said. Across her lap she clipped a tray to the chair arms, wheeled to the kitchen, got out plates and cutlery, salt and pepper cellars. Was Tam so panicked he'd skip dinner? She set four places. Then a sudden image brought a smile. Why not? She wheeled down the hall and out to the greenhouse. She collected two of her lesser chrysanthemums, clipped the pots to the tray, wheeled back slowly and placed them on a mirror in the center of the table. She played with the chandelier dimmer switch until the light brought out the richest gleam from the purple-black petals. Then she took two bottles of Rab's present, Pessac-Léognon, and stood them on the sideboard.

———

It had been Artemus who, years ago, first induced Peter Rabinovich to visit Eaglenest Gallery. Or rather, Rab had allowed himself to be tempted by Artemus Marchand, a man who had gained eminence by becoming a world-renowned expert in locating lost or forgotten fine European paintings. For Rab had conceived a grand idea: if the original Hermitage in St. Petersburg needed Great Works of Art, a disciple Hermitage needed the Best Works Available. Like those produced by the students of the great masters. A shame if it were all to stop now.

Outside the Gallery door he put his hand on Artemus' arm. "Do you concur with Rose that we have to limit our business relationship?"

Artemus frowned. "She's talked to you about that?"

"She mentioned it." Rab waited for Artemus to respond but the man's face had taken on that mask of remote infallibility. "But neither the States nor Canada wants the border to create business difficulties."

"No, but in the short term, security concerns slow things down."

We are stating the obvious, Rab thought.

"After the Thanksgiving show, we can talk. But you know Rosie," Artemus laughed dryly, "when she's made up her mind, nothing can move her." He unlocked the Gallery door.

Years back Rab had chosen Herm 5, Deacon Thywold, to search out potential suppliers. Herm 5 had rounded up possibilities from Copenhagen to Santiago, Chicago to Capetown. And on the island of Gabriola in British Columbia's Strait of Georgia.

In the wilderness? Unlikely. One of the few times Rab doubted Herm 5, despite his Oxford doctorate in European painting, seven major monographs and so many scholarly articles no university could afford him. Rab had bought him. Art on an obscure Canadian island?

Herm 5 had shown the boss dozens of slides of paintings and of characteristic details. And read him records, produced copies of authentication documents, photocopies of bills of sale. Eaglenest Gallery was legit. And Pyotr Rabinovich needed legit.

So he flew his Learjet to Nanaimo, rented a car, and ferried to the island. A pleasant ease took him as he approached Eaglenest Gallery, a comfort found him the moment he saw the wealth of flowers, the handsome house, the sea and mountains behind. Meeting Rose was a happy shock, suddenly a delightful and distant romance, safe and proper. His Caspian Rose. They talked till four in the morning, Artemus long in bed. Rosie and Rab, as he very soon asked her to call him, became twin spirits of the mind. Partly because, they discovered, they shared a sensate yearning for mastery, always had, often hidden but now, privately, kindled again. They agreed: such quintessence, their version of it, could come only from common geographic and, likely, ethnic sources as well, western Asia, Tadzhik, Srinagar, their ancestors near neighbors.

The next day Pyotr returned to Las Vegas after agreeing with Artemus that if he, Peter Rabinovich, wanted to buy one of Marchand's discoveries he would be allowed to bid 10 percent over the highest offer Marchand had obtained.

Rose and Artemus visited The Hermitage the following February. By their second day Rose was swimming, at least afloat in the warm pool as her strong arms pulled her useless legs forward, a freedom she'd not felt in twelve years. No thank you, she wouldn't dive, not just then.

That night too Artemus retired early. Again Rose and Rab talked late. She heard the public part of his story, Russia and the Communists, Israel and the Socialists. She grew to care for him, always treated him as an equal. Few others could, and she knew Rab found it hard to react to this, as if the equality she imposed endeared her to him.

———

Hell with her. Noel made rigatoni with pesto and a green salad for one. He ate it standing inside the balcony door, glaring through glass at the cliffs of Gabriola. He put his plate in the dishwasher, picked up the phone, again dialed Kyra's cell. "Hello. You have almost reached—" He hung up. Sure she was screwing Gill. In disgust he scooped up the photos and spread them out beside his computer. Rose's inner sanctum. The metal cylinders, hinged on the top. The bulby things on the counter— They looked familiar now that he thought about it.

He sat back and contemplated. A person with a double-locked room into which others can't see and into which only that one person can enter is protecting something. What? Herself against outside interference, yes. Something secret, yes. Her plants themselves, yes. In the interest of science? In the interest of herself? All perfectly legal. Or—maybe not? What illegal acts could a botanist with a greenhouse commit? Genetic engineering. Rose does that. Not illegal. Something with drugs. The logical flower to make drugs from is the poppy and yes! that's where I've seen these bulby things before, eureka maybe? He got on the Internet and searched.

———

Kyra's stomach rumbled. She'd probably been hungry for a while. Okay, one piece of wire and maybe a triple fold. She moved up and felt the lock again. Start with double. Long time since that dreadful chowder and garlic bread. Right now she'd eat anything. She untwisted the end of the wire, straightened it, folded it to double thickness, angled the double in the middle. A medium rare Porterhouse steak, little fat drip off the edge, baked potato and salad would do nicely. Sour cream, chives, and bacon bits on the potato. Or a pizza, vegetarian. There was a pizza delivery on Gabriola, Noel had read about it. Maybe the delivery person would unlock— The wire, Rachel.

If she still smoked she'd have a cigarette now, that'd dull the hunger. Except she would've left her cigarettes in her purse. If she still smoked, she'd be really frantic now. Except if she still smoked she'd have brought her purse down— Shit! If her period started, no tampons.

She had made what felt like a simulated ten. Plus the two the wire resembled. Yes, she'd used the ten and two above. She tried them. Nope. She crouched down to fiddle again. Bacon and scrambled eggs with hash browns and toast, hell, a bowl of dry cereal, hell, stale bread. There was water in the bathroom. She wouldn't die immediately. One didn't die for weeks if one could get water. Great.

She recombined the wires, a tighter bend. If she could see the lock, that might help. She felt her way back up the stairs. How to visualize the lock— Yes! She slid down the stairs, fumbled around till she found the camera, back up. She held the camera to one side, her index finger found the switch, her other hand located the lock, she clicked. An explosion of light, instant black and she squeezed her eyes tight. But her memory now held the image she needed. And in her camera a photo of the underside of a Weiser lock.

"Where are they?"

Rose whirled her chair about and glared at Tam. "You scared me!"

"Sorry. Where's Rab? And A.?"

"In the Gallery." His forehead glistened with a thin layer of sweat. She released her tension with a long sigh. "Did you go over to the cabin?"

"Yes. Earlier."

"And?"

"I listened for a while. It's like there's a big rat in the basement. Scurry, scurry."

"She knows everything."

Tam sighed. "I flicked the breaker. But she'd have seen it all. I worked till five this morning and left everything out."

"The present project?"

"I said everything! Five minutes—one!—and she's figured it out."

"What a mess."

"Anyway I know I'm not doing anything wrong. Just practicing my craft."

"Others," she arched her eyebrows, "might disagree."

"Rab won't find out."

"Let us pray. Because," she now believed this, "if he does he could have us killed."

"Don't overdramatize."

"I don't want Rab as an adversary. We have to deal with your detective ourselves."

"I've thought about it." He folded his arms. "I believe she'll keep quiet."

"What, make her your concubine?"

Tam sneered. "Oh Rosie, sometimes you are just so off the wall."

Rab, suddenly in the kitchen, asked, "And why is Rose so off the wall? Share it with us."

Rose shook her head. "Some things one shares only with a brother."

Tam looked from one to the other.

"Very well." Rab sat at one end of the long couch and crossed his legs— And leapt up and strode to the dining table. "Rosie-Rosita! Those are splendid!"

Now Tam too noted the flowers. "Pretty impressive, BSR."

"It's the chrysanthemum—?" ventured Rab.

"*Chrysanthemum morifolium*," Rose elaborated. "A very common plant, but not a common color. Nobody's produced a black one before."

Artemus joined them. He knew instantly here was a breakthrough, an original. His chest filled with love and pride. He laid his palm on Rose's shoulder. "Well done, my dear."

"That black has purple in it," Tam pointed out.

"All black flowers have a purple tinge. It's the nature of the pigment."

"This requires a toast." Rab uncorked one of the wine bottles, and poured. "To beautiful paintings and magnificent chrysanthemums!" They sipped. "And to two very clever people!" Rab saluted his glass, bowed to Artemus, then reached for Rose's hand and kissed it. Rose looked at her brother and her lips copied his small smile. Tam raised his glass in acknowledgment.

"And what will be the accompaniments to Artemus' lamb chops?" Rab sat down on the sofa again. "I hope your vegetable garden is as happy as your flowers."

"I'm afraid not, but we'll make do." Rose wheeled to the deck window beside Tam.

Rab repeated his delight in the splendid chrysanthemums. But not half as splendid as Rosie! As splendid as the angels in that Correggio student's clouds.

Tam stopped listening. It was okay. Rosie held Rab in the creases of the palm of one hand. Like he could hold Kyra Rachel. Rab would be gone in the morning, off to break a neck or make someone disappear. Somebody like Kyra. He went to take a shower.

Quickly Noel learned that the opium poppy is *Papaver somniferum*, that the Sumerians called it flower of joy, that the raw sap, opium, is refined to morphine and further refined to heroin. Ten grams of opium produce one gram of heroin so even a modest habit requires acres of poppies. Hmm, Noel thought, Rose Gill doesn't have acres planted in poppies. Maybe in the spring? Heroin and morphine are white, opium is black and tarry. He looked at the photo of goo in the plastic bags. Opium? Being sent off to be refined? Albert will be most interested. We don't like heroin, do we. Though we do like morphine for pain.

Recent increase of opium use in the Seattle area, the Internet told him, an elite fad for Victorian-style drugs. Well, well. Noel remembered reading about the opium dens of early Vancouver. If people wanted to sit around and smoke themselves some joy, he had no problem. As he recalled, though, the Fathers—and probably Mothers—of early Vancouver did.

He contemplated some more. So our Rose is manufacturing opium? Where is it going? To Seattle? To The Hermitage? They ship pictures there. The opium arrives. With the pictures? And there they turn it into heroin? Oh where the hell is Kyra? He dialed her cell number again. Again the message. Oh come on, you can't screw all afternoon and all evening too!

Suddenly he thought: she could be in deep shit.

⁓

Loin chops of four-month-old Gabriola Island lamb, grilled with shredded tarragon and mustard, on a bed of rosemary. Even to Rab's educated palate, a thorough success. And Rosie's accompanying shallot and red pepper couscous brought an eye-dampening memory to Rab's congratulations. His mother had adored sweet peppers in her couscous. Sweet red peppers had not been easy to find in the Sverdlovsk markets of the fifties.

A shame therefore that only he and Artemus showed much appetite. Rosie picked at the lovely meat as if she feared the mustard glaze. Tam ate little and refused the lamb.

Rab slaked his thirst with some of the Bordeaux. Slaked, such a fine Anglo-Saxon word. Well, whatever bothered Rosie and her boorish brother was more than the turmoil of world politics. Likely tomorrow, before his departure, they would tell him. He smiled in silence.

Rose caught him. "Do you find us humorous tonight?"

"Always, Rosie. Always."

She stared at her plate. With her fork she cut a small slice of potato. Halved it. Brought it to her mouth, between her lips, held it and withdrew the fork.

Tam said, bemused, "Why always?"

Always? Not, thought Rab, on his second visit to Eaglenest Gallery. For example. He glanced out through the small grove of trees to the same thick sea. "You're right. Not always."

"When not?" Tam enjoyed this rich and too powerful fool who bought canvases painted by many students from many schools. Rabinovich who didn't need to say aloud, I'd never buy a Tam Gill painting, just as Artemus had not said aloud, I'd never show a Tam Gill painting. This idea with its two unequal parts now seemed quite funny to Tam, so he gave Rab a smile.

"When not?" Rab repeated. "Early in our acquaintance. You do remember?"

Tam glanced at Artemus, who seemed far away. At Rose, who nodded. "Of course."

That summer evening Rab had expounded on several subtle improvements at The Hermitage, not least his newly acquired original oils, four from the seventeenth century, two from the eighteenth, one from early nineteenth. They hung on the walls of seven elegant period-decorated suites of his hotel casino. "They are lovely to see, but something's missing." He'd shrugged. "I'm not sure."

"I don't understand." Artemus, during their visit to The Hermitage, had felt thoroughly comfortable in the opulent suite.

As if shaping a response to Artemus, Rab waved both hands before him. Then he settled for an idea. "Mastery is the measure of things."

Rose said, "Perfection."

"Perfection?" Artemus squinted at her.

"In the balance." She spoke slowly.

Rab nodded. "Go on."

"A balance in what is close."

"Ah," said Rab.

"The perfection of light. I see this, at times. The perfection of a human body slicing through the air. I was this, long ago. The perfection of a single flower, its balance, its—yes, its power." She glanced away from Rab, almost shy. "I can do this."

No humor in Rose's tone, nor in her intent. Rab had to respond, "What kind of flower?"

"The one I believe you'd like best."

He had nodded. "What I believe, Rosie, is there can be a perfection. My hope is to make perfection available at The Hermitage."

"With a poppy," she said.

Comprehension took his face. "You're amazing."

She tipped her head to the right and smiled, lips closed. "I am."

Artemus said, "A poppy?"

Rab nodded at Rose, offering her the lead. She said, "An opium poppy."

"For pity's sake, Rosie! Heroin kills. The white death—"

She touched her husband's forearm. "Without morphine I couldn't have endured life. I wouldn't be here today. You know that."

"Of course, but not opium."

"Without opium there's no morphine. True, there's no heroin either. But I don't think Rab's talking about heroin."

Rab shook his head. "Pure opium. Three times I've spent time in a perfect place. Once for forty hours, twice for thirty and more. The perfect realm of opium innocence."

Rose, fascinated, nodded. "And what is it like?"

Rab had closed his eyes, searched. "When you make the perfect dive, the air against your face and torso, your legs, the air holds you, yes? You fly. Your flight is timeless, all silk and grace." He opened his eyes.

She'd nodded. Artemus, gazing at her, saw his wife again for a moment as the exquisite young swimmer he had met twenty-five years before, the only other person in the room at a crowded fraternity party. Rose's ethereal face said, Anything is possible. Even perfection.

Now Tam said, "Yeah, I remember that evening. And my comment to my sister: No."

Rab's turn to be bemused. "Charming, Tam."

There had followed weeks of discord between Artemus and Rose. He despised recreational drugs and Rosie must not, *must not*, produce opium. But opium, she had argued, was hardly cut heroin, or crack cocaine, or even ecstasy—hardly a jolly party drug. I won't allow it, Artemus shouted. You allow morphine, Rose argued, you allowed it for me. And what, damn it, is opium's medicinal value!? Opium is another category of things, Rose explained—neither medicinal nor recreational, but a drug to enter the spirit. By what power could she say such a thing, Artemus raged, what hubris to pretend she knew this as a truth? She explained: she had felt the embrace of perfection. I was so close, Rose told him, so nearly there. I have to try to produce it, the finest opium, to test it. If it works, share it with Rab. Tiny quantities, Artemus. No chance of danger or pain. And my way to say thank you to the poppy, for relieving my own despair.

In the end, Artemus acquiesced. Rose made so few demands, he had never reached for the unequivocal No. How could he? He approved of medicinal marijuana and morphine. His principles, he discovered, were not sheltered by absolutes.

Nineteen months after Rab's challenge to achieve the quintessential flower, Rose produced a small harvest of opium poppies with rich sap, three times the quantity available from a normal opium poppy, 82 percent more viscous. Perfect poppies. Or, as she joked, so near perfect you couldn't tell the difference. She'd bred them, grown them, bled, dried, and bagged them. With Tam's help, shipped the bags in narrow tubes inserted in the ornate frames of paintings done by, well, a student of European masters. Her new crop had been set to go next week. Now—

From the start, Rose had made it clear to Artemus: these tubes were not being sold, they were gifts. Because Rab was their friend.

At The Hermitage Rab had constructed a luxury opium den. He estimated it cost him about twenty-two thousand American dollars to give a select friend a unique experience: thirty-six hours in the purity of perfection. A small chamber, an appropriate amount of opium, a constant but concealed attendant, optional escort pleasures according to taste, then twelve hours of steam, massage and sleep.

Rose Marchand's cache of enriched opium was limited. She could produce only enough to supply five guests twice a year. A few people out there, Rose figured, seriously owed Rab.

Twice at The Hermitage Rab and Rose shared a period of opium heaven. They reveled privately for twenty-four hours in their imagined desires. For Rab, his dead young wife walked out of the burning bus and literally, bodily, into his beating heart. For Rose, her powerful legs walked her from the wheelchair to a velvet ocean, she swam, she swam, she needed no legs. For one day, each was a perfect being.

This evening around the dinner table, far less than perfection. With the possible exception of the lamb, Rab noted. But the best of it lay congealing on the platter.

——————

At 8:30 Noel couldn't stand it any longer. He picked up the phone and dialed. After four rings Artemus Marchand answered. "Yes?"

"Artemus, this is Noel Franklin."

"Yes?"

"I'm trying to locate Kyra Rachel. Is she there, by any chance?"

"Of course not. Why should she be?"

"She had an appointment with you earlier. Was she there?"

"Yes."

"Did she mention where she was going?"

"No, nothing."

"Did she talk about staying on Gabriola?"

"I'm afraid I don't remember."

"Did she say she was going back to Nanaimo?"

"Maybe. I'm not sure. Now if that's all, you've disturbed us at dinner."

"Sorry. Thanks." Noel put the phone down. "Damn." He breathed deeply. He walked through each of his rooms. He sat down, instantly got up. He shivered. He'd gone beyond anger and worry, right through to damn scared.

TWENTY-ONE

KYRA CRAWLED UP again, inserted, hmm, tighter fit, ah! a tumbler clicked. Onward. If she drank more water she wouldn't feel so hungry. But the water was over there in the dark. She was thirsty. She had to pee again. Did she care if she peed in the toilet? Pee here. She'd either get out or get killed. Who cared about a cleaning bill. She sighed. Fastidiousness bumped her down the steps, the bent wire held out like a short thin cane. Twelve steps, she counted. And in spite of herself, giggled. She found the toilet and peed. A 12-step program. Head under the tap, and she drank. It did help. She started back to the steps.

A flash of light. The trap opened, things flew down. She throbbed with adrenalin terror.

"Sorry about this, Kyra." Tam's voice, flat. "Here're sandwiches and blankets. You shouldn't have gone where you weren't wanted. You've left us no alternative."

"You fucker, you major fucker, let me out!" She dashed to the stairs but the trap door slammed down again, and clicked. "At least turn the light on!" Damn, damn, damn! The tumbler she'd released had clicked back in locked position.

"Kyra?"

His voice through the wooden door came to her a bit muffled. "What?"

"You want to talk?"

"About what?"

"Well, first you could say thank you for the sandwiches and blankets."

"Fuck off."

"Then you can tell me what I should do with you."

"It's simple." She stared up to where his voice came from. "Let me out."

"I can't. Not till we reach an agreement."

Something was shifting. Likely not for the better. "What agreement?"

"I could promise to let you out and you could leave unharmed. But you'd have to promise something too."

She waited a moment. "Like what?"

"Like, to help me keep my secret."

His voice became more muted, as if he'd moved away from the trap door. "What secret?"

"About my studio. My work."

"Sure, that's no problem. I promise, I really do." Damn! She'd spoken too eagerly—

"But how do I know—"

"Hey, Tam, I can barely hear you."

"Oh. Sorry." Then his voice sounded clearer. "Okay. Tell me this. What do you know about Rose and Artemus?"

"Huh?"

"I'll ask another way. Maybe you don't know anything at all about the Marchands, nothing except Rose Marchand, world-renowned botanist, Artemus Marchand, gallery owner, patron of the arts. Roy's body was dumped here, after being killed elsewhere. Nothing more?"

"Noel's report said that. What more is there?"

"How do I know you'll keep on being ignorant? That I can trust you?"

"Come on, Tam." She forced her grimace into a smile. "You know you can."

"I'm not sure. And we have alternatives."

"Yeah?"

"We could keep you down there. For a long time. Without any sandwiches."

She shuddered. "After a while I'd start to stink."

"But before that you might disappear somewhere else. The strait is deep. And close by."

"Come on, you wouldn't kill me." Or would he? She didn't know.

"I know a man who has no problem with projects like that."

"I understand what you're saying. I'll keep my mouth shut tight. You have my promise." She waited. "Do we have an agreement?"

Silence from Tam, till he said, "The man I know does many things. People can meet with car accidents. Like your friend Noel. Or your father. We wouldn't want his shop to burn down."

"Are you talking about you?"

"I'm not in that league." He snorted a laugh. "This guy's ruthless. And he's as close to us right now as the house."

Oh man, am I in deep shit— No, don't think about it now—"Hey! Tam! I'm not stupid." She forced her voice to stay steady. "We've got a deal. Total silence from me. I'm outta your life, you're outta mine." No response. "Okay?"

"We'll sleep on it."

"Please, let me out."

"Good night." Heavily muffled.

"Hey Tam!" No answer. What man does Tam know? Helldamn-pissfuck.

———

Artemus visited while Rose prepared for bed. They spoke little: Can you get me my robe? Do you want to floss? An avoidance of talk, with Rab in the next bedroom.

That she and Rab had upset each other was clear to Artemus. Rab was too unctuous, Rose too silent. Her unwillingness to send more opium, surely. Which didn't explain why she had undermined the upcoming sales of the paintings. "Rose?"

"Mmn?" She applied cream to her face.

"You told Rab we wouldn't be able to get many paintings in the future. Where do you get information like that?"

"Tam. And keep your voice down. I don't want to talk about this now."

"You left me looking like a fool—"

"I'm sorry." She wiped the last of the cream between her fingers. "Really. But can we wait until Rab's left?" She smiled, looking as if she were about to cry. "Please?" She reached out to touch his hand.

"All right. But you've made me extremely angry." He turned and left the room.

———

Noel turned off his computer and switched on the ten o'clock news. It couldn't distract him. He was royally scared. On the screen, images flashed past. She's driving an unfamiliar car. She had an accident on Gabriola. Do they have a jaws of life over there? He grabbed the phone again, looked up the number for the Gabriola RCMP, dialed.

A machine: Call the Nanaimo number. Nanaimo RCMP: No, no accidents reported today on Gabriola. He disconnected, turned off the TV, on impulse dialed Albert in Victoria. Not at the office, back in the morning. At Albert's apartment a machine, Albert wasn't available. He left a message, Kyra's gone missing, please call. Shit shit! He called Emergency at the hospital. No, no Kyra Rachel had been admitted.

Was she simply with the artist brother-in-law? He picked up the phone and called Tam Gill's number. Another answering machine. Kyra's cell again. The service again.

Okay, he had no idea what to do. He'd never taken a course in criminology, or police work. He didn't even read detective novels much. Though he'd loved John D. McDonald. What would Travis McGee do right now?

How could he ever partner with Kyra if he worried like this.

He turned on the news again. A broadcaster with tight lips bade him good night.

Not a good night. Travis McGee would get his ass over to Gabriola right now. He'd be stuck there, but he'd search all night. He checked his watch. He rushed to the balcony. Shit! The ferry, just pulling out. The last one, always on time. Okay, a water taxi— Sure, get to the island, no car, walk all night— Damn it, there should be a bridge to Gabriola!

His phone was ringing. Kyra! "Yes?"

"Hello, Noel, it's Lucille."

"Oh. Hello."

"You don't sound excited to hear from me."

"Sorry, Lucille. It's, uh, late."

"Well I thought you might want to know, the call I got about Roy Dempster's binoculars? I copied down the calling number on my screen and the next day I got in touch with my friend at Telus. She just called me back. The phone belongs to an island fellow, Jerry Bannister. He's got a bit of a record. A cellphone."

"Very interesting—"

"Franklin! Pay attention! How did Bannister know the binocs were where he said?"

"I get it, Lucille. He planted them there."

"Very good. And where did Bannister get Roy's binoculars from?"

"That's only a surmise. Okay, a pretty good one."

"I should've had the information sooner. But what with the weekend, and I don't have my old clout at the phone company. Not like it used to be. Know what I'm saying?"

"I do. But you ought to tell this to the Mounties."

She laughed. "I write a better story when I'm not my own hero."

"I'll get the information to those who can use it. Thank you."

"Sleep tight." The line went dead.

He called Albert again at home. "Hi. An update on my last call. I have important information. Call when you get in. No matter how late."

He tried Kyra again. Same. Okay. Wherever Kyra was, she couldn't phone. Why not? No answer. First ferry in the morning. He brushed his teeth, pulled off his shirt—

Lucille! Water taxi time. He grabbed the phone, punched in her number.

It rang once. "Maple."

"Hello, Lucille. It's Noel."

A moment of silence. "It's, uh, late, Noel."

He laughed. "Sorry. But listen." He explained his worry, Kyra's absence, not returning from Gabriola this evening, no word. "I need your help. I'm coming over. By water taxi. Could you meet me?"

"I'll send our fellow from here. Cheaper than the Nanaimo rip-offs. And he owes me."

"You sure?"

"If you don't hear from me in fifteen minutes get yourself to the seaplane dock in forty-five. His name's Isaac." Excitement in her voice. "I'll pick you up."

"Okay." But she'd already hung up. He checked his watch. 11:25. A boat was the bridge to Gabriola. Shirt back on, sweater. Windbreaker at the ready. He wrapped his toothbrush bristles in a tissue and stuck it in his shirt pocket. He slid four fifties into his wallet. What else? The flashlight. Computer? No. Notebook and pen.

Quarter to midnight, no call. He waited till midnight, locked, walked down the stairs, out, along the promenade to the quay where the seaplanes dock. Two of Nanaimo's water taxis floated there, bobbing in easy sleep. He waited, hands in pockets. Another fifteen minutes and he heard the hum of a motor, then saw the approaching lamp, and the taxi docked. "Isaac?"

"Let's go."

Noel climbed aboard a flat-bottomed craft, small cabin up front. "Thanks for coming."

The taxi bobbed. "It'll be a hundred." Isaac, tall and skinny, made no move to leave.

"Sure." Noel gave him two bills.

Isaac studied him down and up. "Might want to get into the cabin. It's cool out."

"I'll be fine."

Isaac gave him a two-second stare, turned to the wheel and pointed the taxi across the harbor toward Gabriola. The engine roared, picking up speed quickly. Noel came close to losing his balance. But the sea lay smooth and they skimmed across. "Sorry to get you out so late."

Isaac nodded.

Noel wondered what Isaac owed Lucille. And what to do when he got to Gabriola. Lucille could drive him to Eaglenest, he'd do an all-night stakeout. Should've brought his down jacket. But was Kyra there? Where else could she be? The taxi slowed. Except they weren't landing at the ferry dock. The taxi's beam took in a rickety floating platform. "Where are we?"

Isaac lashed the boat to the dock. "Green Wharf. Across from Mudge."

"Oh."

"Off South Road." He killed the engine, stepped onto the dock, brought out a flashlight. "Near Brickyard." He pointed with the beam to a steep tottering ramp. "Lucille'll be up there."

"Thanks." Noel could see the ramp in the starlight. He turned on his light and climbed the shaky slope up to a higher platform, this one solid. He crossed to shore and heard the low murmur of an engine. Double high beams hit him. He heard Lucille shout, "Climb in!" Yes, her TR6. He sat beside her. "I appreciate this, you know."

"I do know." She backed up, turned, and headed up a potholed dirt road.

Wrong car for here, thought Noel, but the Triumph wound between gullies and over ridges with no bottom scrape. Up on South Road, Noel said, "Can you drive me to the Gallery?"

"Nope."

"Why not?"

"Nothing'll happen till it's light."

Shit. "Lucille, I need to—"

"At night on small islands, people sleep. You do business by day. Legal business or illegal business, no difference."

"So why did I come over?"

"So you can be in place at the first twinkle of dawn."

"For god's sake, Lucille—"

"I understand this island, know what I mean? We'll have a drink, you'll get a little sleep."

He could walk to the Gallery. Or steal her car? Or maybe she was right.

She turned into her driveway and parked in the carport. In the living room the couch had become an impromptu bed. They sipped Scotch. "Okay," she said, "what's going on?"

How much should he tell her? Jerry, Roy, the pot patch? Rose and the opium? Hazardous to dangle unprovable allegations in front of a journalist, right? "All I know is, Kyra's missing. And I'm worried."

"You think the Marchands have done her in? Why?"

"The Gallery's the last place she's known to have been."

"Probably some guy. Tam Gill, maybe."

Noel felt the name grind behind his eyes. "Likely that's all. But I need to find out."

She squinted at him, doubt on her lips. "Okay." She gave him an alarm clock, the time a red glow, and showed him the bathroom.

———

Kyra patted the floor beside the stairs until her hand connected with a packet. Sandwiches in a Baggie. She crawled back up the stairs, pushing a blanket out of the way. Trapped. "You've left us no option." Us. Artemus, Rose, Tam. But Tam made the deal.

She unwrapped the sandwiches and sniffed. Meat and mustard. At least they weren't going to starve her right away. Lamb? One more bite. Slightly charred, barbecued? Delicious! Cheese and lettuce, and a tart herb, probably tarragon. On firm sourdough.

Her jaws stopped. What if they've poisoned it? She moved the suddenly tasteless morsel around her mouth, slowly swallowed. Idiot! Rose knows poisons for sure. Deadly nightshade? Leave me here to die an agonizing death. Kyra poked some meat out from between two teeth and wiped her finger on the stair edge. Yeah, they stay over at the house, don't have to listen to my agony. I should know pretty soon if it's poisoned.

Maybe poisoned, locked in the dark, knowing too much about someone else's business, their knowing you know, what to do? Get control. Keep it in the air, label the balls, around and around. Faked schools-of painting, ball number one, up in the air. She closed her eyes in the dark and the ball was in her hand, lob up, drop down, caught by feel. Second ball, a black basement room, up in the air, the painting down, up again. Ball three a poisoned sandwich, up, around, over, across. Fourth ball, the lock picks, up, over— No wonder she was getting nowhere! Shift in mid-air? She'd never done this, have to try, the great jugglers can. She plucked ball two from on high, flipped it in between three and four, around, around. It worked! Lock pick ball beside door ball, up, over, lock pick perfect among the tumblers, around, over, around. Minutes it felt like, or hours. Till she caught all the balls in one hand, held them tight, opened her hand and they were gone. Opened her eyes. The dark was still here.

She found the wire and crawled up the steps. More careful fiddling. A click. Good. Professional lock picks, a worthwhile invention. Like a plow instead of a stick to dig a hole. She'd rather be digging. Her arms were tired noodles over her head. She let them hang, and shook them. If she escaped, she'd work out again. Hard.

She yawned. Rather, a yawn yawned her. Okay, what do I know, lock-wise? One tumbler loose. She stuck the wire back in, she felt about with it. But her fingers sensed nothing, they'd gone numb. The poison? She pulled her hand down, placed the wire in her lap, shook her hands and pressed them on the step. Normal feel. Her stomach didn't hurt. Maybe just exhausted. The blankets, a couple hours sleep. If she wasn't dead when she woke, the rest of the sandwiches.

She bumped down the stairs and made a blanket-nest just outside the bathroom. She lay down. The film cartridge dug into her hip. She shoved it between her breasts under her bra.

In jagged dreams Lyle and Jerry played some grotesque version of hide-and-seek with Tam, Rose and Artemus. And Noel was it. He woke three times before five o'clock. When he finally pulled his pants on and headed for the toilet he found Lucille in the kitchen, dressed and sipping coffee. "You didn't have to get up. Can I borrow your car?"

"Have some coffee. I'm going with you."

"Lucille, no."

"I can handle the Marchands better than you."

"Look. I don't know what's happening there. And you don't want to be your own hero."

She studied him. "I'll take you. I'll wait in the car. In case anything goes wrong."

"The getaway driver?" He grinned. She didn't.

She drove fast, headlights reflecting ground fog. To keep from talking, Noel played a solitary What-do-we-know? Rose Gill is producing poppy-sap. Being refined into heroin? By whom? Where? Yesterday Kyra went to talk with Art Marchand— Oh god, Marchand. Art Merchant. A name to be cursed with. No wonder he insists on Artemus.

<hr>

Not so much a sleepless night for Artemus, more a lot of darkness with tiny naps. Despite his sleeping pill he lay awake more than ten times between 11:40 and 6:55.

All night he'd felt Rab studying him, from up on the ceiling or from behind the mirror, just as over dinner Rab had searched down and across his face. Rosie's as well, the long glance of a casino owner who needed to know everything all the time. But Rab had asked nothing. Artemus had waited for Rosie to take the lead. She didn't. They all went to sleep. Rather, to bed.

At moments his anger had ebbed. But when thinking about Rose's claim that he couldn't find more paintings— How might it have been, without the successes of the last years? Without doing everything possible for the Foundation? How lucky to have found the world's most single-minded buyer in Rabinovich.

Such pleasure when Tam brought him first the School of Tintoretto his people had located in that little town near Debrecen, and then the School of Schnürer, part of the estate—several minor masters, a few Old Testament groups from schools of the greater masters—of a shoe-and-boot commissar for northern Hungary. How did good communists come to have estates? Likely the commissar had been a clever fellow and a bad communist. For the moment the heirs would sell only one, from the Schnürer school. It was a small complex study for the *Moses in Sinai* now in Munich's Alte Pinakotech, the early rendering already equipped with tablets and horns.

Tam had picked it up, he told Artemus in great excitement on the phone from Budapest, for just over US $11,000. Back on Gabriola, Artemus too bubbled with pleasure. His ardor had communicated itself so well to Rab that he'd bought it after seeing only the slides. Artemus showed it as part of that year's Thanksgiving Day show. Rab had paid US $366,000 for it.

Rosie wanted those times to be over. What was the matter with her?

———

Lucille turned down the absent neighbor's driveway. Daylight glowed over the trees ahead. The two Jaguars in their cages, and another car, a small red Taurus. Maybe Kyra's rental—? Noel said, "Okay. If I'm not back in two hours, come looking. But please, stay here till then."

Lucille looked irked but said, "Okay," and reached for a library book.

Noel inspected the red car, parked where they'd left his for the break-in. On the floor in back, running shoes. Kyra's? Maybe good news. He returned to the road, found the split fir, headed down the trail. Tam's cabin. He crouch-walked up the steps to the porch. Glanced in. No one. Kitchen tidy. He walked around the front. A studio, an easel, paintings. Another glass door. A bedroom. Bed made. Damn! Gill's pad in Nanaimo, is that where she was?

Down the walk to the circular drive. Silence. The two Gallery vans. The BMW. A large black Lexus. Kyra's rental? Unlikely. The rear door of the van beside the black car opened. He sank instantly to the ground. A man got out. Tall, shorts, a black T-shirt. Well-tanned skin. Or naturally dark? From Kyra's description, Tam Gill? A new gardener? The man closed the door, stretched, walked to the carved-eagle door and let himself in. Not likely a gardener.

Noel stayed in place, barely breathing. No one left the house. A rustling behind him. He flicked his eyes as far to the side as he could without moving his head. Slowly he turned it. A deer, munching the wisteria draping down from the pergola. His shoulders sank in relief.

Closer to the house. He skirted the periphery of the circular drive. The deer bolted. Noel sank under the cover of a shrub, astounded at the deer's hoof-clicks on asphalt. Would someone come out to investigate?

No one. He peered around, and breathed in. How easy to forget to breathe. He stepped cautiously around to the far side of the house, up close to the Gallery. He crouched low and zipped over to the van the man had come from, the passenger door side. He turned the handle. It squeaked. He cringed. He stepped onto the running board and climbed in. Behind the seats, a mattress, a crumpled sheet. Where the hell was Kyra?

The house door opened. Noel dropped flat on the van seat, then slowly raised his head. A man in a dressing gown, slender, bald, heavy eyebrows, middling height— And instantly Noel recognized him. Peter Rabinovich walked over to the Lexus, passenger door. A key. He opened the door, leaned in, took out what looked like a camera case. Closed the door, locked. Noel dropped flat. For a long long time. Raised his head. Rabinovich was gone.

Travis McGee would have a gun. He'd ring the doorbell, stick the pistol barrel up Marchand's nose and demand to know what they'd done to Kyra. Noel didn't have a gun. If he had a baseball bat— He didn't. A tree bough from the woods, grab a branch, storm up to Marchand's door, in his hand a thick fir bough with little green needles, shouting charges of abduction, kidnapping. Looking and sounding like an idiot. Like Birnham Wood.

He stepped out of the van. Was Kyra in the house? The side facing the water was mostly glass, he recalled. Try to see them before they saw him. Good luck.

—————

Tam Gill looked like he'd slept in a shed, Rab thought. Same shorts and shirt as yesterday. Chin stubble. Had Gill not slept in his cabin? Strange.

Breakfast turned into a half hour of light and tiny talk. Rab created something like joy by asking Rosie if he could take a photo of her chrysanthemum. She smiled. As Artemus cleared the table, Rab stepped out on the deck and let his gaze follow the ridge of mountains across the channel. A magnificent world these people lived in. A shame if they stopped exporting to him. He would not have a reason to come back. He breathed deeply and returned to the house, sliding the screen closed. Yes, a final cup of coffee in the living room.

Perhaps he'd been wrong and they wouldn't mention their problem today. Perhaps it was only the cessation of their shipment. So he'd raise the subject himself. "Now," he said, "I've considered further, Rosie, your side of our agreement. You may be right, the borders are uncertain these days. Though I believe our arrangements are safe, we shouldn't press our luck."

"Good."

Tam looked bored.

On Artemus' face, that old superiority.

"When the times change, and change they shall, then we can reconsider." He shook his head sadly. "I shall miss your shipments, Rosie. No one can compete with you. So as you produce more, don't sell it in Canada. No one would appreciate its excellence."

"I shall be producing—less, I think."

"However," Rab continued, "I can think of only one reason to cease shipping the paintings, Artemus."

"Hmm?" said Artemus.

"Do you have another market?"

"Of course not!"

Tam grinned. "That whole point's moot anyway. We'll be getting way fewer paintings in the future. If any."

Artemus spoke with great control. "Will you elaborate on that, Tam?"

"Our wonderful idea has become the prototype for both the Rijksmuseum and the Bilbao Guggenheim. A joint E.U. project. They're putting real money into keeping their art at home."

"Outrageous," Artemus said, his lips tight.

"But whatever you acquire," said Rab, "our original agreement still holds. Breaking contracts is a dangerous commercial practice."

"Of course," Artemus said quietly.

"And one more thing. About those detectives you hired—"

⁓

From behind a broad rhododendron below the deck, Noel heard snatches of conversation. He'd come around the corner by the Gallery just as someone inside, a man, it didn't sound like Artemus, so Tam or Rabinovich, had mentioned shipments, something about quality. To hear and see properly he'd have to sneak right up to the glass doors. Not a good idea. Now a few words were coming through clearly: ". . . that was foolish, Artemus. So rash . . ." Another voice: "Rab, I was only trying . . ." The voice disappeared, the first came back: ". . . in our business . . . investigators who . . ." Gone again. Then a woman's voice—no, not Kyra—saying: ". . . incompetent, Rab . . ." And again Rabinovich: ". . . a lot about you . . . and me . . . his computer . . ." and the woman, ". . . wasn't like that, Rab . . ."

What was all that? Where is Kyra? Leave, check the other room. Wrong side to come around but he took the chance and crouch-ran the length of the deck, he figured out of any sightline from inside. At the far end he climbed to the deck and hoped no one would step out. Two big sliding doors here. The first a small room, an unmade bed, a small suitcase open, no obvious person. The next, from the bars around the bed, would be Rose Marchand's room. No one here either. A closet. Not locked. No Kyra. Enough. Off the deck, and he checked underneath. A slab, no basement or even crawl space. Around to the side, a sprint across the bare land, the path to the cabin. He was in the wooded area, and safe. Well, safer.

By Gill's cabin— Something didn't fit. Why wasn't Gill in his cabin? The guy who got out of the van, was that Gill? The cabin. Up the stairs. Noel stared through the window into the kitchen. Still no one visible. Was Kyra in there? Go in? No lock picks or skeleton keys. He tried the handle. The door swung open. How about that. He closed it behind him. He called quietly, "Hello? Tam Gill?" No answer. Kitchen empty, a studio—easel, paintings, paintings everywhere. No one in the bedroom, a bed not slept in. A closet. Shirts hung carefully. On the floor, an anvil. What was that about? And Kyra's purse. Her low boots. "Kyra?" No answer. "Kyra?!" Still nothing. No one here, nothing to lose, and he screamed, "Kyra!!!"

The sound of his shout died from his ears. A voice, muted, said, "Noel?"

"Kyra! Where are you?"

"Down below you."

"You can't get out?"

"No!! There's a trap door."

"I don't see anything."

"You're maybe standing on it."

"Oh." What, under the anvil? He moved it aside, and lifted the rug. A ring in the wood. He tugged. Locked. "What do I do?"

"Get my picks. They're in my purse."

"I don't know—"

"Just get them!"

He scrambled around in her purse— A noise in the living room? He froze. The fridge rumbled into a steady purr. He grasped the picks. "Got them. Now what?"

"Get—I think it's a two and a ten."

Noel separated them. "How do you tell a two?"

"The one with the sort of double chink, right by the tip."

Noel examined the picks. Some were double, some triple, others wedged. "I don't know—" A squeak from the living room. It's nothing, just a wooden house, it shifts.

"Okay— Let me think."

Small creak from the bedroom. He picked up the anvil. Heavy bastard. Slowly he stepped through the doorway. Nothing in the bedroom. To the living room. Just old wooden floors.

He heard Kyra calling, "Noel, for god's sake get back here!"

How to pry the trap open? Smash it with the anvil? He looked around the room, maybe a crowbar? Not even an axe. In the bedroom? In the drawers of the chest? Sweaters, underwear, stationery. On top of the chest, keys! He grabbed the ring, dashed into the closet. "Okay, I found some keys. Hang on."

Nine keys, half of them shaped wrong. Two fit in, wouldn't turn. A third— "It turns!"

"Twist the ring and lift."

He did, and saw her face a metre down. Holding her camera she climbed up, shading her eyes from the sudden light. He grabbed her hand, lifted her out, hugged her for an instant.

Kyra grabbed her purse and slid her feet into her boots. "Bless you, Noel." She shivered.

"Let's get out of here."

"Hold on." Kyra closed the trap, replaced the rug.

"Right." And Noel put the anvil back on top.

They reached the door, looked, saw no one, down the stairs, through the wooded land to the neighbor's drive. "Wait," Noel said. "Lucille drove me here, she's parked next door."

"So am I." Kyra stopped. "What does she know?"

"That I hadn't heard from you since yesterday morning."

"Let's leave it that way. Come on."

In the drive, Lucille's TR6 faced the road. Noel reached her. "She's okay, it's okay."

"But what's going on?"

"I'll explain later, I'll call you. Just get out of here."

"But—"

They ran to the Taurus. Kyra handed him the key, got in the passenger side. Lucille, behind them, hadn't moved. Noel waved to Lucille: back out! Slowly the Triumph did. Noel followed, close. Both cars drove past the Gallery driveway slowly. A hundred metres beyond, Noel floored the accelerator, passed Lucille, reached sixty, seventy. To hell with island speed limits.

TWENTY-TWO

A RED-TAILED HAWK, gliding between the house and a grove of curving arbutus trees, caught Pyotr Rabinovich's eye. His glance followed the bird to a perch high in a tree. A cool wind swept down the channel. Protected by the closed glass door he took pleasure in the bright light and the blue water beyond the grove.

He would not soon be back to Gabriola, and that saddened him. So setting the Gallery and its environs as a mind-picture was important. Because at this moment something was off, wrong. Normally he understood Rosie well. The brother stood transparent, each of his motives clear on his face. The quandary, then, remained Artemus. True, the man had his own fortune. But to spend one's investments when new money could come in so easily? Another WASP idiosyncrasy. As to Tam Gill's argument that ever fewer schools-of were coming onto the market, perhaps he was right. He'd ask Herm 5 to look into it.

Kyra's Taurus arrived at the ferry lineup. No ferry. "Shit." Kyra slouched, cursed again, pulled her hand through her scraggly hair, panicked that a van bearing Tam would instantly be next in line. No, she told herself. She turned to Noel. "Hi."

He leaned her way. "God, you had me scared."

She croaked a small laugh. "I was scared too."

"Did anybody—hurt you?"

"Just my ego."

He reached out, took her hand. "Must've worked you over pretty hard, then."

She covered his hand with her other. "They didn't have to. I was stupid."

"But why did they lock you in?"

"I'll tell you. In a minute."

"As soon as they find out you're gone—"

"Sometimes I hate islands, nowhere to hide—"

"Maybe we should head over to the RCMP office and—"

"No! We can't. We mustn't."

"We could leave, go down some dirt road, come back later. They won't cover every ferry."

"We've got to get off the island." She stared out across the water. "Meanwhile we're sitting here. Two ducks." She shuddered. "They're dangerous."

"The Marchands?"

"Yeah, but they know a guy who's way more dangerous. Tam said he'd kill you or Dad if I said anything."

"About what?" Noel asked.

"The basement. It's Tam second studio. He paints his own schools-of paintings there. I saw one in process."

"We rejected that possibility. How does he get away with it?"

"I don't know," said Kyra. "But we've got a bigger problem than that."

"The dangerous friend."

"The nearby dangerous friend. Tam said he was right there in the house."

"Oh my god. Rabinovich."

"What?"

"I just saw him," Noel said. "Heard him. Recognized him from his award picture."

"Well, Tam said this friend kills people who get in his way. And the Marchands are working for him."

Noel considered this. "You mean, like Roy Dempster?"

She shook her head. "No. I think Tam and Rose killed him. Tam, really."

"And Artemus?"

"I don't think Artemus could kill anything."

"But why Tam? And Rose?"

"If Dempster found the basement and saw what I saw—"

Noel considered this. "No, it doesn't feel right." He told her about searching for her. He included his guess that, from overhearing the Marchands at breakfast, their powerful friend, Rabinovich, had organized the break-in at Noel's condo.

She leaned against the headrest. "I should've had that damn cell-phone with me."

"It mightn't have worked down there. You up to filling me in?"

"I'll try." She told him, from the truncated interview with Artemus to Tam's deal of silence and threat, killing Noel or destroying her father. With each mention of Gill a roll of nausea took her stomach, heaves of disgust. Suddenly she threw the door open and breathed deeply. That pig had been inside her! She gagged, leaped out, and threw up. After a few seconds she straightened, tears in her eyes. "Water. In my purse." He got it for her. She rinsed out her mouth, wiped her lips, got back in the car. "Thank you." They sat silently for half a minute. She said, eyes shut, "Now you tell me what you know."

A small press on her hand. "You sure?"

"Pretty sure."

"Well. I think Rose is shipping out merchandise in two-centimetre cylinders."

"About an inch." She told him about the picture-frame hollows.

"Yes. Maybe. I had the greenhouse photos developed. Opium in cylinders?"

"Could be." Kyra opened her eyes. "And I've got more photos. From Tam's basement."

The ferry approached the dock. Noel looked behind. A long row of cars. A Gallery van?

"The frames." She thought back. "Tam picked them up. From the float plane. They came from somewhere in Oregon. North Bend. Sinbad—no. Sultan. That's it. Sultan Suppliers."

"I'll track them down."

"You sure it's opium? Not heroin?"

"Heroin takes complicated refinement. Anyway, it's not like her. She plays with flowers."

Kyra considered this. "She modifies poppies?"

"Could be."

"Yeah. The highest grade product. Her kind of perfection: I have developed the perfect flower, I am perfect." Kyra sat back. "The Mounties could get them for dealing."

"Shipping it across an international border—"

Her head drooped. "I can't think. I'm wiped."

"I bet."

She rested her head on the headrest and closed her eyes. They waited in silence.

Noel watched people walk off the ferry, followed by the cars. "We'll load in a minute." Foot passengers boarded. The ferry worker signaled. They drove on. Safe. Well, safer.

After they'd waved Rab goodbye, Artemus had turned to his wife and brother-in-law. "Now will someone please tell me what's going on here?"

"What do you mean?" Rose spoke quietly.

"All this about the European Union, that's crazy! Art goes to the highest bidder."

"Which we no longer are," said Tam. "I had a call from Dorstel. Both he and Enfrescu have gone over to the Rijksmuseum consortium. They've got the cash."

"We can compete. Rab has lots of money."

"It's cultural politics, the way Dorstel explained it." Tam hung up the dish towel. "European patrimony—they know the importance of hanging on to their cultural heritage. We don't know much about that in North America." He shrugged. "Anyway, we'll never be able to buy cheap again."

"I can't believe it."

"So all decisions are taken out of our hands. It's best this way." Rose held out her arms

Artemus leaned down and kissed the top of her head. "Well, I don't like it." He headed up the staircase.

Rose said to Tam, "We'll wait till the ferry's gone. We don't want Rab coming back."

"You just trying to put this off?"

"Did you really have a call from Dorstel?"

"I made it up as I went along. Let's walk around the drive." He explained the agreement he'd suggested to Kyra, the threat if she didn't accept.

"Empty threats. Let's hope she's good and scared."

A half hour, and she rolled her way to the cabin, Tam beside her. Up the ramp to the deck, into the front room, the bedroom— "Uh-oh."

"What?"

Tam pointed to the floor. "No purse, no boots."

"Open it. Quick."

To the breaker box, lights on. Unlock. He climbed down. One blanket, one half-eaten sandwich, no Kyra. She found the key in his overalls! He ran to check the pockets. The key was there. How— He climbed up. "Gone."

"How?"

"Beats me." Tam, trying to sound casual.

"This is crazy. She couldn't just disappear."

"Nope."

"Someone had to release her. Somebody broke into your studio."

"Yeah. Who. Her partner?"

"Tam, she's out there. How badly did you scare her?"

"A lot."

"But you don't know so. Would she go to the Mounties?"

"I don't know."

"You don't know much, do you? Are you this stupid about all your girlies?"

"Hey."

"Come on." She rolled to the door so fast her foot rest bumped it.

"Where?"

"To the house."

"Why?"

"To greet the police when they arrive." Each word clipped. She backed up. Tam opened the door. She rolled through. "Or whoever arrives."

"You think the police?"

"Depends on how well you scared her."

He locked the door and jogged after his sister. "You think Rab might come back?"

"If she tells him about your forgeries to save herself, damn right he will."

"She doesn't know anything about Rab."

"She will."

"Rab wouldn't kill you." He strode beside her.

"He'd send a Herm." She approached the drive, Tam barely keeping up. "No, likely Rab himself. He'd want to watch you, at that moment." She slowed. "And me, too. A last time."

The rented Taurus was first on, center lane, fine view, Nanaimo ahead, the mountains beyond. The *Quinsam* chugged across the water. In front of them a young couple, arms about each other. An elderly man, his dog straining its leash as if wanting to swim ahead and tug the ferry on. A man with a motorcycle grooming his machine. A tall man, totally bald, his head glowing, wearing a leather jacket and expensive flannel slacks, walked to the front. He faced forward, in control of all that lay before him.

Noel gestured with his chin. "Uh, see him? Baldy?"

She giggled. "Basket-bald."

"That's Rabinovich."

She slouched low in her seat. "Oh god."

"You hiding from him?"

"Seems like a great idea."

"He doesn't know you. He's never seen you."

"You're right." She pulled up to half-sitting.

He grinned. "Maybe I should go make casual conversation with him."

"Are you crazy?"

"Ask him how he liked Gabriola."

"You are crazy." She grabbed his arm. "Maybe he saw your picture when he broke into your condo."

"He wouldn't. He sent someone."

Question: What's worse than being locked in a concrete basement with no light and decreasing air and a lamb sandwich that could be poisoned?

Answer: Easy. Escaping, and knowing there's no escape.

"Climb into the tub. I'll see what's to eat." Noel pushed down the plug, turned on the water, threw in a handful of special bath salts that bubbled—he never used the stuff—and adjusted the temperature. "Go." He tugged her up from the sofa. She staggered off.

He checked his answering machine. Albert. "I'm in the office all day. Call."

Damn. He'd completely forgotten Albert. Albert answered on the second ring. Noel reported his conversation with Lucille—Jerry Bannister, the binoculars in Danny's shed.

For a moment the line stayed silent. Then: "Thank you. And what about Kyra?"

"Oh, she's okay." Not a story for Albert. "But she was gone all night. I was worried."

"She's a big girl, right? And remember, Noel, not everyone's gonna leave you."

"I know." Albert was Cop again, with his Pop-Cop Psychology. "Thanks." Noel set the phone down and got two snifters from the cabinet. He checked his watch. Not too early, not on a day like today. He poured two fingers of brandy into each. He sorted through the freezer: turkey soup, July 27; *boeuf bourguignon*, no date; pasta w/ Eng. Chesh. & cream, August 15. Perfect, closest thing to comfort food, macaroni and cheese. Into the microwave. All the while the brunt of Tam Gill's threat hovered. Noel figured they weren't done with Eaglenest.

He picked up her glass, and knocked. No answer. He opened the bathroom door a crack. "Here. A drink in the tub." No answer. "Kyra?" He peeked in. Shampoo a froth in her hair. Damn it, she was asleep under bubbles. Feet propped on the tap end. "Wake up, Kyra." She opened her eyes. "Rinse your hair." In the kitchen lunch had defrosted. He tore lettuce into the salad bowl. He was hungry.

Kyra lying in the tub, Kyra here safe. Noel knocked firmly on the door. "You out yet? Or I'm coming in!"

A loud splash. "Hmmm?"

"Sleeping in the tub is unsafe. Get out and I'll feed you."

"Ummh, coming—" She felt weepy, sleepy, sudsy. She sat up, pulled herself to the tap, turned it on, rinsed her hair. Legs, arms, gone limp. She pulled the plug, knelt, held on to the faucet, stood sort of, dried sort of, pulled on Noel's dressing gown, picked up the film cartridge that had clunked from her bra to the floor when she'd gotten undressed, staggered out. "Here."

"What's this?"

"Photos of what I saw. Another roll still in my camera."

He stuck it into his pocket. "I'll take them in. Eat this."

"What."

"Macaroni and cheese."

She ate half the macaroni, not really macaroni, way more subtle, but okay macaroni. Even the word comforted her. Three mouthfuls of salad and her eyes were closing. Noel's hands pulled her up, steered her, his voice far away, Sleep. She did as she hit the bed.

Noel finished her macaroni, and the salad. Dirty dishes to the dishwasher. The snifters on the counter? He combined their contents, carried one glass to the living room and lay on the couch, feet on one arm, head on the other. To you, Kyra. On being alive. He sipped. He felt a slowly increasing glow of elation: someone to worry about again. And after worry comes relief. It felt good.

He took the film in, ordered triplicates. He spent part of the afternoon watering and deadheading Brendan's flowers. He needed to talk with Kyra, get Lyle and Jerry straight in his head. And Jerry and Roy. At suppertime he ordered Indian food for two. But Kyra slept on.

⸺

"Never say my name. Not to me or anyone. Call me Partner."

That's what he'd said to Jerry. What a weirdo, Jerry had figured. But if that's the way he wanted it, well what the hell, eh? Nobody, but nobody, had seeds as good as, uh, Partner.

"Never say my name." He'd said that at the faggy restaurant where Roy saw them talking and eating together. Then a couple days later Roy comes up to him saying, I'm here to save you, Jerry, save you from being a homo, the man was a homo and Jerry'd get infected. Funniest thing Jerry ever heard. Only Roy wasn't laughing. Jerry wondered if Roy'd gone bonkers.

Jerry had said to the man, "And what if I say it? Your name?"

Then electricity shot out of the man's eyes as if he were being electrocuted. The man whispered, "Late at night, on the street or in your bed, I'll get you." And a smile that said, Partner does not lie.

Nope, no reason to mention the guy's name to anyone. Finish the harvesting, give him his half, never see the guy again. Jerry whistled while he worked. The tune had been haunting him. He smoked, too. The male plants were great this year, already a couple of weeks ago when dumb Roy had picked those two. Wrong. Roy'd torn them out by the roots. The asshole. Pulled out a couple females too, getting bushy on top, not yet bushy enough. Dumb fuck Roy. Back in the old days, you could talk to Roy. Should never have talked about using the land in the clearcut. But hell, he'd only wanted real bad to remember the old days with Roy, go back to before the religious stuff fucked up Roy's head. Maybe if he hadn't been stoned he mightn't have told Roy. Roy'd been so pissed off about Jerry being stoned, what a goddamn asshole. But not so assholish as Roy pulling the plants out, for pissake.

Jerry glanced about. Three black garbage sacks full, maybe a quarter of the crop. Jerry stood, stretched, breathed deep. Great air, yessir. He lit up again and toked. Goddamn stupid Roy, fuckin' idiot. Jerry whipped another bag open, knelt beside a row of fine little girlies, a few buds still clearish whitish but maybe two-three times that many going nice and brown. He should've waited another coupla days. But the cops, had to be the cops, who else uses equipment like that? they found the patch. Except they didn't know whose patch it was. That's why they needed him on camera when he harvested. So he had to jump the gun. Stupid cops.

Half and half, sure, but not till Jerry took out a quarter of the crop first. Gotta even things up. Give the guy a full half when Jerry did all the work? Shit, no way. Jerry giggled. Guy didn't even have a place to plant, all he had was the seeds. And his drying shed. Thanks, Partner.

As if Jerry couldn't read the terrain. You don't spend your life on an island and not know the terrain, ground trampled under those videocams gave them right away. Easy, easiest thing in the world, deactivate the cams each time he came up, do the weeding and watering, reactivate and, yeah! home free. Tomorrow he'd tell the man how astute he'd been. Astute, yeah, damn astute. He'd found all four of the videocams, one for each point of the compass. Mounties thinking they were smart. So dumb.

Jerry whistled the tune again. In his head he'd changed the words. So he hummed, to the tune of "American Pie"— Buy, buy, the best dope you can buy. Then he went back to whistling it. Faith Bearing makes you stupid. Fart Bearing was more like it. Jesus says you shouldn't smoke dope, says Roy. Well imagine that. So, says Roy, I can't let you harvest those plants. But Jerry managed to cool Roy out—okay, Roy, okay, we'll let it go to seed. Off they went, both of them. Except, a few minutes later, Jerry knew Roy hadn't cooled out. So Jerry jumped in his truck, up here to the plot, and in the middle of the blackberries, there was Roy. Half a dozen uprooted plants. Some gorgeous females. Enough destruction to make you go blind mad. Jerry didn't even know where the rock in his hand had come from. Or how it made contact with Roy's head. Or why Roy fell so hard. And didn't move. Jerry knew Roy'd wake up soon, right then Jerry had to save those plants, get them in the ground. He got them back. Roy was still asleep. Jerry shook Roy. He didn't wake up. Jerry took his pulse. Other hand maybe. No pulse. Oh shit.

Buy, buy, the best dope you can buy. Buy, buy—

Albert let the phone ring three times before he picked it up. "Matthew."

"Corporal Yardley here."

"Yes, Jim?"

"The pot perp, Gerald Arnold Bannister—"

Yardley the stickler. Oh well, good to have some of that on the Force.

"—he located the usual four videocams again, deactivated them, 19 to 2300 hours—"

Albert hated the international clock. Getting old, guy.

"—but again he didn't find the fifth. We got some first-rate shots."

Yardley sounded chuffed, and well he should. "Good work, Corporal. Got his record?"

"Four priors, sir. One conviction, assault. Suspended sentence, 1997. Delivery boy, low level enforcer. He'll go in this time."

"I want him, and I want his contact. But mainly I want to lean on him for the Dempster murder."

"You got real evidence?"

"Yep." He shut his eyes. "First for trafficking. And some new links."

"Yes, sir."

Albert recalled a beautiful barred owl that had decided to investigate camera one a few days ago, activating the cam. A shame to end the stakeout. "What are the shots on video five?"

"Great, sir! Bannister lugging reams of heavy bulgy plastic bags out of the blackberries." Yardley was in full chuff. A little chuff was fine but keep it in control, man. "Go on."

"Hot work lugging them out all the way."

"Hot the first of October? At night?"

"Well—"

"Surveillance?"

"Sir. All bases covered." A pause, a breath, still excitement. "You want to arrest him soon as he tries to leave?"

"No, Corporal. I've got things organized this end. Don't lose him, but don't spook him either. Once we've got him, go back to the blackberry patch and secure it."

"Sir."

Albert hung up. He sort of liked the sirs.

———

Jerry Bannister exhaled. He lay, alone, on his bed. All done, all of it out of the ground, all safe and hidden. And four days ahead of schedule. Tomorrow he'd drive it over to Nanaimo, deliver it to the man four days early. Well, not all, a quarter for himself, he'd dry that here. The rest they'd dry in the man's shed. Then Jerry would take his half. Or let the man sell some of it for him, nobody could smoke all that not even giving it away. Surprise time tomorrow. Jerry hadn't talked to the man more than a couple of times since the night he'd called him, saying Roy was lying up there by the clearcut dead and all. The man was pissed, shit was he pissed. Ditch the body the man had screamed, get it away from the clearcut! Where? Anywhere, just away from there! Suddenly Jerry knew exactly where. Down where Roy worked! That was funny. He figured the man would find it funny too. Tomorrow he'd ask him if he'd thought it was funny. "Hey Lyle, was that funny or what, Roy down there dead at your favorite gallery?" Except he wouldn't call him anything except Partner: "Hey Partner, was that ever funny." The last thing the man had asked Jerry was, How long till you harvest? And Jerry had told him. Except now the harvest was four days early. Gonna be a big surprise.

TWENTY-THREE

NOEL, AT 6:50 in the morning, heard Kyra making noises. He dressed and headed for the kitchen. Awake at last, was she? He had to talk. Out loud, not in his head. The parade had gone on for hours: Lyle and Jerry, Jerry and Roy. Lyle and Roy? All three together? Sleep had brought little clarity.

Ah, Kyra was busy with eggs, milk, bowl, bread in the frying pan— French toast, her specialty. A bowl of fruit salad on the counter next to butter, sugar-cinnamon mix, plates, cutlery.

She gave him a brilliant smile. "Good morning. Coffee?" Without waiting, she poured.

"Thanks. Feel okay?"

"Yep. And ready to eat."

"Right." He looked out the window at a thin grey sky and back to Kyra flipping toast over, checking the underside. "Nice and golden."

"Of course. I had three husbands."

"Look. We have to talk."

"About my three husbands?"

"About this whole case."

"Yep." She plopped a slice of toast on his plate. "Here, eat."

He took a forkful. "Great." Another. "This is about Jerry, Lyle, Roy. I'm betting they're all three connected." As he ate he tried to clarify a hypothesis: Lyle contracts Jerry to set up a grow operation. Jerry plants on some land at the edge of the clearcut, Roy finds out about it, something goes wrong, Roy gets killed. A yardman who's born again, a slob of a doper, a high-style painter. The first, dead. One or both of the others, murderers?

"Maybe," said Kyra.

"Just trying to make sense of things. Don't dismiss it out of hand."

"Okay."

"You sure you're feeling okay?" He stared at her face.

"Yep. Mostly." She thought for a moment. "Rabinovich is scary. His power. But that's kind of abstract. It's Tam who's really got to me."

Noel set his hand on hers.

"Feeling way better today than last night." She squeezed his hand. "Maybe Lyle really did contract Jerry for some clearing."

Noel told her about Lyle's place. Nothing to be cleared. Just a large shed. No windows.

"Yeah. Like Tam's basement."

"So what's the shed for? A studio? Something more covert?" Noel took his plate and cutlery to the sink. "Maybe I should just ask him."

"Ask what? Lyle, did you and Jerry set up a grow-op? Lyle, did you and Jerry kill Roy?"

Silence for a moment. "Yeah."

Kyra rinsed dishes and set them in the washer. Noel made fresh coffee. Cup at his side, at his laptop, he typed: Wednesday, October 3. "Back to Eaglenest."

"Tam says we remain silent about everything at Eaglenest, what we know about them and The Hermitage. Or some accident happens to someone we love, you, my father, whoever."

Noel typed.

"Tam voiced the threat but they're all in it. Rabinovich works at a level I've never run into." She squeezed her eyes closed then opened them.

"How about a walk? I need to be outside."

She's better, Noel thought, but nowhere near a 100 percent. "Let's go."

The phone rang. Noel answered. "Okay, thanks." He disconnected. "The locksmith. He'll be here in fifteen minutes."

Shit. Kyra didn't know if she wanted to be by herself or not, but she wanted to be outside. But a locksmith— She put on her shoes and jacket and walked up and down the sidewalk in front of Noel's condo until a van pulled up. A man got out with a tool case. Kyra scurried upstairs after him.

———

RCMP Constable Charlotte Fredricks, posted at Silva Bay Marina, reported no large shipment loaded, no bales or crates, not on the boat wharf nor at the seaplane dock. Corporal Jim Yardley received similar negative responses from both the water taxi and Page's Marina.

Inspector Albert Matthew fully expected the suspect to leave the island on the ferry, but he covered all the bases.

They waited till the locksmith left, and went for late lunch at the seaplane pub. Then they strolled for more than an hour along the harbor walkway to the Departure Bay ferry and back. They didn't talk much, which was fine. Many large boats in the marinas. Noel kept the Lyle-Jerry-Roy relationship hidden from conscious thought, Kyra felt the Gill-Marchand-Rabinovich quandary go quiet. After four when they got back. "Meet you upstairs," Kyra said. "I'll go get the photos."

Climbing the stairs Noel was hit by a moment of concern. He checked his new lock. All fine. He unlocked. The rug lay at its correct slant. In the bedroom Brendan's photo stood as before. He turned on his computer. No problems. Okay, Sultan Suppliers. An old firm, recently bought by an art supplies conglomerate, Artifacts International. They mass-produce copies of ethnic art, special prices for museum gift shops. And ornate frames. Two more minutes of probing, and there it was: Artifacts International, owned by Latuis Interest Corp.

Kyra came in, back with her pictures of Tam's basement: the partial forgery, the old frames with slot-out backs. In triplicate.

"First rate." Noel told her about Sultan.

"So neat." She sat on the couch. "Think we should contact the Marchand-Gills, reassure them that we're keeping our side of the bargain?"

"Or let them sweat."

They sat in silence, weighing the options, till Kyra spoke up. "I say we call."

Noel gave a long sigh, and nodded. "You talk."

She went to the phone. "Hey, you've got a couple of messages."

"Play them, okay?"

Kyra pressed play. "Noel, it's Lucille. I'm royally pissed off at you. What's going on with the Dempster murder? Is Rose Gill involved? I need information. Crime makes a better story than this piece on alternative justice I would have to fall back on. My bones are down to their last ounce of patience. Get on the horn and call me back!"

"Oh damn! I completely forgot."

The next message played. A few seconds of silence, then a distorted whisper: "... remember the Buckland fiasco, be cool ..." Another second, then the disconnect.

They stared at each other. Noel said, "Shit."

Kyra took him by the elbow and edged him down on the couch. "Tell me."

"Not Gill's style of intimidation. Two different people making threats."

"Has to be."

"Right." An empty part in him was filling with anger. "So do I wait for his next call? Or another obit? Or worse?"

She got up and poured him a Scotch. And one for herself. "To hell with him."

He topped his off with water. "Do I have a choice?" He glanced at Kyra's photos of Tam's cellar. "Couldn't be someone from Eaglenest. How would they know about Buckland?"

"Anybody could check you out. Lots of publicity when you wrote that series. Didn't Marchand know you'd been a reporter?"

Noel shrugged, sipped the Scotch. "Could it have been Marchand, disguising his voice?"

"Didn't sound like Marchand. Or Tam."

Noel flipped through the photos. "What do they have to protect?" He stared at a picture of Tam's easel. "They're pretty much like any entrepreneurs. Artemus buys for less and sells for more, Tam works for him and paints on the side, Rose develops a product to market. They have a Foundation that supports small sustainable projects. It gives them tax breaks."

"You make it sound like a mom and pop shop." She laughed without humor. "What about the poppies. Rose develops small quantities, opium-wise. Really strong stuff?"

He got up. "Let's go back to their threat." He paced. "Try it differently. One," ticking off his index finger, "we have no proof for anything. Small amounts of opium maybe in frames for The Hermitage. Two," middle finger, "Tam paints in many styles, including Old Masters, but if he doesn't sign them are they technically forgeries? Three," ring finger, "maybe Artemus has actually bought some art from Europe that has been authenticated. Four, they've somehow figured a way to get

Gill's paintings through the authentication process. Five," the thumb, "the stuff Marchand sells to The Hermitage might or might not include a Gill." He turned, pacing hard. "Six," the other index, "Peter Rabinovich, a friend of the family, is their best customer and owns a luxury casino-hotel in Vegas. Six and a half," Noel stuck up his left thumb knuckle, "likely, and we can only guess, he has control of more things than we've ever thought of." He came to rest by the window. "Such as picture frame companies."

"And seven." Kyra took over, "We've fulfilled our obligation to our client and the rest is none of our business."

Noel whirled about. "Oh yes it is. Seven, eight, nine and ten, those are big threats. Threatening us is bad, threatening people we love is diabolical. They control us with threats."

"Go on."

"We have two options." He nodded, agreeing with himself. "We let them know we'll abide by their demands, hope Tam and Co. honor the bargain, report to Lucas that we couldn't learn anything more, get on with our lives. Or—we defuse the threat."

"Let's take a step back. What if Rose isn't selling drugs. What it she gives them away. Where's the criminal offense?"

"Producing opium. Even in tiny amounts. It's like a pot plant on the window ledge. They're both illegal."

"It's a law you broke, too. For Brendan."

"Yeah but come on, the police are looking for heroin from Thailand, Colombian coke. Terrorists making bombs. Half a dozen vials of opium from Gabriola? Technically illegal, but get serious. Hey. Did you return the rental car?"

"Oh shit!" She leapt up, looked at her watch. "Too late. I'm into a full third day."

—————

Rose wheeled her way up the ramp to Tam's deck. Tam opened a beer for her, and one for himself. "More than twenty-four hours."

Rose said, "You should make sure she's agreed to be silent."

"Let's not provoke them. Easier to talk in a couple of days."

Rose said nothing.

"What's with Artemus?"

"His usual self."

Tam raised his beer. "To the silence of detectives."

"Two days." She sipped.

———

Okay, Noel thought, how do we break the control of Tam's threat? Superior force wouldn't do it, not from say the Mounties, bring them in and the threat becomes reality. Force from us? Go in with pistols blazing? Not likely.

And the other thing, Lyle and Jerry. Either or both as murderers? A circumstance that grew out of control? Noel couldn't see Lyle losing control. Could Lyle hurt someone with cold-blooded intent? Unlikely. Jerry could lose control. Sue had reported the argument between Jerry and Roy. If, say, Jerry and Lyle were in the grow-op together, and Jerry had accidentally killed Roy, and gone to Lyle for help, then Lyle was involved. After the fact. So, talk to Jerry? Put it to him, see how he responds? Except if I've guessed right, Jerry's lack of control could make me suddenly as dead as Roy. Bad idea. Lay it out to Lyle? Make a deal with Albert, get Lyle to turn Jerry in, give evidence against Jerry. A suspended sentence for Lyle? Do I care enough for Lyle, to help him like this?

Lyle, involved in murder? One way to find out.

Why can't I leave it alone. To find a little justice for Roy? Unlikely.

Noel called Albert. The machine. No sense leaving a message. Kyra was off food shopping. They were eating in tonight. A note: Gone to have a chat with Lyle. Back soon. N.

Down the stairs, into the garage. Tires okay. He drove out, headed south. It'd be dark in an hour. How to start this conversation? No, let it happen in the doing.

He stopped the car in front of Lyle's house. Up to the latticed porch. He rang the bell. "Swanee River." He sighed.

The door opened. "Noel. What a surprise."

"Hello, Lyle."

"And what brings you by this evening?"

"To talk to you. May I come in?"

"Of course." Lyle stepped back and Noel entered. Lyle led him along the hall. Noel noted a study on this side, a bedroom on that. They entered the largest room, to the right of the kitchen, the living room.

"Have a seat." Lyle gestured at a fat brown leather chair.

It matched the sofa against the far wall. Two other plush patterned chairs about the room, both away from the wall as if in obeisance to the heavy sofa. A glassed-in fireplace. Half a dozen paintings, three of which Noel recognized as Lyle's. A thick green carpet. "Thanks." Noel sat.

"A drink?"

"Okay."

They agreed on Scotch, neat. Lyle poured and handed Noel one of two heavy cut-crystal glasses. "To what do I owe the honor, and so on?"

"I need to talk to you."

"So you said." He grinned. "Should I put on the soft music?"

"A serious talk."

"What? More tires slashed? More phone calls? I hope not something worse."

"No, luckily." Mention today's call? Remembering it had suddenly put Noel on edge.

"No obituaries? No more computer attacks? Hard to believe, Noel."

"That the guy's leaving me alone?"

"That someone would mess up your computer. I find that implausible."

Something weird about Lyle. Could work out okay, though. "Why implausible?"

"No no, not important, you came to talk." He sipped. "About another of your problems."

"Actually no. I came to talk about you." Noel sipped in return. "Your problem."

"About me? What an intriguing subject."

Noel leaned forward. "Actually to help you, if I can."

"Help me with—?"

"With the trouble you're in."

"Trouble?" Lyle raised his eyebrows.

"It has to do with Jerry Bannister."

Lyle grimaced. "I've decided not to paint him. He's impossible to be with."

"But he's your pot-growing buddy, isn't he."

A strain now on Lyle's face. "Bannister?"

Noel nodded. "In the grow-op. And possibly also in Roy's death."

"You're crazy."

Noel shook his head. "No, sensible. And I can call a Mountie friend, get him to make a deal with you."

"A deal?"

"I think you're an accomplice, you could be charged with murder. You have to tell the RCMP what happened, how Roy died, what Jerry Bannister's role in this is."

While Noel spoke, Lyle stared into his glass. Now he stood. "Let me see if I understand what you're saying here. I made a deal with Bannister to grow pot?"

"Right. You smoke the best dope. Best is what you grow yourself. You offered me some at my place, remember? And you provided Brendan with some good stuff."

Lyle nodded. "Brendan. Yes. But Brendan was a friend. A very very dear friend."

Dear? "Look, you were in this with Bannister, and he killed Roy. Likely by accident."

"This is crazy." Lyle paced to the window. "How can you think I'd get involved in growing pot, let alone murder?"

"I think it was an accident. Maybe you weren't even there."

"Of course I wasn't there." Lyle marched to the fireplace. "There was no there for me not to be at." Back to the window. "Grow pot with that pig Bannister? For shitsake." He finished the Scotch. "You couldn't be more wrong."

He'll react soon. "I'm right. Admit it."

"Come on," pacing again, "I could no more" striding behind the chairs "have been involved in murder than—"

The last words Noel heard because a crystal whisky glass smashed into his head just behind the right temple.

———

Kyra put down the groceries. She was hungry. How could she be hungry after a late lunch? No sign of Noel. His phone caught her eye. He has to change his phone number. She went to the bathroom, looked in the mirror, applied new lipstick.

The door to his room stood ajar. She glanced in. Nope. In the living room? No. She checked the little balcony. She called, "Noel? Noel!"

———

Inside Noel's head, the pain pounded hard. I'm alive, he thought. He tried to touch the place of the pain but his hand had gone wrong, he couldn't move it. The other hand? No. But he felt something with his right hand, with his left too. Then he realized, each hand felt the other. In fact couldn't move from the other. Where was he? He'd gone to see Lyle. He said, "Lyle?" but it came out, "Mmmnbb" because tape covered his mouth, tearing at his lips and cheek.

He was lying on the floor. On his back. Under him, a carpet. He rolled to an elbow, tried to push himself to standing. His feet were connected to each other. He slumped down.

Lyle said, "Good morning. Or rather, good night."

Noel said, "Mmuuyuu dnnnn," which should have been, What're you doing?

"Why did you have to be such a fool, Noel?" Lyle sounded nothing like the Lyle who'd cheerily designed a business for Kyra and him.

Noel mmyed.

"This isn't good." His tone was flat.

"Nnnnnn—"

"Are you religious, Noel? Funny, all the time I've known you and I don't have a clue. Do you believe in an afterlife? Where you'll see Brendan again? If you believe, grunt once. If not, twice."

Noel grunted twice.

"That's good. Because if you did meet Brendan again, I'd be jealous. Extremely." He bent down, staring at Noel's face. "Again."

Noel closed his eyes. Oh shit.

"You never knew about Brendan and me. Just before you arrived on the scene. Brendan never spoke of previous intimates. And who else could tell you? Me?" He laughed.

Triple shit.

"Here's a choice. Die knowing why you'll die, or die in ignorance. Which would you prefer?"

Die? Die?

"If you want to know, grunt once. If not, twice."

Keep him talking, keep him talking. Noel grunted once.

"Good. Don't go away, I'll just get myself another Scotch. Sorry I can't offer you one. I'll only be a moment, I have to get a new glass." He laughed lightly. "Since you broke my first."

Noel worked the tape around his wrists. No give. And his feet were wrapped so tightly they'd gone numb. Multiple shit. Why hadn't he told Albert's machine where he'd gone, what he was doing. He closed his eyes against a surge of panic.

Lyle's voice, quietly menacing: "Now, the famous five journalistic questions. You surely remember them. From your one-time profession. Until you decided you didn't want to be a public person any longer, until your press friends turned on you, exposed you. All those mistakes, how dumb. What was the name of that woman? Oh yes. Buckland. Tanja Buckland. So dumb." He sighed. "Are you wondering, how do I know these things? I like to know my subjects thoroughly." He shook his head. "Too bad Brendan didn't see how stupid you were. Are."

Unbelievable. Who is this Lyle? Changed so completely so fast?

"The five questions. First, how. How it will be done. In this manner." Noel felt a cold tickle on his nose. He opened his eyes. The tip of a broad-bladed knife. "It's served many purposes. Fileting fish, though it's a little large. Hacking chickens apart. It hasn't entered human flesh. At least not to my knowledge. Ooh—now that's wrong, I cut myself once slicing an onion. Wrong tool for the job."

A moment of silence. Then: "Superior Scotch. You I served a common blend. Why waste this lovely Glenmorangie." Silence. "Next, where. Let's do where and when together, shall we? Not here, not now, it'd be a mistake, blood stains on my carpet. Don't you agree? When it's dark, we'll go for a ride. Where? To, let's say, the Third Nanaimo Lake. Oh, in your car, naturally. It wouldn't do to leave my tire tracks up there. Nice new tires, Noel. Then I'll bring your car back. Where? To your garage. It'll be lots easier to get into this time. From the hot tub roof took some daring. And agility too, I might add. You do have an automatic door opener, don't you?"

Noel thought: would Kyra find his note?

"And then why. I think that's out of order. Silly journalistic order. But good in order for me. Why? Because you destroyed something perfectly wonderful, Noel. What? Why, Brendan and me. There has never been a better couple. Never! We were close, intensely close. Hard to achieve such singularity of ideal and purpose between two people. And you destroyed it. One week, all it took you. Which shows your power. Your casual power." Silence. "So good, this Scotch. Ah, you may ask, why did I wait till now? You can't guess. No, you're not swift. Except in your stealth in stealing a man's lover. So I'll tell you. Because I loved Brendan. I still love Brendan. I wouldn't have hurt him. Not for the world. To harm you while he lived would be to hurt Brendan. I couldn't do that."

He's nuts. Out of his fucking head. Would Kyra find this place? Noel hadn't left an address. She'd find it in the phone book! Get here, Kyra—Shit! Lyle's number isn't listed.

"And finally, who. We both know the answer to that. You and me. I and only I could do this. It would have worked out more painfully for you if you hadn't shown up here, I'll give you that. You were going to hurt in three ways, Noel. You've felt the beginning pain of each. What three, you ask. I'll tell you. But wait, a little light, so I can watch your face." A standing lamp came on. "First, psychologically. Your panic from my calls, my breath in your ear. Clever of you to ignore them at night. But you couldn't escape your answering machine, could you. Thank you for suggesting lunch at the Crow and Gate, by the way. And now you see why I insisted on paying. You gave me such pleasure. Of course the obituary was mine, and the tires. But I've already mentioned the tires." Silence. "And devious of you to increase my challenge. Messing with your computer? It never happened. Not what I like to do. All right then, I got to you psychologically." He knelt beside Noel and whispered into his face: "Admit it. Grunt once if I got to you psychologically."

Noel grunted. Lyle disappeared from his view.

"Good. Okay, your second area of pain. Noel Franklin, private investigator. Triple I. Increasing respect for your abilities. The public Franklin once again. Exposed, known. And so, vulnerable in the light of day. When everything is visible."

Noel's glance shot to the window. Getting dark. Damn! He tried to pull against the tape again, the dozenth time. Nothing gave.

"And third, emotionally. The very best. Had we gone on seeing each other, you would have fallen in love with me. Deeply, wildly. When I work at it, Noel, I am irresistible. You were discovering this. That's why you took the initiative and invited me to that pub. You'd come to trust me, to tell me about the dangerous things that were happening to you. You needed my help. You believed I could help, I was a friend. In a few months, maybe only weeks, your passion for me would've been boundless. I'd have allowed it for a short time. Long enough to pierce your heart. And then I'd have hurt you as only a lover can hurt." He laughed, a sad little laugh. "As you hurt me."

A long silence. Noel thought he heard Lyle's throat catch.

"Ah well, dark enough, time to go. Now you've got, once again, two choices. Either I stand you up and you sit in my office chair, it has wheels, and I roll you to your car. I'll first bring it into the driveway. We'll lay you in the back seat. Or, to assure your passivity, I can knock you out again. No, I won't destroy another glass, I'll use a blunt instrument, like the poker. Then I'll drag you out of here in my wheelbarrow. One grunt to stand, two for the poker."

Noel grunted once.

"Don't go away. I'll get the chair."

Kyra arrived in time to catch the last few words of Lyle's speech, badly muffled, from the edge of the living room window. She'd seen Noel's note. Noel surely wasn't going to confront Lyle! Yes he was. She'd tried to locate Lyle's address, only a phone number in Noel's address book, nothing in the phone book, couldn't figure where on his computer he might have it. Then, an idea! She called Artemus Marchand. She gave her voice a bit of a Yiddish accent. Yes, interested in acquiring a painting by Lyle Sempken. Nothing at the Eaglenest Gallery? A shame, she was in Nanaimo for only a day, did Mr. Marchand have Mr. Sempken's address? Yes, she understood that Mr. Marchand was agent for all Mr. Sempken's work, no desire to cheat anyone. She simply wished to make her choice from what she could see of Mr. Sempken's. Marchand gave her the address.

She'd looked around the apartment for some kind of weapon. A hammer? She spotted a carving knife first and dropped it into her purse. The butt stuck out. So be it. She found a map, figured where Lyle's address should be, ran to her car and sped to Angus Drive. Yes, Noel's Honda. But the house seemed dark. No one here? She crept around the carport past a big old car to the back. A weak light came from a rear room. She saw Lyle standing, sipping a drink, staring down, talking. Noel on the floor? Then Lyle left the room. She snuck up to the window, tried to glance in without revealing herself. No one. Except, on the floor, two feet, bound together with duct tape. Noel? Had to be. Damn! Why was Noel tied up? What was Lyle doing? He wouldn't hurt Noel, would he? Yes, Lyle maybe would. But not here, somewhere else. He had to get Noel away. By car? Okay, back to the carport. The carving knife. Right rear tire, farthest from the house. She speared the sidewall, hard. The knife bounced back. She set the point against the sidewall, and worked at it, fifteen seconds, thirty, forty— A small spurt of air, tiny. A bit more. A blast now, still small—

The front door opened. Lyle came out, walked down to the street, got into Noel's Honda. Kyra scurried around to the big car's front bumper and ducked low. The Honda started, backed past the drive-way, stopped, turned onto the drive and parked directly behind the old car. She heard Lyle get out and head back inside. She slipped around to the passenger side and waited, knife in hand. The back door opened. Lyle, pushing a desk chair. Someone sitting there. Noel. She walked out from behind the big car. "Stop right there."

Lyle whirled, his face a massive question. Then it warmed to a smile of pleasure. "Well well, the other half of Triple I."

"Untape him, Lyle."

"No hope of that."

"Then I'll have to." She stepped forward and raised her knife.

Noel saw Lyle step around the chair. In his hand too, a knife. He came toward her, she at him. He raised his knife and slashed for-ward. Noel shouted, "Look out!" but it came out as "Mmmnb o!" She had ducked away, thrown Lyle off-balance, lashed the knife at his free hand, missed. Lyle swung at her with his knife, she ducked under his arm and brought up her knife arm. Their forearms touched halfway between wrist and elbow. Kyra pushed. Her forearm angled below Lyle's, pushing back and up. He was swung to her right, off balance—

From out of nowhere a pickup truck turned into the driveway, head-lights illuminating the battle scene. Before Kyra could take advantage of the moment, before Lyle could regain his balance, Jerry Bannister leapt from his truck. "Hey! What the hell's going on here?"

Lyle said, "Jerry, take the knife away from this woman."

Jerry stared at Noel, at Kyra. Then at Lyle. "Her?"

"Do as I say!"

But Jerry didn't have time to. Three RCMP squad cars and two sedans swept in behind the pickup and across the front of the house. A bullhorn voice called, "Okay everyone, drop your weapons." Mounties everywhere. Albert Matthew personally cut Noel's tapes.

———

Albert took statements from Kyra and a shaky Noel. They left, Noel in his Honda. "I'm fine, I'm okay." Kyra followed in her rental. No, Noel was not okay. But he was driving adequately. They parked, they went upstairs.

"I don't think I'm up for eating much tonight," Noel said.

"Neither am I. But a Scotch would taste good."

"I have a fine single malt." He tried to laugh but his voice trembled. "I didn't get one earlier."

Kyra said, "Huh?"

Noel told her what she'd missed, Lyle's full spiel. By the time he was done his voice was stronger. "I find it hard to believe that the Lyle I had to dinner was the same Lyle as today's."

"Gonna take some time to sift through all the shit in Sempken's psyche," Kyra said.

"I guess. How about you and Tam Gill's shit?"

"I'll get over it." She nodded. "I've started."

"Damn good thing Albert was following Bannister's truck."

"You didn't trust me to save you?"

"Always good to have reinforcements."

They talked around and around it till Noel said, "One down, one to go. We still have to get out from under Gill's threat."

Kyra agreed. "You know, it occurred to me. The best thing we have on our side is exactly what they disparage."

"Which is?"

"They think we're small time. Not even mosquitoes. Gnats." She sounded only a little defensive. "They think we're cowering, heads under blankets. But if we think of smallness as a power, kind of like Tam Gill's karate, going with the force of the approach—"

"Which means we first have to get Rabinovich out of our heads. We concede we can't touch him at the level he's operating on."

"I'm in favor." Kyra sipped. "For now. Pisses me off but it's more important to defuse Tam's threat. How?"

Noel raised his glass. "We brainstorm. As usual."

By the time they quit they'd figured how to deal with the Marchands and Tam Gill. Kyra called Eaglenest.

TWENTY-FOUR

NOEL PARKED IN the ferry lot. On board, he and Kyra stayed in the car. The grey morning sky was their excuse, just too much cold autumn. Noel wore his black jacket, Kyra her Gore-Tex. She hoped she looked okay. Looking okay to Tam was important, today more than ever.

They talked in monosyllables. Talking more would expose tight nerve ends held in place by leftover anger. Best way to take on the Marchand-Gills, keep an edge honed.

The ferry slowed, approached the ramp, and slipped into place. Foot passengers disembarked, front cars off. Noel said, "Something we ought to do."

"What?"

"Figure what we don't know."

Kyra sighed. "Right."

Noel checked his watch. "Ten-twenty."

"We have ten minutes. So we keep them waiting, so what."

Ahead, their line of cars started to move. Noel turned on the engine, drove up the ramp, onto the island. Right turn after the parking lot, up the hill, back down to the water. He stopped at the pullout and turned off the engine.

"Okay," said Kyra. "What don't we know."

"If Rabinovich went back to Eaglenest."

"It didn't sound like it, when I spoke to Rose." Kyra smiled, mock-grim. She'd begun practicing it, a smile of dismissal, while in bed, in the mirror brushing her teeth, through breakfast. She had to carry the smile to Eaglenest. To keep the nausea away.

"If he is, we chicken out and go home."

"How will we know?"

"That big black Lexus. If it's there—"

"Maybe it was a rental, too."

"Any unfamiliar car, okay?" Noel thought a moment. "What else? Okay, we don't know how many of the paintings Rabinovich bought are forgeries."

"Hmmmph. Doesn't matter. It's ace of trumps either way. What else don't we know."

Noel stared at the ocean, small waves riding the surface toward shore. "Lots."

"Does it matter?"

"Who knows?"

She laughed, her stomach tight.

Six minutes later they turned into the Eaglenest grounds. A minute to park. Noel grabbed his attaché case from the back seat. Walking to the door he glanced at his watch: 10:35. He reached for the knocker as the door opened inward. Artemus Marchand, stony, silent, severe.

Marchand stepped aside. Noel passed through the doorway. Kyra followed. Noel said, "Let's try to make this nice and simple."

Marchand followed them to the living room. Rose sat in her wheelchair, her back to them. Tam, waiting but unclear for what, got up from the couch. Kyra noted a sparkle in his eye, a tautness to his movement. Consistent ability to control his image, technique on all levels.

"Hello, Kyra," he said, smiling just for her.

"Hello, Tam." She gave him the practiced smile. It held.

Noel said, "Please, everyone, have a seat." He sat in the middle of the couch, the case on his lap. Rose turned her chair. Kyra sat opposite Noel.

"And in whose house do you think you are?" Artemus muttered, and sat.

Tam, bemused, glanced from Noel to Kyra, again to Noel and remained standing.

Noel held his eye. "And Rabinovich? Back in Vegas, is he?"

Tam said, "He didn't leave us his schedule."

"No, I imagine he wouldn't." Noel took a file folder from his briefcase, opened it, glanced at the top sheet. "What I'm sure we all want," he looked from one to the other to the other, "is a win-win situation. Victories in silence. But silence about what? Well, silence from us about your activities. No. I'll call them what they are. Your crimes."

Kyra held back the smile. It would look nervous now. With good reason.

Noel checked page three in his file. He looked over to Rose. "The growing of poppies for the purpose of manufacturing opium. The sale of this opium—"

Kyra noted Rose's small dismissive outward hand gesture.

"—and the transport of opium across international borders. With a business partner in Las Vegas," casual, Noel, no proof here, "organizing and running an establishment with the intent of sale and use of such opium." He looked again from one to the other. "Activities to keep hidden."

Rose said, "We don't sell opium."

"Ah," Noel nodded. "You give it away."

"That's none of your business."

"No? But you have to tell us. How else will we know what to keep silent about?"

Artemus said, "You're being ridiculous."

Kyra turned to Rose. "Rabinovich overpaid for the oils. But he did pay full value for each unit, painting plus frame plus narrow tube insert."

Tam raised his eyes from his fingers and stared at Kyra. "Prove it."

Noel shook his head. "We don't need to. In fact, to keep our side of the agreement, we don't want to. Oh, we could prove it. It's all in this deposition—"he raised the file for them to see—"plus the bills of lading, plus the photos we have of your studio, Tam, plus another roll, Rose—"

"My lab." Rose rolled her chair to Noel's knees. "You did break into my lab."

"Sorry, Rose. But we didn't contaminate anything. We wore gloves and masks."

"You son of a bitch."

"Yes, well, these things happen when you dabble in opium."

"You stupid little people." She glared at Kyra. "Both of you, ignorant dwarves."

"Ignorance," the mock-grim smile now on Kyra's lips, "is where you find it. Like in casinos. A tax on the poor. Way worse than selling opium to the rich. Which is a crime. But casinos are criminal. Except not illegal. Tell me about ignorance."

"Interesting, if a touch pious." Artemus faked a yawn. "Now tell us please, why did you ask to meet with us?"

Noel leaned forward, his eyes again raking his audience. "You people have committed some serious crimes. Tell me," he looked at Artemus, "does Peter Rabinovich enjoy buying forged paintings at the price of originals?"

Artemus grasped the arms of his chair. "How dare you!"

"Yes," said Tam, "how dare you." He turned and caught Rose's glance. He shrugged at the inevitable. He sat.

"All these paintings have been authenticated. Tam was there when they were authenticated. Tell him, Tam."

Did Marchand really not know at least some were forgeries? How about that.

Rose turned to Tam. "Yes, each was authenticated. Tell them." She spoke quietly.

Tam said, "By the highest authority."

"Except we know where they were painted, and by whom."

"Didn't you hear him?" Artemus half rose from his chair. "They're authentic. Each one."

"Artemus," said Rose, "let him talk." She sighed.

Artemus sank back, his face alone asking his questions.

"Thank you." Noel's gaze flowed from one to another. "The crimes, then. The forging of oil paintings, using some clever masking techniques to obfuscate the possibility for dating the work. Selling these forgeries, thereby profiting from the proceeds of a crime—"

Artemus said, "Rose. What is this man talking about?"

Without turning her head Kyra caught a glimpse of Tam. His own smile was there still, but now unmoving, stuck, forgotten. His eyes ignored Noel, finding much greater fascination with the knuckles of his right hand, his painting hand.

Rose rolled her chair to Artemus' side. "I'm sorry, Artemus."

"But—but he's lying—"

"He's making a point, Artemus. He's leading us somewhere."

"But Rosie, they're not forgeries." He looked from Rose to Tam. "They really aren't."

Tam said, "Oh Artemus, do shut up."

Artemus stood. "Tam, you brought them from all over—Spain, Germany, the Ukraine—"

"I painted some of them, Artemus. Pretty good, eh? Pretty damn good, I'd say. And these people know how good they are. Don't you, Kyra?"

"Pretty damn good, Tam," she said.

Artemus walked slowly to Tam's chair. "You painted them, Tam? Some of them?"

"Only thirteen. The rest are fully authen—"

Artemus' arm flew up and around and his fist caught Tam behind the right ear. Tam, unprepared for the first blow, caught Marchand's wrist before the second landed, directed the thrust, threw him to the floor and catlike pounced to deliver a return blow. But Rose had already positioned her chair and with her Extendiarm grabbed her brother's shoulder. "Stop it!"

Slowly, slowly, Artemus drew himself to his feet. He stood hunched over, staring at his hand. He tried to flex his fingers. His hand wouldn't close. He looked at Rose.

"Come sit, Artemus."

"Rose. They aren't forgeries. They can't be."

Rose nodded, a little smug. "Thirteen are, Artemus."

Again his hand leapt up and slapped Rose across her left cheek. She gasped. Kyra was on her feet but Artemus had pulled back. He slumped down in his chair. Kyra reached her arm out to Rose. Rose flicked her away.

"Shall I go on?" Noel asked.

Artemus' head again began to shake. "But this makes no sense, none at all. Barnabé knows a forgery when he sees one—" his voice broke, "when—when he—sees—"

Rose turned to Noel. "What do you want?"

"The crimes you committed, you have to pay for them."

"Don't try it," said Tam, no smile now. "You talk to the Mounties, no telling what happens to your friends and relatives."

Yep, a nasty hunk of business. Kyra did enjoy seeing the little muscle on the right side of Tam's neck spasming. Not a conscious technique, she was pretty sure. "Did Noel mention speaking with the RCMP? Much better to keep this among ourselves."

"Go on." Rose sat straight in her chair, suddenly taller. She held her hand over her cheek.

"Here's the deal. You've committed acts you'd prefer the Mounties and the FBI didn't know about. We'd rather not send you to rot in jail, particularly at the taxpayer's expense. Maybe we can find another solution. A kind of alternative justice."

"You think we'd get sent to prison for anything you've mentioned?" Near to a sneer from Tam. "Our friend would never let it happen."

Noel shrugged. "No, your friend Rabinovich wouldn't want any of us in jail. He has his own rules, doesn't he? I personally fear your friend. Perhaps you should as well. Half a million for a forged painting? Oh dear."

"Go on," Rose repeated.

"Mostly there's the danger to our—what were Tam's words, Kyra?"

"Friends and relations."

"Right. Not to mention to ourselves, and to yourselves. Who needs that, right?"

None of them answered.

"So. We say nothing. Some conditions. First, no further sales of schools-of paintings, forged or not. Not to anyone. The Internet knows all, and tells all." He looked from Tam to Artemus. No reaction from either.

A tiny smile from Rose. "And?"

Noel turned to her. "No more opium. Anyway, where would you sell it? Without your vials, without selling paintings." Many places, he feared, but waited for their response.

A small breath of a laugh escaped from Tam's nose. These guys just didn't get it about his sister. The sap-rich poppy and the black chrysanthemum were likely the final flowers his BSR would ever breed. If you completely master a task, why continue? He loved the irony, Rab and these guys both misunderstanding Rose in about the same way.

Noel smiled at Rose. "Congratulations, by the way, on masking the pigment age."

Rose smiled at Noel.

"Getting the paintings past all the tests."

Rose's smile widened.

"Assuring that they dated them wrong."

She nodded. "Each time. They test in patches. Often it doesn't read. Normal, they said."

Noel looked from Rose to Tam to Rose. "And your use of the pigments. Very good."

"The stuff Rosie brewed up," Tam grinned, "was great to work with."

Artemus whispered, "Pigments, Rosie?"

She nodded.

"Oh my god." His head drooped. "It's not possible." He pressed his palms to his temples. "You can't fake pigment age."

"I can. I did."

"And the canvas? And the frames?"

Tam laughed quietly. "There's lots of junk out there from the seventeenth century."

"You painted them in Nanaimo? That's why you bought the condo."

"No. In the cabin basement."

"There's no basement." Artemus' face was grey; his hands shook. "Just a crawl space."

Tam looked at him with a pitying smile. "Remember when you went to that conference in Brazil and stayed on for four months exploring South America? I put in a basement. Wondered if you'd ever notice."

To Kyra, Artemus looked ten years older. He asked, "How—did you do the paintings?"

Tam affected modesty. "I flaked the paint from old canvasses and painted on them. And Rosie mixed the old flakes into her non-organic soup. No way to prove fakery, not by elemental analysis or carbon-14 dating. And with the flakes there's so much evidence of authenticity any expert would have to concede the legitimacy of the painting." Modesty shifted to smug: "Especially when the brush strokes confirm the master's signature."

"You used your own flowers, Rosie?"

"Do you really want to know?"

A long silence from Artemus. "No." The tears were back. "No."

"Good." She reached her hand to her face where he'd hit her. "You know, we only did all this to see if we could. And when we'd succeeded, it snowballed. We just kept on going."

Artemus rubbed his eyes. "He'll kill us."

"Why?"

"Oh for christsake, Rosie!"

Tam said, "Listen to me, A. You sold him a painting from, say, the

School of Alphonse Schnürer. Painted by one of Schnürer's students. I, in fact, am a student of Schnürer. One of his best. It's too bad I never met the man, but I doubt I could have learned more from him."

"Don't patronize me—"

"I'm not! What do you think these so-called school-of paintings are? People making a few basic paintings, copies or bits and pieces of a larger work. Some are just studies, not even made for sale. But if a collector's willing to buy? The collector, Rab or whoever, buys and he's happy, he's got a school of this or that on his wall. He hangs it in suites he rents out to others, and they've got an original oil right there, and their snob side's just delighted. You've got a packet of money in your pocket. For the Foundation. The Foundation gives it away, some worthy project in Sumeria or Sumatra has a real lease on life, a village has clean water for the first time, whatever, because of you, because of me. Because of Rab. Everybody benefits. No complaints. Okay?"

A defeated glaze in Artemus' eyes. "The perfect victimless crime."

"No crime, Artemus." Rose again touched her cheek. "Students don't stop painting when the master dies, they go on and on. It makes the master even more famous."

"Say what you will," Artemus breathed, "they're still forgeries. They're not painted in the period they're supposed to represent." He rubbed his knuckles. "Did Dorstel really call you?"

"Not recently."

"But a few of the paintings were real?"

"Yes."

"How many?"

"Eight. The Correggio, the Titian, the—"

Noel cut Tam off. "Here are our conditions for silence. Ready?"

They stared at him. They waited.

"You will found, build and maintain an artists' center, with at least five studios for painters and sculptors. Artists to be selected by a jury of other artists. You don't get to decide who's chosen. Full open competition, except for one slot that always goes to a Gabriola artist."

"What a terrible idea." Tam scowled at Noel. "Anyway, the Official Community Plan won't permit that density. Don't you know anything about building codes?"

"Then you'll just have to buy yourselves a larger piece of land."

"With what?" Tam shook his head. "You just told us we can't sell any more paintings."

"Oh, break my heart. Sell contemporary artists. Dip into the Marchand fortune." Noel glared at them yet spoke softly. "Imagine the glory it'll bring you. Gabriola, womb of the finest young artists from around the world. The School of Artemus Marchand."

Rose gazed at Artemus. His face and hands were wet.

Kyra, all cheer, smiled at Tam. "You'll run the center, Tam. You've got such great technique, you can adapt yourself to anybody's style. You'll be a great teacher."

"Yeah? And if I don't want to?"

"But you do. Especially since it coincides with your very best interests."

Rose turned to Kyra. "I can hardly wait to hear your plans for me."

It was Noel who said, "Nothing you won't enjoy. The art center buildings will be handicap-accessible. You'll design them well, you're too professional not to. Then you'll build a workshop with two purposes. One, a place in a beautiful setting for the disabled to brainstorm new ideas. And two, machines and tools available for guests to build prototypes for making life easier for themselves and others. Just as you did with your gardening tools."

Rose said, "I'm not gregarious."

"It's easy to be friendly with your admirers. Those you give a door to new freedom."

"And," Noel added, "you might think about a swimming pool, Rose. Heated. You'll design all kinds of aids to make a pool more accessible."

"You've destroyed us." Artemus shook his head. "You've destroyed me. Are you done?"

"One more thing. Quarterly you send a check for $23.65 to this lawyer's address." He stood and handed Marchand a card.

"What for?" Rose asked.

Noel gave them his pièce-de-résistance smile. "The price of the safety deposit box that holds a copy of this deposition," he held up the file again, "and the photos and so on." Now he smiled at each of them separately. "A small regular reminder of our agreement."

Kyra said, "A win-win situation."

Rose said, "How nice."

TWENTY-FIVE

THEY ARRIVED BACK at Cameron Island just before two. Kyra needed some space so tramped the seawall to Departure Bay and back. She stopped off at the seaplane office. When she returned she announced, "I lucked into a cancellation tomorrow morning."

"You don't sound happy. How about a celebratory martini and a delivered pizza?"

She shook her head.

"I hope the negative was to the pizza."

She smiled, sort of. "Not hungry." She checked her watch. Nearly five. "A martini, sure."

In the kitchen Noel fixed a shakerful. He got down two glasses and poured. Kyra stared out at the ferry from Gabriola. A mist was descending, the island's cliffs losing solidity. Noel clinked her glass with his. "To a closed investigation," sipped, not bad. "Not going to toast?"

She shrugged, sipped. "Nice drink."

"Great compliment." Noel sat on the sofa. "What's up?"

Kyra sipped again. "Rabinovich. You think maybe Rose was under his spell, in some way?" She put her feet on the coffee table.

Noel raised an eyebrow. If anyone knows about spells, it's you, babe.

"Okay, okay." Kyra contemplated her olive. "And that's all I'm going to say."

"They gave in faster than I'd expected."

"I suspect they liked our idea. It is in fact a stroke of genius."

"You think Rabinovich really values those people?" Noel wondered.

"Oh cases," said Kyra. "You get a glimpse into lives and relationships, then it's over and they're left cryovacced in your mind."

"Like each case is a two-hour movie? No sequel." At the counter he hefted the shaker. "You want to eat out?"

"What are the freezer options?"

"Turkey soup. Or the leftover *bourguignon*. It'll taste better without Lyle's company."

"The latter. And more martinis. I need to get drunk. A little."

He filled a bowl with pistachios.

She scooped a handful. "It's just, they're people I detest. But, as Tam said, who's been hurt? Rabinovich, he's paid fortunes for fake paintings. He deserves to be taken in. Is it wrong to hurt the criminally rich just because they're criminally rich?"

"I hope they run with the art school. At least we got their threat under control."

"Okay." She puffed a sigh. "Tell me we can't do anything about Rabinovich and his obscene power—"

"Really, we can't."

"—and I'll say, Case closed."

"And our report to Lucas?"

"We tell him Marchand's sources have dried up. The truth."

"Let's drink to that." Noel raised his glass.

"Wait." She touched his wrist. "I must say you got the worst of the deal, with Lyle. I didn't like him and now I detest him."

"Yeah. Damn, he was terrifying. For a bit there I thought it was all over." He squeezed her hand. "But then you showed up. And the Mounties."

"Yeah. Like when I heard you when I was in Gill's basement."

They drank to their gratitude.

Kyra's cellphone rang. "Hello? . . . Oh hi, Margery . . . The police think it's suicide?"

Noel noted Kyra's smile, warmed by a new puzzle. The Eaglenest case was the best new thing he'd done in years. He took dinner from the freezer and put it in the microwave.

Kyra was saying, "I'll be back in town tomorrow—" She made scribbling motions. Noel passed her paper and pen. "I'm sure that'll be fine . . . yes, I'll phone first . . . no problem. Thanks, Marge. Goodbye." She stared at the paper. "A Ms. Oswald says she knows who killed her husband and why, but Puget Sound would prefer it to be a suicide."

"So they won't have to pay?"

"Right." She twinkled. "Want to come along?"

"To Bellingham?"

"Orcas Island. Maybe this case will be a simple black-and-whiter."

"A case on Gabriola, a case on Orcas. Islands Investigations

International?" He ruminated. "We better get some cards printed." He pulled out his notebook and scribbled, *cards*.

Kyra held up her glass. "To Triple-I." They drank. "The only thing Lyle was good for."

The microwave beeped. Noel poked the *bourguignon*. Another ten minutes. "Soon."

"I've never been to Orcas Island," Kyra said.

"I was there once, before I met Brendan. Don't remember a thing. Oh, I said I'd phone Lucille." He picked up the phone again. "Hi, it's Noel. The Mounties have charged Jerry Bannister with Dempster's murder, and the painter Lyle Sempken as accessory . . . That's the one . . . You're welcome." He paused. "Oh, I had a little adventure of my own—" And told her. "And you can print any of that you want . . . Yes. Of course I, or my partner," he grinned at Kyra, "will let you know. Bye."

EPILOGUE

NOEL'S FAX BRRR-ED out paper. He picked up the sheet.

Hi Noel,
Since you were so involved with Eaglenest Gallery last year, I thought
you'd want to see my recent column. Hope things are going well for you and
your associate. Drop in for tea sometime, my kettle's getting dusty.
    Lucille

A THRILLING EVENT
By Lucille Maple
Yesterday I attended the GRAND OPENING
of Gabriola's newest institution, The
Marchand School Of Art. Gabriola is indeed
fortunate to have been picked as "home"
by a family so talented and generous as
Artemus Marchand's.

Last year they bought sixty acres of the
old clearcut and, after demolishing foliage
(rumour hath it BLACKBERRIES were used to
hide a forbidden substance) work proceeded
apace all year.

Now there are three buildings: a large
studio-gallery, a large workshop and a
student residence. Everything is wheelchair
accessible, I was assured, and the workshop
is to be used for training the disabled in
making Tools for Self-Help. Rose Gill is in
charge of the workshop, you all recall her
skill with inventing gardening tools for
the disabled. [See Gabriola Gab, April 13,
2000. Ed.]

Unfortunately, Tam Gill who was to be the
primary Art Teacher has not yet returned

from Australia. Yet fortunately two of Gabriola's artists, Linda Preston from the Studio on the Hill, and Stanley Carmichael from Weedbucket, have been selected as instructors. This is a worthy way of creating jobs for Islanders. How fortunate are students able to study with these great Gabriola Artists! There are eight students enrolled this year, five already in residence. They hope to accommodate twenty-two when they're "in full swing." Artemus Marchand introduced me to Phoebe Hanson, a great would-be artist—what a warm, welcoming atmosphere this "gallant" is able to create just by placing his arm across a student's shoulders! [We plan to bring you interviews with the students during the course of their studies. Ed.]

No expense has been spared, as one would expect from the philanthropic Artemus Marchand. I do not know how much the school cost to build, but a building authority assures me it is A LOT.

Landscaping has not been achieved yet and the grounds are a sea of dust or mud, depending on the season. However, I assume Ms. Gill will be in charge of this, now that she has returned from her extended sea voyage.

Artemus Marchand oversees the whole enterprise and one just knows that it will run as smoothly as Eaglecrest Gallery has in the past. He will move the Gallery shows to The Marchand School Of Art and they will concentrate on the students' achievements. Schools of European Masters have "dried up" he informed me. Which is a shame, readers must remember last year's show, the Gallery show of the Great Paintings. AND the unveiling of the new black chrysanthemum! (With the Marchand-Gills all on the same sixty acres, there should be no more conflict such as last year's Fall Fair when I had to dash from the Agi [Agricultural. Ed.] Hall to the Gallery and back again.)

Readers will join me in wishing Artemus and Rose—and Tam, in his new life in Australia—every success in their new endeavours and hoping that soon a young Gabriola Artist can profit from attendance!